HARRY HA...

THE HAMMER AND THE CROSS

TOR®
fantasy

52348-2 ★ $5.99 ($6.99 CAN)

Tor books by Harry Harrison

Galactic Dreams
The Hammer and the Cross
The Jupiter Plague
Montezuma's Revenge
One Step from Earth
Planet of No Return
Planet of the Damned
The QE2 Is Missing
Queen Victoria's Revenge
A Rebel in Time
Skyfall
Stainless Steel Visions
Stonehenge
A Transatlantic Tunnel, Hurrah!

HARRY HARRISON

A TOM DOHERTY ASSOCIATES BOOK
NEW YORK

THE HAMMER AND THE CROSS

Copyright © 1993 by Harry Harrison and John Holm

Cover art by Kevin Johnson
Interior illustrations by Bill Sanderson

A Tor Book
Published by Tom Doherty Associates, Inc.
175 Fifth Avenue
New York, N.Y. 10010

Tor® is a registered trademark of Tom Doherty Associates, Inc.

ISBN: 0-812-52348-2

First edition: September 1993
First mass market edition: November 1994

Printed in the United States of America

0 9 8 7 6 5 4 3 2 1

Qui credit in Filium, habet vitam aeternam; qui autem incredulus est Filio, non videbit vitam, sed ira Dei manet super eum.

He that believeth on the Son hath everlasting life: and he that believeth not the Son shall not see life; but the wrath of God abideth on him.

—John 3 : 36

Angusta est domus : utrosque tenere non poterit. Non vult rex celestis cum paganis et perditis nominetenus regibus communionem habere; quia rex ille aeternus regnat in caelis, ille paganus perditus plangit in inferno.

The house is narrow : it cannot hold both. The king of heaven has no wish to have fellowship with damned and heathen so-called kings; for the one eternal king reigns in Heaven, the other damned heathen groans in Hell.

—Alcuin, deacon of York, A.D. 797

The greatest disaster ever to befall the West was Christianity.

Gravissima calamitas umquam supra Occidentem accidens erat religio Christiana.

—Gore Vidal, A.D. 1987

Thrall

Chapter One

NORTHEAST COAST OF ENGLAND, A.D. 865

Spring. A spring dawn on Flamborough Head, where the rock of the Yorkshire Wolds juts out into the North Sea like a gigantic fishhook, millions of tons in weight. Pointing out to sea, pointing to the ever-present threat of the Vikings. Now the kings of the little kingdoms were uneasily beginning to draw together against this threat from the North. Uneasy and jealous, remembering the long hostilities and the trail of murder that had marked the history of the Angles and the Saxons ever since they came here centuries ago. Proud warsmiths who overcame the Welsh, noble warriors who—as the poets say—obtained the land.

Godwin the Thane cursed to himself as he paced the wooden palisade of the little fort erected on the very tip of Flamborough Head itself. Spring! Maybe in more fortunate parts the lengthening days and the light evenings meant greenery and buttercups and heavy-uddered cows trooping to the byres to be milked. Here on the Head it meant wind. It meant the equinoctial gales and the nor'easter blowing. Behind him the low, gnarled trees stood in line, one behind the other like men with their backs turned, each successive one a few inches higher than the one to windward, so that they formed natural wind-arrows or weathercocks, pointing out to the tormented sea. On three sides all round him the gray water heaved slowly like an immense animal, the waves starting to curl and then flattening out again as the wind tore at them, beating them down and levelling out even the massive surges of the ocean. Gray sea, gray sky, squalls blotting the horizon, no color in the world at all except when the rollers finally crashed into the striated walls of the cliffs, shattering and sending up great plumes of spray. Godwin had been there so long that he no longer heard the roar of the collision, noticed it only when the spray reached so high up the cliff that the water which soaked his cloak and hood and dripped onto his face turned salt instead of fresh.

Not that it made any difference, he thought numbly. It was all just as cold. He could go back into the shelter, kick the slaves aside, warm his frozen hands and feet by the fire. There was no chance of raiders on a day like this. The Vikings were seamen, the greatest seamen in the world, or so they said. You didn't have to be a great seaman to know that there was no point in putting out on a day like this. The wind was due east—no, he reflected, due east a point north. Fine for blowing you across from Denmark, but how could you keep a longship from broaching to in this sea? And how could you steer for a safe landing once you arrived? No, no chance at all. He might as well be by the fire.

Godwin looked longingly at the shelter with its little trail of smoke instantly whipped away by the wind, but turned his pace and began to shuffle along the palisade again. His lord had trained him well. "Don't think, Godwin," he had said. "Don't think maybe they'll come today and maybe they won't. Don't believe that it's worth keeping a lookout some of the time and it's not worth it the rest. While it's day, you stay on the Head. Look out all the time. Or one day you'll be thinking one thing and some Stein or Olaf'll think another and they'll be ashore and twenty miles inland before we can catch up with them—if we ever do. And that's a hundred lives lost and a hundred pounds in silver and cattle and burnt thatch. And the rents not paid for years after. So watch, Thane, or it's your estates that will suffer."

So his lord Ella had said. And behind him the black crow,

Erkenbert, had crouched over his parchment, his quill squeaking as he traced out the mysterious black lines that Godwin feared more than he feared the Vikings. "Two months' service on Flamborough Head to Godwin the thane," he had pronounced. "He is to watch till the third Sunday after *Ramis Palmarum*." The alien syllables had nailed the orders down.

Watch they had said and watch he would. But he didn't have to do it as dry as a reluctant virgin. Godwin bellowed downwind to the slaves, for the hot spiced ale he had commanded half an hour before. Instantly one of them came running out, the leather mug in his hand. Godwin eyed him with deep disfavor as he trotted over to the palisade and up the ladder to the watchkeeper's walkway. A damned fool, this one. Godwin kept him because he had sharp eyes, but that was all. Merla, his name. He had been a fisherman once. Then there had been a hard winter, little to catch, he had fallen behind with the dues he owed to his landlords, the black monks of St. John's Minister at Beverley, twenty miles off. First he had sold his boat to pay his dues and feed his wife and bairns. Then, when he had no money and could not feed them any longer, he had had to sell his family to a richer man, and in the end had sold himself to his former landlords. And they had lent Merla to Godwin. Damned fool. If the slave had been a man of honor he would have sold himself first and given the money to his wife's kin, so at least they would have taken her in. If he had been a man of sense he would have sold his wife and the bairns first and kept the boat. Then maybe he would have had a chance to buy them back. But he was a man of neither sense nor honor. Godwin turned his back on the wind and the sea and took a firm swallow from the brimming mug. At least the slave hadn't been sipping from it. He could learn from a thrashing if from nothing else.

Now what was the wittol staring at? Staring past his master's shoulder, mouth agape, pointing out to sea.

"Ships," he yelled. "Viking ships, two mile out to sea. I see 'em again. Look, master, look!"

Godwin spun automatically, cursed as the hot liquid slopped over his sleeve, peered out into the cloud and rain along the pointing arm. Was there a dot there, out where the cloud met the waves? No, nothing. Or . . . maybe. He could see nothing steadily, but out there the waves would be running twenty feet high, high enough to shelter any ship trying to ride out a storm under bare poles.

"I see 'em," yelled Merla again. "Two ships, a cable apart."

"Longships?"

"No, master, knorrs."

Godwin hurled the mug over his shoulder, seized the slave's thin arm in an iron grasp, and slashed him viciously across the face, forehand, backhand, with a sodden leather gauntlet. Merla gasped and ducked but did not dare to try to shield himself.

"Talk English, you whore's get. And talk sense."

"A knorr, master. It's a merchant ship. Deep-bellied, for cargo." He hesitated, afraid to show further knowledge, afraid to conceal it. "I can recognize 'un by . . . by the shape of the prow. They must be Vikings, master. We don't use 'em."

Godwin stared out to sea again, anger fading, replaced by a cold, hard feeling at the base of his stomach. Doubt. Dread.

"Listen, Merla, to me," he whispered. "Be very sure. If those are Vikings I must call out the entire coast-watch, every man from here to Bridlington. They are only churls and slaves, when all is said and done. No harm if they are dragged from their greasy wives.

"But I must do something else. As soon as the watch is called I must also send riders in to the minister at Beverley, to the monks of good St. John—your masters, remember?"

He paused to note the terror and the old memories in Merla's eyes.

"And they will call out the mounted levy, the thanes of Ella. No good keeping them here, where the pirates could feint at Flamborough and then be twenty miles off round

Spurn Head before they could get their horses out of the marsh. So they stay back, so they can ride in any direction once the threat is seen. But if I call them out, and they ride over here in the wind and the rain on a fool's errand . . . And especially if some Viking sneaks in through the Humber while their backs are turned . . .

"Well, it would be bad for me, Merla." His voice sharpened and he lifted the underfed slave off the ground. "But by almighty God in heaven I'll see you regret it till the last day you live. And after the thrashing you get that may not be long.

"But, Merla, if those are Viking ships out there and you let me *not* report them—I'll hand you back to the black monks and say I could do nothing with you.

"Now, what do you say? Viking ships, or no?"

The slave stared out again to sea, his face working. He would have been wiser, he thought, to say nothing. What was it to him if the Vikings sacked Flamborough, or Bridlington, or Beverley Minster itself? They could not enslave him any more than he was already. Maybe foreign heathens would be better masters than the people of Christ at home. Too late to think that now. The sky was clearing, momentarily. He could see, even if his weak-eyed landlubber of a master could not. He nodded.

"Two Viking ships, master. Two mile out to sea. Southeast."

Godwin was away, bellowing instructions, calling to his other slaves, shouting for his horse, his horn, his small, reluctant force of conscripted freemen. Merla straightened, walked slowly to the southwest angle of the palisade, looked out thoughtfully and carefully. The weather cleared momentarily, and for a few heartbeats he could see plain. He looked at the run of the waves—the turbid yellow line a hundred yards offshore which marked the long, long expanse of tidal sandbanks which ran the full length of this barest and most harborless, wind- and current-swept stretch of English shore—tossed a handful of moss from the pali-

sade into the air and studied the way it flew. Slowly a grim
and humorless smile creased his careworn face.

Great sailors those Vikings might be. But they were in the
wrong place, on a lee shore with a widow-maker blowing.
Unless the wind dropped, or their heathen gods from Valhalla could help them, they stood no chance. They would
never see Jutland or the Vik again.

Two hours later fivescore men stood clustered on the beach
south of the Head, at the north end of the long, long, inlet-
less stretch of coast that ran down to Spurn Head and the
mouth of the Humber. They were armed: leather jackets and
caps, spears, wooden shields, a scattering of the broadaxes
they used to shape their boats and houses. Here and there a
sax, the short chopping sword from which the Saxons to the
south took their name. Only Godwin had a metal helmet and
mail-shirt to pull on, a brass-hilted broadsword to buckle
round his waist. In the normal way of things men like these,
the coast-watch of Bridlington, would not hope or expect to
stand on the shore and trade blows with the professional
warriors of Denmark and Norway. Rather, they would fade
away, taking as much as they could of their goods and
wives with them. Waiting for the mounted levy, the thane-
service of Northumbria, to come down and do the fighting
for which they earned their estates and manor houses. Waiting hopefully for a chance to swarm forward and join in the
harassing of a beaten enemy, the chance of taking loot. It
was not a chance which had come to any Englishman since
Oakley fourteen years before. And that had been in the
south, in the foreign kingdom of Wessex, where all manner
of strange things happened.

Nevertheless the mood of the men watching the knorrs
out in the bay was unalarmed, even cheerful. Almost every
man in the coast-watch was a fisherman, skilled in the ways
of the North Sea. The worst water in the world, with its fogs
and gales, its monstrous tides and unexpected currents. As
the day strengthened and the Viking ships were blown re-
morselessly closer in, Merla's realization had come to ev-

eryone: The Vikings were doomed. It was just a matter of what they could try next. And whether they would try it, lose, and get the wreck over with before the mounted levy Godwin had summoned hours before could arrive, resplendent in its armor, colored cloaks and gold-mounted swords. After which, opinion among the fishermen felt, the chances of any worthwhile plunder for them were low. Unless they marked the spot and tried later, in secret, with grappling irons . . . Quiet conversations ran among the men at the rear, with an occasional low laugh.

"See," the town reeve was explaining to Godwin at the front, "the wind's east a point north. If they put up a scrap of sail they can run west, north or south." He drew briefly in the wet sand at their feet. "If he goes west he hits us. If he goes north he hits the Head. Mind you, if he could get past the Head he'd have a clear run northwest away up to Cleveland. That's why he was trying his sweeps an hour ago. A few hundred yards out to sea and he'd have been free. But what we knows, and what they doesn't, is there's a current. Hell of a current, rips down past the Head. They might as well stir the water with their . . ." He paused, not sure how far informality could go.

"Why doesn't he go south?" cut in Godwin.

"He will. He's tried the sweeps, tried the sea-anchor to check his drift. It's my guess the one in charge, the *jarl* what they call them, he knows his men are exhausted. A rare old night they must have had of it. And a shock in the morning when they saw where they were." The reeve shook his head with a kind of professional sympathy.

"They are not such great sailors," pronounced Godwin with satisfaction. "And God is against them, foul, heathen Church-defilers."

A stir of excitement behind them cut off the reply the reeve might have been incautious enough to make. The two men turned.

On the path that ran along behind high-water mark, a dozen men were dismounting. The levy? thought Godwin. The thanes from Beverley? No, they could not possibly have arrived in this time. They must only now be saddling up. Yet the man in front was a nobleman. Big, burly, fair hair, bright blue eyes, with the upright stance of a man who had never had to plough or hoe for a living. Gold shone beneath his expensive scarlet cape, on buckles and sword-pommel. Behind him strode a smaller, younger version of himself, surely his son. And on the other side of him another youth, tall, straight-backed like a warrior. But dark in complexion, poorly dressed in tunic and wool breeches. Grooms held the horses for half a dozen more armed, competent-looking men—a retinue, surely, a rich thane's hearth-troop.

The leading stranger held his empty hand up. "You do not know me," he said. "I am Wulfgar. I am a thane from King Edmund's country, from the East Angles."

A stir of interest from the crowd, the dawnings his message might be of hostility.

"You wonder what I am doing here. I will tell you." He gestured out at the shore. "I hate Vikings. I know more of them than most men. And, like most men, to my sorrow. In my own country, among the North-folk beyond the Wash, I am the coast-guard, set by King Edmund. But long ago I saw that we would never get rid of these vermin while we English fought only our own battles. I persuaded my king of this, and he sent messages to yours. They agreed that I should come north, to talk with the wise men in Beverley and in Eoforwich about what we might do. I took a wrong road last night, met your messengers riding to Beverley this morning. I have come to help." He paused. "Have I your leave?"

Godwin nodded slowly. Never mind what the lowborn fish-churl of a reeve said. Some of the bastards might come ashore. And if they did, this lot might well scatter. A dozen armed men just might be useful.

"Come and welcome," he said.

Wulfgar nodded with deliberate satisfaction. "I am only just in time," he remarked.

Out to sea the penultimate act of the wreck was about to

take place. One of the two knorrs was fifty yards farther in than the other; her men more tired or maybe less driven by their skipper. Now she was about to pay the price. Her wallowing rolls in the waves changed angle, the bare mast rocking crazily. Suddenly the watching men could see that the yellow line of underwater sandbanks was the other side of the hull. Crewmen exploded from the deck and the planks where they had been lying, ran furiously up and down, grabbing sweeps, thrusting them over the side, trying to pole their ship off and gain a few extra moments of life.

Too late. A cry of despair rang thinly across the water as the Vikings saw it, echoed by a hum of excitement from the Englishmen on the shore: the wave, the big wave, the seventh wave that always rolls farthest up the beach. Suddenly the knorr was up on it, lifted and tilted sideways in a cascade of boxes and barrels and men sliding from the windward into the leeward scuppers. Then the wave was gone and the knorr smashed down, landing with a thump on the hard sand and gravel of the bank. Planks flew, the mast was over the side in a tangle of cordage; for an instant a man could be seen grasping desperately to the ornamented dragon-prow. Then another wave covered everything, and when it passed there were only bobbing fragments.

The fishermen nodded. A few crossed themselves. If the good God spared them from the Vikings, that was the way they expected to go one day—like men, with the cold salt in their mouths, and rings in their ears to pay kindly strangers to bury them. Now, there was one more thing for a skillful captain to try.

The remaining Viking was going to try it, to scud south with the wind abeam and all the easting he could get, rather than wait passively for death like his consort had. A man appeared suddenly at the steering oar. Even from two furlongs' distance the watchers could see his red beard wagging as he bellowed orders, could hear the echo of his urgency rolling across the water. There were men at the ropes, waiting, heaving together. A scrap of sail leapt free from the yard, caught instantly by the wind and tugged out.

As the ship shot urgently towards shore another volley of orders swung the yard round and the boat heeled downwind. Within seconds she was steady on a new course, picking up speed, throwing water wide from her bow-wave as she raced away from the Head down toward the Spurn.

"They're getting away!" yelled Godwin. "Get the horses!" He cuffed his groom out of the way, scrambled astride, and set off at a gallop in pursuit, Wulfgar, the stranger thane, only a pace or two behind, and the rest of their retinues following in strung-out, disorderly lines. Only the dark boy who had come with Wulfgar hesitated.

"You're not hurrying," he said to the motionless reeve. "Why not? Don't you want to catch up with them?"

The reeve grinned, stooped, picked a pinch of sand from the beach and threw it in the air. "They've got to try it," he remarked. "Nothing else to do. But they're not going to get far."

Turning on his heel he indicated a score of men to stay where they were and watch the beach for wreckage or sur-vivors. Another score of mounted men set off along the path behind the thanes. The rest, bunched together, began to trot purposefully but deliberately along the beach after the rac-ing ship.

As the minutes passed even the landsmen realized what the reeve had seen straight away. The Viking skipper was not going to win his gamble. Twice already he had tried to force his ship's head out to sea, two men joining the red-bearded one as he strained at the steering oar, the rest of the crew bracing the yard round till the ropes sang iron-hand in the wind. Both times the waves had heaved, heaved re-morselessly at the prow till it wavered, swung back, the ship's hull shuddering with the forces contending on it. And again the skipper had tried, turning back parallel with the coastline and building up speed for another dash to the safety of the open sea.

But was he parallel with the coastline this time? Even to the inexperienced eyes of Godwin and Wulfgar it looked this time as if something was different: stronger wind, heavier sea, the grip of the inshore current dragging at the bottom. The red-bearded man was still by the oar, still shouting orders for some other maneuver, the ship was still racing along, as the poets said, like a foamy-necked floater, but her prow was turning in inch by inch or foot by foot; the yellow line was perilously close to her bow-wave, it was clear she was going to—

Strike. One instant the ship was running full tilt, the next her prow had slammed into unyielding gravel. The mast snapped off instantly and hurled itself forward, taking half the crew with it. The planks of the clinker-built boat sprang outward from their settings, letting in the onrushing sea. In a heartbeat the whole ship had opened up like a flower. And then vanished, leaving only cordage streaming in the wind for a moment to show where she had been. And, once again, bobbing fragments in the water.

Bobbing fragments, the fishermen noticed interestedly as they panted up, this time rather closer to shore. One of them a head. A red head.

"Is he going to make it, do you think?" asked Wulfgar. They could see the man clearly now, fifty yards out in the water, hanging still and making no effort to swim farther as he eyed the great waves pounding in to destroy themselves on the shore.

"He's going to try," replied Godwin, motioning men forward to the watermark. "If he does, we'll grab him."

Redbeard had made his mind up and started to swim forward, hurling the water aside with great strokes of his arms. He had seen the great wave coming behind him. It lifted him, he was swept forward, straining to keep himself on top of the wave as if he could propel himself up the beach and land as weightlessly as the white foam that crawled almost to the soles of the thanes' leather shoes. For ten strokes he was there, the watchers turning their heads up to look at him as he swung to the crest of the wave. Then the wave in front, retreating, checked his progress in a great swirl of sand and stone, the crest broke, dissolved. Smashed him down with a grunt and a snap. Rolled him helplessly forward. Dragged him back with the undertow.

"Go in and get him," yelled Godwin. "Move, you harehearts! He can't hurt you."

Two of the fishermen darted forward between the waves, grabbed an arm each and hauled him back, for a moment waist-deep amid the smother but then out, the redbeard braced between them.

"He's still alive," muttered Wulfgar in astonishment. "I thought that wave was enough to break his spine."

The redbeard's feet touched the shore, he looked round at the eighty men confronting him, his teeth showed suddenly in a flashing grin.

"What welcome," he remarked.

He turned in the grip of his two rescuers, placed the outside of his foot on one man's shin, raked it down with full weight onto the instep. The man howled and let go the brawny arm he was clutching. Instantly the arm swept across, two fingers extended, driving deep into the eyes of the man still holding on. He, too, shrieked and fell to his knees, blood starting from between his fingers. The Viking plucked the gutting-knife from his belt, stepped forward, seized the nearest Englishman with one hand and stabbed savagely upwards with the other. As the fisherman's mates leapt back, shouting in alarm, he snatched a spear, whipped the knife back and hurled it, grabbed a sax from the hand of the fallen man. Ten heartbeats after his feet touched the shore he was the center of a semicircle of men, all backing away from him, except the two still lying at his feet.

His teeth showed again as he threw his head back in a wild guffaw. "Come now," he shouted gutturally. "I one, you many. Come to fight with Ragnar. Who is great one who comes first? You. Or you." He flourished his spear at Godwin and Wulfgar, now isolated, mouths gaping, by the fishermen still drawing respectfully back.

"We'll have to take him," muttered Godwin, drawing his broadsword with a wheep. "I wish I had my shield."

Wulfgar followed suit, stepping sideways, pushing back

the fair-haired boy who stood a pace behind him. "Go back, Alfgar. If we can disarm him the churls will finish it for us."

The two Englishmen edged forward, swords drawn, facing the bearlike figure which stood grinning, waiting for them, the blood and water still surging round his feet.

Then he was in motion, heading straight for Wulfgar, moving with the speed and ferocity of a charging boar. Wulfgar sprang back in shock, landed awkwardly, a foot twisting under him. The Viking missed with a lefthand slash, poised the right arm for a downward killing thrust.

Something jerked the redbeard off his feet, hurled him backward, struggling helplessly to free an arm, twisted him round and threw him heavily into the wet sand. A net. A fisherman's net. The reeve and two more jumped forward, seized handfuls of tarry cordage, jerked the net tighter. One twitched the sax from an enmeshed hand, another stamped savagely on the fingers holding the spear, breaking shaft and bones in the same movement. They rolled the helpless man quickly, expertly, like a dangerous dogfish or herring-shark. They straightened, looking down, and waited for orders.

Wulfgar limped over, exchanging glances with Godwin. "What have we caught here?" he muttered. "Something tells me this is no two-ship chieftain out of luck."

He eyed the garments of the netted man, reached down and felt them.

"Goatskin," he said. "Goatskin with pitch on. He called himself Ragnar. We've caught Lothbrok himself. Ragnar Lothbrok. Ragnar Hairy-Breeks."

"We can't deal with him," said Godwin in the silence. "He'll have to go to King Ella."

Another voice broke in, the voice of the dark boy who had questioned the reeve.

"King Ella?" he said. "I thought Osbert was king of the Northumbrians."

Godwin turned to Wulfgar with weary politeness. "I don't know how you discipline your people in the North-folk," he remarked. "But if he were mine and said something like that

I'd have his tongue torn out. Unless he's your kin, of course."

In the lightless stable no one could see him. The dark boy leaned his face on the saddle and let himself slump. His back was like fire, the wool tunic sticky with blood, rasping and pulling free at every movement. The beating had been the worst he had ever suffered, and he had suffered many, many thrashings from rope and leather, bent over the horse-trough in the yard of the place he called home.

It was that remark about kin that had done it, he knew. He hoped he had not cried out so that the strangers would hear him. Toward the end he hadn't been able to tell. Pained memories of dragging himself out into the daylight. Then the long ride across the Wolds, trying to hold himself straight. What would happen now they were in Eoforwich? Once upon a time the fabled city, home of the long-departed but mysterious Rome-folk and their legions, had stirred his fervent imagination more than the songs of glory of the minstrels. Now he was here, and he only wanted to escape.

When would he be free of his father's guilt? Of his step-father's hate?

Shef pulled himself together and began to unbuckle the girth, dragging at the heavy leather. Wulfgar, he was sure, would soon formally enslave him, put the iron collar round his neck, ignore the faint protests of his mother, and sell him in the market at Thetford or Lincoln. He would get a good price. In childhood Shef had hung around the village forge, drawn by the fire, hiding from the abuse and the thrashings. Slowly he had come to help the smith, pumping the bellows, holding the tongs, beating out the iron blooms. Making his own tools. Making his own sword.

They would not let him keep it once he was a slave. Maybe he should run now. Slaves sometimes got away. Usually not.

He pulled off the saddle and groped round the unfamiliar stable for a place to stow it. The door opened, bringing in light, a candle, and the familiar cold, scornful voice of Alfgar.

"Not finished yet? Then drop it, I'll send a groom. My father is called to council with the king and the great ones. He must have a servant behind his chair to pour his ale. It is not fitting for me to do it and the companions are too proud. Go, now. The king's bower-thane waits to instruct you."

Shef plodded out into the courtyard of the king's great wooden hall, new-built within the square of the old Roman ramparts, into the dim light of the spring evening, almost too tired to walk straight. And yet, inside him, something stirred, something hot and excited. Council? Great ones? They would decide the fate of the prisoner, the mighty warrior. It would be a story to tell Godive, one that none of the wiseacres of Emneth could match.

"And keep your mouth *shut*," a voice hissed from inside the stable. "Or he *will* have your tongue torn out. And remember: Ella is king in Northumbria now. And you are no kin to my father."

Chapter Two

"We think he's Ragnar Lothbrok," King Ella asked his council. "How do we know?"

He looked down a long table with a dozen men seated round it, all of them on low stools except for the king himself, who was on a great carven high seat. Most of them were dressed like the king, or like Wulfgar, who sat at Ella's left hand: in brightly colored cloaks, still pulled round them against the drafts that swirled in from every corner and closed shutter, making the tallow-dipped torches flare and eddy; gold and silver round wrists and brawny necks; clasps and buckles and heavy sword-belts. They were the military aristocracy of Northumbria, the petty rulers of great blocks of land in the south and east of the kingdom, the men who had put Ella on the throne and driven out his rival Osbert. They sat on their stools awkwardly, like men who spent their lives on foot or in the saddle.

Four other men stood out against them, grouped at the foot of the table as if in conscious isolation. Three wore the black gowns and cowls of the monks of St. Benedict, the fourth the purple and white of a bishop. They sat easily, bending forward over the table, wax tablets and styli ready to record what was said, or to pass their thoughts to one another in secret.

One man made ready to answer his king's question: Cuthred, captain of the bodyguard.

"We can't find anyone to recognize him," he admitted. "Everyone who ever stood face-to-face with Ragnar in battle is dead—except," he remarked courteously, "the gallant thane of King Edmund who has joined us. However, that doesn't prove this one is Ragnar Lothbrok.

"But I think he is. One, he won't talk. I reckon I'm good at getting people to talk, and anyone who won't is not a common pirate. This one for sure thinks he's somebody.

"Another, it fits. What were those ships doing? They were coming back from the south, they'd been blown off course, they hadn't seen sun nor stars for days. Otherwise skippers like that—and the Bridlington reeve says they were good—wouldn't have got into that state. And they were cargo ships. What cargo do you take south? Slaves. They don't want wool, they don't want furs, they don't want ale. Those were slavers on their way back from the countries down south. The man's a slaver who's a somebody, and that fits Ragnar. Doesn't prove it, though."

Cuthred took a heavy pull at his ale-mug, exhausted by eloquence.

"But there's one thing that makes me sure. What do we know about Ragnar?" He looked round the table. "Right, he's a bastard."

"Church-despoiler," agreed Archbishop Wulfhere from

the end of the table. "Ravisher of nuns. Thief of the brides of Christ. Assuredly his sins shall find him out."

"I dare say," agreed Cuthred. "One thing I have heard about him is this, and I've only heard it about him, not all the other Church-despoilers and ravishers there are in the world. Ragnar is very big on information. He's like me. He's good at getting people to talk. The way he does it, I hear, is this"—A note of professional interest crept into the captain's voice.—"If he catches someone, first thing he does—no talk, no argument—is gouge one eye out. Then he still doesn't talk, he reaches round and gets the man's head ready for the next one. If the man thinks of something Ragnar really wants to know while he's getting ready, all right, he's in business. If he doesn't, well, too bad. They say Ragnar wastes a lot of people, but then churls aren't worth a lot on the block. They say he reckons it saves him a lot of time and breath."

"And our prisoner has told you this is his view too?" It was one of the black monks who spoke, his voice dripping condescension. "In the course of a friendly discussion on professional matters?"

"No." Cuthred took another pull at his ale. "But I looked at his nails. All clipped short. Except the right thumbnail. It's been grown an inch long. Hard as steel. I got it here." He tossed a bloody claw onto the table.

"So it's Ragnar," said King Ella in the silence. "So what do we do with him?"

The warriors exchanged puzzled looks. "Like you mean beheading's too good for him?" ventured Cuthred. "We should hang him instead?"

"Or something worse?" put in one of the other nobles. "Like a runaway slave or something? Maybe the monks— what was that story about Holy Saint ... Saint ...? The one with the gridiron, or ...." His imagination ran out; he fell into silence.

"I have another idea," said Ella. "We could let him go."

Consternation faced him. The king leaned forward from

his high seat, his sharp, mobile face and keen eyes passing to each man in turn.

"Think. Why am I king? I'm king because Osbert"—the forbidden name sent a visible shudder through the listening men, and called an answering twinge from the lacerated back of the servant who stood listening behind Wulfgar's stool—"because Osbert could not defend this kingdom against the Viking raiders. He just did what we'd always done. Told everyone to keep a lookout and organize their own defense. So we had ten shiploads land on a town and do what they liked while the other towns and parishes pulled the blankets over their heads and thanked God it wasn't them. What did I do? You know what I did. I pulled everyone back except the lookout stations, I organized the rider teams, I set up the mounted levies at the vital places. Now, they come down on us, we have a chance of coming down on them before they get too far, of teaching them a lesson. New ideas.

"I think we need another new idea here. We can let him go. We can do a deal with him. He stays away from Northumbria, he gives us hostages, we treat him as an honored guest till the hostages come, we send him off with a pile of presents. Doesn't cost us too much. Could save us a lot. By the time he's exchanged he'll have got over Cuthred's conversation with him. All part of the game. What do you say?"

The warriors looked at each other, eyebrows rising, heads shaking in surprise.

"Might work," muttered Cuthred.

Wulfgar cleared his throat to speak, a look of displeasure crossing his reddened face. He was cut off by a voice from the black monks at the end of the table.

"You may not do that, my lord."

"May not?"

"Must not. You have other duties than those in this world. The archbishop, our reverend father and former brother, has reminded us of the foul deeds done by this Ragnar against Christ's Church. Deeds done against us as men and

Christians—those we are commanded to forgive. But deeds done against Holy Church—those we must avenge with all our heart and all our strength. How many churches has this Ragnar burned? How many Christian men and women carried off to sell to the pagans and worse, to the followers of Mohammed? How many precious relics destroyed? And the gifts of the faithful stolen?

"It would be a sin against your soul to forgive these deeds. It would imperil the salvation of every man around this table. No, King, give him to us. Let us show you what we have made for you, for those who molest Mother Church. And when the news of that reaches back to the pagans, the robbers from the sea, let them know that Mother Church's arm is as heavy as her mercy is long. Let us give him to the serpent-pit. Let us make men talk of the worm-yard of King Ella."

The king hesitated, fatally. Before he could speak, the sharp agreement of the other monks and of the archbishop was echoed by the rumble of surprise, curiosity, approval from his warriors.

"I have never seen a man given to the worms," said Wulfgar, his face beaming with pleasure. "It is what every Viking in the world deserves. And so I shall say when I return to my own king, and I shall praise the wisdom and the cunning of King Ella."

The black monk who had spoken rose to his feet: Erkenbert the dreaded archdeacon. "The worms are ready. Have the prisoner taken to them. And let all attend—councillors, warriors, servants—to see the wrake and the vengeance of King Ella and Mother Church."

The council rose, Ella among them, his face still clouded by doubt, but swept along by the agreement of his men. The nobles began to jostle out, calling already for their servants, friends, wives, women to join them, to see the new thing. Shef, turning to follow his stepfather, looked back at the last moment to see the black monks still clustered in a little knot at the end of the table.

"Why did you say that?" muttered Archbishop Wulfhere

to his archdeacon. "We could pay a toll to the Vikings and still save our immortal souls. Why did you force the king to send this Ragnar to the serpents?"

The monk reached in his pouch and, like Cuthred, threw an object on the table. Then another.

"What are those, my lord?"

"This is a coin. A gold coin. With the script of the abominable worshippers of Mohammed on it!"

"It was taken from the prisoner."

"You mean—he is too evil to let live?"

"No, my lord. The other coin?"

"It is a penny. A penny from our own mint here in Eoforwich. It has my own name on it, see—Wulfhere. A silver penny."

The archdeacon picked up both coins and stowed them back in his pouch. "A very bad penny, my lord. Little silver, much lead. All the Church can afford in these days. Our slaves run away, our churls cheat on their tithes. Even the nobles give as little as they dare. Meanwhile the heathens' pouches drip with gold, stolen from believers.

"The Church is in danger, my lord. Not that she may be defeated and pillaged by the heathen, grievous though that is, for from that we may recover. It is that the heathens and the Christians may make common cause. For then they will find that they have no need of us. We must not let them deal."

Nods of agreement, even from the archbishop.

"So. To the serpents."

The serpent-pit was an old stone cistern from the time of the Rome-folk, with a light roof hastily erected over it to keep off the drizzle. The monks of St. Peter's Minster in Eoforwich were tender of their pets, the shining worms. All last summer the word had gone out to their many tenants scattered across the Church lands of Northumbria: Find the adders, seek them out in their basking places on the high fells, bring them in. So much remission of rent, so much remission of tithes for a foot-long worm; more for a foot and a half; more, disproportionately more for the old, the grand-father worms. Not a week had passed without a squirming bag being delivered to the *custos viperarum*—the keeper of the snakes—its contents to be lovingly tended, fed on frogs and mice, and on each other to promote their growth: "Dragon does not become dragon till it has tasted worm," the *custos* would say to his brothers. "Maybe the same is true of our adders."

Now lay brothers racked torches round the walls of the stone court to augment the evening twilight, carried in sacks of warm sand and straw and spread it on the floor of the pit to make the serpents fiery and active. And now the *custos* too appeared, smiling with satisfaction, waving along a gang of novices, each the proud—if careful—bearer of a leather sack that hissed and bulged disconcertingly. The *custos* took each bag in turn, held it up to the crowd now pushing and jostling round the low walls of the cistern, undid the lash-ings, and slowly poured the struggling inhabitants down into the pit. He moved a few paces as he did each one, to dis-tribute his serpents evenly. His task done, he stepped back to the edge of the lane kept open for the great ones by brawny companions—the king's own hearth-troop.

They came at last: the king, his council, their body-servants, the prisoner pushed along in the middle of them. There was a saying among the warriors of the North: "A man should not limp while both his legs are the same length." And Ragnar did not limp now. Yet he found it hard to hold himself straight. Cuthred's ministrations had not been gentle.

The great ones fell back when they came to the edge of the pit, and let the prisoner see what he faced. He grinned through broken teeth, his hands tied behind him, a powerful guard holding each arm. He still wore the strange shaggy clothes of tarred goatskin which had brought him his name. Erkenbert the archdeacon pushed forward to face him.

"That is the worm-yard," he said.

"Orm-garth," corrected Ragnar.

The priest spoke again, in simple English, the trade-talk

of the merchants. "Know this. You have a choice. If you become Christian, you live. As a slave. No orm-garth then for you. But you must become Christian."

The Viking's mouth twisted in contempt. He spoke in reply, still in the trade-tongue. "You priests. I know your talk. You say I live. How? As a slave, you say. What you not say, but I know, is how. No eyes, no tongue. Cut legs, cut hough-sinews, no walk."

His voice rose to a chant. "I fought in the front for thirty winters, always I struck with the sword. Four hundred men I killed, a thousand women I ravished, many minsters I burned, many men's bairns I sold. Many have wept for me, I never wept for them. Now I come to the orm-garth, like Gunnar the god-born. Do your worst, let the shining worm sting me to the heart. I shall not ask for mercy. Always I struck with the sword!"

"Get on with it," snarled Ella from behind the Viking. The guards began to hustle him forward.

"Stop!" Erkenbert called. "First bind his legs."

They tied the unresisting man roughly, pulled him to the edge, balanced him on the wall, then—he looking round at the pushing but silent crowd—shoved him over. He fell a few feet, landing with a thump on top of a pile of crawling snakes. Instantly they hissed, instantly they struck.

The man in the shaggy tunic and breeches laughed once from the ground.

"They cannot bite through," called a voice in disappointment. "His clothes are too thick."

"They may strike at his hands or face," called the serpent-keeper, jealous for the honor of his pets.

One of the largest adders indeed lay a few inches from Ragnar's face, the two staring almost eye-to-eye, the forked tongue of the one almost touching the chin of the other. A long moment of pause.

Then, suddenly, the man's head moved, shooting sideways, teeth agape. A threshing of coils, a mouth spitting blood, the snake lay headless. Again the Viking laughed. Slowly he began to roll, humping his body despite the bound arms and legs, trying to fall on the snakes with the full weight of hip or shoulder.

"He's killing them," cried the *custos* in mortal pain.

Ella moved forward in sudden disgust, clicking his fingers. "You and you. You've stout boots on. Go in and lift him out.

"I'll not forget this," he added in an undertone to the disconcerted Erkenbert. "You've made a damned fool of all of us.

"Now, you men, free his arms, free his legs, cut his clothes off, bind him again. You and you, go fetch hot water. Serpents desire heat. If we warm his skin they will be drawn to it.

"One more thing. He will lie still this time, to thwart us. Bind one arm to his body and tie the left wrist to a rope. Then we can make him move."

They lowered the prisoner again, still grinning, still unspeaking. This time the king himself steered the lowering to the spot where the snakes lay thickest. In a few moments they began to crawl to the warm body steaming in the chill air, writhing over it. Cries of disgust came from the women and servants in the crowd as they imagined the scales of the fat adders brushing over bare skin.

Then the king jerked his rope, again and again. The arm moved, the adders hissed, the disturbed ones struck, felt flesh, struck again and again, filling the man's body with their poison. Slowly, slowly, the awed watchers saw his face begin to change, to puff, to turn blue. As his eyes and tongue began to bulge, finally he called out once more.

"Gnythja mundu grisir ef galtar hag vissi," he remarked.

"What did he say?" muttered the crowd. "What does that mean?"

I know no Norse, thought Shef from his vantage point. But I know that bodes no good.

"Gnythja mundu grisir ef galtar hag vissi." The words still rang in the mind of the massive man, weeks later and hundreds of miles to the east, who was standing in the prow of

the longship easing gently up toward the Sjaelland shore. It was sheer chance that he had ever come to hear them. Had Ragnar been talking to himself alone? he mused. Or had he known someone would hear, would understand and remember? It must have been very long odds against anyone in an English court knowing Norse, or anyway, enough Norse to understand what Ragnar had said. But dying men were supposed to have insight. Maybe they could tell the future. Maybe Ragnar had known, or had guessed, what his words would do.

But if those were the words of fate, which would always find someone to speak them, they had chosen a strange route to come to him! In the crowd pushing round the ormgarth there had been a woman, concubine to an English noble, a *"lemman,"* as the English called such girls. But before she had been bought for her master in the slave-mart of London, she had plied the same trade in the court of King Maelsechnaill in Ireland, where much Norse was spoken. She had heard, she had understood. She had had the wit not to tell her master—lemmans without wit did not live to see their beauty fade—but she had whispered it to her secret lover, a trader going south. He had passed it on to the other members of his caravan. And among them there had been another slave, a former fisherman on the run, one who had taken special interest in it because he had seen the actual capture of Ragnar on the shore. In London, thinking himself safe, the slave had made a story of it to earn himself mugs of ale and hunks of bacon in the waterfront booths where all men were welcome, English or Frankish, Frisian or Dane, as long as their silver was good. And so the tale had come in the end to Northern ears.

The slave had been a fool, a man of no honor. He had seen in the tale of the death of Ragnar only excitement, strangeness, humor.

The massive man in the longship—Brand—saw in it much more. That was why he brought the news.

The boat was gliding in now along a long fjord, reaching into the flat, rich countryside of Sjaelland, easternmost of the Danish islands. There was no wind; the sail was furled up against the yard, the thirty oarsmen rowing a steady, unhurried, practiced stroke, the ripples of their progress fanning out across the flat, pondlike sea to caress the shore. Cows moved gently in rich meadows, fields of thickly shooting grain stretched into the distance.

The air of peace was totally deceptive, Brand knew. He was at the still center of the greatest storm in the North, its peace guaranteed only by hundreds of miles of war-torn sea and burning coastline. As they rowed in he had been challenged three times by naval patrols—heavy coastal warships never designed for the open sea, filled with men. They had let him through with increasing amusement, always keen to see a man try his luck. Even now two ships twice the size of his were cruising behind him, just to make certain there was no escape. He knew, his men knew, that worse lay ahead.

Behind him the helmsman passed the steering-oar to a crewman and strolled forward to the prow. For a few moments he stood behind his skipper, his head barely reaching the huge man's shoulder blade, and then spoke. He spoke softly, taking care not to be overheard even by the foremost rowers.

"You know I'm not one to question decisions," he murmured. "But since we're here, and we've all stuck our pizzles well and truly in the wasps' nest, maybe you won't mind me asking why?"

"Since you came so far without asking," replied Brand in the same low tones, "I'll give you three reasons and charge you for none of them.

"One: This is our chance to gain lasting glory. This will be a scene for sagamakers and for poets until the Last Day, when the gods fight the giants and the brood of Loki is loosed on the world."

The helmsman grinned. "You have enough glory already, champion of the men of Halogaland. And some men say the ones we are going to meet *are* the brood of Loki. Especially one of them."

"Two, then: That English slave, the runaway who told us the tale, the fisherman running from the Christ-monks—did you see his back? His masters deserve all the woe in the world, and I can send it to them."

This time the helmsman laughed aloud, but gently. "Did you ever see anyone after Ragnar had finished talking to him? And those we are going to visit are worse. Especially one of them. Maybe he and the Christ-monks deserve each other. But what of all the others?"

"So, then, Steinulf, it comes to three." Brand lifted gently the silver pendant which hung round his neck and lay on his chest, outside the tunic: a short-hafted, double-headed hammer. "I was asked to do this, as a service."

"By whom?"

"Someone we both know. In the name of the one who will come from the North."

"Ah. Well. That is good enough for both of us. Maybe for all of us. But I am going to do one thing before we get too close to the shore."

Deliberately, making certain his skipper saw what he was doing, the helmsman took the pendant which hung round his own neck and tucked it inside his tunic, pulling the collar so that no trace of the chain showed.

Slowly, Brand turned to face his crew and followed suit. At a word, the steady beat of the oars in the calm water checked. The oarsmen shuffled chains and pendants out of sight. Then the beat of oars resumed.

At the jetty ahead men could now be seen sitting or strolling, never looking at the approaching warboat, giving a perfect impression of total indifference. Behind them a vast dragon-hall lay like an upturned keel; behind it and round it, a vast confusion of sheds, bunkhouses, rollers, boatyards on the edge of the fjord, smithies, stores, rope-walks, corrals, barracoons. This was the heart of a naval empire, the power center of men intent on challenging kingdoms, the home of the homeless warriors.

The man sitting on the very end of the jetty ahead of him stood up, yawned, stretched elaborately and looked in the other direction. Danger. Brand turned to shout orders. Two of his men standing by the halliards ran a shield up to the masthead, its new-painted white face a sign of peace. Two others ran forward and eased the gaping dragon-head off its pegs on the prow, turning it carefully away from the shore and wrapping it in a cloth.

More men onshore suddenly became visible, now prepared to look directly at the boat. They gave no sign of welcome, but Brand knew that if he had not observed proper ceremonial his welcome would have been very different. At the thought of what might have happened—might still happen—he felt his belly give an unaccustomed twinge, as if his manhood was trying to crawl back within him. He turned his face out to the far shore, to ensure no expression betrayed him. He had been taught since he could crawl, *Never show fear. Never show pain.* He valued this more than life itself.

He knew also that in the gamble he was about to take, nothing could be less safe than a show of insecurity. He meant to bait his deadly hosts, draw them into his story: appear as a challenger, not a suppliant.

He meant to offer them a dare so shocking and so public that they would have no choice but to take it. It was not a plan that allowed half measures.

As the boat nosed into the jetty ropes were thrown, caught, snubbed round bollards, still with the same elaborate air of carelessness. A man was looking down into the boat. If this had been a trading port he might have asked the sailors what cargo, what name, where from? Here the man raised one eyebrow.

"Brand. From England."

"There are many men called Brand."

At a sign two of the ship's crewmen swung a gangplank from ship to jetty. Brand strolled across it, thumbs in belt, and stood facing the dockmaster. On the level boards he was looking down. Far down. He noted with inner pleasure the slight shift of the eyes as the dockmaster, no stripling himself, weighed up Brand's bulk, realized that man-to-man, at least, he was outmatched.

"Some men call me Viga-Brand. I come from Halogaland, in Norway, where men grow bigger than Danes."

"Killer-Brand. I have heard of you. But there are many killers here. It needs more than a name to be welcome."

"I have news. News for the kinsmen."

"It had better be news worth hearing if you disturb the kinsmen, coming here without leave or passport."

"News worth hearing it is." Brand looked directly into the dockmaster's eyes. "Come to hear it yourself. Tell your men to come and hear it. Anyone who cannot be bothered to hear what I have to say will curse his laziness till the last day he lives. But of course if you all have an urgent appointment in the privy let me not ask you to keep your breeches up."

Brand brushed past the other and strode wordlessly toward the plume of smoke rising from the great longhouse, the hall of the noble kinsmen, the place no enemy had seen and left alive and free to tell the tale—the Braethraborg itself. His men trooped off the ship and silently began to follow him.

The dockmaster's lips twitched, finally, with amusement. He made a sign and his men, picking their spears and bows from concealment, began to straggle inland. A flag dipped in acknowledgement from the still-vigilant outposts on the headland two miles off.

Light shone into the hall from many open shutters, but Brand halted when he got inside to let his eyes adjust, to look around, to get the feel of his audience. In later years, he knew, this scene would be famous in song and saga—if he played it right. In the next few minutes he would gain either imperishable glory or unthinkable death.

Inside the hall many men were sitting, standing, loitering, playing at one game or another. None looked at him as he came in, or at the other men silently filtering in behind him, but he knew they had registered his presence. As his eyes cleared he saw slowly that though there was no apparent order in the hall, indeed a careful avoidance of it—a pretense that all warriors, all true *drengir*, were equal—still the groupings of the men were all subtly poised on one center. At the end of the hall, there was a little space no one ventured into. There four men were grouped, all seeming intent on their own concerns.

He walked toward them, the padding of his soft seaman's shoes audible in what had indiscernibly become silence.

He reached the four men. "Greetings!" he said, pitching his voice loud for the audience clustered around and behind him. "I have news. News for the sons of Ragnar."

One of the four glanced over his shoulder at him, went back to paring his fingernails with a knife. "Great news it must be, for a man to come to the Braethraborg without invitation or passport."

"Great news it is." Brand filled his lungs and controlled his breathing. "For it is news of the death of Ragnar."

Utter silence now. The man who had spoken continued his paring, intent on his left index finger, the knife slicing, slicing. Blood sprang out, the knife cut on down, down to the quick and the bone. The man made no sound and no movement.

A second one of the four spoke, picking up a stone piece from the checkerboard to make his move, a powerful, thick-shouldered man with grizzled hair. "Tell us," he remarked, his voice carefully unperturbed, deliberately refusing to show unmanly emotion. "How did our old father Ragnar die? For it is not to be surprised at, since he was getting on in years."

"It all began on the coast of England, where he was wrecked. According to the story I heard, he was caught by the men of King Ella." Brand changed his voice slightly, as if to match, or to mock, the second Ragnarsson's studied pretense of imperturbability. "I do not suppose they had much trouble, for, as you say, he was getting on in years. Maybe he offered no resistance."

The grizzled man still held his draughtsman, his fingers closing on it tighter, tighter. Blood spurted out from under his fingernails, splashed on the board. The man put the piece down, moved it once, twice, lifted the captured draughtsman to the side. "I take, Ivar," he remarked.

The man he was playing with spoke. He was a man with hair so fair it was almost white, swept back off his pale face and held with a linen headband. He looked at Brand with eyes as colorless as frozen water, under lashes that never blinked.

"What did they do once they had caught him?"

Brand looked carefully into the pale man's unblinking stare. He shrugged, still elaborately unconcerned.

"They took him to King Ella's court at Eoforwich. It was no great matter, for they thought him only a common pirate, of no importance. I believe they asked him some questions, had some little sport with him. But then, tiring of him, they decided they might as well put him to death."

In the dead silence Brand studied his fingernails, conscious that his baiting of the Ragnarssons had almost reached its climax of danger. He shrugged again.

"Well. They gave him to the Christ-priests in the end. I expect he did not seem worthy of death from the warriors."

A flush shot into the pale man's cheeks. He seemed to be holding his breath, almost choking. The flush deepened, deepened till his face was scarlet. He began to sway to and fro in his chair, a kind of coughing coming from deep in his throat. His eyes bulged, the scarlet deepened to purple—in the dim light of the hall, almost to black. Slowly the swaying stopped, the man seemed to win some deep internal battle within himself, the coughing died, the face ebbed back to a startling pallor.

The fourth man who stood by his three brothers, watching the draughts game, was leaning on a spear. He had not moved or spoken, had kept his eyes down. Slowly now he raised them to look at Brand. For the first time the tall messenger flinched. There was something in the eyes he had heard of but had never believed: the pupils astonishingly black, the iris around them as white as new-fallen snow—startlingly clear—and surrounding the black totally, like the paint around an iron shield-boss. The eyes glinted like moonlight on metal.

"How did King Ella and the Christ-priests decide to kill the old man, in the end?" asked the fourth of the Ragnarssons, his voice low, almost gentle. "I suppose you will be telling us it did not take much doing."

Brand answered bluntly and truthfully, taking no more risks. "They put him in the serpent-pit, the worm-yard, the orm-garth. I understand there was some little trouble, as to begin with the snakes would not bite and then—from what I heard—Ragnar bit them first. But in the end they bit him and he died. It was a slow death, and no weapon-mark on him. Not one to be proud of in Valhalla."

The man with the strange eyes did not move a muscle. There was a pause, a long pause, as the intently watching audience waited for him to make some sign that he had heard, for him to show some failure in self-control like his brothers. It did not come. The man straightened finally, tossed the spear he had been leaning on to a bystander, hooked his thumbs in his belt, prepared to speak.

A grunt from the bystander, a grunt of surprise, drawing all eyes to him. Silently he held up the tough ashwood spear he had been thrown. On it men could see indentations, marks where fingers had gripped. A slight hum of satisfaction ran round the hall.

Before the man with the strange eyes could speak, Brand interrupted, seizing the moment. Pulling his mustache thoughtfully, he remarked, "There was one other thing."

"Yes?"

"After the snakes had bitten him, as he lay dying, Ragnar spoke. They did not understand him, of course, for he spoke in our tongue, in the *norroent mal*, but someone heard, someone passed it on; in the end I was fortunate enough to come by it. I have no invitation and no passport, as you said just now, but it occurred to me you might be interested enough to want to know."

"What did he say, then, the old man dying?"

Brand lifted his voice loudly so that it filled the whole

hall, like a herald issuing a challenge. "He said, *'Gynthja mundu grisir ef galtar hag vissi.'*"

This time there was no need to translate. The whole hall knew what Ragnar had said: "If they knew how the old boar died, how the little pigs would grunt."

"So that is why I came uninvited," called Brand, his voice still high and challenging. "Though some told me it might be dangerous. I am a man who likes to hear grunting. And so I came to tell the little pigs. And you must be the little pigs, from what men tell me. You, Halvdan Ragnarsson"—he nodded to the man with the knife. "You, Ubbi Ragnarsson"—the first draughts-player. "You, Ivar Ragnarsson, famous for your white hair. And you, Sigurth Ragnarsson. I see now why men call you Orm-i-auga, the Snake-eye.

"It is not likely that my news has pleased you. But I hope you will agree that it was news you should be told."

The four men were on their feet now, all facing him, the pretense of indifference gone. As they took in his words, they nodded. Slowly, they were beginning to grin, their expressions all the same, looking for the first time as if they were all a family, all brothers, all sons of the same man. Their teeth showed.

It was the prayer of the monks and minister-men in those days: *Domine, libera nos a furore normannorum*—"Lord, deliver us from the fury of the Northmen." If they had seen those faces, any sensible monk would have added immediately: *Sed praesepe, Domine, a humore eorum*—"But especially, Lord, from their mirth."

"It was news we should be told," said the Snake-eye, "and we thank you for bringing it. At the start we thought you might not be telling all the truth about this matter, and that was why we may have seemed displeased. But what you said at the end—ah, that was our father's voice. He knew someone would hear it. He knew someone would tell us. And he knew what we would do. Didn't he, boys?"

A gesture, and someone rolled forward a great round chopping block, an oak trunk sawn off. A heave from the four brothers together, and it crashed down firm on the floor. The sons of Ragnar clustered round it, facing their men, each raising one foot and placing it on the block. They spoke together, following the ritual:

"Now we stand on this block, and we make this boast, that we will—"

". . . invade England in vengeance for our father"—so Halvdan said.

". . . capture King Ella and kill him with torments for Ragnar's death"—so Ubbi.

". . . defeat all the kings of the English and bring the land into subjection to us"—so Sigurth the Snake-eye.

". . . wreak vengeance on the black crows, the Christ-priests who counseled the orm-garth"—so Ivar spoke. They ended again together:

". . . and if we go back on our words let the gods of Asgarth despise us and reject us, and may we never join our father and our ancestors in their dwellings."

As they ended, the smoke-blackened beams of the longhouse were filled with a roar of approval from four hundred throats, the jarls, the nobles, the skippers, and the helmsmen of the whole pirate fleet in unison. Outside, the rank and file gathering from their booths and bunkhouses nudged each other with excitement and anticipation, knowing that a decision had been made.

"And now," the Snake-eye yelled over the din, "pull out the tables, spread the boards. No man may inherit from his father till he has drunk the funeral ale. And so we shall drink the arval for Ragnar, drink like heroes. And in the morning we shall gather every man and every ship and take our way to England, so that they shall never forget us nor be quit of us!

"But now, drink. And, stranger, sit at our board and tell us more of our father. There will be a place for you in England once it is ours."

Far away, Shef, the dark boy, the stepson of Wulfgar, lay on a straw pallet. The mist was still rising from the dank

ground of Emneth, and only a thin old blanket covered him
from it. Inside the stout-timbered wooden hall, his stepfather
Wulfgar lay in comfort, if not in love, with the boy's
mother, the lady Thryth. Alfgar lay in a warm bed in a room
by his parents, and so too did Godive, the concubine's child,
Wulfgar's daughter. At Wulfgar's homecoming they had all
eaten lavishly of the roasted and the boiled, the baked and
the brewed—duck and goose from the fens, pike and lam-
prey from the rivers.

Shef had eaten rye porridge and gone out to his solitary
hut by the smithy where he worked, to have his only friend
dress his new-got scars. Now he was tossing in the grip of
a dream. If dream it was.

*He saw a dark field somewhere on the edge of the world, lit
only by a purple sky. On the field lay shapeless huddles of
rags and bone and skin, white skulls and rib cages showing
through the remains of gorgeous garments. Round the huddles, everywhere on the field, hopped and swarmed a great
army of birds—huge black birds with black beaks, stabbing
savagely into eye sockets and pecking bone-joints for a mor-
sel of flesh or marrow. But the bodies had been picked over
many times, the bones were dry; the birds began to croak
loudly and peck at each other instead.*

*They ceased, they grew quiet, they clustered together to
where four black birds were standing. They listened as the
four croaked and croaked in ever louder and more menacing
tones. Then the whole flock rose as one into the purple sky,
circled and closed formation, then banked slowly like a single
organism and flew directly toward him, toward Shef, to where
he was standing. The leader flew straight at him, he could
see the remorseless unblinking golden eye, the black beak
pointed at his face. It did not pull back, he could not move;
something was holding his head firm and rigid; he felt the
black beak driving deep into the soft jelly of his eye.*

Shef woke with a shout and a start, leaping straight off the
pallet, clutching his thin blanket round him as he stared out

of the hole in his hut's wall into a marshy dawn. His friend
Hund called from the other pallet.

"What is it, Shef? What frightened you?"

For a moment he could not reply. Then it came out as a
croak—he did not know what he was saying.

"The ravens! The ravens are on the wing!"

Chapter Three

"Are you certain it is the Great Army itself which has
landed?" Wulfgar's voice was angry but unsure. It
was news he did not want to believe. But he did not dare to
challenge the messenger openly.

"There is no doubt," said Edrich, the king's thane, trusted
servant of Edmund, king of the East Angles.

"And this army is led by the sons of Ragnar?"

Even more fearful news for Wulfgar, thought Shef as he
listened to the debate from the back of the room. Every
freeman in Emneth had crowded into their lord's hall, summoned by runners. For though a freeman in England could
lose everything—land-right, folk-right, even kin-right—for
failing to answer a lawful summons to arms, for that very
reason it was also their right to hear all issues debated publicly before they answered any call.

Whether Shef had any right to join them was another
matter. But he had not been collared as a slave yet, and the
freeman standing by the door to verify presence and absence still owed Shef for his mended ploughshare. He had
grunted doubtfully, looked at the sword and shabby scabbard at Shef's side, and decided not to press the point. Now
Shef stood at the very back of the room among the poorest
cottagers of Emneth, trying to hear without being seen.

"My men have spoken to many churls who have seen
them," said Edrich. "They say this army is led by four great

warriors, the sons of Ragnar, all of equal status. Every day the warriors gather round a great banner with the sign of a black raven. It is the Raven Banner."

Which the daughters of Ragnar wove all in one night, which spreads its wings for victory and droops them for defeat. It was a familiar story, and a fearful one. The deeds of the sons of Ragnar were famous all over Northern Europe, wherever their ships had sailed: England, Ireland, France, Spain, and even the lands beyond in the Middle Sea, from which they had returned years before laden with booty. So why had they now turned their fury on the poor and puny kingdom of the East Angles? Anxiety grew on Wulfgar's face as he pulled his long mustache.

"And where are they camped?"

"In the meadows by the Stour, south of Bedricsward." Edrich the King's Thane was visibly beginning to lose his patience. He had been over this several times before, and in more than one place. It was the same with every petty landowner. They didn't want information, they wanted a way out of their duty. But he had expected better from this one, famous for his hatred of the Vikings, a man—so he told it— who had stood sword to sword with the famous Ragnar himself.

"So what are we to do?"

"The order of King Edmund is that every freeman of the East Angles capable of bearing arms is to muster at Norwich. Every man over fifteen winters and under fifty. We will match their host with ours."

"How many of them are there?" called one of the richer tenants from the front.

"Three hundred ships."

"How many men is that?"

"They row three dozen oars, mostly," said the king's thane, briefly and reluctantly. This was the sticking point. Once the yokels realized what they were up against, they might be hard to move. But it was his duty to tell them the truth.

There was a silence while every mind confronted the same problem. Shef, faster than the others, spoke aloud.

"Three hundred ships, and three dozen oars. That's nine hundred dozen. Ten dozen is a long hundred. More than ten thousand men. All of them warriors," he added, more in amazement than fear.

"We can't fight them," said Wulfgar decisively, turning his glare away from his stepson. "We must pay tribute instead."

Edrich's patience was at an end. "That is for King Edmund to decide. And he will pay less if the Great Army sees that it is matched by a host of equal size. But I am not here to listen to talk—I bring a summons to obey. You and the landholders of Upwell and Outwell and every village between Ely and Wisbech. The king's order is that we shall muster here and set out for Norwich tomorrow. Every man liable for military service from the village of Emneth must ride or be liable to penalty and punishment from the king. Those are my orders and they are your orders too." He turned on his heel, facing the room full of stirring, unhappy men. "Freemen of Emneth, what do you say?"

"Aye," said Shef compulsively.

"He's not a freeman," snarled Alfgar from his place by his father.

"Then he damned well should be. Or he shouldn't be here. Can't you people make your minds up about anything? You've heard your king's commands."

But Edrich's words were drowned by a slow, reluctant mutter of assent from sixty throats.

In the Viking camp by the Stour, things were very different. Here the four sons of Ragnar made the decisions. They knew each others' minds too well for more than the briefest discussion.

"They'll pay in the end," said Ubbi. He and Halvdan were very much like the rest of their army, in both physique and temperament. Halvdan ruddy, the other already grizzled, both of them powerful and dangerous fighters. Not men to be trifled with.

"We must decide now," grunted Halvdan.

"Who shall it be then?" asked Sigurth.

All four men considered for a few moments. Someone who could do the job, someone experienced. At the same time someone they could afford to lose.

"Sigvarth," said Ivar finally. His pale face did not move; his colorless eyes remained fixed on the sky; he spoke only the one word. What he said was not a suggestion, but the answer. He who was called the Boneless One, though never in his presence, did not make suggestions. His brothers considered, approved.

"Sigvarth!" called out Sigurth Snake-eye.

A few yards away the jarl of the Small Isles bent over his game at knucklebones. He finished his cast, to show a proper spirit of independence, but then straightened and walked hopefully over to the little group of leaders.

"You called out my name, Sigurth."

"You have five ships? Good. We think the English and their little King Edmund are trying to play stupid games with us. Resisting, trying to bargain. No good. We want you to go out and show them who they're dealing with. Take your ships up the coast, then round to the west. Push inland, do as much damage as you can, burn some villages. Show them what could happen if they provoke us. You know what to do."

"Yes. Done it before." He hesitated. "But what about spoils?"

"Anything you get, it's yours. But loot isn't what this is about. Do something that they will remember. Do it as Ivar would do it."

The jarl grinned again, but more hesitantly, as most men did when the name of Ivar Ragnarsson the Boneless was mentioned.

"Where will you land?" asked Ubbi.

"Place called Emneth. I was there once before. Found me

a nice little chicken." The jarl's grin was cut off this time by a sudden movement from Ivar.

Sigvarth had given a stupid reason. He was not going on this mission to repeat the escapades of his youth. It was unwarriorlike. It was also the kind of thing Ivar did not discuss.

The moment passed. Ivar leaned back in his chair and turned his attention elsewhere. They knew Sigvarth was not the best in the Army—one of the reasons they were letting him go.

"Do the job and never mind chickens," said Sigurth. He waved a hand in dismissal.

At least Sigvarth knew the mechanics of his profession. At dawn two days later his five ships were sweeping cautiously into the mouth of the river Ouse, with the tide still on the flow. An hour's rowing at high tide took them as far inland as the water would bear, until the boats' keels grated on the sand. The dragon-prows nuzzled in, the men poured ashore. Instantly the assigned ship-guards backed water, pulled their wave-coursers offshore to the mudbanks, and waited there for the ebb tide to ground them out of reach of any counterattack from the local levies.

The youngest and swiftest men of Sigvarth's command had already moved out. Finding a small stud of ponies they cut down the lad in charge and raced off to round up more. As they captured the horses they sent them back to the main body. By the time the sun struggled through the morning mists a hundred and twenty men were pounding along the twisted and muddy paths towards their goal.

They rode in a hard, disciplined group. Keeping together, without advance or flank guards, counting upon strength and surprise to drive through any resistance. When their path took them up to any inhabited place—farmhouse, garth, or hamlet—the main body halted for as long as it might take a man to piss. The lighter men on the better horses swept round to the flanks and rear and halted, to prevent any escapes that might raise the alarm. Then the main body attacked. Their orders were simple, so simple that Sigvarth had not even bothered to repeat them.

They killed every person they met—man, woman, child, or babe in cradle—immediately, without halting to ask questions or seek for entertainment. Then they remounted and drove on. No looting, not yet. And, on the strictest of instructions, no fire.

By midday a corridor of death was slashed through the peaceful English countryside. Not a single person was left alive. Far behind the attackers men were beginning to notice that their neighbors were not astir, were finding horses missing and corpses in fields, were ringing the church bells and lighting their alarm beacons. But ahead of the Vikings there was not the slightest suspicion of their deadly presence.

The party from Emneth had set out considerably later in the day than Sigvarth's men. They had had to wait for the reluctant contingents from Upwell, Outwell, and beyond. Then there was a long delay while the landholders of the area greeted each other and ponderously exchanged courtesies. Next Wulfgar decided that they could not start on empty bellies and generously called for mulled ale for the leaders and small beer for the men. It was hours after sunrise when the hundred and fifty armed men, the military service of four parishes, set off down the road through the marsh which would lead them across the Ouse and in the end to Norwich. Even at this early stage they were already trailed by stragglers whose girths had broken, or whose bowels had loosened, or who had slipped off to make their farewells to their own wives or to other men's. The troop rode without precautions and without suspicion. The first inkling they had of the Vikings' presence was as they came round a bend in the road and saw heading toward them a tight-packed column of armed men.

Shef was riding just behind the leaders, as close to Edrich the King's Thane as he dared to go. Speaking up at the council had got him Edrich's favor. No one would send him back while Edrich was watching. Yet he was still there, as

Alfgar had taken pains to point out to him, as a smith, not as a freeman on military service. At least he still had his self-forged sword.

Shef saw them as soon as the others, and heard the startled cries of the leaders.

"Who are those men?"

"It's the Vikings!"

"No—it can't be! They're in Suffolk. We're still negotiating."

"It's the Vikings, you porridge-brains! Get your fat arses off your horses and form up for battle. You there, dismount, dismount! Horse-holders to the rear. Get your shields off your backs and form up."

Edrich the king's thane was by this time bellowing at the top of his voice, whirling his horse round and riding into the tangled confusion of the English column. Slowly men began to appreciate the situation, to drop from their saddles, to root desperately for weapons that they had stowed for comfortable riding. To edge toward the front or toward the rear, depending on personal inclination, boldness or cowardice.

Shef had few preparations to make—the poorest man in the column. He dropped the reins of his nag, a grudging loan from his stepfather, pulled the wooden shield from his back, and loosened his only weapon in its sheath. All the armor he had was a leather jacket with such studs as he had been able to collect sewn onto it. He took position immediately behind Edrich and stood ready, his heart beating fast and excitement clutching his throat—but all outweighed by a vast curiosity. How would the Vikings fight? What was the nature of battle?

On the Viking side, Sigvarth had grasped the situation as soon as he saw the first riders coming toward him. Dropping his heels from their tucked-up riding position, he rose in his saddle, turned, and bellowed a brief command to the men behind him. Instantly the Viking column dissolved in practiced disarray. In a moment they had all dismounted. One man in five, already told off for the task, seized horse-

reins and led the mounts to the rear, bending down, as soon
as they were clear of the throng, to drive pegs into the
ground and knot the reins to them. As soon as this was
done, the two dozen horse handlers clustered in the rear and
formed a reserve.

Meanwhile the others halted for the space of twenty
heartbeats. Some in grim silence, others swiftly reknotting
their shoes, or gulping water or pissing as they stood. Then
all simultaneously unslung shields, loosened swords, passed
their axes to shield-hands, poised the long battle-spears in
their casting-hands. Without further words they spread into
a line two-deep, from edge to edge of the road, where it dissolved into swamp on either side. At a single shouted word
from Sigvarth at they stepped forward at a brisk walk, the
flanks falling back until the line formed a broad shallow arrow pointing directly at the English levies. At its apex was
Sigvarth himself. Behind him his son Hjörvarth led a picked
dozen—the men who, when the English line was broken,
would sweep through and round to the rear, cutting men
down from behind and turning setback into rout.

Facing them, the English had formed into a rough line
three- or four-deep, also extending from edge to edge of the
road. They had solved their problem with the horses by
abandoning them, dropping reins and leaving the animals to
stand or trot away. Among the mob of ponies there were
also a few men who had slunk quietly to the rear. Not many.
After three generations of raid and war many of the English
had personal grudges to pay off—while none wished to be
exposed to the derision of his neighbors. Shouts of encouragement rose from all the men who thought their rank enti-
tled them to do so. But no orders. Glancing round, Shef saw
that he was very much alone, immediately behind the group
of armored nobles. As the Viking arrow drove toward the
English line, men had unconsciously edged to left or right.
Only the most determined were there to take the first blow,
where the weight would fall if Wulfgar and his colleagues
were to fail. The wedge formation was said to be the inven-

tion of the Viking war-god. What would happen when it struck?

Spears began to fly from the English line, some falling short, some batted aside by the shields of the leaders. Suddenly, simultaneously, the Vikings began to trot forward. One, two, three paces, and the throwing arms of the leaders drew back and a shower of javelins whirred at the English center. In front of him, Shef saw Edrich adroitly twist his shield-boss so that one spear flew over his head and far to the back of the line, and smash another with the edge so that it fell at his feet. A few paces to one side, a noble dropped his shield to block a spear aimed at his belly, choked, and fell sideways as another ripped through his beard and throat. Another landholder cursed as three spears found his shield at once, tried to knock them free with his sword, then frenziedly struggled to pull the strap from his elbow and drop the now-clumsy encumbrance dragging down his arm. Before he could succeed the Viking wedge was on them.

In front of him Shef saw the Viking leader swing a mighty blow at Wulfgar. The Englishman caught it on his shield, tried to stab in reply with his sword. But the Viking had already recovered and swung again with all his force, backhand. Once more Wulfgar parried, with a mighty clang as his own blade met the Viking's, but he was already off balance. With a sudden thrust the Viking clubbed him in the face with his sword-pommel, thrust a shield-boss into his ribs, and hurled him aside by main force. As he stepped forward to stab, Shef sprang at him.

For all his size the Viking leader was amazingly fast on his feet. He jumped back a pace and slashed at the boy's unarmed head. Shef had realized two things already from his three heartbeats' observation of real battle: One, in battle everything must be done with full force, with none of the unconscious restraint of training or practice. He put all his smithy-hardened muscle into the parry. Two, in battle there could be no interval or pause between blows. As the Viking swung again, Shef was already braced for him. This time his parry caught the blow higher up. He felt a clang and a snap and the fragment of a blade whirred over his head. Not mine, thought Shef. Not mine! He stepped forward and stabbed exultantly for the groin.

Something knocked him sideways and backwards. He staggered, caught his balance, and found himself shoved aside again by the figure of Edrich, bellowing something in his ear. As he glanced round Shef realized that while he exchanged blows with their leader, the tip of the Viking wedge had broken through. Half a dozen English nobles lay on the ground. Wulfgar, still on his feet, was backing dazedly toward Shef, but a dozen Vikings were facing him, pouring through the broken line. Shef found himself shouting, brandishing his sword, daring the foremost of the Vikings to come on. For a heartbeat the man and the boy stared into each other's eyes. Then the man wheeled left, following his orders, moving through the gap to roll up the English line and drive the flankers into the swamp in disorder and confusion.

"Run for it!" shouted Edrich. "We're beat. Nothing to do now. Run now and we can get away."

"My father," shouted Shef, lunging forward to try to grasp Wulfgar by the belt and haul him back.

"Too late, he's down."

It was true. The dazed thane had taken another smashing blow on the helmet and staggered forward, to be enveloped by a wave of enemies. The Vikings were still fanning sideways, but at any moment some would press forward and overwhelm the few men left standing in the center. Shef found himself seized by the collar and hustled, half-choking to the rear.

"Damned fools. Half-trained levies. What can you expect? Grab a horse, boy."

In seconds Shef was cantering down the track the way he had come. His first battle was over.

And he had run from it within seconds of the first blow being struck.

Chapter Four

The reeds at the marsh's edge moved slightly in the morning breeze. They moved again and Shef peered out at the empty countryside. The Viking raiders were gone.

He turned and waded back through the reeds to the path he had found the previous evening. The small island was hidden by low trees. Edrich the king's thane was eating the cold remains of their dinner from the night before. He wiped greasy fingers on the grass and raised his eyebrows.

"Nothing in sight," Shef said. "Quiet. No smoke that I could see."

They had fled the battle, knowing it was lost, seeking only to save their own lives. There had been no sign of pursuit when they abandoned their horses and fled on foot into the marsh where they had spent the night—an oddly comfortable and pleasant night for Shef. He thought about it with mixed feelings of both pleasure and guilt. It had been an island of peace in a sea of anxiety and trouble. Just for one evening there had been no work to do, no duty that could possibly be performed. All they had to do was hide, protect themselves, and stay as comfortable as possible. Shef had splashed off into the marsh and quickly found them a dry island in the midst of the pathless fen, where it was certain that no stranger would ever penetrate. It had been easy to put up a shelter made out of the reed which the marsh-folk used for thatching. Eels had been snared in the sluggish water, and Edrich, after brief consideration, had

seen no harm in making a fire. The Vikings had other things
to do and weren't going to come splashing all the way over
here just because of a bit of smoke.

In any case, before darkness fell, they could see smoke
rising all around them. "The raiders on their way back,"
said Edrich. "They don't mind sending up signals when
they're retreating."

Had he ever run from a battle before? Shef asked cautiously, nagged by the worry that kept on surfacing every
time memory brought back the picture of his stepfather going down, engulfed by a tide of enemies. "Many times,"
Edrich replied, in the curious camaraderie of this day stolen
out of time. "And don't think that was a battle. Just a skirmish. But I've run for it often. Too often. And if everybody
did that we'd have a lot fewer dead men on our side. We
never lose very many while we're standing and fighting, but
once the Vikings break through it's just a slaughter. Just
stop a moment and think of it—every man who gets off the
field is saved for another stand-up fight on even terms another day.

"Trouble is," he smiled grimly, "the more often it happens the less likely most people are to be willing to try
again. They lose heart. And there's no need for it. We lost
yesterday because nobody was ready, not physically, not in
their minds either. If they'd spend a tenth of the time they
spend in whining afterwards in getting ready beforehand,
we'd have no need ever to lose a battle. As the proverb
says: 'Often the deed—late in doom diminishes, in all suc-
cesses. Starves he later.' Now show me your blade."

Face unmoving, Shef drew it from its scuffed leather
scabbard and passed it over. Edrich turned it thoughtfully in
his hands.

"It looks like a hedger's tool," he remarked. "Or a reed-
cutter's bill. Not a real weapon. Yet I saw the Viking jarl's
sword snap on it. How did that happen?"

"It is a good blade," Shef replied. "Maybe the best in
Emneth. I made it myself, forged in strips. Much of it is soft
iron. I beat it out myself from the iron blooms they send us

from the South. But there are layers too of hard steel. A thane from March gave me some good spearheads in payment for work I did for him. I melted and beat them out, and then I twisted the iron and steel strips round each other and forged the whole into a blade. The iron lets it bend, the steel gives it strength. In the end I welded on a cutting edge of the hardest steel I could find. Four man-loads of charcoal the whole work cost me."

"And with all that work you made it short and single-edged, like a work-tool. Put on a plain ox-bone handle, with no guard. And then you left it out in the wet and let it get rusty."

Shef shrugged. "If I swaggered round Emneth with a warrior's weapon on my hip and serpent-patterns glittering on the blade, how long would I have kept it? The rust is just enough to discolor the blade. I make sure it eats no further."

"That was the other question I meant to ask you. The young thane said you were not a freeman. You behave as if you were in hiding. Yet in the fight you called Wulfgar 'father.' There is some mystery here. The world is full of thanes' bastards, God knows. But no one tries to enslave them."

Shef had faced the same question many times, and in another time or place would not have answered. But in the island in the fen, speaking one to another, status forgotten, the words came.

"He is not my father, though I call him that. Eighteen summers ago the Vikings raided here. Wulfgar was away from Emneth then, but my mother, the lady Thryth, was here, with her baby son Alfgar—my half brother, her child and Wulfgar's. A servant got Alfgar away when the raiders came in the night, but my mother was taken."

Edrich nodded slowly. All this was familiar enough. But still his question was not answered. There was a system in these matters, at least for those of rank. After a while, surely, the husband might have expected to hear from the slave-marts of Hedeby or Kaupang, to tell him such and such a lady was ransomable, at a price. If he did not, then he could have considered himself a widower, free to marry again, to set his fine silver bracelets on another woman who would rear his son. Sometimes, it was true, such arrangements were disturbed by the arrival, twenty years later, of some withered crone who had managed to outlive her usefulness in the North and bribe her way, God knew how, onto a ship that would take her home. But not often. Neither case explained the young man sitting before him.

"My mother returned, only a few weeks later. Pregnant with me. She swore that my father was the jarl of the Vikings himself. When I was born she wanted me named Halfden, because I am half a Dane. But Wulfgar cursed her. He said that was a hero's name, the name of the king who founded the race of the Shieldings, from whom the kings of England and Denmark both claim descent. Too good for me. And so I was given a dog's name instead. Shef."

The young man dropped his eyes. "That is why my stepfather hates me and wants to make me a slave, why my half brother Alfgar has everything, and I nothing."

He had not told the full story: How Wulfgar had pressed and pressed his pregnant wife to take birthwort, to kill the rapist's child in her womb. How he himself had only been saved by the intervention of Father Andreas, who had denounced fiercely the sin of child-murder, even of a Viking's child. How Wulfgar in his rage and jealousy had taken a concubine, and bred on her Godive the beautiful, so that in the end there had been three children growing up in Emneth: Alfgar the trueborn; Godive, child of Wulfgar and his slave-lemman; Shef, child of Thryth and the Viking.

The king's thane passed back the hand-forged blade in silence. Still a mystery, he thought. How had the woman escaped? Viking slavers were not usually so careless.

"What was the name of this jarl?" he asked. "Of your . . ."

"Of my father? My mother says his name was Sigvarth. The jarl of the Small Isles. Wherever they are."

They sat for a while in silence, then stretched out for sleep.

* * *

It was late the next day when Shef and Edrich walked cautiously out of the reeds. Well-fed and unharmed, they approached what they could already see were the ruins of Emneth.

All the buildings were burnt, some mere heaps of ash, others with blackened timbers protruding. The thane's house and stockade were gone, the church, the smithy, the huddle of wattle-and-daub houses for the freemen, the lean-tos and sandpit-houses of the slaves. A few people still moved, stumbling haphazardly here and there, poking in the ashes or joining those already clustered round the well.

As they came into the village area, Shef called to one of the survivors, one of his mother's maids.

"Truda. Tell me what happened. Are there more . . . ?"

She was shaking, gaping up at him with horror and amazement, looking at him unharmed, his shield, sword. "You better . . . come see your mother."

"My mother's still here?" Shef felt a slight lift of hope at his heart. Maybe the others would be there too. Could Alfgar have got away? And Godive? What of Godive?

They followed the maid as she hobbled clumsily along.

"Why does she walk like that?" muttered Shef, looking at her painful limp.

"Been raped," said Edrich briefly.

"But . . . But Truda's no virgin."

Edrich answered the unspoken question. "Rape's different. If you have four men hauling at you while another does it, all of them excited, tear sinews, breaks bones sometimes. Even worse if the woman tries to fight them."

Shef thought of Godive again, and his knuckles whitened as he gripped the inside of his shield-boss. It was not only the menfolk who paid for lost battles.

They followed Truda in silence as she limped before them to a makeshift shelter, a collection of planks propped on half-burnt timbers and leaning against a fragment of stockade saved from the flames. She reached the shelter, looked inside, muttered a few words, and waved them in.

The lady Thryth lay inside, on a heap of old sacking. From the grim look of pain on her face and the awkward way she sprawled, it was obvious that she too had been through Truda's experience. Shef knelt beside her and felt for her hand.

Her voice was just a whisper, weakened by terrible memory. "We had no warning, no time to prepare. No one seemed to know what to do. The men rode straight here after the battle. They couldn't make up their minds. Those pigs caught us while they were still arguing. They were all round us before anyone knew that they had come."

She grew silent, writhed a bit in pain, looked up at her son with empty eyes.

"They are beasts. They killed everyone who showed fight. Then they gathered the rest of us together outside the church. It was beginning to rain by then. First they picked out the young girls and the pretty girls, and some of the boys. For the slave markets. And then . . . then they brought out their prisoners from the battle and then . . ."

Her voice began to quake and she pulled her stained apron up to her eyes.

"And then they made us watch . . ."

Her voice was drowned in tears. After a few moments she seemed to remember something and moved suddenly. She gripped Shef's hand and for the first time looked directly at him.

"But Shef. It was him. It was the same one as last time."

"Sigvarth Jarl?" asked Shef, his mouth thick.

"Yes. Your . . . your . . ."

"What did he look like? Was he a big man, dark hair, white teeth?"

"Yes. With gold bracelets all up his arm." Shef thought back to the moments of conflict, felt again the snap of the sword breaking and the moment of delight with which he had stepped forward to stab. Could it be that God had saved him from a terrible sin? But if that were the case—what had God been doing afterward?

"Couldn't he protect you, mother?"

"No. He didn't even try." Thryth's voice had gone hard and controlled again. "When they broke ranks after . . . after the show, he told them to loot and enjoy themselves till the warhorns blew. They kept their slaves, tied them together; but the rest of us, Truda and the ones they weren't keeping . . . We were just handed over.

"He recognized me, Shef! And he remembered me. But when I begged him just to keep me for himself he laughed. He said . . . he said I was a hen now, not a chicken, and hens must look after themselves. Especially hens who flew away. So they used me like Truda. They used me more because I was the lady, and some of them thought that this was something very funny." Her face twisted with anger and hatred, her pain forgotten for the moment.

"But I told him, Shef! I told him that he had a son. And that his son would one day seek him out and kill him!"

"I did my best, mother." Shef hesitated, another question forming on his lips. But Edrich, behind him, spoke first.

"What did they make you watch, lady?"

Again Thryth's eyes filled with tears. Unable to speak, she waved vaguely at the outside of the shelter.

"Come," said Truda. "I will show you the Vikings' mercy."

The two men followed her out, across the ashy remains of the village green, to where another makeshift shelter had been set up near the ruin of the thane's house. A small huddle of people stood outside it. Occasionally one would break away and walk inside, look, and come out again. Their expressions were unreadable. Grief? Anger? Mostly, thought Shef, it was just plain fear.

Inside the shelter stood a horse-trough, half filled with straw. Shef recognized at once Wulfgar's blond hair and beard, but the face between them was that of a corpse: white, waxy, the nose pinched and the bones sticking through the flesh. Yet the man was not dead.

For a moment Shef could make no sense of what he saw. How could Wulfgar lie in a horse-trough? He was too big. He was six feet tall, and the horse-trough—Shef knew it well from the beatings of his youth—was barely five feet long. . . . There was something missing.

Wulfgar had something wrong with his legs. His knees reached the bottom of the trough, but then there were only clumsy bandages, wrapped round and round the stumps, with dark blood and foul matter clotted in them. A smell of corruption, and of burning, drifted up to Shef.

With growing horror he saw that Wulfgar appeared to have no arms either. The bits that were left were crossed on his breast, the limbs ending in stumps and bandages just below the elbows.

A voice murmured behind them. "They brought him out in front of us all. Then they held him over a log and chopped off his arms and legs with an axe. Legs first. After each one they seared the stump with a red-hot iron, so that he would not die from loss of blood. First he cursed them and fought, but then he began to beg them to leave him just one hand, so that he could feed himself. They laughed. The big one, the jarl, said they would leave him everything else. Leave him his eyes so he could see fair women, and his balls, so he could desire them. But he would never be able to take down his own breeches, never again."

Never do anything for himself again, Shef realized. He would depend on others for every action of life, from eating to pissing.

"They've made him a *heimnar*," said Edrich, using the Norse word. "A living corpse. I've heard of this before. Never seen it. But don't trouble yourself, boy. Infection, pain, loss of blood. He won't live long."

Incredibly, the wasted eyes in front of them opened. They shone with pure malevolence on Shef and Edrich. The lips parted and a dry snakelike whisper came forth.

"The runaways. You ran and left me, boy. I will remember. And you, king's thane. You came, exhorted us, would have us fight. But where were you when the fighting ended? Have no fear, I will live yet, to be avenged on you both. And on your father, boy. I should never have reared his get. Or taken back his whore either."

The eyes closed, the voice was still. Shef and Edrich walked out into the thin drizzle that was beginning once again.

"I don't understand," said Shef. "What did they do it for?"

"That I do not know. But I can tell you one thing. When King Edmund hears of this he will be in a fury. Raid and murder under truce, that's normal enough, but this, done to one of his men, a former companion . . . He will be of two minds, perhaps feeling that he must spare his people more of the same. But then again he may decide he is honor-bound to seek vengeance. It will be a difficult decision for him." He turned to look at Shef.

"Will you come with me, lad, when I take him the news? You are not a freeman here, but it is plain to see that you are a fighter. There is nothing for you now in this place. Come with me and you will be my servant till we can get you proper equipment and armor. If you can fight well enough to stand up to a jarl of the heathens the king will make you his companion, no matter what you were here in Emneth."

The lady Thryth was walking toward them, leaning heavily on a stick. Shef asked her the question that had been burning in his mind since first he saw the smoke from ravaged Emneth.

"Godive. What has happened to Godive?"

"Sigvarth took her. She has gone to the Vikings' camp."

Shef turned to Edrich. He spoke firmly, without apology.

"They say I am a runaway and a slave. Now I will be both." He unbuckled his shield and dropped it on the ground. "I shall make for the Viking camp down by the Stour. One more slave—they may take me in. I must do something to rescue Godive."

"You won't last a week," said Edrich, voice cold with anger. "And you will die a traitor. A traitor to your people and to King Edmund." He turned on his heel and walked away.

"And to the blessed Christ Himself," added Father Andreas, appearing from the shelter. "You have seen the pagans' deeds. Better to be a slave in Christendom than a king among such as they."

Shef realized that he had made the decision quickly—perhaps too quickly, without thinking. But having done this he was now committed. Thoughts tumbled in his head: I have tried to kill my father. I have lost my foster father to a living death. My mother now hates me for what my father did. I have lost my chance to be free and have lost one who would have been my friend.

Such thoughts would not help him now. He had done this all for Godive. Now he must finish what he had begun.

Godive woke with a splitting pain in her head, smoke in her nostrils and someone struggling beneath her. Terrified, she struck out and pushed herself away. The girl on whom she had been lying began to whimper.

As her eyes cleared, Godive realized she was in a wagon, a moving wagon creaking along a puddled road. Through its thin canvas tilt, light shown on its cramped interior packed with humanity, half the girls of Emneth lying one on top of another. A steady chorus of moans and sobbing rose from them. The small square of light at the back of the wagon suddenly darkened and a bearded face showed at it. The sobbing dissolved into shrieks and the girls clutched at each other or tried to hide themselves behind their companions. But the face only grinned—its white teeth gleaming brilliantly—shook a finger in warning, and withdrew.

The Vikings! Godive remembered it all in one instant, everything that had happened: the wave of men, the panic, her dart for the marsh, the man rising in front of her to catch her by the skirt, the overmastering terror she had felt at being held by a grown man for the first time in her uneventful life . . .

Her hand flew suddenly to her thighs. What had they done while she was unconscious? But though the pain in her head grew and grew, there was no throb, no soreness in her body. She was a virgin. She had been a virgin. Surely they could not have raped her and left her feeling nothing?

The girl next to her, a cottager's daughter—one of Alfgar's playmates—saw the movement and said, not without malice, "Don't be afraid. They did nothing to any of us. They're keeping us for sale. And you a maiden too. You have nothing to fear till they find you a buyer. Then you will be like the rest of us."

The memories kept arranging themselves. The square of people, with armed Vikings all round the outside. And inside the square her father being dragged forward, shouting and offering terms, to the log . . . The log. The horror when she realized what they were going to do as they had spread-eagled her father and the axeman had stepped forward. Yes. She had run forward, screaming and clawing at the big man. But the other, the one he had called "son," had caught her. Then what? She felt her head gingerly. A lump. A splitting pain on the other side from the lump. But—she looked at her fingers—no blood.

She was not the only one treated like that; the Viking had hit her with a sandbag. The pirates had been in the trade a long time and were used to dealing with human cattle. At the start of a raid, charge in with axe and sword, spear and shield, to kill the menfolk or the warriors. But after that even the flat of a sword or the back of an axe were unhandy weapons for stunning. Too easy to slip, to fracture a skull or slice an ear from some valuable piece of merchandise. Even a clenched fist was unsafe, given the oar-pulling strength of the man behind it. Who would buy a girl with a broken jaw, or one with her cheekbone smashed and set awry? The skinflints of the outer isles, maybe, but never the buyers for Spain or the choosy kings of Dublin.

So, in Sigvarth's command and in many others, the men detailed for slave-taking carried in their belts or hooked inside their shields a "quietener"—a long sausage of canvas stoutly sewn and filled inside with dry sand collected carefully from the dunes of Jutland or of Skåane. A smart blow with that, and the merchandise lay still, and gave no further trouble. No risk of damage.

Slowly the girls began to whisper to each other, their

voices trembling with fear. They told Godive what had happened to her father. Then what had happened to Truda, to Thryth, and to the rest. How they had finally been loaded into the wagon and pulled off down the track toward the coast. But what would happen next?

Late the next day, Sigvarth, jarl of the Small Isles, also felt an inner chill, though with far less apparent cause. He sat now at his ease in the great tent of the Army of the sons of Ragnar, at the jarls' table, comfortably full of best English beef, a horn of strong ale in his hand, listening to his son Hjörvarth tell the story of their raid. Though he was only a young warrior he spoke well. It was good also to let the other jarls, and the Ragnarssons, see that he had a strong young son who would, in the future, have to be taken account of.

What could be wrong? Sigvarth was not a man given to self-examination, but he had also lived a long time, and had learned not to ignore the prickles of oncoming danger.

There had been no trouble coming back from the raid. He had taken the column of wagons and booty, not back along the Ouse, but down the channel of the Nene. The shipguards, meanwhile, had waited on their mudbank till an English force appeared, had traded jeers and stray arrows with them for a while, watched them slowly assemble a force of rowing-boats and fishercraft, and then at the appointed time had kedged themselves off on the tide and sailed gently upcoast to the rendezvous, leaving the English behind fuming.

And the march to the rendezvous had gone well. The most important thing was that Sigvarth had done exactly what the Snake-eye had said. Torches in every thatch and every field. Every well with a few corpses down it. Examples too, brutal ones. Nailed to trees or mutilated, not dead, to tell their tale to everyone they knew.

Do it like Ivar would do it, the Snake-eye had said. Well, Sigvarth had no illusions about being in the Boneless One's class when it came to brutality, but no one could say he hadn't tried. He had done well. That countryside would not recover for years.

No, it wasn't that disturbing him; that had been a good idea. If there was anything wrong it was further back. Reluctantly, Sigvarth realized that it was the memory of the skirmish that was troubling him. He had fought in the front for a quarter of a century, killed a hundred men, taken a score of battle-wounds. That skirmish should have been easy. It hadn't been. He had broken through the English front line like so many times before, brushed the fair-haired thane out of his way almost with contempt, and got through to the second line, as ragged and disorganized as ever.

And then that boy had come out of the ground. He hadn't even a helmet or a proper sword. Only a freedman, or the poorest of the cottagers' children. Yet two parries and Sigvarth's own sword was in pieces and he himself off balance with his guard too high. The fact was, Sigvarth concluded, if that had been single combat he would have been a dead man. It was the others coming up on each side who had saved him. He did not think anyone had noticed, but if they had—if they had, some one of the bolder heads, the frontmen or the duelers, might be thinking of calling him out even now.

Could he face them? Was his son Hjörvarth strong enough yet for his vengeance to be feared? Maybe he was getting too old for the business. If he couldn't settle a half-armed boy, and an English boy at that, then perhaps he was.

At least he was doing the right thing now. Getting the Ragnarssons on your side—that could never be a bad idea. Hjörvarth was coming to the end of his tale. Sigvarth turned in his chair and nodded at his two henchmen waiting near the entrance. They nodded back and hastened out.

". . . so we burned the wagons on the shore, threw in a couple of churls that my father in his wisdom had kept back, as sacrifice to Aegir and to Ran, boarded ship, ran down the coast to the rivermouth—and here we are! The men of the Small Isles, under famous Sigvarth Jarl—and I his lawful son Hjörvarth—at your service, sons of Ragnar, and ready for more!"

The tent erupted in applause, horns banged on tables, feet stamped, knives clashed. The men were in a good temper at this fair start to the campaign.

The Snake-eye rose to his feet and spoke.

"Well, Sigvarth, we said you could keep your plunder, and you have earned it, so you need have no fear of telling us your good luck. Tell us, how much did you take? Enough to retire and buy yourself a summer home in Sjaelland?"

"Little enough, little enough," called Sigvarth, to groans of disbelief. "Not enough to make me turn farmer. There are only poor pickings to be expected from country thanes. Wait till the great, the invincible Army sacks Norwich. Or York! Or London!" Cries of approval now, and a smile from the Snake-eye. "It is the ministers we must sack, full of gold which the Christ-priests have wrung from the fools of the South. No gold and little silver from the countryside.

"But some things we did take, and I am ready to share the best of it. Here, let me show you the finest thing that we found!"

He turned and waved his followers in. They pushed through the tables, leading with them a figure draped completely in sacking, a rope round its waist. The figure was pushed to the front of the center table, and then in two movements the rope was cut, the sacking whisked away.

Godive emerged blinking into the light, facing a horde of bearded faces, open mouths, clutching hands. She shrank back, tried to turn away, and found herself staring into the eyes of the tallest of the chieftains, a pale man, no expression on his face and eyes like ice, eyes that never blinked. She turned again, looking almost with relief at Sigvarth, the only face she could even recognize.

In this cruel company she was like a flower in a patch of dank undergrowth. Pale hair, fine skin, full lips more attractive now as they parted with fear. Sigvarth nodded again, and one of his men ripped down at the back of her gown. Tearing at it until the fabric tore, then stripping it from her

despite screams and struggles until the young girl stood naked but for her shift, her youthful body clear for all to see.
In an agony of fear and shame she crossed her hands over
her breasts and hung her head, waiting for whatever they
would do with her.

"I will not share her," called out Sigvarth. "She is too
precious for sharing. So I will give her away! I give her to
the man who chose me for this expedition, in thanks and in
hope. May he use her well, and long, and vigorously. I give
her to the man who chose me out, wisest of all the Army.
It is to you I give her. You, Ivar!"

Sigvarth ended with a shout, and a raise of his horn.
Slowly he realized that there was no answering shout, only
a confused murmur, and that from the men farthest away
from the center, the ones who, like him, knew the Ragnarssons least and were the latest comers to the Army. No horns
were raised. Faces seemed suddenly troubled, or blank. Men
looked away.

The chill at Sigvarth's heart came back. Maybe he should
have asked first, he thought to himself. Maybe something
was going on that he didn't know about. But where could
the harm be in this? He was giving away a piece of plunder,
one that any man would be glad to own, doing it publicly
and honorably. Where could be the harm in making a gift
of this girl, a maiden—a beautiful maiden—to Ivar? Ivar
Ragnarsson. Nicknamed—Oh, Thor aid him, why was he so
nicknamed? A terrible thought possessed Sigvarth. Was
there meaning in that nickname?

The Boneless.

Chapter Five

Five days later, Shef and his companion lay in the slight
shelter of a copse, staring across flat watermeadows to

the earthworks of the Viking camp a long mile away. For
the moment, at least, their nerve had failed.

They had had no trouble getting away from ruined
Emneth, which normally might have been the most difficult
task for the runaway slave. But Emneth had had troubles of
its own. No one in any case considered himself Shef's master, and Edrich, who might have thought it his duty to keep
anyone from going over to the Vikings, seemed to have
washed his hands of the whole business. Without opposi-
tion, Shef had gathered his few possessions, quietly lifted a
small store of food which he kept in an outlying shelter, and
had made his preparations to leave.

Still, someone had noticed. As he stood hesitating over
whether to bid a farewell to his mother, he had become
aware of a slight figure standing silently next to him. It was
Hund, boyhood friend, child of slaves on both sides, perhaps the least important and lowest ranking person in the
whole of Emneth. Yet Shef had learned to value him. There
was no one who knew the marshes better, not even Shef.
Hund could slide through the water and take moorhens on
their nests. In the foul and crowded hut he shared with his
parents and their litter of children there was often an otter
cub playing. The very fish seemed to come to his hands to
be caught without rod or line or net. As for the herbs of the
countryside, Hund knew them all, their names, their uses.
Already—though he was two winters younger than Shef—
the humble folk were beginning to come to him for simples
and for cures. In time to come he might be the cunning man
of the district, respected and feared even by the mighty. Or
action might be taken against him. Even the kindly Father
Andreas, Shef's preserver, had several times been seen to
look at him with doubt in his eyes. Mother Church had no
love for competitors.

"I want to come," Hund had said.

"It will be dangerous," Shef had replied.

Hund had said nothing, as was his custom when he felt
nothing more needed to be said. It was dangerous to stay in

Emneth too. And Shef and Hund, in their different ways, increased each other's chances.

"If you are coming you will have to get that collar off," Shef had said, glancing at the iron collar which had been fitted round Hund's neck at puberty. "Now is the time. No one is interested in us. I'll get some tools."

They had sought shelter in the marsh, not wanting to draw attention. It had been a difficult business getting the collar off even so. Shef had filed through it, first putting rags inside the collar to save Hund's neck from rasps, but once broken through it had been hard to get the tongs inside the circlet to bend it open. In the end Shef had lost patience, wrapped the rags round his hands, and pulled the collar open by main strength.

Hund had rubbed the calluses and weals where the iron had worn his neck and stared at the U-shape of the bent collar. "Not many men could do that," he had observed.

"Need will make the old wife trot," Shef had answered dismissively. Yet secretly he was pleased. He was coming into his strength, he had faced a grown warrior in battle, he was free to go where he would. He did not yet know how he could do it, but there must be a way to free Godive, and then leave the disasters of his family behind.

They had set out without further words. But trouble had begun at once. Shef had expected to have to dodge a few inquisitive people, sentries, maybe levies heading for the muster. Yet from the first day of travel he had realized that the whole countryside was beginning to buzz like a wasps' nest stirred with a stick. Men cantered down every road. Outside every village groups waited, armed and hostile, suspicious of every stranger. After one such group had decided to hold them, ignoring their story of being sent to borrow cattle from a relative of Wulfgar's, they had had to break and run for it, dodging spears and outdistancing their pursuers. But clearly orders had gone out and the folk of East Anglia had for once decided to obey wholeheartedly. There was fury in the air.

For the last two days Shef and Hund had crept through

the fields and hedges, going painfully slowly, often on their bellies in the mud. Even so, they had seen patrols out, some of them horsemen commanded by a thane or a king's companion, but others—and these the more dangerous ones— moved quietly on foot like themselves, armor and weapons padded to prevent jingle or clink; marshmen in the lead, carrying bows and hunters' slings for ambush or stalk. They meant, Shef realized, to keep the Vikings in, or at least to prevent them coming out in small parties for private plunder. But at the same time they would be only too happy to catch and hold, or kill, anyone they thought might have any intention of giving the Vikings aid, information, or reinforcement.

Only in the last couple of miles had the danger receded; and that, the pair soon understood, was only because they were now within the range of the Vikings' own patrols— these easier to avoid, but at the same time more menacing. They had spotted one group of men waiting silently within the borders of a small wood, maybe fifty of them, all mounted, all armored, great axes resting on shoulders, the man-killing battle-spears bristling above them like a gray-tipped thorn thicket. Easy to see, quite easy to avoid. But it would take a full-scale incursion by the English to drive them off or defeat them. The village patrols would stand no chance.

These were the men to whose mercy they now had to trust themselves. It did not seem as easy now as it had at Emneth. To begin with, Shef had had a vague idea of reaching the camp and declaring his relationship to Sigvarth. But there would be far too much chance of being recognized, even from the few seconds of contact they had had. It was terrible luck that had brought him into hand-to-hand combat with the one person in the camp who might—or might not—have accepted him. But now Sigvarth was one person they had to avoid at all costs.

Would the Vikings accept recruits? Shef had an uneasy feeling that much more would be needed than willingness and a hand-forged sword. But they could always use slaves.

Again, Shef had an uneasy feeling that he himself might do for a laborer or galley-slave in some far-off country. But Hund had nothing visibly valuable about him. Might the Vikings just let him go, like a fish that was too small for the pan? Or would they take the easy way out of dealing with an encumbrance? The evening before, when they had first caught sight of the camp, the two youths' keen eyes saw a party come out of one of the gates and start digging a hole. A little later there had been no doubt about the contents of the cart that creaked out and emptied a dozen bodies unceremoniously down the pit. Pirates' camps had a high wastage rate.

Shef sighed. "It doesn't look any better than it did last night," he said. "But we'll have to move sometime."

Hund gripped is arm. "Wait. Listen. Can you hear something?"

The sound strengthened as the two youths turned their heads this way and that. Noise. Song. Many men singing together. The sound, they realized, was coming from the other side of a slight rise maybe a hundred yards to their left, where the watermeadows ran into a tangle of uncultivated common.

"It sounds like the monks singing at the great minster at Ely," murmured Shef. A foolish thought. There would be neither monk nor priest left within twenty miles of this place.

"Shall we look?" whispered Hund.

Shef made no reply, but began to crawl slowly and carefully toward the sound of deep-voiced singing. It could only be the pagans in this spot. But maybe a small group of them would be easier to approach than the whole army. Anything was better than simply walking out across that flat plain.

After they had covered half the distance on their bellies, Hund gripped Shef's wrist. Silently he pointed up a slight slope. Twenty yards away, beneath a huge old hawthorn, stood a man, motionless, his eyes scanning the ground. He leaned on an axe two-thirds his own weight. A burly man, thick-necked, broad across paunch and hip.

At least he did not seem built for speed, Shef reflected. And he was standing in the wrong place if he wanted to be a sentry. The two youths exchanged a glance. The Vikings might be great seamen. They had much to learn about the art of stealth.

Gently Shef snaked forward, angling away from the sentry, round a thicket of bracken, between and beneath a tangle of gorse, Hund crawling immediately behind him. Ahead, the noise of singing had ceased. Replaced by a single voice talking. Not talking. Exhorting. Preaching. Could there be secret Christians even among the heathen? Shef wondered.

A few yards on, he parted the bracken stems and peered silently down into a little dell, hidden from view. There, forty or fifty men sat on the ground in a rough circle. All carried swords or axes, but their spears and shields were propped up or planted in the ground. They sat within a corded-off enclosure made of a dozen spears with a thread running between them. From the thread, at intervals, dangled clumps of the bright red berry that the English called "quickbeam," now in autumn brilliance. At the center of the enclosure, with the men seated round it, a fire burned. Next to it was planted a single spear, point up, its shaft gleaming silver.

One man stood by the fire and the spear, his back to the hidden watchers, speaking to the men round him in tones of persuasion, of command. Unlike the others, and unlike anyone else Shef had ever seen, his tunic and breeches were neither natural homespun in color nor dyed green or brown or blue, but a brilliant white, white as the inside of an egg.

From his right hand there dangled a hammer, short-hafted, double-headed—a blacksmith's hammer. Shef's keen sight locked on the front row of sitting men. Round every neck, a chain. On every chain, a pendant displayed on the chest. They were of different kinds: he could see a sword, a horn, a phallus, a boat. But at least half the men wore the sign of a hammer.

Shef rose abruptly from his concealment and walked forward into the dell. As they saw him, fifty men leap simultaneously to their feet, swords coming out, voices raised in warning. A grunt of amazement behind him, a crashing of feet through the bracken. The sentry was behind him now, Shef knew. He did not turn to look.

Slowly the man in white turned to meet him, the two facing each other across the berry-fringed thread, looking each other up and down.

"And where are you come from?" said the man in white. He spoke English with a strong, burring accent.

What shall I say? thought Shef. From Emneth? From Norfolk? That will mean nothing to them.

"I come from the North," he said aloud.

The faces in front of him changed. Surprise? Recognition? Suspicion?

The man in white gestured his followers to hold still. "And what is your business with us, the followers of the *Asgarthsvegr*, the Asgarth Way?"

Shef pointed to the hammer in the other's hand, the hammer-pendant round his neck. "I am a smith, like you. My business is to learn."

Someone was translating his words now to the others. Shef realized Hund had materialized at his left, and there was a threatening presence just behind them both. He kept his eyes fixed on those of the man in white.

"Show me a sign of your craft."

Shef pulled his sword from its sheath and passed it over, as he had to Edrich. The hammer-bearer turned it over and over, looked at it intently, flexed it gently, noting the surprising play in the thick, single-edged blade, scratched with his thumbnail at the surface discoloration of old rust. Carefully, he shaved a patch of hair from his forearm.

"Your forge was not hot enough," he remarked. "Or you lost patience. Those steel strips were not even when you twisted them. But it is a good blade. It is not what it seems.

"And neither are you. Now tell me, young man—and remember, death is just behind you—what it is that you want? If you are just a runaway slave like your friend"—he ges-

tured toward Hund's neck, with the telltale marks on it—
"maybe we will let you go. If you are a coward who wants
to join the winning side, maybe we will kill you. But maybe
you are something else. Or someone else. Say then, what do
you want?"

I want Godive back, thought Shef. He looked into the pagan priest's eyes and said, with all the sincerity he could
muster, "You are a master-smith. The Christians will let me
learn no more. I want to be your apprentice. Your learning-
knave."

The man in white grunted, handed back Shef's sword,
bone hilt first. "Lower your axe, Kari," he said to the man
behind the pair. "There is more here than meets the eye.

"I will take you as a knave, young man. And if your
friend has any skill, he may join us too. Sit, both of you, to
one side, till we have finished what we were doing. My
name is Thorvin, which is to say, 'the friend of Thor,' the
god of the smiths. What are yours?"

Shef flushed with shame, dropped his eyes.

"My friend's name is Hund," he said, "which is to say,
'dog.' And I too, I have only a dog's name. My father—
No, I have no father. They call me Shef."

For the first time Thorvin's face showed surprise, and
more. "Fatherless?" he muttered. "And your name is Shef.
But that is not only a dog's name. Truly you are unin-
structed."

Shef felt his spirits sinking as they moved toward the camp.
He was not afraid for himself, but for Hund. Thorvin had
told the pair of them to sit to one side while they finished
their strange meeting: first him talking, then some kind of
discussion in the burring Norse Shef could almost follow,
and then a skin of some drink passed ceremoniously from
hand to hand. At the end all the men had gathered in little
groups and joined hands in silence on one object or another:
Thorvin's hammer, a bow, a horn, a sword, what looked like
a dried horse's penis. No one had touched the silver spear
till Thorvin had gone over, pulled it briskly into two parts

and rolled them up in a cloth bag. A few moments later the enclosure had been broken up, the fire put out, the spears reclaimed, the men of the group already drifting away in fours and fives, moving warily and taking different directions.

"We are followers of the Way," Thorvin had said in partial explanation to the two youths, still speaking his careful English. "Not everyone wishes to be known as such—not in the camp of the Ragnarssons. Me they accept." He tugged at the hammer pendant on his chest. "I have a skill. You have a skill, young smith-to-be. Maybe it will protect you.

"What of your friend? What can you do?"

"I can pull teeth," replied Hund unexpectedly.

The half dozen men still standing round had grunted in amusement. *"Tenn draga,"* remarked one of them. *"That er ithrott."*

"He says, 'To draw teeth, that is an accomplishment,' " Thorvin translated. "Is it true?"

"It is true," supplied Shef for his friend. "He says it is not strength you need. It is a twist of the wrist—that, and knowing how the teeth grow. He can cure fevers too."

"Tooth-drawing, bone-setting, fever-curing," said Thorvin. "There is always trade for a leech among women and warriors. He can go to my friend Ingulf. If we can get him there. See, you two, if we can get to our own places in the camp—my forge, Ingulf's booth—we may be safe. Till then—" He shook his head. "We have many ill-wishers. Some friends. Will you take the risk?"

They had followed him mutely. But wisely?

As they came toward it, the camp looked more and more formidable. It was enclosed by a high earth rampart, with a ditch outside it, each side at least a furlong in length. Lot of work in that, thought Shef. Lot of spadefuls. Did that mean they were going to stay a long time, that they thought it worth doing so much? Or was it a matter of course to the Vikings? A routine?

The rampart was crowned with a stockade of sharpened logs. A furlong. Two hundred and twenty yards. Four sides—No, from the lay of the land Shef realized suddenly that one side of the camp was bounded here by the river Stour. On that side he could even see prows projecting into the sluggish stream. He was puzzled—until he realized that the Vikings must have pulled their ships, their most precious possessions, up on the mudflats there, then grappled them together so that they themselves formed one wall of the enclosure. Big. How big? Three sides. Three times two hundred and twenty yards. Each log in the stockade maybe a foot wide. Three feet to a yard.

Shef's mind, as it so often did, tried to grapple with the problem of numbers. Three times three times two hundred and twenty. There must be a way to know the answer to that, but this time Shef could see no shortcut to finding it. It was a lot of logs, anyway, and big ones too, cut from trees hard to find down here on the flats. They must have brought the logs with them. Dimly, Shef began to discover an unfamiliar notion. He knew no word for it. Making plans, perhaps. Planning ahead. Thinking things out before they happened. No detail was too small for these men to trouble with. He suddenly realized that they did not think war was only a matter of the spirit, of glory and speeches and inherited swords. It was a trade, a matter of logs and spades, preparation and profit.

More and more men came into view as they trudged up to the ramparts, some of them simply lounging at ease, a group round a fire apparently cooking bacon, others throwing spears at a mark. They looked very much like Englishmen in their grubby woolens, Shef decided. But there was a difference. Every group of men Shef had ever seen before had had in it its proportion of casualties, men not fit to stand in the line of battle: men whose legs had broken and had been set awry; men undersized, deformed; men with bleared eyes from the marsh fever or with old head injuries that affected the way they talked. There were none like that here. Not all were of great stature, Shef was rather surprised to see, but all looked competent, hard-bitten, ready. Some adolescents, but no boys. Bald men and grizzled men, but no palsied elders.

Horses, too. The plain was covered with horses, all hobbled, all grazing. It must take a lot of horses for this army, Shef thought, and a lot of grazing for those horses. In a way that might be a weak point. Shef realized that he was thinking as an enemy, an enemy scouting for opportunities. He was not a king or a thane, but he knew from experience that there was no way to guard all those herds at night, whatever you did. A few true marshmen could reach them however many patrols you had out, could cut them loose and frighten them off. Maybe ambush the horse-guards in the night as well. Then how would the Vikings feel about going on guard duty—if the guards made a habit of never coming back?

Shef felt his spirits sink again as they came up to the entrance. There was no gate, and that was ominous in itself. The track led straight up to a gap in the rampart ten yards broad. It was as if the Vikings were saying, "Our walls protect our goods and keep in our slaves. But we don't need them to hide behind. If you want to fight, march up to us. See if you can get past our gate-guards. It is not these logs that protect us, but the axes that felled them."

Forty or fifty men stood or sprawled by the gap. They had an air of permanence. Unlike those outside, they all wore mail or leather. Spears were propped against each other in clumps, and shields were in easy reach. These men would be ready for battle within seconds—wherever an enemy might erupt from. They had been scanning Shef, Hund, Thorvin, and party—eight men all told—for minutes as they came into sight. Would they be challenged?

At the gate itself a big man in mail strolled forward and stared at them thoughtfully, making it clear he had noted the two newcomers and everything about them. After a few moments he nodded and jerked a thumb towards the inside. As they passed into the camp itself he called a few words after them.

"What does he say?" hissed Shef.

"He says, 'On your own head be it.' Something like that."

They walked on into the camp.

Inside, all appeared to be confusion; yet it was a confusion with an underlying regularity, a sense of overriding purpose. Men were everywhere—cooking, talking, playing at knucklebones or squatting over game boards. Canvas tents stretched in all directions, their guy-ropes an inextricable tangle. Yet the path in front of them was never obscured or encroached on. It stretched straight forward, ten paces broad, even its puddles neatly filled with loads or gravel, and the signs of passing carts barely visible on the beaten earth. These men work hard, Shef thought again.

The little group pressed forward. After a hundred yards, when by Shef's calculation they must have been almost in the middle of the camp, Thorvin stopped and beckoned the other two up close.

"I whisper, for there is great danger. Many in this camp speak many languages. We are going to cross the main track that runs north to south. To the right, to the south, down by the river with the ships, is the encampment of the Ragnarssons themselves and their personal followers. No wise man willingly goes there. We shall cross the track and go straight on to my forge near the gate opposite. We will walk straight forward, not even looking down to our right. When we reach the place we will go right into it. Now move. And take heart. Not far now."

Shef kept his eyes rigidly down as they crossed the broad track, but he wished he could have ventured a moment's gaze. He had come here because of Godive—but where would she be? Did he dare ask for Sigvarth Jarl?

Slowly they moved through the crowds again, till they could see the east stockade almost in front of them. There, a little separated from the others, stood a roughly constructed shelter, open to the side facing them, inside it the familiar apparatus of the smithy: anvil, clay hearth, pipes and bellows. Round it all ran the threads, with the vivid scarlet splashes of quickbeam berries dangling from them.

"We are here," said Thorvin, turning with a sigh of relief. As he turned his eyes passed beyond Shef and the color drained suddenly from his face.

Shef turned with a sense of doom already on him. In front of him there stood a man, a tall man. Shef realized he was looking up at him—realized too how rarely he had done that in the last few months. But this was a man strange for reasons well beyond size.

He was wearing the same wide homespun breeches as everyone else, but no shirt or overtunic. Instead his upper body was wrapped in something like a wide blanket, of a plaid colored a startling yellow. It was pinned over his left shoulder, leaving his right arm bare. Projecting above his left shoulder was the handle of an enormous sword, so great it would have trailed along the ground if slung from a belt. In his left hand he carried a small round buckler with a central grip. An iron spike a foot long stuck out from the center of it. Behind him crowded a dozen others in the same garb.

"Who are these?" he snarled. "Who let they in?" The words were strangely accented but Shef could understand him.

"The gate-wards let them in," Thorvin replied. "They will do no harm."

"These two. They are English. *Enzkir.*"

"The camp is full of English."

"Aye. Wi' chains round their necks. Give them to me. I'll see they fettered."

Thorvin paced forward, between Shef and Hund. His five friends spread out, facing the dozen half-naked men in yellow plaids. He gripped Shef's shoulder.

"I have taken this one into the forge, to be my learning-knave."

The grim face, long-mustached, sneered. "A bonny weight. Maybe ye have other uses for him. The other?" He jerked a thumb at Hund.

"He goes to Ingulf."

"He's no' there yet. He's had a collar on his neck. Give him to me. I'll see he does no spying."

Shef felt himself taking a slow pace forward, stomach contracting with fear. He knew resistance was hopeless. There were a dozen of them, all fully armed. In a moment one of those mighty swords would be hacking the limbs from his body or the head from his neck. Yet he could not let his friend be taken. His hand crept to the hilt of his short sword.

The tall men leapt back, hand reaching over shoulder. Before Shef could draw, the longsword had wheeped free. All round, weapons flashed, men sprang on guard.

"Hold," cried a voice. An immense voice.

While Thorvin and the plaid-wearer had been talking, their group had become the focus of total attention for yards around. Sixty or eighty men now stood in a ring, watching and listening. From the ring now stepped the biggest man Shef had ever seen, taller than Shef by head and shoulders, taller than the man in the plaid, and broader, heavier by far.

"Thorvin," he said. "Muirtach," nodding to the strangely dressed one. "What's the stir?"

"I'm taking that thrall there."

"No." Thorvin seized Hund suddenly and pushed him through the gap in the enclosure, clenching his hand round the berries. "He is under the protection of Thor."

Muirtach strode forward, sword raised.

"Hold." The immense voice again, threatening this time. "You have no right, Muirtach."

"What's it to you?"

Slowly, reluctantly, the immense man reached inside his tunic, fumbled, brought out a silver emblem on a chain. A hammer.

Muirtach cursed, swept his sword back, spat on the ground "Take him then. But you, boy—" His eye turned to Shef. "You touched yer hilt to me. I catch you on yer own before long. Then ye're dead, boy." He nodded to Thorvin. "And Thor is nothing to me. No more than Christ and his hoor of a mother. Ye'll not fool me like ye've done him."

He jerked a thumb at the immense man, turned, and walked away down the track, head high, swaggering like one who has met a defeat and will not show it, his fellows straggling after.

Shef realized he had been holding his breath and let it out with careful and affected ease.

"Who are those?" he asked, looking at the retreating men.

Thorvin replied not in English, but in the Norse they had been using, speaking slowly, with stress on the many words the languages had in common. "They are the Gaddgedlar. Christian Irishmen who have left their god and their people and turned Viking. Ivar Ragnarsson has many in his following and hopes to use them to become king of England and Ireland as well. Before he and his brother Sigurth turn their minds back to their own country, to Denmark, and Norway beyond."

"And there may they never come," added the immense man who had saved them. He bobbed his head to Thorvin with odd respect, even deference, looked Shef up and down. "That was bold, young swain. But you have irked a mighty man. I too. But for me it has been long in the coming. If you need me again, Thorvin, call. You know that since I took the news to the Braethraborg the Ragnarssons have kept me with them. How long that will last now that I have shown my hammer, I do not know. But in any case I am growing tired of Ivar's hounds."

He strolled away.

"Who was that?" asked Shef.

"A great champion, from Halogaland in Norway. He is called Viga-Brand. Brand the Killer."

"And he is a friend of yours?"

"A friend of the Way. A friend of Thor. And so of smiths."

I do not know what I have got into, thought Shef to himself. But I must not forget why I am here. Unwillingly his eyes drifted away from the enclosure where Hund still stood, toward the danger-center, the southern river-wall of the Viking base, the encampment of the Ragnarssons. She must be there, he thought suddenly. Godive.

Chapter Six

For many days Shef had no time to think of his quest for Godive—or anything else for that matter. The work was too hard. Thorvin rose at dawn and worked on sometimes into the night, hammering, reforging, filing, tempering. In an army of this size there seemed to be innumerable men whose axe-heads had come loose, whose shields needed a rivet, who had decided that their spears needed reshafting. Sometimes there would be a line of men twenty-long, stretched from the forge to the edge of the precinct and on down the lane that led to it. There were also harder and more complex jobs. Several times men brought in mail shirts, torn and bloody, asking for them to be repaired, let out, altered for a new owner. One at a time each link of the mail had to be laboriously fitted into four others, and each of the four others into four others. "Mail is easy to wear, and it gives freedom to the arms," Thorvin had remarked when Shef finally ventured to grumble. "But it does not give protection against a fierce stroke—and it is hell on earth for smiths."

As time went by Thorvin handed over the routine jobs more and more to Shef, and concentrated on the difficult or special items. Yet he was rarely far away. He talked continually in Norse, repeating himself as often as was necessary. Sometimes, in the beginning, using mime until he was sure Shef understood. He spoke English well enough, Shef knew, but he would never use it. He insisted too that his apprentice spoke back to him in Norse, even if all he did was repeat what had been said to him. In fact the languages were close to each other in vocabulary and in basic style. After a while Shef caught the trick of repronunciation, and began to think of Norse as a bizarre and aberrant dialect of English, which had only to be imitated, not really learned from the beginning. After that matters went well.

Thorvin's conversation was also a good cure for boredom or frustration. From him, and from the men who stood waiting their turn, Shef learned a great many things that he had never heard before. The Vikings all seemed enormously well-informed about everything that had been decided or intended by their leaders, and had no scruples about discussing it or criticizing it. One thing that soon became clear was that the Great Army of the pagans, feared throughout Christendom, was by no means a unit. At its heart were the Ragnarssons and their followers, maybe half the total. But to these were attached any number of separate contingents, joined to share the loot, of any size from the twenty ships brought down by the Orkney jarl to single crews from villages in Jutland or Skaane. Many of these were already dissatisfied. The campaign had started well enough, they said, with the descent on East Anglia and the establishment of the fortress as a base. Yet the idea had always been not to stay too long, but to gather horses, acquire guides, and then move suddenly from a firm base in the East Anglian kingdom against the true enemy and target, the kingdom of Northumbria.

"Why not land with the ships in Northumbria in the first place?" Shef had asked once, wiping the sweat from his forehead and signaling to the next customer. The stocky, balding Viking with the dented helmet had laughed, loudly but without malice. The really tricky part of a campaign, he had said, was always getting started. Getting the ships up the river. Finding a place to beach them. Getting horses for thousands of men. Contingents turning up late and going down the wrong river. "If the Christians had the sense they were born with," he had said emphatically, spitting on the ground, "they would pick us off before we got started almost every time." "Not with the Snakeeye in charge," another man had remarked. "Maybe not," the first Viking had agreed. "Maybe not with the Snakeeye. But lesser commanders. Do you remember Ulfketil down in Frankland?"

So, better to get your feet planted before you tried to hit, they had agreed. Good idea. But this time it had gone wrong. Their feet were planted too long. It was that there King Edmund, most of the customers agreed—or "Jatmund" as they pronounced it—and the only question was, what was making him act so stupid? Easy to ravage his country till he gave in. But they didn't want to ravage East Anglia, the customers complained. Takes too long. Too thin pickings. Why in Hell didn't the king just pay up and come to a sensible deal? He'd had a warning.

Maybe too much of a warning, Shef thought, remembering the wasted face of Wulfgar in the horse-trough, and that indefinable buzz of rage which he had felt in the fields and woods on their journey. When he asked why the Vikings were so determined to march on Northumbria, largest but not by any means richest of the English kingdoms, the laughter at that question took a long time to die down. Eventually, when he unraveled the tale of Ragnar Lothbrok and King Ella, of the old boar and the little pigs who would grunt, of Viga-Brand and his taunting of the Ragnarssons themselves in the Braethraborg, a chill fell on him. He remembered the strange words he had heard from the blue-swelling face in the snake-pit of the archbishop, the sense of foreboding he had known at the time.

Now he understood the need for revenge—but there were other things about which he remained curious.

"Why do you say 'Hell'?" he asked Thorvin one night after they had put their gear away and were sitting mulling a tankard of ale on the cooling forge. "Do you believe there is a place where sins are punished after death? Christians believe in Hell—but you're no Christian."

"What makes you think Hell is a Christian word?" answered Thorvin. "What does heaven mean?" For once he used the English word, *heofon.*

"Well—it's the sky," answered Shef, startled.

"Also the Christian place of bliss after death. The word

was there before the Christians came. They just borrowed it, gave it a new meaning. Same with Hell. What does *hulda* mean?" This time he used the Norse word.

"It means to cover, to hide something. Like *helian* in English."

"So. Hell is what is covered. What's underground. Simple word, just like heaven. You can put what meaning you like to it after that.

"But your other question: Yes, we do believe there is a place of punishment for your sins after death. Some of us have seen it."

Thorvin sat silent for a while, as if brooding, unsure how far to speak further. When he broke the silence it was in a half chant, slow and sonorous, like the monks of Ely Minster Shef had heard once, long ago, singing on the vigil of Christmas Eve.

> *"A hall stands, no sunlight on it,*
> *On Dead Man's Strand: its doors face northward.*
> *From its roof rain poison drops.*
> *Its walls are made of woven serpents.*
> *There men writhe in woe and anguish:*
> *Murder-wolves and men forsworn,*
> *Those who lie to lie with women."*

Thorvin shook his head. "Yes, we believe in punishment for sins. Maybe we have a different idea from the Christians about what is a sin and what is not."

"Who are 'we'?"

"It is time I told you. It has come to me several times that you were meant to know." As they sipped their warm, herb-scented ale in the glow of the dying fire, the camp quietening around them, Thorvin, fingering his amulet, spoke. "This is how it was."

All this began, he said, many generations before, maybe a hundred and fifty years ago. At that time a great jarl of the Frisians—the people on the North Sea coast opposite England—had been a pagan. But because of the tales that had been told him by missionaries from Frankland and from England, and because of the old kinship felt between his people and the now-Christian English, he had decided to take baptism.

As was the custom, baptism was to take place publicly, in the open air, in a great tank that the missionaries had constructed for all to see. After the jarl Radbod had been immersed and baptized, the nobles of his court were to follow and soon after that the whole earldom, all the Frisians. Earldom, not kingdom, for the Frisians were too proud and independent to allow anyone the title of king.

So the jarl had stepped to the side of the tank, clad in his robes of ermine and scarlet over the white baptismal garment, and put one foot down onto the first step of the tank. He actually had his foot in the water, Thorvin asserted. But then he turned and asked the head of the missionaries—a Frank, whom the Franks called Wulfhramn, or Wolfraven— whether it was true that as soon as he, Radbod, accepted baptism, his ancestors, who now lurked in Hell along with the other damned, would be released and allowed to wait for their descendants' coming in the courts of heaven.

No, said the Wolfraven, they were pagans who had never been baptized, and they could not receive salvation. No salvation except in the Church, reinforcing what he said with the Latin words: *Nulla salvatio extra ecclesiam.* And for that matter no redemption once in hell. *De infernis nulla est redemptio.*

But my ancestors, said the jarl Radbod, never had anyone speak to them of baptism. They had not even the chance to refuse it. Why should they be tormented forever for something they knew nothing about?

Such is the will of God, said the Frankish missionary, perhaps shrugging his shoulders. At that Radbod took his foot out of the baptismal tank and declared with oaths that he would never become a Christian. If he had to choose, he said, he would rather live in Hell with his blameless ancestors than go to heaven with saints and bishops who had no sense of what was right. And he began a great persecution of Christians throughout all the jarldom of the Frisians, arousing the fury of the Frankish king.

Thorvin drank deep of the ale, then touched the small hammer that hung about his neck.

"Thus it began," he said. "Radbod Jarl was a man of great vision. He foresaw that as long as the Christians were the only ones with priests and books and writing, then what they said would come in the end to be accepted. And that is the strength and at the same time the sin of the Christians. They will not accept that anyone else has so much as a splinter of the truth. They will not deal. They will not go halfway. So to defeat them, or even to hold them at arm's length, Radbod decided that the lands of the North must have their own priests and their own tales of what is the truth. That was the foundation of the Way."

"The Way," prompted Shef, when Thorvin seemed disinclined to continue.

"That is who *we* are. We are the priests of the Way. And our duties are threefold, and ever have been since first the Way came to the lands of the North. One is to preach the worship of the old gods, the Aesir: Thor and Othin, Frey and Ull, Tyr and Njörth and Heimdall and Balder. Those who put full faith in these gods carry an amulet like mine, made in the sign of whichever god they love the best: a sword for Tyr, a bow for Ull, a horn for Heimdall. Or a hammer for Thor, such as I wear. Many men carry that sign.

"Our second duty is to support ourselves by some trade, as I support myself by smithcraft. For we are not permitted to be like the priests of the Christ-god, who do no work themselves but take tithes and offerings from those who do, and enrich themselves and their minsters till the land groans beneath their exactions.

"But our third duty is hard to explain. We must take thought for what is coming, what will happen in this world—not the next. The Christian priests, you see, believe that this world is only a resting place on the way to eternity, and that the true duty of mankind is to get through it with as little harm to the soul as possible. They do not believe

that this world is in any way important. They are not curious about it. They do not want to know any more about it.

"But we of the Way, we believe that in the end a battle
will be joined, so great that no man can conceive of it. Yet
it will be fought in this world, and it is the duty of us all to
make our side, the side of gods and men, stronger when that
day comes.

"So the duty laid on us all, besides practicing our skill or
art, is to make that skill or art the better for what we learn.
Always we must try to think what we can do that is different, that is new. And the most honored among us are those
who can think of a skill or art that is entirely new in itself,
that no man has ever heard of or thought of before. I am far
from the heights of such men as those. Yet many new things
have been learned in the North since the time of Radbod the
Jarl.

"Even in the South they have heard of us. In the cities of
the Moors, in Córdoba and Cairo and the lands of the blue
men, there is talk of the Way and what is happening in the
North among the *majus*, the 'fire-worshippers' as they call
us. They have sent emissaries to watch and learn.

"But the Christians do not send to us. They are still confident in their single truth. They alone know what is salvation and what is sin."

"Is it not a sin to make a man a *heimnar*?" asked Shef.

Thorvin looked up sharply. "That is not a word I have
taught you. But I forgot—you know more of many things
than I have thought fit to ask you.

"Yes, it is a sin to make a man a *heimnar*, whatever he
has done. It is a work of Loki—the god in whose memory
we burn the fire in our enclosures next to the spear of his
father Othin. But few of us wear the sign of Othin, and none
wear that of Loki.

"To make a man a *heimnar*. No. That has the mark of the
Boneless One about it, whether he did it himself or not.
There are more ways than one of defeating the Christians,
and Ivar Ragnarsson's way is foolish. It would come to
nothing in the end. But there—you have seen already for

yourself that I have no love for the creatures and the hirelings of Ivar.

"Now. Go to sleep." And with that Thorvin swilled down
his mug, retired to the sleeping tent, and left Shef to follow
him thoughtfully.

Working for Thorvin had given Shef no chance at all to pursue his quest. Hund had been taken off almost immediately
to the booth of Ingulf the Leech, also a priest of the Way,
but one dedicated to Ithun the Healer, some distance away.
After that the two had not seen each other. Shef was left to
the routine duties of a smith's assistant, made more trying
by being confined to the enclosure of Thor: the forge itself,
near it a small sleeping tent and an outhouse with a deep-
dug latrine, the whole surrounded by the cords and the
quickbeam berries, which Thorvin called *rowan*. "Don't
step outside the cords," Thorvin had told him. "Inside you
are under the peace and protection of Thor, and killing you
would bring down vengeance on the killers. Outside"—he
shrugged—"Muirtach would think himself happy to find
you wandering around on your own." Inside the precinct
Shef had stayed.

It was the following morning when Hund came.

"I have seen her. I saw her this morning," he whispered
as he slipped into place beside the squatting Shef. For once
Shef was alone. Thorvin had gone off to see about their turn
for baking bread in the communal ovens. He had left Shef
grinding wheat kernels into flour in the hand quern.

Shef jumped to his feet, spilling flour and unground kernels all over the beaten earth. "Who? You mean—Godive!
Where? How? Is she—"

"Sit down, I beg," Hund started to scrape hurriedly at the
spilt mess. "We must look normal. There are always people
watching in this place. Please listen. The bad news is this:
She is the woman of Ivar Ragnarsson, the one they call the
Boneless. But she has not been harmed. She is alive and
well. I know because as a leech, Ingulf gets everywhere.
Now he has seen what I can do, he often takes me with him.

A few days ago he was called to see the Boneless One.
They would not let me enter—there is a strong guard round
all their tents—but while I was waiting outside for him I
saw her pass. There could be no mistake. She was not five
yards off, though she did not see me."

"How did she look?" asked Shef, painful memory of his
mother and Truda forcing itself forward.

"She was laughing. She looked—happy." Both youths fell
silent. From all that both had heard there was something
ominous in anyone feeling or seeming happy anywhere
within the range of Ivar Ragnarsson's power.

"But listen, Shef. She is in terrible danger. She does not
understand. She thinks that because Ivar is courteous and
speaks well and does not use her immediately as a whore,
then she is safe. But there is something wrong with Ivar,
maybe in his body, maybe in his head. He has ways of easing it. Maybe, one day, Godive will be one of them.

"You have to get her out, Shef, and soon. And the first
thing is to let her see you. What we do after that I cannot
guess, but if she knows you are near at least she will maybe
be thinking of a chance of passing a message. Now I have
heard another thing. All the women, of all the Ragnarssons
and their highest chiefs, will be going out from the tents today. I have heard them complaining. They say they have not
had a chance to wash anywhere except in the filthy river for
weeks. They mean to go out this afternoon and wash their
clothes and themselves. They are going out to a backwater
maybe a mile off."

"Could we get her away?"

"Don't even think about it. There are thousands of men in
the army, all of them desperate for women. There will be so
many trusted guards on that trip you won't be able to see
between them. The best thing you can do is make sure she
sees you. Now this is where they are going to go." Hund began to explain the lay of the land hastily, pointing to add
emphasis to his words.

"But how am I to get away from here? Thorvin—"

"I thought of that. As soon as the women start to leave I

will come here and say to Thorvin that my master needs him to come and put a final edge on the tools he uses for opening men's bellies and heads. Ingulf can do marvelous things," Hund added, shaking his head in admiration. "More than any church-leech I have ever heard of.

"When Thorvin hears that, he will come with me. Then you must leave here, slip over the wall, and get well ahead of the women and the guards so you can meet them accidentally on the path."

Hund was right about Thorvin's reactions. As soon as Hund sidled up to him with the request, and explanation of why he was needed, Thorvin had agreed. "I will come," he said, putting down his hammer and searching for whetstone, oilstone, sleekstone. He went off without further ado.

And then things went wrong. Two customers in line, and neither of them ready to be put off, both of them knowing full well that Shef never left the precinct. Those got rid of, a third wandered up full of inquiries and surprise and desire to talk. When he finally stepped over the rowan-festooned cords for the first time, Shef realized that he was now bound to do the most dangerous thing he could in this crowded campment full of eyes and bored intelligences: hurry.

Yet hurry he did, loping through the crowded lanes with never a look at the interested faces, cutting suddenly through the ropes of a few deserted tents, up to the wall with its stockade of logs, two hands on the sharp, man-high poles, and over them in one powerful vault. A shout from somewhere told him that he had been seen, but there was no hue and cry. He was going out, not in, and no one had reason to call "Thief."

Now, he was out on the plain, still dotted with horses and exercising men, with the tree-line of the backwater a mile away. The women would make their way along the river, but it would be suicide to run up after them. He had to get there first and had to be walking innocently back, or better still, to be standing where they would pass. Nor could he go near the gateway where the guards stood noting all that went on. Heedless of the danger, Shef stretched his legs and began to run across the meadow.

Within ten minutes he had reached the backwater and was strolling along the muddy lane which led beside it. No one there yet. Now all he had to do was look like a member of the Army taking his ease. Difficult: There was one thing that set him off from the others. He was on his own. Outside the camp and even inside it, the Vikings went round in ship's crews, or at least with an oarmate to bear company.

He had no choice. Just walk by them. Hope that Godive had the eyes to see him and the wit to say nothing.

He could hear voices ahead, women calling out and laughing, men's voices among them. Shef stepped round a bank of hawthorn and saw Godive in front of him. Their eyes met.

At the same moment he saw a blaze of saffron plaids all round her. He looked convulsively to either side, and there was Muirtach, not five yards away, striding towards him, a cry of triumph on his lips. Before he could move, hard hands had him by each arm. The rest were crowding up behind their leader, their female charges for the moment forgotten.

"The little cock-sparrow," gloated Muirtach, thumbs in belt. "The one who showed his hilt to me. Come out for a look at the womenfolk, is it? And an expensive look it's bound to be. Here, boys, take him aside a few paces." He unsheathed his longsword with a chilling *wheep*. "We don't want the ladies to be dashed by the sight of blood."

"I'll fight you," said Shef.

"That you won't. Am I a chieftain of the Gaddgedlar and to be matched with a runaway with the collar hardly off his neck?"

"There's never been collar on my neck," snarled Shef. He could feel a heat rising within him from somewhere, driving out the chill of fear and panic. There was only one small chance here. If he could draw them into treating him as an equal he might live. Otherwise he would be a headless corpse in a bush within a minute. "My birth is as good as yours. And I speak the Danish tongue a deal better!"

"That is true," said a chilly voice from somewhere behind the plaids. "Muirtach, your men are all watching you. They should be watching the womenfolk. Or does it need all of you to deal with this lad?"

The crowd in front of Shef melted away, and he found himself staring into the eyes of the speaker. Almost white eyes. They were as pale, Shef thought, as pale as ice in a dish—a dish of the thinnest maplewood, carved so thin it was almost transparent. They did not blink, and they waited for Shef's eyes to drop. Shef tore his own eyes away with an effort. Felt fear that instant, knew death was very close.

"You have a grudge, Muirtach?"

"Yes, lord." The Irishman's eyes too were dropped.

"Then fight him."

"*Och,* now, I said before—"

"Then if you won't—let one of your men fight him. Pick the youngest. Let a boy fight a boy. If your man wins I'll give him this." Ivar plucked a silver ring from his arm, threw it in the air, replaced it. "Step back and give them room. Let the women watch as well. No rules, no surrender," he added, teeth flashing in a chill and humorless smile. "To the death."

Seconds later Shef found himself staring once more into Godive's eyes, round now with terror. She stood at the front of a ring, two-deep, women's clothes intermixed with bright saffron plaids, and scattered through them also the scarlet cloaks and gold armrings of jarls and champions, the aristocracy of the Viking army. In the midst of them Shef caught sight of a familiar figure, the giant frame of Killer-Brand. On impulse Shef stepped over to him as the others prepared his opponent for battle on the far side of the ring.

"Sir. Lend me your amulet. I will return it—if I can."

Impassively the champion pulled it over his head and handed it over. "Kick your shoes off, lad. Ground's slippery."

Shef took the advice. He was beginning, consciously, to

breathe hard. He had been in many wrestling matches and had learned that it would prevent that momentary stillness, the unreadiness to fight that looked like fear. He peeled his shirt off too, donned the hammer amulet, drew his sword and threw the sheath and belt aside. It was a big ring, he thought. Speed would have to do it.

His enemy was coming out of his corner, plaid also thrown aside, stripped like Shef to his breeches. In one hand he held the longsword of the Gaddgedlar, thinner than the usual broadsword but a foot longer. In the other hand he had the same spiked targe as his fellows. A helmet was pulled down over his braided hair. He did not look much older than Shef, and in a wrestle Shef would not have feared him. But he had the longsword, the shield, a weapon in each hand. He was a warrior who had seen battle, fought in a dozen skirmishes.

From somewhere outside him, an image formed in Shef's mind. He heard again the solemn voice of Thorvin chanting. He stooped, picked a twig from the ground, threw it over his adversary's head like a javelin. "I give you to Hell," he called. "I give you to Dead Man's Strand."

A buzz of interest rose from the crowd, cries of encouragement: "Go on, Flann boy!" "Get him with your buckler!"

No voice encouraged Shef.

The Irish Norseman padded forward—then attacked swiftly. He feinted a thrust at Shef's face, turned it into a sideways backhand slash, aimed at the neck. Shef ducked under it, stepped away to his right, dodged the thrust with the spiked buckler. The Viking paced forward, swung again, backhand up, forehand down. Again Shef stepped back, feinted to step right, stepped left again. For an instant he was to his adversary's side, with a thrust possible at the bare right shoulder. He leapt back instead and moved rapidly to the center of the ring. He had already decided what to do, and he felt his body answering perfectly, light as a feather, buoyed up by a force that swelled his lungs and raced the blood through his veins. He remembered for an instant the way that Sigvarth's sword had broken and the fierce joy that had filled him.

Flann the Irishman came in again, swinging the sword faster and faster, trying to box Shef in against the bodies of the ring. He was quick. But he was used to men standing up to him to trade blows and catching them on blade or buckler. He did not know how to deal with an opponent who simply tried to avoid him. Shef jumped a wide sweep at knee level and saw that the Irishman was beginning to pant already. The Viking Army was made of sailors and horsemen, strong in the arm and shoulder, but men who walked little, and ran even less.

The shouting in the background was getting angry as the watchers grasped Shef's tactic. They might start to close in and narrow the ring. As Flann tried his favorite backhand sweep downward—a little slower now, a little too predictable—Shef stepped forward for the first time and parried fiercely, aiming the base of his thick blade at the tip of the longsword. No snap. But as the Irishman hesitated, Shef slashed out of the parry at the back of the other man's arm—a quick spurt of blood.

Shef was out of reach again, refusing to follow up his advantage, circling to his right, changing step as the other man advanced and then moving to his left again. He had seen the momentary shock in the warrior's eyes. Now there was blood running down over Flann's sword-hand, quite a lot of it, enough to weaken him in a few minutes if he did not finish things quickly.

For a hundred heartbeats they stood close to the center of the ring, Flann trying now to thrust as well as cut, stabbing out with his buckler; Shef parrying as well as dodging, trying to knock the sword from his enemy's blood-smeared hand.

Then Shef felt, suddenly, the confidence draining from his enemy's blows. Shef began to move again, springing on tireless feet, circling his opponent, moving always to the left, trying to get behind the other's sword-arm, careless of the energy he expended.

Flann's breath came almost as a sob. He hurled the buckler at Shef's face and followed it with a ripping upward stab. But Shef was in a crouch, knuckles of his sword-hand on the ground. His parry deflected the thrust far over his left shoulder. In an instant Shef straightened and drove his own sword deep beneath the naked, sweating ribs. As the stricken man shuddered and staggered away, Shef seized him in a wrestler's grip round the neck and poised his sword again.

Shef heard through the yelling the voice of Killer-Brand. "You gave him to Naströnd," it shouted. "You must finish him."

Shef looked down at the pallid, terror-stricken, still-living face in the crook of his arm, and felt a surge of fury. He drove the sword deeply home through the chest and felt the pain of death leap through Flann's body. Slowly, he dropped the corpse, retrieved his sword. Saw Muirtach's face, pale with rage. He stepped over to Ivar, where he stood with Godive now at his side.

"Most instructive," said Ivar. "I like to see someone who can fight with his head as well as his sword-arm. You have saved me a silver ring too. But you have cost me a man. How are you going to pay me back?"

"I am a man as well, lord."

"Join my ships, then. You will do as a rower. But not with Muirtach. Come to my tent this evening and my marshal will find you a place."

Ivar looked down for a moment, considering. "There is a notch on your blade. I did not see Flann put it there. Whose blade was it?"

Shef hesitated an instant. But with these men the bold course was always wisest. He spoke loudly, challengingly. "It was the sword of Sigvarth Jarl!"

Ivar's face tightened. "Well," he said, "this is no way to wash women or sheets. Let us be on our way." He turned, pulling Godive with him, though for an instant her face remained fixed, looking agonizedly at Shef.

Shef found himself staring up at the bulk of Viga-Brand. He slowly pulled off the amulet.

Brand weighed it in his hand. "Normally I would say keep it, boy, you earned it. If you live you will be a champion one day; I say it, Brand, champion of the men of Halogaland.

"But something tells me the hammer of Thor is not the right sign for you, smith though you are. I think you are a man of Othin, who is called also Bileyg, and Baleyg, and Bölverk."

"Bölverk?" said Shef. "And am I a doer of evil, a bale-worker?"

"Not yet. But you may be the instrument of one who is. Bale follows you." The big man shook his head. "But you did well today, for a beginner. Your first kill, I believe, and I am talking like a spaewife. Look, they have taken his body, but they have left the sword and shield and helmet. They are yours. It is the custom."

He spoke like one setting a test.

Slowly Shef shook his head. "I cannot profit from one I gave to Naströnd, to Dead Man's Strand." He picked up the helmet, threw it into the muddy water of the stream, hurled the buckler up into a bush, put his foot on the long thin sword, bent it once, twice, into unusability, left it lying.

"You see," said Brand. "Thorvin never taught you to do that. That is the sign of Othin."

Chapter Seven

Thorvin showed no surprise when Shef returned to the smithy and told him what had happened. He grunted a little wearily when Shef finally told him that he would be joining the contingent of Ivar, but said only, "Well, you'd better not go looking like that. The others would laugh at you—then you'll lose your temper and worse will happen."

From the pile at the back of the smithy he dug out a spear, recently reshafted, and a leather-bound shield. "With these you'll look respectable."

"Are they yours?"

"Sometimes people leave things in for repair, don't come back for them."

Shef took the gifts and then stood awkwardly, his rolled blanket and few possessions on his shoulder.

"I must thank you for what you did for me."

"I did it because it was my duty to the Way. Or so I thought. Maybe I was wrong. But I'm not a fool, boy. I am sure that you're after something I don't know about. I just hope it doesn't get you into trouble. Maybe our paths will run together again another day."

They parted with no more words, Shef stepping for only the second time over the rowan-berry cords of the precinct and for the first time walking down the lane between the tents without fear, face forward, not looking furtively around him. He headed not for the encampment of Ivar and the other Ragnarssons, but for the tent of Ingulf the leech.

As usual there was a small crowd standing round it, watching something. It dispersed as Shef strolled up, the last few men to leave carrying a stretcher with a bandaged shape on it. Hund came to meet his friend, wiping his hands on a rag.

"What were you doing?" Shef asked.

"Helping Ingulf. It's amazing what he can do. That man there was wrestling, fell awkwardly—leg broken, just like that. What would you do with that if you were back at home?"

Shef shrugged. "Bandage it up. Nothing else you can do. In the end it would heal."

"But the man would never walk straight again. The bones would just join each other wherever they happened to be. The leg would be all lumps and twists—like Crubba, who was rolled on by his horse. Well, what Ingulf does is pull the leg out straight before he starts bandaging, squeezes hard to feel if the broken ends of the bone are together. Then he bandages the leg between two stakes, so that the whole thing stays straight while it is healing. But what is even more marvelous is what he does in cases like this one, when it's broken so badly that the bones are sticking up through the skin. If he has to he even cuts back the bone, and opens the leg so that he can push the bone back straight! I didn't think that anyone would live through being opened and cut like that. But he is so quick—and he knows exactly what to do."

"Could you learn to do it?" Shef asked, watching the glow of enthusiasm on his friend's normally sallow face.

"With enough practice. Enough instruction. And something else. Ingulf studies the bodies of the dead, you know, to see how bones fit together. What would Father Andreas say to that?"

"So you mean to stay with Ingulf?"

The runaway slave nodded slowly. He pulled from under his tunic a chain. On it was a small silver pendant, an apple.

"Ingulf gave it me. The apple of Ithun the Healer. I am a believer now. I believe in Ingulf and the Way. Maybe not in Ithun." Hund looked at his friend's neck. "Thorvin has not converted you. You are not wearing a hammer."

"I wore one for a bit." Shef spoke briefly about what had happened. "I may have a chance now of rescuing Godive and getting away. Maybe if I watch for long enough God will be good to me."

"God?"

"Or Thor. Or Othin. I'm beginning to think that it makes no difference to me. Maybe one of them is watching."

"Is there anything I can do?"

"No." Shef gripped his friend's arm. "We may not see each other again. But if you leave the Vikings I hope one day I will have a place for you. Even if it's just a hut in the fen."

He turned and headed for the place he had not dared even

to look at when they first entered the Viking camp days before: the Vikings' command tents.

The domain of the four Ragnarsson brothers ran from east wall to west wall, a full furlong along the riverfront. At its heart, in the center, were the great meeting tent—with room in it for tables for a hundred men—and the decorated tents of the brothers themselves. Round each of these four clustered the tents of women, dependents, the most trusted immediate bodyguards. Further away ran the lines of bivouac tents of the soldiers, usually three or four tents for every ship's crew, sometimes with smaller ones scattered through for the captains, helmsmen, and champions. The retinues of the brothers for the most part kept separate, if close together.

The Snakeeye's men were mostly Danes: It was common knowledge throughout the army that in time Sigurth would return to Denmark to challenge for the kingdom in Sjaelland and Skaane which his father had owned, and would go on one day to challenge for the rule of Denmark from the Baltic to the North Sea—a kingdom no man had possessed since the days of that King Guthfrith who fought Charlemagne. Ubbi and Halvdan, men with no stake and no claim to any throne other than that which their strength might bring them, recruited from anywhere: Swedes, Gauts, Norwegians, men from Gotland and Bornholm and all the islands.

Ivar's men were mostly exiles of one sort or another. Many no doubt were mere murderers escaping vengeance or the rule of one law or another. But the bulk of his following came from the floating population of Norsemen who for generations had been moving into the Outer Isles of the Celtic regions: the Orkneys and Shetlands, then the Hebrides, the Scottish mainland. For years these men had been tempered in the constant skirmishes of Ireland and Man, Strathclyde and Galloway and Cumbria. Among themselves they boasted—but the claim was fiercely rejected by many, especially the Norwegians, who viewed Ireland as their own property to keep or dispose of—that one day Ivar

Ragnarsson would rule the whole of Ireland from his castle by the black pool, the Dubh Linn itself, and would then lead his victorious navies in triumph against the feeble kingdoms of the Christian West. The Ui Niall might still have a say in that, muttered the Gaddgedlar among themselves, speaking Irish as none of the Hebridean or Scottish Norsemen would deign to. But they said it quietly. For all their race pride they knew that they themselves were the most hated of all by their countrymen, apostates from Christ, accomplices of those who had brought fire and slaughter to every part of Ireland. Who had done it for pay and for power, not merely for joy and for glory, as had been the Irish custom since the days of Finn and Cuchulainn and the champions of Ulster.

Into this touchy and tinder-dry encampment, graded with differences and with excuses for quarrel, Shef walked as the cooking fires were lighting for the night meal.

He was met by a marshal who heard his name, listened to his story, ran a disapproving eye over his shabby equipment, and grunted. He called a young man from the throng to show Shef his tent, sleeping place and oar, and to introduce him to his duties. The man—Shef never caught his name, nor did he want to—told him that there were four jobs at which he would have to take his turn: ship-guard, gate-guard, pen-guard, and if necessary, guard on the tent of Ivar. Mostly they were assigned by crew.

"I thought the Gaddgedlar guarded Ivar," Shef said.

The young man spat. "When he's here. When he's not they go with him. But the treasure and the womenfolk stay behind. Someone has to look after them. Anyway, if the Gaddgedlar got too far from Ivar someone would take a dislike to them—Ketil Flatnose and his men have a spite against them, and Thorvald the Deaf too. And a dozen more."

"Would we be trusted to guard the tent of Ivar?"

The young man looked at him aslant. "Shouldn't we be? I tell you, *Enzkr*, if you are thinking of Ivar's treasure you had better cut your thoughts right out of your head. It will be less painful that way. Did you even hear what Ivar did to the Irish king at Knowth?"

As they walked round, he told him in detail what Ivar had done to kings and lesser men who had displeased him. Shef took little notice, looking with great interest at the camp. The tales were clearly meant to frighten him.

The ships, he thought, were the weak point of the camp. Space had to be left clear for them to be drawn up on the muddy banks, so there could be no fortifications there. The ships themselves represented a sort of obstacle, but they were also the Vikings' most precious possession. If anyone got past the riverbank-guards, they could be in among the ships with torch and axe, and they would be difficult to dislodge.

The gate-guards were a different matter. Surprising them would be hard. Any fight would be on level ground and on even terms, where the Vikings' great axes and iron-shafted javelins would have easy play. Anyone who did manage to get through them would in any case only find himself fighting his way through rank after rank of warriors, in a tangle of tents and ropes.

The pens, now . . . They occupied an area of their own near the east wall: a sorry strip of posts hammered into the ground, leather ropes binding them together. Inside, men huddled under makeshift coverings of canvas against the rain. Iron fetters on their feet, iron manacles on their hands. Held together, though, Shef noted, only by leather. Chain was too dear. But by the time a man had chewed through the leather bonds, even the least alert guard should have noticed—and penalty for any disobedience in the slave-pens was fierce. As Shef's guide pointed out, if you marked up a slave too much you couldn't sell him anyway, so you might as well go ahead and finish the job to frighten the others.

As he peered over the logs into the pen, Shef noticed a familiar-looking head lying on the ground, its owner sunk in a depth of despair: a blond head, curls matted with grime. His half brother, son of the same mother. Alfgar. Part of the prey of Emneth. The head stirred as if sensing the eyes upon it, and Shef dropped his gaze instantly, as he would have done had he been stalking a doe or a wild pig of the marshes.

"You haven't sold any slaves since you arrived?"

"Nay. Too much trouble getting them out to sea, with the English ambushing all the time. Sigvarth owns that lot." The young man spat again, eloquently. "He's waiting for someone else to clear the road for him. Will, too."

"Clear the road?"

"Ivar's taking half the army out in two days, to make the kinglet Jatmund—Edmund, you English call him—fight, or destroy his country for him. We'd rather have done it the easy way, but we wasted too much time already. Be bad news for Jatmund when Ivar catches up with him, I tell you. . . ."

"Are we going out or staying here?"

"Our crew stays." Again, the young man looked half curiously, half angrily at Shef. "Why you think I'm telling you all this? We'll be providing guards all the time. I wish I was going. I'd like to see what they'll do to that king when he's caught. I told you about Knowth. Well, I was there at the Boyne when Ivar robbed the tombs of the dead kings and this Christ-priest tried to stop us. What Ivar did, he . . ."

The subject occupied the young man and his mates all through the dinner of broth, salt pork and cabbage. There was a barrel of ale, someone had taken a hatchet or an axe to its top, and they all dipped into it liberally. Shef drank more than he realized, the day's events circling in his head. His mind was revolving what he had learned, trying to put together the rudiments of a plan. He lay down that night exhausted. The Irishman leaping in death in his arms was a detail, a matter of the past.

Then exhaustion seized him, drove him into sleep, into something more than sleep.

He was looking out from a building, through a half-shuttered window. It was night. A bright moonlit night, so bright that the racing clouds above threw dim shadows even in the dark. And out there something had flashed. Something had flashed.

There was a man standing next to him, gabbling out explanations of what the something might be. But he did not need them. He knew. A dull feeling of doom grew within him. Against it, a rising tide of fury. He cut the explanations short.

"That is not dawn from the east," said the Shef-who-was-not-Shef. "Nor is it a dragon flying, nor the gables of this hall burning. That is the flashing of drawn weapons, of secret foes coming to take us in our sleep. For now war awakens, war that will bring about disaster for all the people. So rise now, my warriors, think of courage, guard the doors, fight heroically."

In the dream, a stirring behind him as the warriors rose, gripped their shields, buckled their sword-belts.

But in the dream and over the dream, not in the hall, not part of the hero-tale that was unfolding before his eyes, he heard a mighty voice, too mighty to come from a human throat. It was a god's voice, Shef knew. But not the voice anyone would have imagined of a god. Not dignified, not honorable. An amused, chuckling, sardonic voice.

"Oh half-Dane who is not of the Half-Danes," it said. "Do not listen to the warrior, the brave one. When trouble comes, do not rise to fight. Seek the ground. Seek the ground."

Shef woke with a start, the smell of burning in his nostrils. For several seconds, half-drugged with fatigue, his mind circled around that: strange smell, something acrid, like tar— what could be burning tar? Then there was a confusion of movement all around him, a foot stamping on his guts jerked him into full wakefulness. The tent was abroil with men scrambling for breeches, boots, weapons, all in full darkness; there was a glare of fire on one side of the tent. Shef realized suddenly that there was a continuous roar in the background. Voices shouting, timber crackling, and over it all a deafening metallic clanging, the impact of blade on blade and blade on shield. The noise of full-scale battle.

The men in the tent were shouting, crowding past each other. Voices outside shouting, yelling in English, voices suddenly only yards away. Shef understood suddenly, the mighty voice still ringing in his ears. He hurled himself back to the ground again, fighting his way to the middle of the floor, away from the walls. As he did so the whole side of the tent caved in and through it there flashed a spear-blade. The young man who had guided him turned half to-ward it, his feet still trapped in folds of blanket, met the spear full in the chest. Shef grabbed the falling body and pulled it on top of him, feeling for the second time in a dozen hours the convulsive leap and start of a heart burst-ing.

As he did so, the whole tent collapsed and a wave of trampling feet ran over it, spears stabbing down into the trapped pile of struggling men. The body in his arms jerked again and again; in the darkness inches away there came screams of pain and fear; a blade plunged into the dirt, scraping against Shef's sprawling knee. Then suddenly the feet were gone, a rush of bodies and voices swarmed past in the lane outside, a new hubbub of clanging and shrieking broke out ten yards toward the center of the camp.

Shef knew what had happened. The English king had taken the Vikings' dare, had attacked their camp in the night, and by some miracle of organization and his enemies' overconfidence, had broken through or over the stockade, driving for the ships and the tents of the leaders, killing as many trapped in their blankets as they could. The English were pouring on, driving toward the center of the river-line. Shef seized his breeches, his boots and his sword-belt and wriggled past the corpses of his temporary fellows into the open. Pulled the gear on, ran, keeping low to the ground.

There was no one standing within twenty yards. Between himself and the stockade was a swathe of leveled tents with bodies sprawled among them, some calling feebly for help or trying to struggle to their feet. The English raiders had charged through the camp hacking frenziedly at anything that moved. They had left few survivors.

Before the Vikings could recover, join together, the raiders would be deep in the heart of their enemies' fortress, the battle irrecoverably won or lost.

All along the river-line there was glare and smoke, leaping up as sails caught or the fire took hold of some new-tarred timber hull; against the blaze a frieze of capering demons, hurling spears, swinging swords and axes. The English must have met little resistance down by the ships in their first charge. But the Vikings closest to the ships had rallied swiftly and fiercely to defend their wave-stallions. What was going on by the tents of the Ragnarssons? Was this the moment? Shef thought with a calm and intent calculation which left no room for self-doubt. Was this the moment to try to get Godive out?

No. Clearly there was battle and fierce resistance on all sides. If the Vikings beat off the assault, then she would remain as she was: a slave, the bedslave of Ivar. But if the attack succeeded—and if he were there to save her . . .

He ran, heading not toward the fighting, where one more half-armed man would find nothing but quick death; but in the opposite direction, toward the stockade walls, still dark, still quiet. Not completely. Shef realized now that there was battle not only close to him but also far away, in all directions round the further walls of the stockade. Spears were flying in the blackness, firebrands coming looping over the logs of the stockade. King Edmund had sent in simultaneous assaults from all sides at once. Each Viking had rushed to the nearest point of danger. By the time they realized where help was needed most, again Edmund would have won or lost.

Like a shadow Shef ran towards the slave-pens. As he neared them a figure lurched towards him in the fire-lit dark, its thigh black with blood, a longsword drooping in its hand. *"Fraendi,"* it said, "help me a moment, stop the bleeding—" Shef stabbed once from below, twisted the sword, withdrew.

One, he thought, grabbing up the sword.

The pen-guards were still there, clustered in tight formation in front of the pen's gates, clearly determined to resist any attempt to break through. All along the logs of the slave-stockade heads were bobbing as the tethered slaves tried to peer over, to see what was happening. Shef lobbed the longsword over the nearest wall, followed it in one surge of motion. There was a yell as the guards spotted him, but no movement. Undecided whether to guard the gate or to follow him.

Figures all round him, stinking, clutching. Shef snarled abuse in English, pushed them away. With the longsword he slashed the leather bonds between one pair of hand manacles, did the same for the man's foot fetters, pushed the sword into the freed hands.

"Start cutting them free," he hissed, turning instantly to the next man and drawing his own sword from its scabbard. The slaves saw what was happening, thrust their hands out, then snatched their leg-bonds, held them up for an easy cut. In twenty heartbeats half a score of slaves were free.

The palisade gate creaked open, the guards deciding to come in and catch the intruder. As the first Viking came through, hands caught his arms and legs, a fist slammed into his face. In seconds he was on the ground, his axe and spear snatched away, blows swinging at his fellows who crowded after him from the light into the darkness of the pen. Shef slashed furiously at leather, then saw suddenly the hands of his half brother Alfgar, a face staring at him in amazement and twisted rage.

"We have to get Godive."

The face nodded.

"Come with me. You others, there's weapons at the gate, cut yourselves free. Those with weapons, who want to strike a blow for Edmund, over the wall and follow me."

Shef's voice rose to a bellow. He sheathed sword, stepped to the wall, caught the top of the logs and heaved himself over in a second powerful roll. Alfgar was with him a moment later, staggering from the shock of release, a score of half-naked figures swarming after him and more pouring over the wall. Some ran instantly into the friendly dark, others turned in rage toward their guards, still embroiled in their struggle round the gate. Shef ran back through the leveled tents with a dozen men behind him.

Weapons lay everywhere for the snatching, dropped where their owners had died or still lying where they had been piled for the night. Shef hauled aside a tent flap, rolled over a corpse, seized a spear and a shield. For a long, hard-breathing pause he studied the men who had followed him as they armed themselves too. Peasants mostly, he judged. But angry and desperate ones, maddened by what had happened to them in the pens. The one in the front, though, staring at him intently, rolls of muscle on arm and shoulder, he carried himself like a warrior.

Shef pointed ahead, to the struggle still going on round the untouched command tents of the Viking Army. "There is King Edmund," he said, "trying to kill the Ragnarssons. If he succeeds the Vikings will break and flee and never recover. If he fails they will hunt us all down again and no village of any shire will be safe. We are fresh, and armed. Let us join them, break through together."

The released slaves surged as one toward the fighting.

Alfgar held back. "You did not come with Edmund, half-armed and half-naked. How do you know where to find Godive?"

"Shut up and follow." Shef sprinted ahead again, hurdling through the confusion towards the tents of the women of Ivar.

Chapter Eight

Edmund—son of Edwold, descendant of Raedwald the Great, last of the Wuffingas, and now by God's grace

king of the East Angles—glared through the eyeholes of his
war-mask in frustration and rage.

They had to break through! One more thrust and the desperate resistance of the Viking chiefs would crumble, the
Ragnarssons would all die together in blood and fire, the
rest of the Great Army would fall back in doubt and confusion. . . . But if they held . . . If they held, he knew, in a few
more minutes the war-wise Vikings would realize that the
assaults on their perimeter were no more than angry peasants with torches, that the real attack was here, here. . . .
And then they would be down on the struggle by the riverbank with their overwhelming numbers, and it would be the
English who were caught like rats in the last unmown
square of the hayfield. He, Edmund, had no sons. The
whole future of his dynasty and his kingdom had now narrowed down to this yelling, clanging tumult, maybe one
hundred men on each side, as the picked champions of the
East English and the last hard core of the Ragnarssons' personal forces fought it out: the one side straining every nerve
in their bodies to break into the three-sided square of the
Ragnarssons' tents down by the river; the other, standing
poised and confident among the tangle of their guy-ropes,
bracing themselves to hold out for five minutes more after
the unimaginable shock of the English assault.

And they were doing it too. Edmund's hand tensed on the
bloody sword-hilt and he swayed as if to move forward. Instantly the brawny shadows on either side of him, the captains of his bodyguard, edged slightly forward, blocking
him in with shield and body. They would not let him throw
himself into the melee. As soon as the initial slaughter of
sleeping men had stopped and the fight had begun, they had
been in front of him.

"Easy, lord," muttered Wigga. "See Totta and the boys
there. They'll get through these bastards yet."

As he spoke the battle surged in front of them, first a few
feet forward as a Viking went down and the English rushed
at the momentary gap. Then back, back. Above the helmets
and the raised shields a battle-axe whirled, the thuds as it

struck lindenwood turning to a crash of steel on mail. The swaying mob ejected a body, cleft through its mail from neck to breastbone. For an instant Edmund saw a giant figure twirling its axe in one hand like a boy's ox-goad, daring the English to come on. They did, fiercely, and all he could see was straining backs.

"We must have killed a thousand of the bastards already," said Eddi on his other hand. In a moment, Edmund knew, one or the other of them would say "Time to get out of here, lord," and he would be hustled away. If they could get away. Most of his army, the country thanes and their levies, were already making for the rear. They had done their job: burst over the stockade behind the king and his picked strikers, massacred the sleepers, overwhelmed the ship-guards and set fire to as many beached longships as they could. But they had never expected to stand in line and exchange blows with the professional champions of the North, nor did they mean to. Catch them asleep and unarmored, yes. Fight them awake and enraged, man to man, toe to toe—that was the duty of their betters.

One break, Edmund prayed. Almighty God eternal, one break in this square and we will be through and attacking them from all sides. The war will be over and the pagans destroyed. No more dead boys in meadows and children's corpses tossed down wells. But if they stand another minute, long enough for a mower to whet his scythe . . . Then it is we who will break and, for me, it will be the fate of Wulfgar.

The thought of his tormented thane swelled his heart till it seemed the links of his mail must snap. The king shoved Wigga aside and strode forward, sword raised, looking for a gap in the fighters where he could thrust forward. He shouted full-throatedly, so that his voice echoed inside the metal of his ancient visor:

"Break through! Break through! The hoard of Raedwald, I swear it, to the man who breaks their ranks. And five hundreds to the man who brings me the head of Ivar!"

* * *

Twenty paces away, Shef gathered his little band of rescued prisoners in the night. Many of the tarred longships along the river were now blazing furiously, throwing lurid light on the battle. All around them, the Vikings' bivouac tents were down, flattened by the English charge, their occupants dead or wounded. Only in one place, in front of them, eight or ten pavilions still stood: the homes of the Ragnarssons, their chieftains, their guards—and their women. Round these the battle raged.

Shef turned to Alfgar and to the heavily-muscled thane beside him, standing a pace in front of the little knot of half-armed, heavy-breathing peasants.

"We have to break into those tents there. That's where the Ragnarssons are." And Godive, he thought silently. But only Alfgar would care about that.

In the firelight the thane's teeth showed, a mirthless smile.

"Look," he pointed.

For an instant again, as the battle cleared, two warriors showed in black silhouette, each leap of flame seeming to catch them in another contorted pose. The swords whirled, each blow parried *forte à forte*, the strokes coming fore-hand, backhand, at all angles, each one meeting a precisely timed counter. The warriors twisted and stamped, raising their shields, leaping over low strokes, moving with each blow into position for the next, trying to gain leverage even from the strokes of their enemy for a tiny advantage on the next counter, a weakened wrist, a strain, a hesitation.

The thane's voice was almost affectionate. "Look at them, both sides. Those are the king's warmen and the best of the pirates. They are the *drengir*, the hard *here-chempan*. How long would we last against them? Me—maybe I could give one a little trouble for half a minute. You—I don't know. These—" He gestured with his thumb at the peasants behind him. "Make sausage meat of them."

"Let's get out of here," said Alfgar abruptly. The peasants stirred and muttered.

Suddenly the thane had Alfgar by the arm, fingers sinking deep.

"No. Listen. That is the king's voice. He is calling on his true men. Hear what he wants."

"He wants the head of Ivar," snarled a peasant.

Suddenly they were all moving forward, raising spears, bracing shields, the thane among them.

He knows it won't work, Shef realized—but I know what will!

He leapt in front of them, pointing, gesturing. Slowly the men caught his meaning, turned away, dropped their weapons, headed for the nearest of the blazing longships.

Over the clash of steel the Vikings too heard the king's voice calling, and understood him—many of them had had English bedslaves for years, and their fathers before them.

"King Jatmund wants your head," cried one of the jarls.

"I don't want Jatmund's head," Ivar called back. "He must be taken alive."

"What do you want him for?"

"I will give that much thought. Something new. Something instructive."

Something to put heart back into the men. This had all been much too close for comfort, Ivar reflected, edging from side to side to keep a clear view of the action. He would never have thought that the king of a little kingdom like this would have had the guts to challenge the Great Army in its own base.

"All right," he said quietly to the Gaddgedlar, waiting behind the battle-line as his personal reserve. "No need to wait much longer. They aren't going to break through. Over here, between the tents. Now, when I give the word we are going to charge. Go right through them, don't bother to fight. I want you to catch the kinglet, King Jatmund. See him. There. The little man, the one with the war-mask over his face."

Ivar filled his lungs to shout, over the din of battle, in mockery of the cry of Edmund. "Twenty ounces, twenty ounces of gold to the man who brings me the English king. But don't kill him. He must be taken alive."

But before he could speak he felt Muirtach and the Irish gasp and stiffen around him.

"Will you look at that!"

"It's a fiery cross coming for us!"

"Mac na hoige slan."

"Mother of God be merciful."

"What in the name of Othin is it?"

Over the heads of the struggling men a giant shape rushed toward them like a cross, a monstrous, blazing cross. The ranks of the English parted, Killer-Brand leapt forward with his axe raised. Then the huge timber fell forward, half hurled by the capering furies who grasped it.

Brand sprang aside, tripped over a rope and fell with a clang to the ground. Something struck Ivar a numbing blow on the shoulder. The Gaddgedlar scattered in all directions as the waxed flax walls of the tents started to blaze. The shrieking of women rose to add itself to all the other noises of the battle.

And instantly, running along the blazing timber itself, his face contorted with rage and delight, there came a half-naked churl, the slave manacles still on his wrist, hurtling through the scattered ranks of his captors. A spear stabbed at Ivar's face. Without thought he parried it, slicing the point from its shaft at the same moment his shoulder shrieked protest. The peasant raced on, reversing his clumsy weapon and smashing it at the side of Ivar's head.

The blow, the ground rising up, the fall into burning wax and skin. Struck by a peasant, Ivar's brain thought in the last instant of consciousness, darkness embracing him. But I am the champion of the North.

Through the flames other figures came leaping. It's that boy, thought Ivan, the one who fought the duel by the washing-place. But I thought he was one of mine. . . .

A bare foot landed in his testicles, and his body gave up the fight.

* * *

Shef raced along the still-smoldering timber of the long-ship's mast. He was aware that his hands were burned, swelling, puffy already with blisters. There was no time for that. He and the thane and Alfgar had seized the smoldering timber, its yard still attached, as soon as the peasants had pulled it from the flame, had grasped the upper end and had run toward the fighting battle-line, struggling desperately to keep it upright till they could throw it into the warriors. But the instant they hurled it a wave of furious peasants had run straight past them and over them. And behind him, he knew, came King Edmund's champions, all beside themselves with rage and fear and the passion to kill. He had to reach Godive first.

In front of him a churl rained blows on an amazed Viking with a broken spear-staff. Something groaned and squirmed under his feet. Another peasant was down with a slash from the side. Yellow plaids seemed to be scattering in flight everywhere—the Gaddgedlar, in superstitious panic and fear of the fiery cross that had come to avenge their apostasy. And women shrieking.

Shef swerved instantly to the left round a tent. Bulging sides, the screaming just beyond it. He drew his sword, bent, and scored it open at knee level, instantly catching the flap and hauling at it with all his strength.

A wail of women erupted from it like water from a bro-ken milldam, in their shifts, in their gowns, at least one still naked from her sleep. Godive—where! That one, there, the scarf over her head. Shef seized her shoulder, hauling her round to him, dragging the scarf down. A blaze of yellow hair, turned copper by the flames in the sky, and furious pale eyes, nothing like Godive's gray ones. A fist caught him full in the face and he staggered back, full of shock and incongruous pain: all around him heroes were dying and he had just been punched on the nose!

Then the woman was away, and Shef glimpsed a familiar body-shape, not scuttling like the other women but running full stride like a young deer. Straight into disaster. The En-glish were everywhere now, inside the Viking square, taking their enemies from front and rear simultaneously, determined to wipe out the pirates' leadership and aristocracy in the scant seconds they had before rescue and revenge came down from the main camp. They were cutting at everything that moved, carried away with fear and triumph and long frustration.

Shef was on her, throwing himself forward, catching her round the hips and bowling her over just as a furious warrior, seeing something moving behind him, swung round and launched a body-severing blow at waist level. The two rolled sideways in a tangle of legs and dress and nails as new combat clashed above them. Then he had a grip round her waist and was hauling her by main force into the shadow of a pavilion, tenanted only by corpses.

"Shef!"

"Me." He put his hand over her mouth. "Listen. We have to get away now. There won't be another chance. Go back to where I broke in. Everyone there is dead now. If we can just get through the fight we'll be out there, by the river. Understood? Now, let's go."

Sword in one hand, clutching Godive tightly with the other, Shef stepped crouching into the night, eyes darting for a route through the fifty single combats that raged around him.

The battle was over, Edmund thought. And he had lost. He had broken the Vikings' last ring, sure enough, thanks to that rabble of churls that had sprung from nowhere with the half-naked youth in their midst. In the last few minutes he had done crippling execution among the Great Army's hardest of hard cores, so much that the Army would never be quite the same again. Or remember the camp on the Stour without a shudder. But he had not yet seen a Ragnarsson dead. There were little knots of men still fighting back-to-back and the Ragnarssons must be among them. Only if he held this place of slaughter, defeated and killed every one of them, could he be sure of lasting victory.

He would not get the chance to do it. Edmund felt the

blood-rage inside him cooling, cooling to a slow and wary calculation. Ominously, the noise from the main camp above the Ragnarssons' tents by the river had lessened. Stung by arrows from the palisades, harassed by mock assaults and parties of running knifemen in their rear, the Vikings had let the Ragnarssons deal with their own troubles in their own way. But you could not fool these veterans for long; they would not stand by forever while their leaders were destroyed.

Edmund sensed that men were gathering beyond the reach of the flames. Those were orders being given. Someone was getting ready to come down like a warhammer on a hazelnut, with a thousand men together. How many had he left on their feet and not escaped into the night? Fifty?

"Time to go, lord," muttered Wigga.

Edmund nodded, knowing that he had reached the absolute last instant. His escape route was still clear, and he had a handful of champions round him to brush aside any scattered interceptors there might be between him and the east stockade.

"Back," he ordered. "Back to where we broke in. We'll run for the stockade from there. But kill everyone, everyone on the ground, ours as well as theirs. Don't leave them for Ivar. And make certain every single one is dead!"

Ivar felt consciousness returning. Yet it would not come back all at once; it was there and not there. He had to grasp it, grasp it quickly. Something terrible was coming toward him. He could feel the thump, thump, thump of heavy footsteps. It was a *draugr*—giant, swollen, blue as a three-day corpse, strong as ten men, with all the strength of those who live in the Halls of the Mighty, but come back to earth to vex their descendants. Or to avenge their deaths.

Ivar remembered who he was. In the same instant he realized who the *draugr* must be. It was the Irish king Maelguala, whom he had killed years before. Ivar remembered still his contorted face, glistening with sweat from rage and pain, but still cursing Ivar steadily and fearlessly as the wheels turned and the strongest men of the Army threw their weight on the levers. They had bent him back and back over the stone till suddenly—

As his mind registered the snap of broken spine, Ivar awoke fully. Something over his face; skin, cloth—had they wrapped him in his cloak already for burial? An instinctive movement checked a stab of agony from the right shoulder, but the pain burned away the mist from his head. He sat up instantly, more pain from his head, not the right side, the left side, the side opposite from where he had been hit. Concussion, then. He had felt that before. Get down and stay down. No time to do that now. He could tell where he was.

Ivar lurched slowly to his feet, the effort sending a wave of nausea and giddiness through him. His sword was still in his hand, and he tried to lift it. No strength there. He dropped the blade and leaned heavily on it, feeling the point sink into the close-packed earth. He stared to the west, between the ripped-open tents, toward an arena where still threescore of men fought desperately to buy time, or to annihilate their enemies, and saw doom approaching him.

No *draugr*, but a king. Heading straight toward him, evidently bent on escape, was the short, broad-shouldered figure in the war-mask. The English kinglet. Jatmund. Flanking and following him were a half dozen enormous men, big as Vikings, big as Viga-Brand, obviously the king's own personal bodyguard—the very heart and soul of the king's warriors, the *chempan* as the English called them. As they came they were stabbing carefully, economically, professionally, at every figure that still lay on the ground. They were doing it just right. One of them he would have squared off to, if he had been fighting fit and unwounded and the men had needed to be encouraged. Six. And he could hardly hold a weapon, still less could he wield it. Ivar tried to shuffle his feet round to face them, so that no one could say afterward that Ivar Ragnarsson, the champion of the North, had been caught unawares or trying to flee. As he did so, the war-mask turned toward him.

A cry of recognition broke from it, a wave, a pointing

arm. All the English together broke into a run, charging toward him, swords raised, the bodyguards striving vainly to outstrip their king.

As Edmund attacked, Shef, dodging from dark space to dark space round the edges of the conflict, saw the gap between the tangled tents, pushed Godive violently into it, and tensed his muscles for the final dart to liberty.

Without warning she had torn free of his grasp, was rushing ahead of him. She had seized a man by the arm, a wounded man, was holding him up. By Christ, it was Ivar! Hurt, done for, staggering as he stood.

Shef's lips pulled back in a killing snarl, and he paced forward like a leopard—one step, two, three—sword dropped to hip level, already aiming the fierce thrust upward beneath the chin where no armor covered.

Then Godive was in front of him, clutching at his sword-hand. He tried to throw her off but Godive clung on, pounding his naked chest with her free hand. Shrieking.

"Behind you! Behind you!"

Shef flung her off and spun to see a sword already slicing at his neck. His own sword met it with a clang, driving it up; a second blow came instantly after the first. He ducked under it and heard the whizz as it slashed the air. Realized in the same instant that Godive was behind him and that he had to keep his own body between the swords and her.

Then he was backing between a maze of guy-ropes, half a dozen men crowding toward him behind the short figure in the fantastically molded and gilded war-mask. It was the king. But no matter who it was or how many supporters he had, for just this one moment it was Shef the slave, Shef the dog and the king of the East Angles facing each other.

"Get out of the way," said Edmund, pacing forward. "You are an Englishman. You brought the ship's timber, you broke the line. I saw you. That is Ivar behind you. Kill him, let me kill him, and you will have the reward I promised."

"The woman," Shef stammered. He had meant to say "Just leave me the woman." But he had no time.

Too late. As the gap between the tents widened, the

champions of Edmund saw their chance. One was by the side of his king in an instant, stabbing furiously upward at the unarmored youth in front of him, converting the stab instantly into a slash, jerking his shield forward as the slash missed, to break a rib or smash a wrist. Shef stepped back, ducked, twisted, as he had against the Irishman Flann, making no attempt to strike back or parry.

"You can have him," he yelled.

He beat a thrust aside, ducked into a shield-boss, and with the strength of desperation grappled a wrist as thick as a horse's fetlock, twisted, and hurled Wigga the champion over his thigh in a village-green cross-buttock throw.

He was on the ground and legs were all around him; cries and blows and the clang of metal. A dozen Vikings had appeared, Viga-Brand at their head, to protect their chief. Now it was the English king whose men had to close round him, to die one by one while all the time Ivar called out for Jatmund to be spared, for the kinglet not to be killed.

Taking no notice of the fray Shef wriggled clear, saw Godive standing a few yards away from the edge of the battle, staring round in panic. He seized her by the arm and dragged her at full speed toward the dying fires of the longships and the muddy waters of the Stour. The English kingdom lay in ruins behind him, and if the pirates ever caught him again his fate would be terrible. But Godive was unhurt. He had saved her.

Though she had saved Ivar.

Chapter Nine

The stars were paling in the eastern sky behind them as the young man and the girl stole carefully and cautiously through the depths of the wood. If he looked back Shef could see the topmost branches now silhouetted against the sky, moving slightly in the breeze, the little wind that comes before dawn. Down at ground level nothing of it could be felt. Where the two crossed the occasional clearing created by the fall of oak or ash, the dew soaked their feet. It would be a hot day, Shef thought, one of the last of the late, event-filled summer.

It could not come soon enough for him. Both were cold. Shef wore only the boots and woolen breeches which he had snatched up when the English attack came in. Godive had only her shift. She had stripped off her long dress before slipping into the water by the fired ships. She could swim like a fish, like an otter; and like otters they had swum out, underwater for as many strokes as they could, concentrating on noiselessness and cutting out both splash and gasp. A hundred slow strokes and ten breaths up the river, against the slow, weedy current; eyes alert every time they came up for watchers on the bank. Then a careful filling of the lungs while Shef warily eyed the stockade edge, where surely guards might still be posted. Then the deep dive and the long swim underwater, till it was time to come up and repeat the otter stroke, on, on, for another quarter mile before he decided it might be safe to creep ashore.

He had felt no chill while they were escaping, only a momentary prickle on his burned hands and body as he dashed into the water the first time. But now he was beginning to shiver uncontrollably, the great shudders wracking his body. Shef knew that he was close to collapse. He would have to let go soon, lie down, let his muscles relax. And let his mind come to terms with the events of the last twenty-four hours. He had killed a man; no, two men. He had seen the king, something he might have expected to do once or twice in a lifetime. But this time the king had seen him, had even spoken to him! And he had stood toe to toe with Ivar the Boneless, champion of the North. Shef knew he would have killed him if it had not been for Godive. He could have been the hero of all England, of all Christianity.

But she had stopped him. And then he had betrayed his king, delayed him, all but handed him over to the power of the pagans. If anyone were ever to know about that . . . But his mind shied away from the thought. They had escaped. He would ask Godive about her and Ivar when he could.

As the light strengthened, Shef's eye caught the faint trace of a trail. It was overgrown, had not been used for weeks. That was good. Used last to flee from the Viking landing. But at the end of the trail there might be something: a hut, a shed. Anything left behind would now be worth its weight in silver.

Now, the trees were thinning, there was something in front of him: not a hut, he realized, but a shelter, a lean-to made of branches. The coppicers must have made it to store their gear in as they worked through the forest cutting the poles that all farmers relied on for hurdles and fencing, for handles, and for the centerpieces for their flimsy wattle-and-daub walls.

There was no one there. Shef led Godive over. Turning her toward him, he held her hands in his own and looked down into her eyes.

"What we have here," he said, "is nothing. One day, I hope we will have a real house of our own, somewhere we can live together untroubled. That is why I came to take you back from the Vikings. It will not be safe to travel in the day. Let us rest as well as we can till evening."

The coppicers had rigged up a bark gutter beneath the roof of rough shingles. It led to a large broken crock, full to overflowing with clear rainwater: one more proof that no one had been there for weeks. The boughs inside were covered with old, torn strips of blanket. Stiffly the pair wrapped themselves, lay down huddled together, fell immediately into an exhausted slumber.

Shef woke as the sun began to pierce through the branches. He rose, careful not to disturb the still-sleeping girl, and crawled out of the shelter. Concealed beneath the boughs he found flint and steel. Should he risk a fire? he wondered. Better not. They had water and warmth, but there was no food to cook. He would take what he had found with them

when they left. Slowly, Shef was beginning to think of the
future. He owned nothing now, save his breeches, so every
single possession he accumulated would be precious.

He did not think they would be disturbed, not this day.
They were still well within range of the Viking fighting patrols he had seen on his way into the camp, but the Vikings
would have other things to think about for a while. Everyone would be at the camp, counting casualties, deciding
what to do—probably fighting among themselves for control of the Army. Had Sigurth the Snakeeye survived? Shef
wondered. If he had, even he might have trouble in reim-
posing his authority on a shaken army.

As for the English, Shef knew that as he and Godive had
left the river and started to make their way into the woods
there had been other folk about. The refugees from King
Edmund's army, the ones who had fled, or at any rate decided to retreat before the crisis of the battle. They were all
making their way to their respective homes as fast as ever
they could. Shef doubted if there would be an Englishman
within five miles of the Viking encampment by now. They
had guessed that their lord's attack had failed, and that he
was dead.

Shef hoped so, remembering what his pirate guide had
told him about Ivar's ways with defeated kings.

He lay in the sun on the blanket, feeling his body relax.
A muscle jumped irregularly in his thigh. He waited for it
to stop, looking at the puffed blisters on both hands.

"Will it be better if I prick them?" Godive was at his
side, kneeling in her shift, holding up a long thorn. He nodded.

As she began to work on his left hand and he felt the
slow tears rolling down his arm, he held her warm shoulder
with his right.

"Tell me," he said. "Why did you stand between me and
Ivar? How was it with you and him?"

Her eyes lowered, Godive seemed unsure what to say.
"You know I was given to him? By—by Sigvarth."

"By my father. Yes. I know. What happened then?"

She kept her eyes down, studying his blisters attentively.

"They gave me to him at a banquet, with everyone watching. I—I only had this to wear. Some of them do terrible things to their women, you know, like Ubbi. They say he takes them in front of his men, and if things do not go to his liking he hands them over to the men then and there, to be used by all. You know I was a virgin—I am a virgin. I was very frightened."

"You are virgin still?"

She nodded. "Ivar said nothing to me then, but he had me brought to him in his tent that night, and he talked to me. He told me—he told me that he was not like other men.

"He is not a gelding, you know. He has sired children, or so he says. But he told me where other men can feel desire just at the sight of flesh, he needs—something else."

"Do you know what that something is?" asked Shef sharply, remembering the hints Hund had given.

Godive shook her head. "I do not know. I do not understand. But he says that if men were to know how it is with him, they would mock him. In his youth the other young men called him the Boneless One because he could not do as they do. But, he says, he killed many men for mocking him and discovered it was a pleasure to him. Now all those who laughed are dead, and only the closest suspect how it is with him. If everyone had known, Sigvarth would not have dared to hand me over to him openly and publicly, as he did. Now, he says, men call him the Boneless because they fear him. They say that at night he turns—not into a wolf or a bear, like other skin-changers—but into a dragon, a great long-worm, that creeps out in the night for its prey. Anyway, that is what they think now."

"And what do you think?" asked Shef. "Do you remember what they did to your father? He is your father, not mine, but even I felt sorrow for him. And though Ivar did not do that, he gave the orders. That is the kind of thing he does. He may have spared you rape, but who knows what else he had in mind for you. You say he has children. Has anyone seen the mothers?"

Godive turned over Shef's palm and began to lance the blisters that covered it.

"I don't know. He is hateful and cruel to men, but that is because he fears them. He fears they are more manly than he is. But how do they show it, this manliness? By violating those who are too weak, by taking their pleasure from pain. Maybe Ivar has been sent by God—as a punishment for men's sins."

"Do you wish I had left you with him?" Hardness edged Shef's voice.

Slowly Godive bent over him, abandoning her thorn. He felt her cheek against his naked chest, her hands sliding along his sides. As he pulled her up next to him, her loose shift slid from one bare shoulder. Shef found himself staring at a naked breast, its nipple girlish pink. The only woman he had seen before like this was the slut Truda—heavy, sallow, coarse-fleshed. His roughened hands began to stroke Godive's skin with disbelieving tenderness. If he had thought of this happening—and he had, often, lying by himself in fisherman's hut or deserted forge—it was years in the future, after they had found a place, after he had deserved her and made a home where they could be safe. Now, in the wood, in the clearing, in the sunlight, without blessing of priest or consent from parents . . .

"You are a better man than Ivar or Sigvarth or any other man I have ever met," sobbed Godive, her face still buried in his shoulder. "I knew you would come for me. I only feared they would kill you for it."

He pulled at her shift, her legs squirming beneath him as she turned onto her back.

"We should both be dead by now. It is so good to be alive, with you—"

"There is no blood between us, we have different fathers, different mothers—"

In the sunlight he entered her. Eyes watched from a bush; breath drew in, in envy.

* * *

An hour later, Shef lay on the soft grass, in the sunshine where the rays of the now-hot sun came through the upper branches of the oak trees. He was torpid, completely relaxed. He was not asleep. Or he was, but at some dim level he remained awake, conscious that Godive had slipped away. He had been thinking of the future, of where they could go: into the marshes, he thought, remembering his night spent with the king's thane Edrich. He was still conscious of the sun on his skin, of the soft turf beneath his body, but they seemed further away. This had happened before—in the Viking camp. His mind was rising from the forest clearing, traveling out beyond the body, beyond the heart's confines. . . .

A voice spoke to him—rough, gravelly, laden with authority.
   "Of mighty men," it said, "the maid you have taken."
   Shef knew he was somewhere else. He was at a forge. Everything was familiar: the hiss as he wound the wet rags round the scorching handles of the tongs, the heft in his back and shoulder muscles as he lifted the red-hot metal out of the heart of the fire, the scrape and scratch of the top of his leather apron across his chest, the automatic duck and shake of the head as the sparks flew up toward his hair. But it was not his forge, back in Emneth, nor Thorvin's forge within the enclosure of the rowan berries. He sensed round him an enormous space, a gigantic open hall so high he could not see the top, just mighty pillars and columns leading away to the top where the smoke clung.
   He took the heavy hammer and began to beat out a shape from the formless mass glowing on his anvil. What that shape should be he did not know. Yet his hands knew, for they moved expertly and without hesitation, shifting the tongs, turning the bloom, striking from one direction and then another. It was no spear-blade or axe-head, no ploughshare or coulter. It seemed to be a wheel, but a wheel with many teeth, sharp-pointed ones, like a dog's. Shef watched with fascination as the thing came to life beneath his blows.

He knew, in his heart, that what he was doing was impossible. No one could make a shape like that straight from a forge. And yet—he could see how it might be done, if you made the teeth separately and then fitted them all together on the wheel you had originally made. But what would the point of it all be? Maybe, if you had one wheel like that, turning one way, up and down like a wall, and another wheel, turning the other way, flat and level with the ground, then, if the teeth on the one wheel matched with the teeth on the other, the first could drive the second round.

But what would be the point of that? There was a point. It had something to do with the object, the giant construction, twice man-height over by one wall, just beyond his vision in the dimness.

Shef realized as his senses cleared that there were other figures looking at him, figures on the same enormous scale as the hall. He could not see them clearly, and he did not dare look up for more than moments from his work, but he caught their presence unmistakably. They were standing together and watching him, even discussing him, he thought. They were Thorvin's gods, the gods of the Way.

Nearest to him was a broad and powerful shape, an immensely scaled-up Viga-Brand, giant biceps muscles rolling beneath a short-sleeved tunic. That must be Thor, thought Shef. His expression was scornful, hostile, faintly anxious. Behind the shape was another god—keen-eyed, sharp-faced, thumbs stuck into a silver belt, eyeing Shef with a kind of concealed approval, as if he were a horse to be bought, a thoroughbred going at a bargain price from a foolish owner.

That one is on my side, thought Shef. Or maybe he thinks I am on his.

Others clustered behind the two: tallest of them, and furthest away, a god leaning on a mighty spear with a triangular head.

Shef became aware of two other things. He was hamstrung. As he moved around the forge, his legs trailed behind him uselessly, making him take the weight on his arms and pull himself from one place to another. High stools,

stocks of wood and benches were littered around in seemingly random fashion, but actually, he realized, to support
him as he went from one workplace to another. He could
prop himself on his legs, stand, like a man balancing on two
stout props, but there was no spring, no movement at all
from the thigh muscles to the calf. A dull ache spread upward from his knees.

And there was someone else watching him, not one of the
mighty figures, but a tiny one, down in the shadows of the
smoke-filled hall, like an ant, or a mouse peering out from
the wainscoting. It was Thorvin! No, it was not Thorvin, but
a smaller and a slighter man with a long face and sharp expression, both accentuated by the thinning hair falling back
from the high forehead. But it was someone dressed like
Thorvin, all in white, with the rowan berries round his neck.
He had something of the same expression too, thoughtful,
intensely interested, but here also, cautious and fearful. The
small figure was trying to speak to him.

"Who are you, boy? Are you a wanderer from the realms
of men, set for a while in Völund's place? How have you
come here, and by what fortune did you find the Way?"

Shef shook his head, pretending it was just a toss to keep
the sparks out of his eyes. He tossed the wheel aside into a
bucket of water and began to set to another piece of work.
The three quick raps, the turn, the three raps again, and a
glowing something flying through the air into the cold water, to be instantly replaced on the anvil by another. What he
was doing Shef did not know, but it filled him with wild excitement and a furious impatient glee, like a man who would
one day be free and did not want his jailer to know the joy
inside him.

Shef realized that one of the giant figures was coming toward him—the tallest of them, the one with the spear. The
mouse-man saw too and ducked back into the shadows, now
visible only as the palest of blurs in the gloom.

A finger like the trunk of an ash turned Shef's chin upward. One eye looked down at him, from a face like the
blade of an axe: straight nose, jutting chin, sharp gray

*beard, wide, wide cheekbones. It was a face that would have
made Ivar's seem a relief, as something at least comprehensible, ravaged only by human passions like envy, hate and
cruelty. This was far different: One touch of the thoughts
behind that mask, Shef knew, and any human mind would go
insane.*

Yet it did not seem entirely hostile, more thoughtful, considering.

"You have far to go, mannikin," it said. "Yet you have begun well. Pray that I do not call you to me too soon."

*"Why would you call me, High One?" said Shef, amazing
himself with his own temerity.*

*The face smiled like a glacier calving. "Do not ask," it
said. "The wise man does not pry or peek like a maiden
searching for a lover. He looks even now, the gray fierce
wolf, into Asgarth's doors."*

*The finger dropped, the great hand came sweeping
across, over forge and anvil and tools, over benches and
buckets and the smith all together, brushing them all away
like a man sweeping nutshells from a blanket. Shef felt himself hurled into the air, spinning end over end, apron flying
away from him, his last memory the little face-shaped blur
in the shadows, watching and marking him.*

In a heartbeat he was back on the grass, back beneath the
open sky of England in the forest clearing. But the sun had
moved off him, leaving him in shadow, cold and suddenly
afraid.

Where was Godive? She had crept from his side for a
moment, but then—

Shef was on his feet, wide awake, staring round for an
enemy. Tumult in the bushes, thrashing and fighting and the
sound of a woman trying to scream with a hand over her
mouth and an arm round her throat.

As Shef sprang toward the struggle, men rose from their
cover behind the tree-trunks, and closed on him like the fingers of doom. Leading them came Muirtach the Gaddgedil,

a newly livid weal across his face and an expression of bitter, contained, contented fury twisting it.

"Nearly you got away, boy," he said. "You should have kept running, not stopped to try out Ivar's woman. But a hot prick knows no sense. It will be cold soon enough."

Hard hands closed on Shef's shoulders as he lunged towards the bushes, desperate to reach Godive. Had they seized her already? How had they found them? Had they left some trail?

A jeering laugh rose above the babble of Gaddgedlar voices. Shef recognized it, even as he writhed and fought, drawing all the Vikings to him. It was the laugh of an Englishman. Of his half brother. Alfgar.

Chapter Ten

When Muirtach and the others had dragged him back inside the stockade, Shef had been close to collapse. He had been exhausted in the first place. The shock of recapture had also bitten deep into him. The Vikings had been rough with him as well as they pulled him back, punching and cuffing him repeatedly as they hustled him through the woods, eyes alert all the time for any fringe of scattered Englishmen still lurking in the trees. Then, as they came out onto the meadows and sighted their comrades rounding up such horses as remained, jerking their captive off his feet again and again in rough triumph. They had been badly scared. Having one trophy to take back to Ivar was not much of a set off against all they had lost. Dimly, through weariness and horror, Shef realized that they were in the mood now to work out all their earlier fears on such little satisfaction as they could find. But before he could take in much of that thought, they dragged him to the pen, beat him unconscious.

He only wished he had not had to come round. They had thrown him inside the stockade at mid-morning. He had been unconscious the whole of the long, warm late-summer day. When he finally blinked his blood-sealed eyelids open he was sore, stiff, bruised—but no longer dizzy or bone weary. But he was also chilled to the bone, dry-mouthed with thirst, weak from hunger—in a state of deadly fear. At nightfall he looked round to try to see some prospect of escape or rescue. There was none. Iron anklets on his feet were lashed to stout pegs. His hands were bound in front of him. In time he might have worked the pegs out or chewed through the rawhide lashings on his wrists, but the slightest movement in either direction brought a growl and a kick from the nearby guard. They had, Shef realized, almost no prisoners to watch. In the confusion of the night attack almost all the accumulated slave-booty of the campaign had fought itself free and vanished, taking the Vikings' profits with them. Only a few other figures, newly captured prisoners secured like himself, dotted the floor space of the pen.

What they said brought Shef no comfort. They were the very few survivors of King Edmund's picked men, who had fought to the last in the final attempt to destroy the Ragnarssons and cripple the Viking army's leadership. All were wounded, usually badly. They expected to die, and talked quietly among themselves as they waited. Mostly, they regretted their failure to make a clean sweep of their enemies in the first few minutes of their attack. But then, they said, it could never have been expected that they could get to the heart of the Great Army without resistance. They had done well: burned the ships, killed the crews. "We have gained great glory," said one. "We stand like eagles on the bodies of the slain. Let us not repent, whether we die now or later."

"I wish they had not taken the king," said one of the warrior's comrades after a silence, speaking with difficulty through the wheezing of his pierced lung. At that they nodded soberly, and their eyes moved together toward a corner of the pen.

Shef shivered. He had no wish to face the aggrieved King Edmund. He remembered the moments when the king had come toward him, pleading with him—the gadderling, the thrall, the child of no father—to stand out of the way. If he had done so, the English would be counting the night still as a victory. And he would not have to face the wrath of Ivar. Dazed as he had been, Shef had heard the taunts of his captors about what their chief would do with him. He remembered the fool of a boy who had shown him round these selfsame pens only the evening before, and his stories of how Ivar dealt with those who crossed him. And he, Shef, had taken his woman. Taken her away, taken her carnally, taken her so that she would not be returned. What had happened to her? Shef wondered detachedly. She had not been dragged back with him. Someone had taken her off. But he could hardly worry about her anymore. His own fate was too all-encompassing. Above the fear of death, the shame of treachery, there loomed the fear of Ivar. If only, Shef thought again and again during the night, if only he could die now of cold. He did not wish to see the morning.

The thump of a boot in the back stirred him from torpor in the growing light of the next day. Shef sat up, conscious above all of the dry, swollen stick of his tongue. Round him the guards were cutting lashings, hauling bodies away; some had been granted Shef's wish in the night. But in front of him squatted a small, slight figure in a stained and dirty tunic, drawn lines of fatigue on the sallow face. It was Hund. He was holding a crock of water. For some minutes Shef thought of nothing else, while Hund carefully, and with many agonizing pauses, allowed him to drink a mouthful at a time. Only when he felt the blessed fullness under his breastbone, and knew the luxury of being able to roll an excess mouthful round his tongue and spit it onto the grass, did Shef realize that Hund was trying to speak to him.

"Shef, Shef, try to take this in. We have to know some things. Where is Godive?"

"I don't know. I got her away. Then I think someone else

snatched her. But they had me before I could do anything about it."

"Who do you think took her?"

Shef remembered the laugh in the thickets, the sense he had had, and had dismissed, that there were other fugitives in the wood. "Alfgar. He was always a good tracker. He must have followed us."

Shef paused again for thought, dispelling the lethargy of cold and weariness. "I think he must have gone back, led Muirtach and the others to us. Maybe they did a deal. They got me, he got her. Or maybe he just snatched her while they were busy with me. There weren't enough of them to risk following very far. Not after the fright they'd had."

"So. Ivar is more concerned about you than about her. But he knows you got her away from the camp. That's bad." Hund passed a hand worriedly across his sparse, scanty beard. "Shef, think back. Did anyone see you actually kill any of the Vikings with your own hands?"

"I only killed one. That was in the dark and no one saw. It was no great deed. But someone may have seen me get into the pen and start freeing the prisoners—freeing Alfgar." Shef's mouth twisted. "And do you know, I broke the Viking shield-wall with a burning timber when all the king's comrades could not do it." Shef turned his palms and looked mutely at the pads of white skin, the tiny thorn holes where the blisters had been.

"Yes. Still, that might not be a cause for blood-vengeance. Ingulf and I have done a lot of favors during this last day and a night. There are many chieftains who would be dead or crippled for life if it had not been for us. You know, he will even stitch together entrails, and sometimes the man will live, if he is strong enough to stand the pain and there is no poison inside the body."

Shef looked more attentively at the stains on his friend's tunic.

"You are trying to beg me off? From Ivar?"

"Yes."

"You and Ingulf? But what do I matter to him?"

Hund dipped a lump of hard bread in the remaining water and passed it over.

"It's Thorvin. He says it is business of the Way. He says you have to be saved. I don't know why, but he is totally set on it. Someone spoke to him yesterday and he came running over to see us at once. Have you done something I don't know about?"

Shef lay back in his bonds. "A lot of things, Hund. But I'm sure of one thing. Nothing is going to get me away from Ivar. I took his woman. How can I pay boot for that?"

"When bale is highest, boot is nighest." Hund filled the crock with water once again from a skin, placed a handful of bread beside it on the ground, and passed over the length of dirty homespun he had been carrying over his arm. "Food is short in the camp, and half the blankets are being used for shrouds. That's all I can find for now. Make it last. If you want to pay boot—see what the king can do."

Hund jerked a chin toward the corner of the pen, beyond where the dying warriors had sat, called something to the watching guards, rose, and left.

The king, thought Shef. What boot will Ivar take for him?

"Is there any hope?" hissed Thorvin across the table.

Killer-Brand looked at him with mild surprise. "What sort of language is that from a priest of the Way? Hope? Hope is the spittle that runs from the jaws of Fenris Wolf, chained till the day of Ragnarök. If we start only doing things because we think there may be some hope—why, we will end up no better than Christians, singing hymns to their God because they think he may give them a better bargain after death. You are forgetting yourself, Thorvin."

Brand looked with interest at his own right hand, spread out on the rough table next to Thorvin's forge. It had been split open by a sword-blade between second and third fingers, cut clean open almost down to the wrist. Ingulf the leech was bending over it, washing the wound with warm water from which a faint scent of herbs drifted. Then he slowly, carefully, pulled the lips of the gash apart. White bone showed for an instant before the oozing blood covered it in the track of Ingulf's fingers.

"This would have been easier if you had come to me straight away, instead of waiting a day and a half," said the leech. "Then I could have treated it while it was fresh. Now the wound has started to clot together, and I have to do this. I could take a chance and stitch it up as it is. But we do not know what was on the blade of the man who struck you."

A trickle of sweat broke out on Brand's eyebrow, but his voice remained mild, contemplative. "You go ahead, Ingulf. I have seen too many wounds go bad to take that risk. This is just pain. The flesh-rot is certain death."

"Still, you should have come earlier."

"I was lying among the corpses for half a day, till some clever warrior noticed they had all gone cold and I hadn't. And when I came round and decided that this was really the worst wound I had, you were busy with more difficult tasks. Is it true you pulled old Bjor's entrails out, stitched them together and pushed them back in again?"

Ingulf nodded, pulling with sudden decision at a bone splinter with a pair of tweezers. "They tell me he calls himself 'Grind-Bjor' now, because he swears he saw the gates of Hell itself."

Thorvin sighed gustily, and pushed a tankard closer to Brand's left hand. "Very well. You have punished me enough with your chatter. Tell me, then. Is there any chance?"

Brand's face was paling now, but he answered with the same even tone. "I don't think so. You know how it is with Ivar."

"I know," said Thorvin.

"That makes it hard for him to be sensible over some things. I do not say 'forgive'—we are none of us Christians to pass over an injury or an insult. But he will not even listen, or think about where his interest lies. The boy took his woman. Took a woman that Ivar—had plans for. If that fool Muirtach had brought her back, then maybe—But even then

I don't think so. Because the girl went willingly. That means the boy did something Ivar could not. He must have blood."

"There has to be something that would make him change his mind, accept compensation."

Ingulf was stitching now, needle rising high over his right shoulder as he pierced and pulled, pierced and pulled again.

Thorvin placed his hand on the silver hammer that hung on his chest. "I swear, this may be the greatest service you or I may ever do for the Way, Brand. You know there are some among us who have the Sight?"

"I have heard you talk of it," admitted Brand.

"They travel into the realms of the Mighty, of the gods themselves, and return, to report what they saw. Some think these are just visions, no better than dreams, a kind of poetry only.

"But they see the same things. Or sometimes they do. More often it is as if they all saw different parts of the same thing, as there might be many reports of the battle the other night, and some would say the English had the best of it, and some would say we did, and yet all would be telling the truth and all would have been at the same place. If they confirm each other, that means it must be true."

Brand grunted. Perhaps in disbelief, perhaps in pain.

"We are sure that there is a world out there, and that people can go into it. Well, something very odd happened only yesterday. Farman came to see me, Farman who is priest of Frey in this Army as I am priest of Thor, or Ingulf of Ithun. He has been in the Otherworld many times, as I have not. He says—he says he was in the Great Hall itself, the place where the gods meet to decide the affairs of the nine worlds. He was down on the floor, a tiny creature, like a mouse in the wainscoting of one of our own halls. He saw the gods in conclave.

"And he saw my apprentice Shef. He is in no doubt. He had seen him at the forge; he saw him in the vision. He was dressed oddly, like a hunter in our own forests in Rogaland or Halogaland, and he stood badly, like one who has been— crippled. But there was no mistaking the face. And the Father of gods and men himself—he spoke to him. If Shef can remember what he said . . .

"It is rare," Thorvin concluded, "for any wanderer in the Otherworld to see another one. It is rare for the gods to speak to or notice a wanderer. For both to happen . . .

"And there is another thing. Whoever gave that boy a name did not know what he was doing. It is a dog's name now. But that was not always so. You have heard of Skiold?"

"Founder of the Skioldungs, the old Danish kings. The ones whom Ragnar and his sons would drive out if they could."

"The English call him Scyld Sceafing—Shield with the Sheaf—and they tell a foolish tale of how he drifted over the ocean on a shield with a sheaf beside him, and that was how he got his name. But anyone can tell that Sceafing means 'the son of Sheaf,' not 'with a sheaf.' So who, then, is Sheaf? Whoever he was, he was the one who sent the mightiest king of all over the waves, and taught him all that he knew to make the lives of men better and more glorious. It is a name of great good luck. Especially if given in ignorance. Shef is only the way the English in these parts say 'Sheaf.'

"We have to save that boy from Ivar. Ivar the Boneless. People have seen him on the other side too, you know. But he did not have the shape of a human being."

"He is not a man of one skin," agreed Brand.

"He is one of the brood of Loki, sent to bring destruction on the world. We have to get my apprentice away from him. How can we do it? If he will not do it on your urging, Brand, or on mine, can we bribe him? Is there something he wants more than vengeance?"

"I do not know how to take this talk of other worlds and wanderers," said Brand. "You know I am with the Way because of the skills it teaches, like Ingulf's here, and because I have no love for the Christians or for the madmen like Ivar. But the boy did a brave deed to come into this camp for a girl. It took guts to do that. I know. I went into the

Braethraborg to bait the Ragnarssons into this venture, as
your colleagues told me to, Thorvin.

"So I wish the boy well. Now I do not know what Ivar
wants—who does? But I can tell you what he needs. Ivar
may see that too, even if he is mad. But if he does not, then
the Snakeeye will make him."

As he spoke on, the other two nodded, thoughtfully.

They were not Ivar's men who came for him, Shef noticed
as soon as they appeared. Just from his few days in the Viking camp he had come to be able to discriminate at least
in an elementary way between the various grades of heathen. These were not the Gaddgedlar, nor did they have the
somehow non-Norse or half-Norse air of the Hebrideans and
Manxmen whom Ivar recruited in such numbers, nor did
they even have that vaguely footloose and less-than-
respectable look that so many of even his Norse followers
had. Younger sons and outlaws, the bulk of them, detached
from their parent communities and with no homes to go to
and no lives outside the camp. The men who came into the
stockade now were heavily built, mature in years, almost
middle-aged; their hair was grizzled. Their belts were silver,
gold armlets and neck-rings shone on them, to prove years
or decades of success. When the warden of the pen blocked
their self-assured way, ordering them back, Shef could not
hear the reply. It was given in a low voice, as if the speaker
no longer expected to have to shout. The warden replied
again, crying out and pointing down the ruined campsite, as
if to the burned tents of Ivar. But before his sentence had
ended there was a thud and a groan. The leader of the newcomers looked down for a moment, as if to see if there was
any chance of further resistance, slid the sandbag back up
his sleeve, and marched on without deigning to look round
again.

In a moment Shef found the lashings on his ankles cut
and himself jerked to his feet. His heart leapt suddenly and
uncontrollably. Was this death? Were they dragging him out
of the pen to a clear patch of ground, where in an instant

they could force him to his knees and behead him? He bit his lip savagely for an instant. He would not speak or plead for mercy. Then the savages would have the chance to laugh, to mock the way an Englishman died. He stumbled along in grim silence.

Only a few yards. Outside the gate, along the fence-posts of the pen, and then, jerked to a stop in front of another gate. Shef realized that the leader of the newcomers was staring hard at him, deep into his eyes, as if trying to burn an understanding into the tough hide of Shef's face.

"You understand Norse?"

Shef nodded.

"Then understand this. If you talk—doesn't matter. But if he in there talks—maybe you live. Maybe. Lot to be answered for. But there's something in there that could mean life for you. Could mean more for me. Whether you live or die, you may need a friend pretty soon. Friend in court. Friend on the execution ground. There's more than one way to die. All right. Throw him in. Rivet him good."

Shef found himself hauled inside a shelter propped up against the side of the pen. An iron ring hung from a stout post; a chain from it to another ring. In an instant the collar was being fitted round his neck, a bolt of soft iron forced through its two holes. A couple of blows with a hammer, a quick inspection, another blow. The men turned and tramped out. Shef's legs were free, but his hands still bound. The collar and chain round his neck gave him only a few feet of space to walk.

There was another man in the shelter, Shef realized, secured as he was; he could see the chain running down from a post into the half-darkness. Something about the figure sprawled there on the ground filled him with unease, with shame and fear.

"Lord," he said doubtfully. "Lord. Are you the king?"

The figure stirred. "King Edmund I am, son of Edwold, king of the East Angles. But who are you, that talk like a Norfolk man? You are not one of my warriors. Did you come with the levies? Did they catch you in the woods? Move, so I can see your face."

Shef moved round. The sun, now westering, streamed in through the open door of the shelter and caught his face as he stood at the limit of his chain. He waited in dread for what the king would say.

"So. You are the one who stood between me and Ivar. I remember you. You had no armor and no weapon, but you stood before Wigga my champion, and held him for ten heartbeats. If it had not been for you those would have been the last heartbeats of the Boneless One's life. Why would an Englishman wish to save Ivar? You ran from your master? Were you a slave to the Church?"

"My master was your thane Wulfgar," Shef said. "When the pirates came—you know what they did to him?"

The king nodded. With his eyes adjusting to the light Shef could see the face that turned to him. It was pitiless, resolute.

"They took his daughter, my—my foster sister. I came to try to get her back. I was not trying to protect Ivar, but your men were going to kill both of them, all of them. I just wanted you to let me pull her aside! Then I would have joined you. I am no Viking, I killed two of them myself. And I did one thing for you, king, when you had need of it. I . . ."

"So you did. I called out for someone to break the ring, and you did it. You and a gang of churls from nowhere, with a ship's timber. If Wigga had thought of that, or Totta, or Eddi, or any of the others, I would have made him the richest man in the kingdom. What did I promise?"

He shook his head in silence, then looked up at Shef.

"You know what they are going to do to me? They are building an altar now, to their heathen gods. Tomorrow sometime they will take me out and lay me on it. Then Ivar will get to work. Killing kings is his trade. One of the men who guarded me told me he was standing by when Ivar killed the Irish king of Munster, told me how he stood there while Ivar's men twisted the rope and twisted the rope and the veins stood out on the king's neck and he called out curses by all the saints on Ivar's name. And then the crack as his back broke over the stone. They all remember that.

"But tomorrow Ivar prepares a new fate. They tell me that he meant to save this for the man who killed their father, for Ella of Northumbria. But they have decided I merit it just as much.

"They will take me out, and lay me on their altar, face down. In the hollow of my back, Ivar will place a sword. Then—you have felt how your ribs make a house of bone, and how each of the ribs fits into its place on the backbone? Ivar will cut each of them away, working up from the lowest to the highest. They say he will use a sword only for the first cut. After that he will use hammer and chisel. When he has cut them all away, he will cut the flesh free, and then he will put his hands in and pull the ribs up and out.

"I expect I will die then. They say he can keep a man alive to that point, if he is careful not to cut deep. But when they pull the ribs out, your heart must burst. When it is done, they pull your lungs out of your back, and then turn the ribs out so they look like a raven's wings, or an eagle's. They call it 'cutting the blood-eagle.'

"I wonder what it will feel like when he first puts the sword in the hollow of my back. You know, young churl, I think that if I can hold my courage at that point, the rest will be easier. But the feel of the cold steel on skin, before the pain begins . . .

"I never thought that I would come to this. I have defended my people, kept all my oaths, been charitable to orphans.

"Do you know, churl, what the Christ said when he hung dying on the cross?"

Father Andreas's lessons had been confined usually to the merits of chastity or the importance of paying contributions duly to the Church. Shef shook his head dumbly.

"My God, my God, why hast thou forsaken me?"

The king paused for a long while.

"I know why he means to do it, though. After all, I am

a king too. I know what his men need. These few months have been bad ones for the Army. They thought they would have an easy start here for their real march on York. And so they might have—if they had not done what they did to your foster father. But since then they have made no gains, caught few slaves, had to fight for every few beeves. And now—say what anyone wishes, there are many fewer of them than there were two nights ago. They have seen their friends die of wounds, and more of them are sitting waiting for the flesh-rot. If there is nothing grand for them to see, then they will lose heart. Ships will row off in the night.

"Ivar needs a display. A triumph. An execution. Or . . ."

Shef remembered the warning of the man who had pushed him into the pen.

"Do not speak too freely, lord. They want you to speak. And me to listen."

Edmund laughed, in one sharp bark. The light had almost gone by now, the sun well down, though the long English twilight lingered.

"Then listen. I promised you a half of Raedwald's hoard if you broke the Viking line, and break it you did. So I will give you the whole of it, and you may make your own bargain. The man who gives them this can have his life and more. If I gave it to them, I could be a Viking jarl. But Wigga and all the others died rather than speak. It would not be fitting for a king, one of the line of Wuffa, to give way out of fear.

"But you, boy. Who knows? You may gain something.

"Now listen and do not forget. I will tell you the secret of the hoard of the Wuffingas, and from that I swear by God a wise man can find the hoard.

"Listen and I will tell you."

The king's voice dropped to a hoarse murmur and Shef strained to hear.

"In willow-ford, by woody bridge,
The old kings lie, keels beneath them.
On down they sleep, deep home guarding.

Four fingers push   in flattest line,
From underground,   Grave the northmost.
There lies Wuffa,   Wehha's offspring.
On secret hoard.   Seek who dares it."

The voice tailed away. "My last night, young churl.
Maybe yours too. You must think what you will do to save
yourself tomorrow. But I do not think the riddle of an Englishman will prove easy to the Vikings.

"And, if churl you are, the riddle of the kings will do you
no good either."

The king spoke no more, though after a while Shef tried
faintly and despondently to rouse him. After an age Shef's
battered body too began to drift off into uneasy dozing. In
his sleep the king's words repeated themselves, twining
round and round and running into each other like the
dragon-shapes carved on a burning stem-post.

Chapter Eleven

This time the Great Army was troubled and unsure. So
much King Edmund had foreseen. It had been taken
in its own base, by a small state and a petty kinglet of
whom no one had ever heard, and while they knew the matter had ended well enough, too many also knew in their
hearts that for a time they had been outfought. The dead had
been buried, the irreparable ships dragged onshore, the
wounded had been treated. Arrangements had been made
between this chieftain and that to sell or trade ships, to
transfer or exchange men to bring contingents up to the
mark. But the warriors, the rank-and-file oar-pullers and
axe-wielders, still needed reassurance. Something that
would show their leaders still had confidence. Some ritual

to demonstrate that they were still the Great Army, the terror of the Christians, the invincibles of the North.

From the early morning, men were crowding down to the marked-out space outside the camp, which would be the site of the wapentake: the meeting where men could show their assent by *vapna takr*, the clashing of weapons, of blade on shield. Or, on rare occasions, under careless leaders, their dissent. From even earlier in the morning, from well before day, the Viking leaders had been making their plan, and considering the balance of forces, the sentiments that might swing their dangerous and unpredictable followers one way or the other.

When they came for him, Shef was ready, at least physically. His hunger was a hole inside him, thirst once more drying his tongue and his lips, but he was awake, alert and fully conscious. Edmund too was awake, he knew, but made no sign. Shef was ashamed to disturb him.

The Snakeeye's men arrived with the same brisk certainty as the day before. In a moment one had Shef's iron collar in his tongs and was forcing the rivet out. It came free, the collar jerked off, and brawny hands were pulling Shef out into the cold murk of an early-autumn morning. Fog still clung to the river, condensed in drops on the bracken roof of the shelter. Shef stared at it for a moment, wondering if he might lick it off.

"You were talking yesterday. What did he tell you?"

Shef shook his head and gestured with bound hands to the leather bottle at a man's belt. Silently the man passed it over. It was full of beer—muddy, thick with barley husks, drawn all too obviously from the bottom of a cask; Shef drank it down in steady gulps, till he could tilt his head back and drain out the last drops. He finished, wiped his mouth, feeling as if the beer had swollen him out like an empty skin, handed the bottle back. There was a grunt of amusement as the pirates watched his face.

"Good, eh? Beer is good. Life is good. If you want more of both, you'd better tell us. Tell us everything he said."

Dolgfinn the Viking watched Shef's face with his usual,

unblinking intensity. He saw on it doubt, but no fear. Also, stubbornness, knowledge. The lad would do a deal, he reflected. It would have to be the right one. He turned away and beckoned, a preconcerted signal. From a group a little way off, a large man came walking, gold round his neck, left hand resting on the silver pommel of a sword. Shef recognized him instantly. It was the big man he had fought in the skirmish on the causeway. Sigvarth, jarl of the Small Isles. His father.

As he strolled forward, the others drew back a few paces, leaving the two face-to-face. They studied one another for a few seconds, each staring the other up and down, the older man looking at the younger's physique, the younger staring intently into his father's face. He's looking at me the same way I'm looking at him, thought Shef. He's looking to see if he can recognize himself in me, just as I am at him. He knows.

"We've met before," remarked Sigvarth. "On the causeway in the marsh. Muirtach told me there was a young Englishman walking round claiming he'd fought me. Now they tell me you're my son. The leech's assistant, the boy who came with you. He says so. Is that true?"

Shef nodded.

"Good. You're a burly lad, and you fought well that day. See here, son"—Sigvarth stepped forward and put a broad hand round Shef's biceps, squeezing gently—"You're on the wrong side. I know your mother's English. That's true of half the men in the Army. English, or Irish, or Frankish, or Finnish or Lapp for that matter. But blood goes with the father. And I know you were brought up by the English—by that fool you were trying to rescue. But what have they ever done for you? If they knew you were my son I dare say you had a hard life of it. Eh?"

He looked into Shef's eyes, conscious that he had scored a point.

"Now, you may be thinking that I just ditched you, and that's true, I did. But then I didn't know you were there. I didn't know how you'd grown up. But now you're here, and

I see how you've turned out, well, I reckon you'll be a credit to me. And to all our kin.

"So, say the word. I'm offering to recognize you as my true son. You'll have the same rights you'd have had if you'd been born on Falster. Leave the English. Leave the Christians. Forget your mother.

"And, as my son, I'll speak for you to Ivar. And what I say, the Snakeeye will back up. You're in trouble here. Let's get you out of it."

Shef looked over his father's shoulder, considering. He remembered the horse-trough and the beatings. He remembered the curse his stepfather had laid on him, and the accusation of cowardice. He remembered the incompetence, the dillydallying, the exasperation of Edrich at the way the English thanes preened and hesitated. How could anyone be victorious with people like that on one's side? Over his father's shoulder he could see, in the front of the group that Sigvarth had left, a young man gazing at them—a young man with decorated armor, a pale face, strong, projecting front teeth like a horse. He too is a son of Sigvarth, Shef thought. Another half brother for me. And he does not like what is going on.

Shef remembered the laugh of Alfgar from the thickets. "What do I have to do?" he asked.

"Say what the king Jatmund told you. Or find out from him what we need to know."

Deliberately, Shef took aim, blessing the draft of beer that had moistened his mouth, and spat on his father's leather shoe.

"You cut Wulfgar's arms and legs off while men held him. You let the men rape my mother, after she had borne you a son. You are no *drengr*. You are nothing. I curse the blood I had from you."

In an instant the Snakeeye's men were between them, hustling Sigvarth away, holding his arms down as he struggled to draw his sword. He did not struggle very hard, Shef thought. As they forced him back he was still staring at his son with a kind of baffled longing. He still thinks there is more to be said, thought Shef. The fool.

"You've done it now," remarked Dolgfinn, the Snake-eye's emissary, jerking his captive along by the rawhide round his wrists. "All right. Take him along to the wapen-take. And get the kinglet out of there and let's see if he's decided to be reasonable before the assembly sees him."

"No chance," remarked one of his henchmen. "These English can't fight, but they haven't the sense to give in. He's for Ivar now, and Othin before nightfall."

The Viking army was drawn up outside the east stockade, not far from the place where Shef had vaulted over to inter-cept Godive and kill Flann the Gaddgedil barely three days before. It filled three sides of a hollow square; the fourth, nearest the stockade, occupied only by the jarls, the chief-tains, the Ragnarssons and their immediate followers. Else-where, the men crowded together behind their skippers and helmsmen, talking to each other, calling out to men from other crews, offering advice and opinion without reproof and without control. The army was a democracy, in its way: Status and hierarchy were important, especially when it came to taking shares. But no man could be entirely si-lenced, if he cared to take the risk of giving offense.

As they shoved their way into the square with Shef, a great yell went up, and a simultaneous clash of metal. Vi-kings were hustling a tall man away toward a block in the corner of the square, the man's face standing out even from thirty yards away in a crowd. All the rest had the usual windburned faces of men who spend their time out-of-doors, even in an English summer. The tall one was deathly pale. Without ceremony they thrust him over the block, one Viking seizing his hair and pulling it forward over the nape of his neck. A flash, a thud, and the head rolling free. Shef stared at it for an instant. He had seen several corpses in Emneth, and many in the last few days. But hardly one in broad daylight, and with a moment to look. There will be no time once they give their decision, he thought. I must be ready as soon as they clash their weapons.

"What was that?" he asked, nodding towards the head being thrown into a pile.

"One of the English warriors. Someone said he had fought well and truly for his lord and we should take ransom. But the Ragnarssons say now is not the time for ransoms, it is time to give a lesson. Now you."

The warriors pushed him forward and left him standing ten feet in front of the chieftains.

"Who wishes to press this case?" called one of the chieftains, in a voice that could compete with a North Sea gale. Slowly, the hubbub faded to a buzz. Ivar Ragnarsson stepped forward from the ranks of the leaders. His right arm was bound in front of him in a sling. Broken collarbone, thought Shef, noting the angle at which the arm was slung. That's why he could not wield a weapon against Edmund's warriors.

"I present the case," said Ivar. "This is not an enemy, but a traitor, a truth-breaker. He was not one of Jatmund's men, he was one of my men. I took him into my band, I fed and lodged him. When the English came, he did not fight for me. He did not fight at all. He ran in while the warriors fought and took a girl from my quarters. He stole her away, and she had never been returned. She is lost to me, though she was lawfully mine, given to me by Sigvarth Jarl in the sight of all men.

"I claim ransom for the girl, and he cannot pay it. Even if he could pay it, I would still kill him for the insult done me. But even more than that, the whole Army has a claim against him for treachery. Who supports me?"

"I support you," called another voice: a burly, grizzled man standing close to Ivar. Ubbi, perhaps, or Halvdan? One of the Ragnarssons, at any rate, but not the leader, not Sigurth, who still stood aloof in the middle of the line of men. "I support you. He has had a chance to show his true loyalty, he has refused it. He came to our camp as a spy and a thief and a stealer of women."

"What penalty do you assess?" called the herald's voice again.

"Death is too easy," cried Ivar. "I claim his eyes for the insult put on me. I claim his balls as compensation for the woman. I claim his hands for the treachery against the Army. After that he may keep his life."

Shef felt the shudder running through him. His spine seemed to have turned to ice. In an instant, he thought, the cry would go up, and the clash of arms, and then in ten heartbeats he would be facing the block and the knife.

A figure strolled slowly forward from the ranks—a massive, bearded, leather-jacketed figure. His hand was in a great white bandage, with spots of dark blood showing through it.

"I am Brand. Many men know me." A yell of approval and agreement came from the men behind him.

"I have two things to say. First, Ivar, where did you get the girl? Or where did Sigvarth get her? If Sigvarth stole her, and the lad here stole her back, where is the wrong in that? You should have killed him when he tried it. But since you did not, it is too late to start calling for vengeance now.

"And there is a second thing, Ivar. I was coming to help you when the warriors of Jatmund advanced on you—I, Brand, champion of the men of Halogaland. I have stood in the front for twenty years. Who can say that I ever held back when the spearmen were fighting? I got this wound there, right by you, when you yourself were hurt. And I challenge you to tell me I lie; when the fight was nearly over, and the English king was breaking out, he came straight toward you with his men. You were hurt and could not raise a sword. Your men were dead, and I had only my left hand, and no other man stood by you. Who stood in front of you with his sword but this youth here? He held them off—till I and Arnketil came down with his band and trapped the king. Tell me, Arnketil, do I lie?"

A voice from the other side of the square. "As you say, Brand. I saw Ivar, I saw the Englishmen, I saw the boy. I thought they had killed him in the stir, and was sorry. He stood bravely."

"So, Ivar, the claim for the woman falls. The claim for treachery cannot be true. You owe him your life. I do not know what he has to do with Jatmund, but I say this: If he is good at stealing women, I have a place for him in my crew. We need some new ones. And if you cannot look after your women, Ivar—well, what is that to do with the Army?"

Shef saw Ivar stepping forward towards Brand, his eyes fixed on him, a pale tongue flickering on his lips like a snake. A hum of interest came from the crowd, not a hostile sound. The warriors of the Army liked entertainment, and here some was promised.

Brand did not move, but thrust his left hand into his broad sword-belt. As Ivar got to three paces of him, he held up his bandaged hand for the crowd to see.

"When your hand is mended, I will remember what you say, Brand," remarked Ivar.

"When your shoulder is whole, I will remind you of it."

A voice called out behind them, cold as stone—the voice of Sigurth Ragnarsson, the Snakeeye.

"The Army has more important things to do than talk of boys. I say this: My brother Ivar must pursue his own claim for the stolen woman. In payment for his life, Ivar must give the boy his own life, and not cripple him so that he cannot live it. But the boy came into this camp as one of us. He did not behave as a true comrade when we were attacked, but thought first of his own advantage. If he is to join the crew of Killer-Brand we must teach him a lesson. Not a hand, or he cannot fight. Not a testicle, for no woman-theft is involved. But the Army will take an eye."

With great effort Shef stood firm as he heard the beginnings of the cry of assent.

"Not both eyes. One. What does the Army say?"

A roar of approval. A clash of weapons. Hands dragging him, not to the block, but to the opposite corner of the square. Men parting, pushing each other aside to reveal a

brazier, coals glowing red, Thorvin pumping at a bellows.
From a bench rose Hund, face pale with emotion.

"Hold still," he muttered in English, as the men kicked
Shef's legs from beneath him and thrust his head back.
Dimly, Shef realized that the brawny arms holding his head
in a grip like a clamp were Thorvin's. He tried to struggle,
to call out, to accuse them of treachery. A cloth thrust into
his mouth, pushing the tongue back from his teeth. The
white-hot needle coming closer, closer, a thumb pushing his
eyelid back while he tried to scream, to twist his head, to
clench his eyes tight shut.

Inexorable pressure. Only the searing point coming closer
and closer to his right eye. Pain, agony, the white fire running from the eyeball into every corner of his brain, tears
and blood streaming down his face. Through it all, dimly,
the sound of sizzling, of steel being tempered in the tub.

*He was hanging in the air. There was a spike through his
eye, a continuous burning pain that made him twist his face
and clench the muscles in his neck to try to reduce it. But
the pain never went away or grew less; it was there all the
time. Yet it did not seem to matter. His mind was unaffected,
continuing to think and to ponder without distraction from
the screaming pain.*

*Nor was his other eye affected. It remained open all the
time, never even blinking. Through it, and from wherever in
all the worlds he was, he could see out across a vast panorama. He was high up, very high up. Below him he could
see mountains, plains, rivers, and here and there on the seas
little collections of colored sails that were Viking fleets. On
the plains scattered dust clouds that were giant armies
marching, the Christian kings of Europe and the pagan no-
mads of the steppe permanently mustering for war. He felt
that if he narrowed his eyes—his eye—a certain way, just
so, he could focus in on anything he wanted to: read the lips
of the commanders and the cavalrymen, see the words of the
emperor of the Greeks or the khakhan of the Tartars even as
they formed them.*

Between himself and the world below, he realized, birds were floating—giant ones keeping station with never a flap or a flutter, just the little tremor along the trailing feathers of the wings. Close to him two passed by, staring at him with brilliant and intelligent yellow dots of eyes. Their feathers were glossy black, their beaks threatening, stained: ravens. The ravens that came to peck out the eyes of hanged men. He stared at them as unblinkingly as they at him; they slanted their wings hastily and swooped away.

The spike through his eye. Was that all that was holding him? So it seemed. But then he must be dead, no one could survive a spike through the brain and the skull, into the wood behind. Through the feel of the bark he could sense a bursting of sap, a steady pumping of fluid, up from roots unimaginably deep to branches far above him, so high that no man could ever climb them.

His eye stabbed him again and he twisted, his hands still hanging loose below him like a dead man's. There were the ravens again—curious, greedy, cowardly, clever, alert for any sign of weakness. They drifted in toward him, flapped their wings, came suddenly closer, landed heavily on his shoulders. Yet this time, he knew, he need not fear their beaks. They clung to him for reassurance. A king was coming.

The figure appeared in front of him, moving upward from a spot on Earth from which he had averted his eye. It was a terrible shape, naked, blood running from it down its ruined loins, an expression of ghastly pain on its face. Its back lifted up behind its shoulders in a parody of the ravens' wings; its chest was shrunken and twisted in; gobbets of spongy matter hung over its nipples. It carried its own backbone in its hand.

For a moment the two figures hung there, eye to eye. The creature recognized him, the hanged one thought. It pitied him. But it was going beyond the nine worlds now, to some other destiny where few if any would follow. Its blackened mouth twisted.

"Remember," it said. "Remember the verse I taught you."

* * *

The pain in Shef's eye redoubled, and he shrieked out loud, shrieked and twisted against the spike that restrained him, the bonds that held him down, the soft, gentle, immovable hands. He opened his eye and stared out, not at the panorama of the nine worlds from the great ashtree, but into the face of Hund. Hund with the needle. He shrieked again and threw up a hand to fend him off, and the hand clutched Hund's arm with desperate force.

"Easy, easy," said Hund. "It's all over now. No one can touch you. You are a carl of the army, in the crew of Brand of Halogaland, and the past is forgotten."

"But I must remember," cried Shef.

"Remember what?"

Water filled both his eyes, the good one and the ruined socket. "I don't remember it," he whispered.

"I have forgotten the king's message."

Carl

Chapter One

For many miles the track had run over flat, well-drained land—the southern half of the great Vale of York, rolling up from the marshes of the Humber. Even so, it had been hard going for the Great Army: eight thousand men, as many horses, hundreds of camp-followers and bedfellows and slaves for the market, all trampling along together. Behind them even the great stone-laid roads built by the Rome-folk of old turned into muddy tracks splashing as high as the horses' bellies. Where the Army marched along English lanes or drover roads it left nothing but a morass behind.

Brand the Champion lifted his still-bandaged hand and the troop of men behind him—three ships' crews, a long hundred and five—eased their reins. The ones at the very rear, the last men in the Army, immediately faced about, peering at the gray, wet landscape behind them, from which the autumn light was already beginning to seep.

The two men at the very point of the troop stared closely at what lay in front of them: a deeply mudded track, four arm-spans wide, descending down and round a bend to what must be the bed of another small stream. A few hundred yards ahead the men could see the land rising again and the unhedged track running across it. But in between, along the bed of the stream, ran a belt of tangled forest, large oak and chestnut trees swaying their brown leaves in the rising wind, crowding up to the very edge of the road.

"What do you think, young marshal?" asked Brand, pulling at his beard with his left hand. "It may be that with your one eye you can see further than most men with two."

"I can see one thing with half an eye, old kay-handed one," replied Shef equably. "Which is that that horse-turd by the side of the road there has stopped steaming. The main body is getting further away from us. We're too slow. Plenty of time for the Yorkshiremen to get in behind them and in front of us."

"And how would you deal with that, young defier-of-Ivar?"

"I would get us all off the road and all go down the right-hand side. The right hand, because they might expect us to go down the left, with our shields toward the trees and the ambush. Get down to the stream. When we get to it, blow all our horns and charge it as if it were the gap in an enemy stockade. If there's no one there, we look stupid. If there's an ambush there we'll flush them out. But if we're going to do it—let's do it fast."

Brand shook his massive head with a kind of exasperation. "You are not a fool, young man. That is the right answer. But it is the answer of a follower of your one-eyed patron, Othin the Betrayer of Warriors. Not of a carl of the Great Army. What we are here for is to pick up the stragglers, to see that no one falls into the hands of the English. The Snakeeye does not care for heads thrown into the encampment every morning. It makes the men restless. They like to think every one of them is important, and that anyone who gets killed gets killed for a good reason, not just by accident. If we went off the road we might miss someone, and then his mates would come round asking for him sooner or later. We will take the risk and go down the track."

Shef nodded, and swung his shield off his back, pushing his arm through the elbow-strap to grip the handle behind the boss. Behind him there was a clanking and rustling as a hundred and twenty-five men moved their weapons to a ready position and urged their horses forward. Shef realized that Brand had these conversations in a way to train him, to teach him to think like a leader. He bore no grudge when his advice was overruled.

Yet deep down he struggled with the thought that these wise men, these great and experienced warriors—Brand the Champion, Ivar the Boneless, even the matchless Snakeeye himself—were wrong. They were doing things the wrong way. Their wrong way had smashed every kingdom they had ventured against, not just the tiny and petty kingdom of the East Anglians. Even so, he, Shef—once thrall, slayer of two men, a man who had never stood in a battle line for ten heartbeats together—he was sure that he knew better how to array an army than did they.

Had he seen it in his visions? Was the knowledge sent to him by his father-god in Valhalla—Othin the Traitor, God of the Hanged, Betrayer of Warriors—as Brand obliquely continued to suggest?

Whatever the cause, Shef thought, if I were the marshal of the Army, I would call a halt six times a day, and blow the trumpets, so the flank-guards and the rear-guard would know where I was. And I would move no further till I heard the trumpets in reply.

It would be better if everyone knew the time when the trumpets would blow. But how could that be, once we are all out of sight of each other? How do the black monks in the minsters know when it is time for their services? Shef chewed on the problem as his horse took him down between the trees and shadows began to fall across the path. Again and again these days his head swam with thoughts, with ideas, with difficulties to which there seemed to be no solution in the wisdom of his time. Shef's fingers itched to hold a hammer again, to work in the forge. He felt he could beat out a solution on an anvil instead of restlessly brooding in his own brain.

There was a figure on the road ahead of them. He spun about when he heard the horses—then let his sword slide back down when he recognized them.

"I am Stuf," the man said. "One of the band of Humli, out of Ribe."

Brand nodded. A small band, not very well organized. The sort of group that would let a man slip out of line and not think to inquire what had happened to him till too late.

"My horse went lame and I dropped behind. Then I decided to turn him loose and go on with just my own pack."

Brand nodded again. "We have spare horses here. I will let you have one. It will cost you a mark of silver."

Stuf opened his mouth to protest, to start the automatic haggling expected of any deal in horseflesh, but then closed it suddenly as Brand waved his men on. He grabbed the reins of the horse Brand was leading.

"Your price is high," he said. "But maybe now is not the time to be arguing. There are Englishmen around. I can smell them."

As he said the words Shef saw a flicker of movement out of the corner of his eye. A branch moving. No, the whole tree sweeping downward in a stately arc, the ropes tied to its top suddenly visible as they tightened into a straight line. An instant later, movement all along the left-hand edge of the track.

Shef threw his shield up. A thump, an arrow-point just protruding through the soft lindenwood an inch from his hand. Shouts and screams behind him, horses rearing and kicking. Already he had hurled himself off the horse and was crouching below its neck, its body between him and the ambush. His mind registered a dozen facts as if in one flash of lightning, far quicker than any words.

That tree had been cut through after the Great Army had passed through. The rear-guard was even further behind than they had thought. The attack would be coming from the left; they wanted to drive their enemies into the wood to the right. No escape forward over the felled tree, none back through the confusion of shot horses and startled men. Do what they least suspected!

Shef ran round the front of his horse, shield up, and hurled himself straight at the steep left bank of the track, his spear gripped underhand. One leap, two, three—not pausing lest the muddy bank give way. A makeshift barricade of branches and a face glaring over it at him, an Englishman fumbling an arrow out of his quiver. Shef drove the spear through the barricade at groin level and saw the face contort in agony. Twist, wrench backward, reach over and drag the man forward through his own barricade. Shef drove his spear-point into the ground and vaulted over body and branches, turning instantly and stabbing at the ambushers, first one side then the other.

He realized suddenly that his throat was raw with shouting. A much bigger voice was bellowing in unison: Brand down on the track, not fit to fight one-handed but directing the startled Vikings up the bank and into the breach he had made. One instant a dozen figures were closing on Shef, with him stabbing furiously in all directions to keep them off. The next there was an elbow in his back, he was stumbling forward, there were mailed men on either side, and the English were backing hastily, turning suddenly in open flight.

Churls, Shef realized. Leather jackets, hunting bows and bill-hooks. Used to driving boar, not to fighting men. If the Vikings had fled into the woods as they had been expected to, no doubt they would have been in a killing ground of nets and pits, where they would have wallowed helpless till speared. But these Englishmen were not warriors to stand and hew at each other over the war-linden.

No point, certainly, in trying to pursue them through their own woods. The Vikings looked down, stabbed or cut thoughtfully at the few men their charge had caught, making sure none would live to boast of the day. Shef felt a hard hand slap him on the back.

"You did right, boy. Never stand still in an ambush. Always run away—or else run straight toward it. But how do you know these things? Maybe Thorvin is right about you."

Brand clasped the hammer pendant round his neck, and then began once more to bellow orders, hustling his men off the track and round the felled tree-trunk, stripping gear off

dead or crippled horses, looking briefly at the ten or twelve
men wounded in the skirmish.

"At this range," he said, "these short bows will send an
arrow through mail. But only just. Not enough punch in
them to get through the ribs or into the belly. Bows and arrows never won a battle yet."

The cortege wound its way up the slope on the other side
of the little stream, out of the woods and into the last of the
autumn light.

Something lay on the track in front of them. No, some
things. As the Vikings crowded forward again, Shef realized
that they were warriors of the Army—two of them, stragglers like Stuf, dressed in the grubby wadmal of the long-
service campaigner. But there was something else about
them, something horrifying, something he had seen before. . . .

With the same shock of recognition he had experienced in
Emneth, Shef realized the men were too small. Their arms
were hacked off at the elbow, their legs at the knee; a reek
of seared flesh told how they had lived. For they were still
alive. One of them lifted his head from the ground as the
riders came toward him, saw the shocked and angry faces.

"Bersi," he called. "Skuli the Bald's crew. *Fraendir, vinir,*
do what you must. Give us the warrior's death."

Brand swung from his horse, his face gray, drawing his
dagger left-handed. Gently he patted the living corpse's face
with his bandaged right hand, steadied it, drove the dagger
home with one hard thrust behind the ear. Did the same for
the other man, lying mercifully unconscious.

"Pull them out of the road," he said, "and let's get on.
Heimnars," he added to Shef. "Now I wonder who has
taught them to do that."

Shef made no reply. Far off, but caught in the last rays of
the sun now streaming almost horizontally through a breach
in the clouds, he could see yellow stone walls, a thicket of
distant houses on a slight hill in front of them, smoke
streaming away from a thousand chimneys. He had seen
them before. Another moment of recognition.

"Eoforwich," he said.

"*Yovrvik,*" repeated the Viking standing next to him, struggling with the unfamiliar consonants and diphthongs.

"To Hell with that," said Brand. "Just call it York."

After dark the men on the city walls looked down on the innumerable twinkling points of the Great Army's cooking fires. They were on the round bastion of the southeast corner of the old and impressive square Roman fortress, once home of the Sixth Legion, placed there to hold the North in awe. Behind them, inside the three-hundred-and-twenty-acre defended site, bulked St. Peter's Minster, once the most famous home of learning and scholarship in the whole northern world. Inside the walls, too, lay the king's quarters, the houses of a hundred noble families, the jammed-together barracks of their thanes and companions and hired swords. And the forges, the arsenals, the weapon-shops, the tanneries, the sinews of power. Outside there lay a sprawling town with its warehouses and jetties down on the Ouse. But this was dispensable. What mattered lay inside the walls: those of the old legionary fortress or its matching walled site across the river, centered on St. Mary's—once the Roman *colonia* where the time-expired legionaries had settled and had walled themselves in as was their custom, against the turmoil or resentment of the natives.

King Ella stared down grimly at the countless fires, the burly captain of his guard, Cuthred, at his side. Close by stood the archbishop of York, Wulfhere, still in his purple and white, and flanked by the black figure of Erkenbert the deacon.

"They have not been much delayed," said Ella. "I thought they might be held up by the Humber marshes, but they slipped across. I hoped they might run out of supplies, but they seem to have managed well enough."

He might have added that he hoped they might have been discouraged by the desperate assault of King Edmund and the East Anglians, of which so many tales already were told. But that thought sent a chill to his heart. All the tales that were told ended with a description of the death by torment of the king. And Ella knew—he had known ever since the Ragnarssons were identified in England—that they had the same or worse in store for him. The eight thousand men camped round the cooking fires out there had come for him. If he fled, they would come after him. If he hid, they would offer money for his body. Wulfhere, even Cuthred, could hope to survive a defeat. Ella knew he must beat the Army or die.

"They have lost many men!" Erkenbert the deacon said. "Even the churls are out, to delay them, to cut off their rear-guards and their forage parties. They must have lost hundreds of men already, maybe thousands. All our people are rallying to the defense."

"That's true," agreed Cuthred. "But you know to whose credit that is."

The group turned together to look at the strange contrivance a few yards from them. It was like a shallow box, on long handles so that it could be carried like a stretcher. Between one pair of handles ran an axle with wheels on it, so that it could be trundled on level ground. Inside the box lay the trunk of a man, though now that the box was tipped forward he was upright, able to see over the battlements like the rest. Most of his weight was taken by a broad strap round his chest and under his armpits. His groin rested on a padded projection. He braced himself on the bandaged stumps of his knees.

"I serve as a warning," rumbled Wulfgar, his voice shockingly deep-toned coming from such a seemingly small man. "One day I will serve as vengeance. For this and all the heathens have done to me."

The other men did not reply. They knew the effect the mutilated East Anglian thane had had, the almost triumphal progress he had made from his home, ahead of the Army, halting in every village to tell the churls what lay in store for them and for their womenfolk.

"What good has all the rallying done?" King Ella asked bitterly.

Cuthred screwed up his face in calculation. "Not slowed them. Not lost them many. Made them keep together. May even have tightened them up. Still around eight thousand of them."

"We can put half as many again in the field," said Arch Deacon Erkenbert. "We are not the East Anglians. Two thousand men of military age live in Eoforwich itself. And we are strong in the strength of the Lord of Hosts."

"I don't think we've got enough," said Cuthred slowly. "Not even counting the Lord of Hosts. It sounds good to say you're three-to-two. But if it's a fight on level ground it's always one to one. We've got champions as good as theirs, but not enough of them. If we marched out to fight them we would lose."

"Then we will not march out against them?"

"We stay here. They have to come to us, try and climb the walls."

"They will destroy our properties," cried Erkenbert. "Kill the stock, carry off the young people, cut down the fruit trees. Burn the harvest. And there is worse. The rents on Church properties are not due till Michaelmas, none have yet been paid. The churls still have their money in their pouches, or hidden in the ground, but if they see their lands ravaged and their lords penned inside a wall, will they pay?"

He threw his hands up theatrically. "It would be a disaster! All over Northumbria the houses of God would fall into ruin, the servants of God would starve."

"They won't starve for loss of a year's rents," said Cuthred. "How much of last year's have you got set aside in the minster?"

"There is another solution," said Ella. "I have proposed it before. We could make peace with them. Offer them tribute—we could call it wergild for their father. It would need to be a mighty tribute to attract them. But there must be ten households in Northumbria for every man out there in the Army. Ten households of churls can buy off a carl. Ten households of thanes can buy off one of their nobles.

Some of them will not want to accept, but if we make the offer publicly, the rest may argue them round. What we would ask for from them is a year's peace. And in that year—for they will come again—we will train every man of military age in the kingdom till he can stand against Ivar the Boneless or the devil himself. Then we can fight them three to two, eh, Cuthred? Or one to one if we have to."

The burly captain snorted in amusement. "Brave words, lord, and a good plan. I'd like to do it. Problem is . . ." He pulled the laces on the pouch at his belt and tipped the contents into his palm. "Look at this stuff. A few good silver pennies that I got from selling a horse when I was down South. The rest is imitations from the archbishop's mint here—mostly lead, if it's not copper. I don't know where all the silver's gone—we used to have plenty of it. But there's been less and less of it all over the North for twenty years now. We use the archbishop's money, but the Southerners won't take it; you have to have something to trade to deal with them. You can be damned sure the Army out there won't take it. And it's no good offering them grain or honeycombs."

"But they're here," said Ella. "We must have something they want. The Church must have reserves of gold and silver. . . ."

"You mean to give Church treasures to the Vikings, to buy them off?" gasped Erkenbert. "Instead of marching out to fight them, as is your Christian duty? What you say is sacrilege, Church-breach! If a churl steals a silver plate from the least of God's houses, he is flayed and his hide nailed to the church door. What you suggest is a thousand times worse."

"You imperil your immortal soul even to think of it," cried the archbishop.

Erkenbert's voice hissed like an adder. "It was not for this that we made you king."

The *heimnar* Wulfgar's voice cut across them both. "And you forget, besides, who you are dealing with. These are not men. They are spawn from the pit—all of them. We cannot deal with them. We cannot have them out there for months—we must destroy them...." Spittle began to show round his pale lips, and he lifted an arm for an instant as if to wipe it away before the truncated limb fell back. "Lord king, *heathens are not men*. They have no souls."

Six months ago, Ella thought, I would have led the host of the Northumbrians out to fight. It's what they expect. If I order anything else there is the risk of being called a coward. No one will follow a coward. Erkenbert has as good as told me: If I do not fight they will bring that simpleton Osbert back. He is still hiding up there in the North somewhere. He would march out to fight like a gallant fool.

But Edmund has shown what happens if you fight on even ground, even when you catch them by surprise. If we march out in the old style, I know we will lose. I *know* we will lose, and I will die. I must do something else. Something Erkenbert will accept. But he will not accept an open payment of tribute.

Ella spoke with sudden decision, the weight of kingship in his voice.

"We will stand a siege and hope to weaken them. Cuthred, check defenses and provisioning, send away all useless mouths. Lord archbishop, men have told me that in your library there are learned books by the old Rome-folk who wrote on matters of war, especially of siegecraft. See what aid they can give us in destroying the Vikings."

He turned away, left the wall, Cuthred and a trail of lesser nobles following; Wulfgar was tipped back on his stretcher and carried off by two stout thralls down the stone steps.

"The East Anglian thane is right," whispered Erkenbert to his archbishop. "We must get these people away before they destroy our rents and seduce our thralls. Even our nobles. I can think of some who might be tempted into thinking they can do without us."

"Look it out—Vegetius," Wulfhere replied. "The book called *De Re Militari.* I had not known our lord was so learned."

* * *

"He has been in the forge four days now," observed Brand. He and Thorvin, with Hund and Hund's master Ingulf, stood in a little knot a few yards away from the glowing fire of a smithy. The Vikings had found it, still stocked with charcoal, in the village of Osbaldwich a few miles outside York. Shef had taken it over immediately, called urgently for men, iron and fuel. The four stared at him through the wide-flung doors of the smithy.

"Four days," repeated Brand. "He has hardly eaten. He would not have slept except the men told him if he did not sleep, they still had to, and made him cease the din of hammering a few hours a night."

"It doesn't seem to have done him much harm," said Hund.

Indeed his friend, who he still thought of as a boy, a youth, seemed to have changed totally in the course of the past summer. His frame was not massive by the demanding standards of the Army, full of giants. But there seemed to be no excess flesh on it. Shef had stripped to the waist in spite of the gusts of an English October. As he moved round the forge, pecking now at something small and delicate, shifting the red-hot metal with tongs, barking quickly at his iron-collared English assistant to pump harder at the bellows, his muscles moved under the skin as if they lay directly beneath it, without blurring fat or tissue. A quick jerk, metal sizzling into a tub, another piece snatched from the fire. Each time he moved, separate muscles slid smoothly over each other. In the red light of the forge he might have seemed a bronze statue of the ancient days.

Except that he had not their beauty. Even in the light of the forge the sunken right eye seemed a crater of decay. On his back the thrall-marks of flogging showed vividly. Few men in the Army would have been so careless as to display such shame.

"No harm in the body, maybe," replied Thorvin. "I cannot speak for the mind. You know what it says in the *Völund-lay*:

"He sat, he did not sleep, he struck with the hammer.
Always he beat out the baleful work for Nithhad."

"I do not know what cunning thing our friend is beating out in his mind. Or who he is doing it for. I hope he will be more successful than Völund—more successful at gaining the desire of his heart."

Ingulf turned the questioning. "What has he been making these four days?"

"This, to begin with." Thorvin held a helmet up for the others to scrutinize.

What Thorvin held up was like no helmet they had ever seen. It was too big, bulbous as the head of a giant insect. A rim had been welded round it, filed to bright razor-sharpness in the front. A nose-guard ran down in front, ending in bars running back to cheek-protectors. A flared skirt of solid metal covered the nape of the neck.

More surprising to the watchers was the inside. A leather lining had been fitted to the helmet, suspended by straps. Once the helmet was on, the lining would fit the head snugly but the metal would not touch it. A broad strap and a buckle fitted under the jaw, to hold all firm.

"Never seen the likes," said Brand. "A blow on the metal will not crash into the skull. Still, it's better not to get hit, I say."

As they talked, the racket at the forge had ceased, and Shef had been seen diligently fitting small pieces together. Now he walked over to them, smiling and sweating.

Brand raised his voice. "I say, young waker-of-warriors-untimely, if you avoid the blow you don't need the helmet. And what in the name of Thor is that you are holding?"

Shef grinned again, and held up the strange weapon from the forge. He held it out horizontally, balancing it after an instant on the edge of one hand, just where wood joined metal.

"And what do you call that?" asked Thorvin. "A hewing-spear? A haft-axe?"

"A beard-axe that's had bastards by a ploughshare?" suggested Brand. "I don't see the use of it."

Shef picked up Brand's still-bandaged hand and gently rolled back the sleeve. He put his own forearm next to his friend's.

"How good a swordsman am I?" he asked.

"Poor. No training. Some talent."

"If I had the training, would I ever be fit to stand against a man like you? Never. Look at our arms. Is yours twice as thick round as mine? Or just half as thick again? And I am not a weak man. But I am a different shape from you, and yours is the shape for a swordsman, even more, an axeman. You swing a weapon as if it were a stick for a boy to slash thistles. I cannot do that. So if I were ever to face a champion like you ... And one day I will have to face a champion like you. Muirtach maybe. Or worse."

All five men nodded silently.

"So I have to even things up. With this, you see ..." Shef began to twirl the weapon slowly. "I can thrust. I can cut forehand. I can strike backhand without reversing the weapon. I can change grip and strike with the butt. I can block a blow from any direction. I can use two hands. I need no shield. Most of all—a blow from this, even in my hands, is like a blow from Brand, which few survive."

"But your hands are exposed," said Brand.

Shef beckoned, and the Englishman in the forge nervously moved over. He held two more metal objects. Shef took them and passed them over.

They were gauntlets: leather-lined, leather-palmed, with long metal projections designed to fit halfway up the forearm. Yet the striking thing about them, the men saw as they peered more closely, was the way the metal moved. Each finger had five plates, each plate fitted to the next on small rivets. Larger plates fitted over the knuckles and the backs of the hands, but they too moved. Shef pulled them on, and slowly flexed his hands, opening and closing them round the shaft of his weapon.

"They are like the scales of Fafnir the dragon," said Thorvin.

"Fafnir was stabbed in the belly, from below. I hope to be harder to murder." Shef turned away. "I have another task to do. I could not have done all this in time without Halfi here. He is a good leather-worker, though he is slow with the bellows."

Motioning the Englishman to kneel before him he began to file at the iron collar. "You will say there is not much point in freeing him, since someone will enslave him again immediately. But I will see him outside the Army's watch fires in the night, and his master is shut up tight in York. If he has any sense or luck he will run away, run far away, and never be caught again."

The Englishman looked up as Shef began gently to pry the soft iron from his throat. "You are heathens," the slave said, not understanding. "Priest said you're men with no mercy. You cut the arms and legs from the thane—I saw him! How can it be that you set a man free where the Christ-priests hold him a slave?"

Shef lifted him to his feet. He replied in English, not in the Norse they had been using before. "The men who crippled the thane should not have done what they did. Yet I say nothing of Christians and heathens, except that there are evil men everywhere. I can give you only one rede. If you do not know who to trust, try a man who wears one of those." He gestured at the four men watching, who, following the speech, silently raised their silver pendants: hammers for Brand and Thorvin, the apples of Ithun for the two leeches, Hund and Ingulf.

"Or others like them. It may be a boat for Njörth, a hammer for Thor, a penis for Frey. I do not say they will help you. But they will treat you as a man, not as a horse or a heifer."

"You do not wear one," said Halfi.

"I do not know what to wear."

Around them, the normal noise of the camp was turning to hubbub as news spread; voices were raised, warriors shouted to each other. The men in the smithy looked up as one of Brand's men appeared, a broad grin splitting the tangle of his beard.

"We're off!" he cried. "The jarls and the Ragnarssons and the Snakeeye have all stopped riding round and round and pondering and scratching their arses. We take the wall tomorrow! Let the women and girls there beware!"

Shef looked darkly at the man, finding no humor in his words. "My girl was called Godive," he said. "That is, 'God's gift.' " He pulled on his gauntlets, swung his halberd thoughtfully. "I shall call this 'Thrall's-wreak'—the vengeance of the slave. One day it will do vengeance for Godive. And other girls as well."

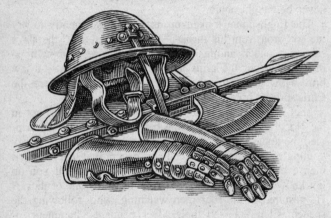

Chapter Two

In the gray morning light the Army began to filter through the narrow, hovel-lined streets of the outer town of York. All three main bridges over the Ouse were commanded by the walls of the old *colonia*, on the south bank of the river, but this had caused no difficulty for the skilled shipwrights and axemen who filled the Viking ranks. They had torn down a few houses and an outlying church for some bigger timbers, and had thrown a wide bridge over the Ouse close to their own encampment. The Army had crossed, and were now lapping their way up, like the tide, toward the yellow stone walls at the heart of the town. There was no sense of hurry, no shouting of commands, just eight thousand men, less the crews detailed to guard the camp, pressing forward toward their obvious goal.

As they tramped up through the narrow streets, men turned aside in small groups to kick down doors or break open shutters. Shef turned his head, stiff and clumsy with the unaccustomed weight of the helmet, and raised brows in silent inquiry at Brand, strolling peacefully by his side, flexing the scarred hand just unwrapped from its bandages.

"There are fools everywhere," remarked Brand. "The runaways say the king here ordered the place cleared days ago, the men inside the fortress, all the others off into the hills somewhere. But there's always someone who knows better, thinks it won't happen."

Commotion broke out ahead of them to lend force to his words: voices shouting, a woman shrieking, the sound of a sudden blow. Out from a shattered doorway squeezed four men, grins splitting their faces, a grubby, slatternly young woman writhing and twisting in their grip. The other men pushing up the hill stopped to exchange jokes.

"Make you too weak to fight, Tosti! You'd be better off with another pancake, keep your strength up."

One of the men pulled the girl's gown up over her head like a sack, pinning her arms and muffling her shrieks. Two others seized her bare legs and pulled them roughly apart. The mood of the crowd passing by changed. Men began to stop and watch.

"Room for more when you're finished, Skakul?"

Shef's gauntleted hands clenched on the shaft of "Thrall's-wreak," and he too turned toward the writhing, grunting group. Brand's enormous fist closed gently over Shef's biceps.

"Leave it, boy. If there's a fight she'll be killed for sure. Easy targets always are. Leave them to it, and maybe they'll let her go at the end. They've a battle to fight, so they can't take too long."

Reluctantly Shef turned his eyes and walked on, trying not to hear the sounds coming from behind—and, as they walked further, from other sides as well. The town, he realized, was like a cornfield in autumn. It seemed to be empty, but as the scythemen walked through it, cutting the wheat down into a smaller and smaller square, so its inhabitants became more and more visible, anxious, terrified, finally running anywhere to get away from the voices and the blades. They should have gone when they were told, he told himself. The king should have made sure. Why can no one see sense in this world?

The buildings ended and before them was a cleared zone of mud and rubble with the yellow stone wall some eighty yards off, the wall the Rome-folk had made. Brand and his crew emerged from the alley, looked up at the top of the wall where figures moved and called jeeringly. A zip in the air, and an arrow thumped into the wattle and daub of a house wall. Another, and a Viking swore in anger as he looked at the shaft sticking from his hip. Brand reached over and pulled it out, glanced at it, tossed it over his shoulder.

"Hurt, Arnthor?"

"Just got through the leather. Six inches higher and it would have bounced off my jacket."

"No punch," remarked Brand again. "Don't look at those fellows. Someone gets one in the eye now and then."

Shef plodded forward, trying to ignore the zips and thuds like the others. "Have you done this kind of thing before?" he asked.

Brand halted, called to his crews to halt as well, turned toward the wall and promptly hunkered down on his heels.

"Can't say I have. Not on this scale. But today we just do

what we're told. The Ragnarssons say they've a plan and they will take the city if everybody stands by to lend their weight where needed. So we watch and wait.

"Mind you, if anyone knows what they're doing it should be them. Do you know, their old man, their father Ragnar, tried to take the city of the Franks—oh, it must be twenty years ago. Paris, it's called. So the Ragnarssons have thought a lot about stone walls and cities ever since. Though it's a far cry from some rath in Kilkenny or Meath to this. I'd like to see how they go about it."

Shef leaned on his halberd and stared around him. To his front ran the stone wall, topped with battlements, men loosely scattered along it, no longer wasting arrows on the mass of the Army drawn up on the fringe of the cleared zone facing them, but clearly ready to shoot at any forward movement. Surprising, Shef thought, how little range even a great stone wall could give you. The men on top of their walls thirty feet were impregnable, unreachable. Yet the archers on the wall could do virtually nothing to the men standing watching them. At fifty yards' range you were in danger, at ten you might well be dead. At eighty you could stand in the open and make your preparations at leisure.

He looked more closely at the wall. To the left, two hundred yards away, it ended in a round, jutting tower, from which men could shoot along the line of the wall, at least for as far as their bows would carry. Beyond the tower the ground dropped toward the brown and muddy Ouse, immediately beyond it on the other bank, the wooden stockade that guarded the river fringe of the *colonia*—Marystown, as the locals called it. It too carried a frieze of men, watching anxiously the preparations of the heathen so close, so out of range.

The Army waited, six- and eight-deep, facing the wall on a five-hundred-yard front; more packed into the mouths of the streets and alleyways, the steam of their breath rising into the air. Dull metal, grubby wool and leather were picked out only here and there by the bright paint on

shields. The warriors looked calm, patient, like farmhands
waiting for the owner.

There came a blare of horns from the center of the waiting ranks, maybe fifty or sixty yards to Shef's right. Shef
realized suddenly that he should have been studying the
gate in the center of the wall. A wide street ran out from it,
no longer prominent in the waste of mud and trampled wattle where houses had been, but clearly the main road out to
the east. The gate itself was new, not work of the Rome-
folk, but massively formidable for that. Its timbers were
seasoned oak tree-trunks, fully as high as the towers on either side of it. Its hinges were the heaviest iron that English
smiths could make.

Yet it was weaker than stone. Opposite it now, the four
Ragnarssons strode forward. Shef picked out the tallest of
them, looking almost frail beside his mighty brothers. Ivar
the Boneless. Clad for the occasion in flaring scarlet cloak,
grass-green breeches beneath his long mail-coat, shield and
helmet silver-painted. He paused and waved to his nearest
supporters, to a roar of recognition. The horns blew again,
and the English on the wall responded with a cloud of arrows, to hiss by, thud into shields, bounce away from mail.

This time the Snakeeye waved, and suddenly hundreds of
men were trotting forward, the Ragnarssons' own picked
followers. The first line of them carried shields, not the
usual round ones for combat, but large rectangles, capable
of covering the body from ankle to neck. They ran forward
through the arrow-sleet and halted, forming a V aimed at
the gate. The second and third line were bowmen. They too
ran forward, crouched behind the shields and began to shoot
up. Now men began to fall on both sides, shot through
throat or brain. Shef could see others crouching, struggling
with arrows this time deeply embedded through mail and
flesh. A trickle of wounded men was already beginning to
walk back from the Viking ranks.

But the job of these first attackers was only to sweep the
battlements clear.

Crawling forward from the mouth of the street up which

it had been towed came the Ragnarssons' pride. Shef, looking at it as it emerged from the ranks of men, saw it for a moment as a monstrous boar. The legs of the men who pushed it from inside could not be seen. Twenty feet long, it was armored on either side with heavy, overlapping shields, roofed over with more.

Inside was an oak-trunk ram which swung on iron chains from its frame. Fifty men picked for strength heaved it along, pushing it on eight double-size cartwheels. From its front poked the iron snout of the ram. As it rolled ponderously forward, the warriors on either side of it cheered and began to surge forward with it, ignoring the English arrows. The Ragnarssons were on either side of the ram, waving their men back and trying to get them into some sort of column. Shef looked grimly at the flurry of saffron plaids. Muirtach was there, his longsword still not drawn, also waving and cursing.

"Well, that's the plan," said Brand—he had still not bothered to stand up. "The ram bashes the door down and then we all walk in."

"Will it work?"

"That's what we're fighting the battle to find out."

The ram was only twenty yards from the gate now, level with the foremost archers, accelerating to a rapid walk as the men pushing saw their goal through the frontal slit. On the battlement men appeared suddenly, drawing an instant hail of shot from the Viking archers. They leveled their bows, and fire-arrows shot down from wall to ram, thumping into the heavy timbers.

"Won't work," Brand said. "Somewhere else maybe, but in England? After harvest? You'd have to dry that wood for a day at your forge before you could get it to take light."

The fires fizzled and guttered. The ram was at the gate, still accelerating till it stopped with a crash. A pause, as the champions left their drag-ropes and stepped across to the handles on the ram itself. The whole structure shifted as they swung it back on the iron chains hanging from the roof of the frame. Then a heave forward, propelled by a hundred arms and the massive weight of the tree-trunk itself. The gate shook.

Shef realized suddenly that the excitement of battle was beginning to take hold. Even Brand was on his feet now, and everyone was beginning to edge forward. He himself was ten yards further forward than he had been. No reply from the battlements, no harassing fire hoping to take its toll.

Now all attention on both sides was fixed on the gate. The ponderous frame of the boar was shifting again as the men heaved the trunk back. Another drive forward, a crash which carried even over the noise of thousands of voices, another tremor from the massive gate. What were the English doing? If they let the boar carry on its routing, their gate would soon be in splinters and the Army surging through.

Heads began to appear at the gate towers, bobbing up in spite of the waves of shafts directed at them. Each man—they must be strong men up there—held a boulder, heaved it over his head, hurled it over and down at the overlapped shields of the ram. It was a target that could not be missed. Shields cracked and broke. But they were nailed firmly in place, and sloping. The boulders fell, rolled to one side.

Something else was happening. He was closer now, just behind the line of the Ragnarsson archers, men behind him darting forward with bundles of retrieved arrows. What was it? Ropes. They had ropes in the gate towers, both of them, lots of ropes, and the men in the towers, still out of arrowshot, were heaving mightily at them. A Ragnarsson ran across his view—Ubbi, it seemed to be—shouting at the men pressing forward. He was telling them to throw javelins up over the battlements, to come down where the men seemed to be pulling. A few men ran forward to cast; not many. It was blind shooting, and a costly throwing spear was not something to waste idly. The ropes tightened.

Up over the edge of the gate came a round object, a great roller teetering slowly toward the edge. It was a pillar: a stone pillar from the Roman days, sawn off at both ends. Falling from thirty feet no frame could stop it.

Shef passed "Thrall's-wreak" to Brand and ran forward, yelling inarticulately. The men inside the boar could see nothing of what was happening above their heads, but others could. The trouble was, no one had a clear idea of what to do. As Shef reached the frame several men were clustered at its rear, urging its crew to drop the handles, turn back to the drag-ropes, and haul the whole contrivance back to safety. Others were calling to Muirtach and his stormers to come to the outside and add their weight to the withdrawal. As they did so, the English archers rallied again and the air was once more full of the zip and thud of missiles, this time coming at killing range.

Shef pushed a man aside, another, and ducked into the rear entrance of the ram. Inside there was an immediate reeking fog of sweat and steaming breath, fifty heroes gasping with exertion and confusion, some already at the drag-ropes, others turning away from the massive swinging trunk.

"No," Shef bellowed at the top of his lungs. "Get back to the handles."

Faces gaped at him, men began to throw their weight on the ropes.

"You don't need to push the whole thing back, just swing back the ram—"

An arm caught him in the back, he was hurled forward, other bodies charged past him, he found a rope thrust in his hand.

"Pull, ye useless bodach, or I'll cut yer liver out," screamed Muirtach in his ear.

Shef felt the frame tremble, the wheel behind him start to turn. He threw his weight on the rope—two feet would do it, maybe three—they couldn't throw that great thing right out from the gate. . . .

A ground-trembling crash, another violent blow in the back, his head making contact with a timber, a sudden terrible shrieking like a woman's that this time went on and on . . .

Shef stumbled to his feet and looked around. The Vikings had been too slow. The stone pillar, finally hauled over the edge by a hundred arms, had come down squarely on the iron snout of the ram, driving it into the ground, snapping chains and tearing out their fixing bolts. It had also smashed the front of the frame, and come down finally across the hips of one of the crew. He was the one—a massive grizzled man in his forties—who was shrieking. His mates backed away—frightened, shamed, ignoring the three or four silent bodies caught by flailing chain or smashing timber. At least, apart from the one man, no one was making any noise. They would begin to babble in a moment, but for a moment, Shef knew, he could bend them to his will. He knew what must be done.

"Muirtach. Stop that noise." The cruel dark face gaped at him, seemingly without recognition, then stepped forward, pulling a dirk from his hose-top.

"The rest of you. Roll the ram back. Not far. Six feet. Stop. Now—" He was at the timbers at the front, examining the damage. "Ten of you, outside; take broken wood, spear-shafts, anything, roll that column right hard up against the gate. It's only a few feet wide—if we get the front wheel right up to it we can still swing the ram.

"Now, rerig these chains. I need a hammer, two hammers. Start pulling the ram back, right back on its slings . . ."

Time passed in a frenzy. Shef was aware of faces staring at him, of a silver helmet pushing in and out of the rear entrance, of Muirtach wiping a dirk. He paid no attention. For him, the chains and posts, the nails and broken timbers, were glowing lines in his head, shifting as he thought how they should be. He had no doubt what to do.

A roar of excitement outside as the Army tried a sudden escalade with makeshift ladders against a seemingly unde-fended wall. Only to be hurled back and off as the English rallied in defense.

Inside, gasps of effort, mutters: "It's the smith, the one-eyed smith. Do as he says."

Ready. Shuffling to the back, Shef waved the champions

to their ropes again, saw the ram rumble forward till its wheels lay against the column and its head; the shattered iron snout, chopped off and discarded, was once again flush with the gate, oak against oak. The champion seized their handles once more, waited for the word, swung back all together, and forward. And forward. They were singing now, a rowing song, putting their bodies into the stroke, heaving mindlessly and without direction. Shef ducked out of the frame once more and into the daylight.

Round him the aimless muddy waste of the morning had taken on the look of a battlefield. Bodies on the ground, hurt men walking or being carried away, spent shafts littering the earth or being picked up by scavenging archers. Anxious faces turning first toward him. Then toward the gate.

It was beginning to split. Movement ran across it now as the ram struck; one post was slightly out of line with the other. The men inside were inching the ram forward, to get a better stroke. In fifty breaths, maybe a hundred, it would go. The champions of Northumbria would surge out, waving their gold-handled swords, to meet the champions of Denmark and the Vik and the apostates of Ireland. It was the turning point of the battle.

Shef found himself staring into the face of Ivar the Boneless, only a few feet away, the pale eyes fixed on him, full of hatred and suspicion. Then Ivar's attention changed. He too knew the battle had reached its crisis. Turning, he waved both arms in prearranged signal. From the houses down toward the Ouse a horde of figures trotted. They carried long ladders, not makeshifts like those of the last escalade, but carefully made and concealed ones. Fresh men, who knew what they were doing. If the champions were at the gate, Ivar would send a wave in at the corner tower, which all the bravest and the best of the English would have left, to join the climactic struggle at the gate.

The English are finished, Shef thought. Their defenses are down in two places. Now the Army will go through.

Why did I do this to them? Why have I helped Ivar and the Army—the ones who burned out my eye?

From the other side of the quaking gate there came a curious dull twang, like a harp-string snapping, but immensely louder, fit to be heard above the din of battle. Up into the air there rose a mass, a mighty mass, a boulder bigger than ten men could lift. That's impossible, Shef thought. Impossible.

But the boulder continued to rise, up and up till Shef had to tilt his head back to look at it. It appeared to hang for an instant.

Then down.

It landed square on the center of the ram, smashing through shields and frame and supports as if they were a child's house of bark. The ram's head kicked up in the air and jerked sideways like a dying fish. From inside, hoarse cries of pain.

The scaling parties now had ladders up against the wall; they were scrambling up; one ladder had been pushed away, the rest were standing firm. Two hundred yards further off, across the Ouse, something was happening on top of the wooden stockade of Marystown: men crouched round some kind of machine.

Not a boulder this time, a line, rising as it streaked across the river, then falling as it headed for the ladders. The hero' on top of the one nearest them had his hand on the stone battlement, and was just reaching over to scramble across. The streak intersected with his body.

He smashed forward as if struck in the back by a giant, smashed so hard the ladder broke under him with the impact. As the ladder fell beneath him and he turned, arms flung wide, Shef saw the giant bolt projecting from the man's spine. He folded over backward as if in two pieces and fell slowly onto the heap of his mates scrambling beneath him.

An arrow. But not an arrow. No human being could have shot it, nor heaved the boulder. Yet these things had happened. Shef walked forward slowly and considered the rock lying amid the ruins of the ram, ignoring the pitiful struggles and cries for help beneath it.

These things had been done by machines. And such machines! Somewhere inside the fort, maybe among the black monks, there must be a machine-master such as he had never imagined. He must find out. But now, anyway, he knew why he had helped the Army. Because he could not bear to see a machine mishandled. But now there were machines on both sides.

Brand had seized him, thrust "Thrall's-wreak" into his hands, was hustling him away, snarling angrily at him.

". . . standing there like a wittol, they'll have a war-band out any moment!"

Shef saw they were almost the last men left on the cleared ground, the place of slaughter. The rest had filtered back down the hill as they had filtered up.

The Ragnarssons' assault on York had failed.

Very carefully, tongue protruding between his teeth, Shef laid the keen blade of his meat-knife to the thread. It snapped. The weight on the end of the wooden arm dropped, the other end flew up. A pebble arced lazily across the forge.

Shef sat up with a sigh. "That is how it works," he said to Thorvin. "A short arm, a heavy weight; a long arm, a lighter weight. There it is."

"I am glad you are satisfied at last," replied Thorvin. "Two days you have been playing with bits of wood and string, while I do all the work. Now maybe you can bear a hand."

"I will, yes, but this is important too. This is the new knowledge that those of the Way must seek."

"It is. And important. But there is the day's work to be done as well."

Thorvin was as keenly interested as Shef in the experiments, but, after a few attempts to help, had realized that he was merely standing in the way of the excited imagination of his former apprentice, and had gone back to the enor-

mous pile of work an army, in being, created for its armor-
ers.

"But is it *new* knowledge?" Hund asked. "Ingulf can do
things no Englishman has ever been able to. And he learns
how to do them by trial, and by taking to pieces the bodies
of the dead. You are learning by trial, but you are only trying to learn what the black monks already know. And they
are not playing with models."

Shef nodded. "I know. I am wasting my time. I understand now how it can be done, but there are all kinds of
things I do not understand. If I had a real weight here, like
the one they really shot, then what kind of weight would I
need to put in the other arm? It would be far greater than a
dozen men could lift. And if it was as heavy as that, how
could I wind down the long arm, the shooting arm? It would
need some sort of a windlass. But I know now what the
sound was that I heard just before the rock came over. It
was the sound of someone cutting the rope, to release the
rock.

"And there is another thing that bothers me even more.
They shot one rock—that smashed the ram. If they had not
hit with that one shot, the gate would have been down and
all the machine-masters would be dead. They must have
been very sure they could hit with the first shot."

He swept suddenly at the lines he had been drawing in
the dirt. "It is a waste of time. Do you see what I mean,
Thorvin? There must be some sort of skill, some sort of
craft, which would tell men where it would go without me
having to try again and again. When I first saw the stockade
round your camp by the Stour, I was amazed. I thought,
how do the leaders know how many logs to bring with them
to build a stockade that will hold all their men? But now I
know how even the Ragnarssons do it. They notch a stick
for each ship, ten notches to a stick, and then they throw the
sticks down in turn in separate piles, one pile for each one
of the three walls, or the four walls, or however many there
are, and when there are no more sticks they pick the piles
up and count them. And that is the reckoning of the greatest

leaders and captains in the world. A pile of sticks. But what they have over there in the city is the knowledge of the Rome-folk, who could write in numbers as easily as they could write in letters. If I could learn to write in Roman numbers, then I would build a machine!"

Thorvin laid down the tongs and looked thoughtfully at the silver hammer displayed on his chest.

"You should not think the Rome-folk had the answers to everything," he remarked. "If they had they would still be ruling England from York. And they were only Christians, when all is said and done."

Shef jumped impatiently to his feet. "Hah! How do you explain the other instrument then? The one that shot the great arrow. I have thought and thought about that. Nothing will do. You could not make a bow big enough. The wood would break. But what can shoot except a bow?"

"What you need," said Hund, "is a runaway from the city, or from Marystown. One who has seen the machines work."

"Maybe one will come," said Thorvin.

A silence fell, broken only by the renewed pounding of Thorvin's hammer and the puffing of the bellows as Shef blew angrily at the forge. Runaways were a subject better avoided. After the failure of the assault the Ragnarssons, in rage, had turned on the countryside around the city of York—a defenseless countryside, since its armed men and nobles, its thanes and champions, were shut up with King Ella inside the city. "If we cannot take the town," Ivar had cried, "we will ravage the shire." Ravage it they had.

"I'm getting sick of it," Brand had confided to Shef after the last sweep of an already-gutted countryside, all crews taking their turn. "Don't think I'm a milksop, or a Christian. I want to get rich and there are few things I won't do for money. But there's no money in what we're doing. Not much sport either, to my eye, in what the Ragnarssons and the Gaddgedlar and the riffraff are doing. No fun going through a village after they've been through. They're only

Christians, I know, and maybe they deserve what they get for cringing to the Christ-god and his priests.

"It still won't do. We're picking up slaves by the hundred, good quality stuff. But where to sell them. Down South? If you do that you need to go with a strong fleet and a sharp eye open. We aren't popular down there—and I blame Ragnar and his brood for that. Round in Ireland? A long way, and a long time before you get your cash. And slaves apart, there's nothing. The churches got their gold and silver into York before we arrived. What money the peasants have got, or the thanes—it's poor stuff. Very poor stuff. Strange. It's a rich land, anyone can see. Where's all their silver gone? We'll never get rich the way we're going. Sometimes I wish I had not taken the news of Ragnar's death to the Braethraborg, no matter what the priests of the Way said to me. It's little enough I have got out of it."

But Brand had taken the crews out again, probing up across the shire to the shrine of Strenshall, hoping for a haul of gold or silver. Shef had asked not to accompany him, sickened with the sights and sounds of a land crisscrossed by the Ragnarssons and their followers, each one intent on showing to the others his skill on racking secrets and information and buried treasure out of churls and thralls who had no information, and certainly no treasure, to yield. Brand had hesitated, scowling.

"We are all in the Army together," he had said. "What we decide together, all must do, even if some of us don't like it. If we don't like it we have to talk the others round, in open meeting. But I don't like the way you think you can take some bits of the Army and leave the others, young man. You are a carl now. Carls do what is best for each other. That is why we are all given a voice."

"I did what was best when the ram broke."

Brand had grunted, doubtfully, and had muttered, "For your own reasons." But he had left Shef behind, with Thorvin and a mountain of smith-work, in the guarded camp that watched York, ever alert for a sally. Shef had begun immediately to play with models, to imagine giant bows, sling-stones, mallets. One problem at least he had solved—if not in practice or even in theory.

Outside the smithy there was a pad of running feet, a gasping of exhaustion. The three men inside moved as one to the wide, open doors. A few feet beyond them Thorvin had set up a line of poles, connected with yarn, from which he had hung the rowan berries that indicated the limits of his precinct, the holy place. To one of the posts clung a panting figure, dressed in rough sacking. The iron collar round his neck indicated his status. Desperately his eyes moved from one to the other of the three faces staring at him, then brightened with relief as he saw, finally, the hammer round Thorvin's burly neck.

"Sanctuary," he gasped, "give me sanctuary." He spoke in English, but used the Latin word.

"What is *'sanctuarium'*?" asked Thorvin.

"Safe-keeping. He wants to come under your protection. Among the Christians, a runaway may grasp a church door in some churches, and then he is under the protection of the bishop till his case is tried."

Thorvin shook his head slowly. He could see now the pursuers coming into view—half a dozen of them, Hebrideans by the look of them, among the most ardent of the slave-takers, not hurrying now that they could see their quarry.

"We don't have that custom here," he said.

The slave wailed with fear as he saw the gesture and felt the presences behind him, and clung tighter to the fragile poles. Shef remembered the moment when he too had walked forward to Thorvin inside his enclosure, not knowing if he was walking to his death or not. But he had been able to call himself a smith, a fellow of the craft. This man looked as if he was just extra labor, knowing nothing of any value.

"Come along, you." The leader of the Hebrideans said, clouting the cringing figure round one ear, and began to pry his fingers from the pole.

"How much do you want for him?" said Shef impulsively. "I'll buy him off you."

Guffaws of laughter. "What for, One-eye? You want a bum-boy? I've got better down in the pen."

"I said I'll buy him. Look, I've got money." Shef turned towards "Thrall's-wreak," stuck in the ground at the entrance to the precinct. From it he had hung his purse with the few coins in it that Brand had doled out as his share of the meager plunder so far.

"No chance. Come down to the pens if you want a slave, sell you one anytime. I've got to take this one back, make an example of him. Too many down there run from one master, think they might run from another. Got to show them it doesn't pay."

The slave had caught something of the dialogue, and wailed with fear again, this time more desperately. As the men gripped his arms and hands and began to pull him off, trying as they did so not to damage the precinct-markers, he thrashed and fought. "The pendants," he cried. "They said the pendant-men were safe."

"We cannot help you," Shef replied, speaking again in English. "You should have stayed with your English master."

"My masters were the black monks. You know what they are like to their slaves. And my master was the worst of all—Erkenbert the deacon, who makes the machines. . . ."

An angry Hebridean lost patience with the man's struggles, whipped a sandbag from his belt, and struck out. He missed his blow, caught the slave along the jaw instead of on the temple. A crack, the jaw lolling forward, blood trickling from the corner of the mouth.

"Er'en'ert. He' a de'il. Ma' 'e de'il-'chines."

Shef seized his gauntlets, pulled them on, ready to jerk his halberd out of the ground. The knot of struggling men swayed back a few paces.

"Hold on," he said. "The man's valuable. Don't hit him again." Ten words, he thought, ten words might be all I need. Then I will know the principle of the great bow.

The slave, fighting now with the frenzy of a tormented weasel, got a foot free, kicked out. A Hebridean grunted, bent forward cursing.

"That's enough," snapped the head of the gang. As Shef leapt forward in entreaty he whipped a knife from his belt, stepped forward and drove upward, backhand. The slave, still held, arched and contorted, went limp.

"You blockhead!" yelled Shef. "You killed one of the machine-men!"

The Hebridean turned back to him, mouth twisting with anger. As he started to speak, Shef punched him full in the face with his armored glove. He sprawled backward, landed on the ground. A dead silence fell.

The Hebridean climbed slowly to his feet, spat one tooth, then another, into his hand. He looked at his men, shrugged. They dropped the slave's corpse, turned, walked off together toward their camp.

"You've done it now, boy," said Thorvin.

"What do you mean?"

"Only one thing can happen now."

"What's that?"

"*Holmgang.*"

Chapter Three

Shef lay on the straw pallet close to the banked fire of the forge, moving uneasily in his sleep. Thorvin had forced a heavy dinner on him, which should have been welcome after days of increasingly short commons in a camp dependent entirely on foraging for its food. But the rye bread and fried bullock lay heavy on his stomach. Heavier still were his thoughts. They had explained the rules of *holmgang* to him, far different from the impromptu brawl in which he had killed the Irishman Flann months before. He knew he was at terrible disadvantage. But there was no getting out of this. The whole Army knew, looked forward to the morning's duel as a major distraction. He was trapped.

And he still thought about the machines. How were they built? How could better ones be built? How could the walls of York be breached? Slowly, he slipped into heavier slumber.

He was on some distant plain. In front of him loomed monstrous walls. On a scale to dwarf the walls of York, or any other walls that had ever been built by mortal man. High above were the figures he had seen before in his dreams, his "visions" as Thorvin called them—the massive figures with the faces like axe-blades and the expressions of severe gravity. But now their expressions were also of concern, alarm. In the foreground, moving up to the walls, he saw there was a figure even more gigantic than those of the gods, so enormous that it towered up even to the height of the walls on which the gods were standing. But it did not have the proportions of a human being: stumpy-legged, fat-armed, swollen-bellied and gap-toothed, it looked like an immense clown. A wittol, one of the children born deformed, who, if Father Andreas were not on hand very swiftly, would quietly have found their way into the fen in Emneth. The giant was urging on an immense horse, fully built to his own scale, and drawing a cart, on it a block of stone large as a mountain.

Shef realized the block was to fill a gap in the great wall. The wall was not complete—but nearly so. The sun in this strange world was setting, and he knew that if the wall were finished before the sunset, something appalling, something incurably dreadful would take place. That was why the gods looked their alarm, and why the giant was urging on his horse—his stallion, Shef saw—with whoops of glee and anticipation.

A whicker from behind. Another horse, this time a more normally proportioned one. A mare, too, with chestnut hair and mane blowing around her eyes. She whickered again,

then turned coyly as if unaware of the effect her call had
had. But the stallion had heard. His head rose. He shook in
his traces. His member started to slide out of its sheath.

The giant shouted, beat the stallion round the head, tried
to cover its eyes. Its nostrils flared, a whinny of rage, yet
another encouraging whicker from the mare, now close by,
heels kicking skittishly. The stallion reared, lashed out with
mighty hooves at the giant, at the traces. Over went the
cart, out tipped the stone, the giant dancing with vexation.
The stallion was free, lunging towards the mare to sheathe
his erect, chain-long penis. But she was coy, prancing away,
provoking him to follow, then darting sideways. The two
horses gyrated, suddenly dashed off at full gallop, the stallion slowly gaining on the mare but both rapidly out of
sight. Behind them, the giant cursed and leapt in comic pan-
tomime. The sun set. One of the figures on the wall strode
forward grimly, pulling on a pair of metal gloves.

There is a forfeit to be paid, thought Shef.

Again he was on a plain, facing a walled city. It too was
mighty, the walls rising far above the heights of those at
York, but this time it was at least on a human scale, as were
the thousands of figures milling about within the walls and
outside the walls. Outside the walls the figures were heaving
at a monstrous image—not a boar, like the Ragnarssons'
battering ram, but a giant horse. A wooden horse. What is
the point of a wooden horse? thought Shef. Surely no one
could be deceived by it.

Nor were they. Arrows and missiles flew out against the
horse from the walls, or flew at the men heaving at its
mighty wheels. They bounced away, scattered haulers, did
not dislodge or discourage the hundreds of new hands rushing to take the place of the fallen. The horse edged up to the
walls, overtopping them. What would take place now, Shef
knew, was the crisis of something that had gone on for many
years, that had swallowed thousands of lives and would yet
swallow thousands more. Something told him also that what
happened here would fascinate men for generation upon

generation—but that few men would ever understand it, pre-
ferring instead to make up their own stories.

A voice Shef had heard before spoke suddenly in his
mind. The voice that had warned him before the night battle
by the Stour—still with the same note of deep, interested
amusement.

"Now watch this," it said. "Watch this."

The horse's mouth opened, its tongue slid out to rest on
the walls. From the mouth . . .

Thorvin was shaking him, dragging relentlessly at his shoulder. Shef sat up, still groping for the meaning of his dream.

"Time to rise," said Thorvin. "You have a hard day ahead
of you. I only hope you live to see the end of it."

Erkenbert the archdeacon sat in his tower room high above
the great hall of the minster and pulled the candlestick
closer to him. There were three candles in it, each of best
beeswax, not stinking tallow, and the light they gave was
clear. He viewed them with satisfaction as he took the
goose-feather from its inkpot. What he was about to do was
difficult, was laborious, and its results might be sad.

In front of him lay a confusion of scraps of vellum, written on, crossed out, written on again. Now he took his quill
and a fresh, large, handsome piece. On it he wrote:

De parochia quae dicitur Schirlam desunt nummi   XLVIII
"   "   "   " Fulford   "   "   XXXVI
"   "   "   " Haddinatunus   "   "   LIX

The list crept on and on. At the end he drew a line beneath
the record of the minster's unpaid rents, drew a deep breath,
and began the mind-wrenching toil of adding the numbers
up. *"Octo et sex,"* he muttered to himself, *"quattuordecim.*
Et novo, sunt . . . viginta tres. Et septem." To assist himself
he began to draw little lines on a discarded sheet, hatching
them through when he completed a ten. He began also, as
his finger crawled down the list, to put a little mark between

the XL and the VIII, the L and the IX, to remind himself which bits were to be added and which were to be left. Finally he came to the end of his first calculation, wrote down firmly CDXLIX, and began to work his way down again with the figures he had omitted before. *"Quaranta et triginta sunt septuaginta. Et quinquaginta. Centum et viginta."* The novice who decorously moved an eye round the doorway a few minutes later to see if anything was required returned in awe to his fellows.

"He is saying numbers of which I have never heard," he reported.

"He is a marvelous man," said one of the black monks. "God send there may be no harm in the learning of such black arts."

"Duo milia quattuor centa nonaginta," pronounced Erkenbert, writing it down: MMCDXC. The two figures now lay next to each other: MMCDXC and CDXLIX. After another interval of crossing and hatching, he had the answer: MMCMXXXIX. And now the real toil began. That was the sum of the failed rents for one quarter. What would this represent for a full year, if by divine punishment the scourges of God, the Vikings, were permitted to lie so long upon the backs of the suffering people of God? Many, even among *arithmetici*, would have taken the easier route and added the same figure up four times. But Erkenbert knew himself superior to such subterfuges. Painstakingly, he set up the complex procedure for the most difficult of all diabolic skills: multiplication in Roman numerals.

When all was done he stared at the figure, disbelievingly. Never in all his experience had he come upon such a sum. Slowly, with shaking fingers, he snuffed the candles in recognition of the growing gray light of dawn. After matins he would have to seek out the Archbishop.

It was too great. Such losses could not be borne.

Far away, a hundred and fifty miles to the south, the same growing light reached the eyes of a woman, snuggled deep in a nest of down mattress and woolen rugs piled high against the cold. She stirred, shifted. Her hand touched the warm, naked thigh of the man next to her. Recoiled as if it had touched the scales of a mighty adder.

He is my half brother, she thought for the thousandth time. Son of my own father. We are in mortal sin. But how could I tell them? I could not tell even the priest who married us. Alfgar told him we had sinned carnally while fleeing from the Vikings and now prayed God's forgiveness and blessing on our union. They think he is a saint. And the kings, the kings of Mercia and of Wessex, they listen to all he says of the menace of the Vikings, of what they did to his father, of how he fought at the Viking camp to set me free. They think he is a hero. They say they will make him an alderman and set him over a shire, they will bring his poor, tormented father home from York, where he is defying the heathens still.

But what will happen when our father sees us together? If only Shef had lived . . .

As she thought the name, Godive's tears started to leak slowly, as they did every morning, through closed eyelids onto the pillow.

Shef marched down the muddy street, between the lines of booths which the Vikings had set up to keep out the winter weather. His halberd rested on his shoulder, and he wore his metal gloves, but the helmet remained at Thorvin's forge. Mail and helmets may not be worn in *holmgang*, they had told him. The duel was fought as a matter of honor, so mere expediencies, like surviving and killing your enemy, were not the point.

That did not mean you would not be killed.

And a *holmgang* was a four-man affair. Each of the two principals took turns to strike at the other. But each principal was covered from the blows of the other by his second, the shieldbearer, who carried a shield for him and intercepted the strokes. Your life depended on the skill of your second.

Shef had no second. Brand and all his crews were still

away. Thorvin had pulled his beard frantically, thumping his hammer again and again into the ground with frustration, but as a priest of the Way he could take no part. If he offered, his offer would be refused by the umpires. The same went for Ingulf, Hund's master. The only person he might have asked was Hund, and as soon as Shef framed the thought, he knew that Hund—once he realized the situation—would surely volunteer. But he had immediately told his friend he must not think of helping. All other considerations apart, he was sure that at the critical moment, with a sword-blow descending, Hund would stop to observe a heron in the marsh or a newt in the fen, and would probably kill them both.

"I will see it through myself," he told the priests of the Way, who had gathered together from the whole Army to advise him, much to Shef's surprise.

"This is not why we spoke for you to the Snakeeye, and saved you from the vengeance of Ivar," said Farman sharply—Farman the priest of Frey, famous for his wanderings in the other worlds.

"Are you then so sure of the ways of fate?" Shef had replied, and the priests had fallen silent.

But in truth, as he walked toward the place of the *holmgang*, it was not the duel itself which bothered him. What bothered him was whether the umpires would let him fight on his own. If they did not, then he would stand for the second time in his life at the mercy of the Army's collective judgement, the *vapna takr*. At the thought of the roar and the clash of weapons that accompanied a decision, his guts knotted within him.

He marched through the gates of the stockade and out onto the trampled meadow by the river where the Army was assembled. As he walked forward, a buzz of comment rose, and the watching crowd parted to let him through. At their center stood a ring of willow wands, only ten feet across. "The *holmgang* should strictly be fought on an island in a stream," Thorvin had told him, "but where there was no eyot suitable, a symbolic one was marked out instead. In a

holmgang there was to be no maneuvering: The participants
stood and cut at each other till one was dead. Or could fight
no more, or ransomed himself off, or threw down his weapons, or stepped outside the marked area. To do either of the
two last meant submitting yourself to the mercy of your opponent, who could demand death or mutilation. If a fighter
showed cowardice, the judges would certainly order either,
or both.

Shef saw his enemies already standing by the willows:
the Hebridean whose teeth he had knocked out, whose name
he now knew was Magnus. He held a naked broadsword in
his hand, burnished so that the serpent-markings on its blade
wriggled and crawled in the dull, gray light. By him stood
his second: a tall, scarred, powerful-looking man of middle
age. He held an oversized shield of painted wood, with
metal rim and boss. Shef looked at them for a moment, and
then looked deliberately round for the umpires.

His heart checked as he recognized instantly, in a little
group of four, the unmistakable figure of the Boneless One.
Still wearing scarlet and green, but the silver helmet put
aside; the pale eyes with their invisible eyebrows and lashes
stared straight into his own. But this time, instead of suspicion they held assurance, amusement, contempt, as they
recognized Shef's uncontrollable start of fear and the immediate attempt to replace it with impassivity.

5Ivar yawned, stretched, turned away. "I disqualify myself from judgement in this case," he said. "This barnyard
cock and I have another score to settle. I will not have him
say that I took advantage to judge unfairly. I leave his death
to Magnus."

A rumble of agreement came from the nearest watchers,
and a buzz as the information was passed to those further
back. Everything in the Army, Shef realized again, was subject to public agreement. It was always best to have public
opinion on your side.

Ivar's withdrawal left three men there, all obviously senior warriors, well armed, necks, belts and arms flashing
with silver to show their status. The middle one, he recog-

nized, was Halvdan Ragnarsson, the eldest of the brothers: a man with a reputation for ferocity, for fighting when there was no need—not as wise as his brother Sigurth nor as dreadful as his brother Ivar, but not a man to show mercy on the unwarlike.

"Where is your second?" said Halvdan, frowning.

"I do not need one," replied Shef.

"You must have one. You cannot fight a *holmgang* with no shield or shield-bearer. If you present yourself without one, then that is as good as surrendering to the mercy of your enemy. Magnus, what do you want to do with him?"

"I do not need one!" This time Shef shouted, stepped forward, jammed the butt of his halberd upright in the earth. "I have a shield." He raised his left forearm, on which he had strapped a square buckler, a foot across, fastened firmly at wrist and at elbow, made entirely of iron. "I do not fight with board and broadsword, but with this and this. I do not need a second. I am an Englishman, not a Dane!"

A growl rose from the audience as they heard him—a growl with a note of amusement in it. The Army liked a drama, Shef knew. They might bend the rules if there was something to bet on. They would support a man who was in the wrong, if he showed enough daring.

"We cannot accept this proposal," said Halvdan to the other two judges. "What do you say?"

A disturbance behind, someone forcing his way through the ring, stepping forward to join Shef as he stood before his judges. Another large and powerful figure, laden with silver. The Hebrideans stood frowning a little way apart. Shef saw with shock that it was his father Sigvarth. Sigvarth looked across at his son, then turned to the judges. He spread his burly arms with a cunning air of conciliation.

"I wish to act as this man's shield-bearer."

"Has he asked you to?"

"No."

"Then what standing do you have in this affair?"

"I am his father."

Another growl from the audience, with a rising note of

excitement. Life in a winter camp was cold and boring. This was easily the best entertainment anyone had had since the failed assault. Like children, the warriors of the Army were anxious not to see the show end too early. They pressed closer, straining to hear and to pass on the news to those further back. Their presence affected the umpires: They had to judge correctly, but also gauge the mood of the crowd.

As they began to mutter quietly among themselves, Sigvarth turned quickly toward Shef. He stepped close, bent the inch or two needed to be on a level, and spoke with a note of entreaty.

"Look, boy, you turned me down once before when you were in a fix. That showed guts, I've got to say. Look what it cost you. Cost you an eye. Don't do it again. I'm sorry—what happened to your mother. If I'd known she'd had a son like you I wouldn't have done it. Many men have told me what you did at the siege, with the ram—the Army's full of it. I'm proud of you.

"Now, let me carry this shield for you. I've done it before. I'm better than Magnus, better than his mate Kolbein. With me as shield-bearer nothing will get through to you. And you—you've knocked that Hebridean fool as dizzy as a dog once already. Do it again! We'll finish the pair of them."

He gripped his son's shoulder hard. His eyes shone with emotion, a mixture of pride, embarrassment, and something else—it was the lust for glory, Shef decided. No one could be a successful warrior for twenty years, a jarl, the leader of warbands, without the urge to be at the front, to have all eyes fixed on one, to break down destiny by sheer violence. Shef felt suddenly calm, composed, even able to think of how to save his father's face while rejecting him. He knew now that his worst fear would not be realized. The umpires would let him fight on his own. It would be too much of an anticlimax to decide anything different.

Shef stepped clear of his father's near embrace.

"I thank Sigvarth Jarl for his offer to bear my shield in this *holmgang*. But there is blood between us—he knows whose it is. I believe that he would support me loyally in this affair, and his help would mean much to a young man like myself. But I would not show *drengskapr* in accepting the offer."

Shef used the word for warriorhood, for honor—the word one used to show that you were above trifles, that you did not care for your own advantage. The word was a challenge. If one man laid claim to *drengskapr*, his opponent would be ashamed to show less.

"I say again: I have a shield, I have a weapon. If this is less than I should have, so much the better for Magnus. I say it is more. If I am wrong, then that is what we are fighting to see."

Halvdan Ragnarsson looked at his two co-arbiters, saw their nods of assent, and added his own. The two Hebrideans walked immediately inside the round of withies and took up their stations one beside the other: they knew any hesitation or further argument would look ill to the Army. Shef walked over to face them, saw the two junior umpires taking their places to either hand, while Halvdan, in the middle, repeated the rules of the combat. Out of the corner of his eye he saw Sigvarth still standing well to the front of the others, joined now by the young man he had seen before, the one with a horse's projecting teeth. Hjörvarth Jarlsson, he thought detachedly. His half brother. Just behind the pair of them stood a rank of men with Thorvin in their center. Even though he strove to keep his mind on Halvdan's exposition he saw that each was wearing a silver pendant, prominently displayed. Thorvin had at least mustered a body of opinion, in case it could have an effect.

". . . combatants must strike alternately. If you try to strike twice, even if your enemy is off guard, you forfeit the *holmgang* and become liable to the judgement of the umpires. And it will not be light! So, begin. Magnus, as injured party, shall be the first to strike."

Halvdan stepped back, eyes wary, sword drawn to strike up any illegal blow. Shef found himself in the midst of a great silence, face-to-face with his two enemies.

He swung his halberd forward and trained the point on
Magnus's face, left hand gripping the weapon just below its
massive and complex head. His right hand down by his
right side, ready to seize the haft to block or parry in any
direction. Magnus frowned, realizing he must now step to
one side or the other and signal his direction. He stepped
forward and right, to the very edge of the line Halvdan had
drawn in the mud to separate the combatants. His sword
swung down, forehand, aimed at the head, the most elementary stroke possible. He wants to get this over with, thought
Shef. The blow was merciless and lightning-quick. He
swung up his left arm to catch it squarely in the center of
the iron buckler.

A clang, a recoil. The blow left a dull line and a dent the
length of the buckler. What it had done to the edge of the
sword-blade, Shef, as a smith, did not like to think.

Magnus was back behind his line now, Kolbein stepping
forward with the shield to cover him. Shef raised the halberd with both hands over his right shoulder, stepped forward to the edge of the line and stabbed point-first straight
forward at Magnus's heart, ignoring the covering of the
shield. The triangular lance-head drove through the lindenwood as if it were cheese, but as it did so, Kolbein jerked
it up, so that the point stabbed past Magnus's cheek. Shef
jerked back, twisted, jerked again, freeing the weapon with
a crunch of broken wood. Now there was a gaping hole in
the gay blue paint of the shield, and Kolbein and Magnus
looked at each other with grave expressions.

Magnus came forward again, and realized that he must
not strike on the buckler side. He swung backhand, but still
at the head, still thinking that a man without proper sword
and shield must needs be at a disadvantage. Without shifting
grip, Shef swung the head of his halberd eighteen inches
sideways at the descending sword, catching it not with the
axe-side but with the reverse, the thumb-wide iron spike.

The sword flew out of Magnus's grasp, to land well on
Shef's side of the line. All eyes flew to the umpires. Shef
stepped back a pace, two paces, looked firmly at the sky. A

buzz as the audience realized what was happening, a low growl of approval—a growl that went on as the keenly intent audience began to realize the potentialities of Shef's weapon and the problem the two Hebrideans were facing. Stone-faced, Magnus stepped forward, recovered his blade, hesitated, then saluted briefly with it and returned to his side of the line.

This time Shef swung the weapon over his left shoulder, and struck like a woodsman felling a tree, left hand sliding down the weapon as it swung, concentrating all his force and all the weight of the seven feet of metal behind the slicing half-yard of blade. Kolbein leapt quickly and decisively to save his partner, and got the shield well up above head height. The axe slashed through its edge and swung on, turned only slightly by the resistance of the metal rim, shore through two feet of lindenwood, and embedded itself with a thunk in the muddy ground. Shef jerked it free and stood once more on guard.

Kolbein looked at the half-shield still strapped to his arm and muttered something to Magnus. Impassive, Halvdan Ragnarsson stepped forward, picked up the severed oval of wood and tossed it to one side.

"Shields may only be replaced at the agreement of both parties," he observed. "Strike."

Magnus stepped forward with something like desperation in his eyes now, and swung a wicked blow with no warning, just above knee height. A swordsman would have jumped it, or tried to—it was just above the height a man might be expected to manage. Shef moved his right hand slightly and stopped the blow dead with his weapon's metal-reinforced shaft. Almost before Magnus could regain the shelter of his partner's shield, he was stepping forward, this time swinging upward, with the spike side foremost. A thump as it met the remnants of the shield, a resistance which this time was not one of wood alone, Kolbein staring at the foot-long spike which had driven through shield and forearm, splitting ulna and humerus bones.

Stone-faced, Shef slid his hand high up the head of the

halberd, gripping tight, and jerked back. Kolbein staggered
forward, put a foot over the line, recovered himself and
straightened up, face white with shock and pain. There was
a simultaneous yell as his foot went down, and then a confusion of cries.

"Fight's over, past the mark!"

"He struck at the shield-bearer!"

"He struck at the man. If the shield-bearer puts his arm
in the way . . ."

"First blood to the smith, settle all bets!"

"Stop it now, stop it now," Thorvin called out. But over
him an even louder voice, that of Sigvarth: "Let them fight
it out! These are warriors, not girls to snivel at a scratch."

Shef looked sideways, saw Halvdan, grave but fascinated,
wave the opponents on.

Kolbein was shaking, starting to fumble with the buckles
of the useless shield, clearly unable to hold it up much
longer. Magnus too had gone white. Each strike with the
halberd had come close to killing him. Now he had no protection left. Yet there was no escape, no chance to run or
surrender.

White-lipped, he stepped forward with the resolution of
despair, raised the sword and swung straight down. It was a
blow any active man could dodge without thinking; but in
a *holmgang* you had to stand still. For the first time in the
contest, Shef twisted his left hand and swung a parry, full
force, with the axe edge of the halberd. It met the descending broadsword halfway down the blade and battered it
aside, knocking Magnus off balance. As he recovered, he
glanced at his weapon. It had not snapped off, but was cut
halfway through, and bent out of line.

"Swords may only be replaced," intoned Halvdan, "by
the agreement of both parties."

Magnus's face sagged with despair. He tried to pull himself together, to stand straight for the deathblow that must
come. Kolbein shuffled a little forward and tried to pull his
shield-arm up into place with his other hand.

Shef looked at the blade of his halberd, running a thumb

over the nick that he had just put in it. Some careful work with a file, he reflected. The weapon was called "Thrall's-wreak." He was fighting because the man over there had murdered a thrall. Now was the time for vengeance, for that thrall and no doubt for many others.

But he had not knocked the Hebridean down because he had murdered a slave, but because he, Shef, had wanted the slave. Wanted to know about the machines the slave had made. Killing Magnus would not bring the knowledge back. Besides, he had more knowledge now.

In the utter silence Shef stepped back, drove his halberd point-first into the mud, unstrapped his buckler, threw it down. He turned to Halvdan and called out in a loud voice, making sure the whole Army could hear him.

"I give up this *holmgang*, and ask for the judgement of the umpires. I regret that I struck Magnus Ragnaldsson in anger, knocking out two of his front teeth, and if he will release me from the *holmgang* I offer him self-doom for that injury, and for the injury just inflicted on Kolbein his partner, and I ask for his friendship and support in the future."

A groan of disappointment mingled with shouts of approval. Yelling and pushing in the crowd as the two points of view found expression. Halvdan and the umpires pushed together to confer, after a few moments calling over the two Hebrideans to join their discussion. Then an agreement, slow quietening as the crowd waited to hear the decision and to ratify it. Shef felt no fear, no memory of the last time he had stood to hear a Ragnarsson pronounce. He knew he had judged the mood of the crowd rightly, and that the umpires would not dare to go against that.

"It is the judgement of all us three umpires that this *holmgang* has been fought well and fairly, with no discredit to any participant, and that you, Shef . . ." He struggled with the English name, could not pronounce it. ". . . *Skjef*, son of Sigvarth, had the right to offer to submit to judgement while it was your turn to strike." Halvdan stared round and repeated the point. "While it was your turn to strike. Accordingly, since Magnus Ragnaldsson is also prepared to accept a judgement, we declare that this contest may be ceased without penalty to either side."

Magnus the Hebridean stepped forward. "And I declare that I accept the offer of Skjef Sigvarthsson to self-doom for the injuries inflicted on me and on Kolbein Kolbrandsson, and we value them at half a mark of silver for each of us . . ." Whistles and hoots at the low rate set by the proverbially grasping islanders. ". . . on one condition:

"That Skjef Sigvarthsson, in his smithy, makes weapons for both of us similar to the one he wields, at the price of half a mark of silver each. And with this we admit him to our full friendship and support."

Magnus walked forward, grinning, clasped hands with Shef as Kolbein too shambled forward. Hund was inside the ring as well, seizing Kolbein's bleeding and already-swollen arm, clucking over the filthy state of the sleeve. Sigvarth was there also, hovering behind the duellers, trying to say something. An icy voice cut through the babble.

"Well, you are all agreed on one thing and another. If you had meant to stop fighting as soon as two drops of blood were shed, you could have done it all behind the privy and not wasted the whole Army's time.

"But tell me this, little dunghill cock—" The Boneless One's voice fell now into a pool of silence as he stalked forward, eyes blazing. "What do you think you can do to get my full friendship and support? Eh? For there is blood between us too. What can you offer me in exchange for it?"

Shef turned and pitched his voice high, allowing once again the note of challenge and contempt to brazen it, so that the Army would know Ivar had been dared.

"I can give you something, Ivar Ragnarsson, that I already tried to get for you once, but that we know you cannot get for yourself. No, I do not mean a woman's skirts . . ." Ivar swayed back, eyes never leaving Shef's face, and Shef knew that now Ivar would never leave him, never forget him till one or the other was dead. "No. Give me five hundred men and I will give you something to share with all of us. I will give you machines stronger than the

Christians'. Weapons greater than the one I used here. And when I have all those I will give you something else.

"I will give you York!"

He ended with a shout, and the Army shouted with him, clashing their weapons in tumult and approval.

"It is a good brag," replied Ivar, glaring round at Sigvarth, at the Hebrideans, at Thorvin and his group of pendant-wearers, all clustered in support of Shef. "But it will be a sad one for the boy if he fails to carry it out."

Chapter Four

Hard to tell when dawn comes in an English winter, Shef thought. The clouds come down to the ground, the showers of rain or sleet come sweeping across—wherever the sun may be, it has to cut through layer after layer before the light gets through. He needed light for his own men, he needed light to see the English. Till he had it, they could all wait.

He moved his aching body beneath the layer of sweat-sodden wool that was his tunic and the layer of stiff boiled leather that was still the only armor he had had time to acquire. The sweat was chilling now, after the hours of gasping, whispering labor. More than anything he would like to strip everything off and rub himself dry on a cloak. The men in the darkness behind him must feel the same.

But each of them now had only one thing to think about, one duty to carry out, and that duty something painfully and repetitively drilled into them. Only Shef had the image in his mind of all the things that had to happen, all the parts that had to fit. Only he could see all the hundreds of things that could go wrong. Shef was not afraid of death or maiming, of pain or shame or disgrace—the usual terrors of the battlefield, to be dispersed by action and excitement and battle-fury. He was afraid of the unpredicted, the unexpected, the broken spoke, the slippery leaves, the unknown machine.

To an experienced jarl of the pirates, Shef would already have done everything wrong. His men were formed-up, but cold, tired, stiff and uncertain as to what was happening.

But this was going to be a new kind of battle. This one did not depend on how men felt or how well they fought. If everyone did as he was supposed to, nothing needed to be done well. It just needed to be done. This would be battle like ploughing a field, or tearing out tree-stumps. No valor, no heroic deeds.

Shef's eyes caught a spark of flame. Yes. More sparks, a growing brush of flame, more flames further away, all from separate sources. The shapes of buildings could be seen now, and smoke was beginning to pour from them, blown by the wind. The flames lit up the long line of wall with the gate that the Ragnarssons' ram had assaulted two weeks before. All along the line facing that eastern wall, men were setting fire to the houses. Long tails of smoke billowing out, men rushing forward through it with ladders raised—a sudden assault, arrows flying, the blast of warhorns, more men coming forward as the first ones withdrew. The noise and flames and rushes were harmless. Soon enough the English leaders would realize this was a feint attack, would turn their attention elsewhere. But Shef remembered the desperate slowness and confusion of the Emneth levies; with the English what the leaders thought hardly mattered much. By the time they persuaded their men not to believe the evidence of their eyes he sincerely hoped that he would have the battle won.

The flame, the smoke. Warhorns on the ramparts blowing an alarm, faint signs of activity on the walls he could now see in front of him. Time to start.

Shef turned to his right and began deliberately to walk along the long line of houses above the north wall, his halberd swinging easily. Four hundred double-paces to count. As he reached forty he saw the great square bulk of the first war-machine, its crew clustered round it in the mouth of the alleyway where they had heaved it up with such immense labor. He nodded to them, reaching out the butt of his halberd and tapped the man in front—Egil the hersir, from Skaane. Egil nodded solemnly and began to tramp his feet up and down, laboriously counting under his breath every time his left foot touched ground.

Nothing in the whole job had been harder than making them do that. It was not warlike. It was not the way *drengir* should behave. Their men might laugh at them. Anyway, how could a man keep count of so many? Five white pebbles Shef had given Egil, one for each hundred, and a black one for the final sixty. At five hundred and sixty paces Egil would move off—if he did not lose the count, if his men did not laugh. By then Shef would have reached the far end of his line, turned, and paced back to his own station in the middle. He did not think Egil's men would laugh. The ten counters he had picked were all famous warriors. Dignity was something they defined.

That was a leader's job in the new kind of battle, Shef thought as he paced on. Picking men the way a carpenter picked pieces of wood for a house-frame. He counted eighty, saw the second war-machine, tapped Skuli the Bald, saw him grip his pebbles and start his count, paced on. And fitting together the pieces of the plan the way a carpenter would.

There had to be an easier way to do it all, he told himself as he passed the third and fourth machines. This would be easy for the Rome-folk, with their numbercraft. But he knew no forge hot enough to beat out this skill for him.

Brand's three crews manned the next three machines in the line. The Hebrideans came next, half a dozen of them clutching their newly forged halberds.

Strange, the volunteers he had got. After the *holmgang* he had asked Sigurth Snakeeye for five hundred men. He had needed more like two thousand in the end, not only to man the machines and make up the diversion squads, but above all else to form the labor gangs to forage for wood, to cut it into shape, to find or forge the massive nails he needed, to manhandle the great contrivances up the muddy slope from the Foss. But the men who had done the work had not been provided by Sigurth, Ivar, or any of the Ragnarssons, who after a few days had held aloof. They had been the men from the small crews, the uncommitted, the fringes of the Army. A high proportion of them wore the pendants of the Way.

Shef was uneasily aware that Thorvin's and Brand's beliefs about him were beginning to leak out into the ranks. People were beginning to tell stories about him.

If all went well they would have another to tell soon enough.

He reached the last machine at the count of four hundred and twelve, turned on his heel, striding out more briskly now as he realized his count was over. The light was strengthening all the time; the din was at its peak over by the eastern wall, smoke still rising in the murky air.

Unbidden, a verse came into his mind, a little English verse from his childhood:

In willow-ford, by woody bridge,
The old kings lie, keels beneath them . . .

No, that was wrong! It was *"Dust rose to heaven, dew fell to earth, night went forth"*—that was the verse . . . So what was the other verse . . . ?

He stopped, doubled over as if stricken by cramp. Something horrible, in his head, just when he had no time to deal with it. He struggled to rise. Saw Brand approaching, concern on his face.

"I lost my count."

"No matter. We can see forty paces now. We'll move when Gummi does. Just one thing . . ." Brand bent and muttered in Shef's ear. "A man's come up from the rear. He says the Ragnarssons aren't behind us. They're not following our lead."

"We'll do this ourselves, then. But I tell you: the Ragnarssons, anyone—those who don't fight, don't share!"

"They're moving."

Shef was back by his own machine, in the comforting smell of sawdust. He ducked inside its shell, hooked the axe-blade of his halberd over a broken nail he had hammered in himself last night, stepped to his appointed place at the rearmost push-bar, and hurled his weight forward. Slowly, the machine began to creak along the level ground toward the waiting wall.

To the English sentries, it seemed as if the houses moved. But not the little, squat wattle-and-daub houses they knew were there. Rather, it seemed to them as if thane's halls, church towers, belfries, were rolling toward them out of the rising mist. For weeks they had looked down from their wall at everything the eye could see. Now things were coming toward them at their own level. Were they rams? Disguised ladders? Screens for some other kind of devil-work? A hundred bows bent, loosed arrows. Useless. Anyone could see the constructions coming toward them would take no heed of bolts from a breast-bow.

But they had better weapons than that. Snarling, the thane of the northern gate hurled a white-faced fyrdman, a conscript in the service of some petty lord, back to his place on the battlements, seized one of his slave errand-runners, and barked at him.

"Go to the eastern tower! Tell the machine-folk there to shoot. You! Same tale, western tower. You! Back to the square, tell the men with the stone-hurler that there are machines coming up to the northern wall. Tell them *machines*! Definitely! Whatever is going on over there, this is not a feint attack. Go on, all of you, move!"

As they scattered he turned his attentions to his own troops, the ones off guard pounding up the ladders to their places, the ones who had seen already shouting and pointing at the shapes rolling closer.

"Keep your minds on what you're doing," he bellowed.

"Look down, for God's sake! Whatever these things are, they can't come up to the wall. And once they get close enough the priests' weapons will destroy them!"

If the Rome-soldiers still had been in the fortress, Shef, had realized, there would have been a deep ditch at the base of the wall, which any stormer would have had to cross before trying any kind of escalade. Centuries of neglect and refuse-tipping had filled this in, had created a swelling, turf-grown mound five feet high and as many broad. A man who ran up it would still be a dozen feet below the often-patched battlements. It had not seemed dangerous to the defenders. Indeed, without their knowing it, it had become one more hindrance to the enemy.

As the siege-tower rolled up to the wall the man at the front raised a yell, the push-teams stepped up their pace to a half-trot. The machine rolled forward, met resistance from the swelling mound, shuddered to a halt. Immediately a dozen men ran forward from their positions behind the tower. Half of them held up heavy square shields to block the arrow-shower. The others carried picks and shovels. Without words they set instantly to cutting a track along the marks of the front wheels, throwing the earth aside like badgers.

Shef walked forward between the sweating push-teams and peered through the light planking across the machine's front. Weight, that had been the problem. In essence the tower was simply a square frame eight feet wide, twelve feet long, thirty feet high, running on six cartwheels. It was unstable and unwieldy, and the whole of both lower sides were made of the heaviest beams the houses and churches of Northumbria could provide. As defense against the English bolt-throwers. They had had to save weight somewhere, and Shef had decided to skimp at the front. The wood there was only shield-thickness. As he looked out, arrows thumped into it, driving their points through. Only inches away the diggers shoveled frantically to gain the extra two feet to advance the wheels.

That was it. As he turned to call to the push-teams there was a tumult of yells behind him, and a great crash. Shef spun round, heart leaping. A bolt? One of the giant boulders? No, not so bad. Some burly Englishman on the wall had hurled down a rock, weighing fifty pounds at least. It had crashed through the shielding and bounced into the front of the machine, splintering the planks. No matter. But there was a man down, too—Eystein, lying with his leg crooked right under the left-hand wheel, gaping up at the engine towering over him.

"Hold it!" The men checked as they gathered their muscles for the final heave that would have gone straight over Eystein's smashed leg.

"Hold it. Drag him clear, Stubbi. All right. Pick-and-shovel party back into cover. Heave now, boys, and make it a good one. There—she's home! Hammer in the piles, Brand, so she doesn't roll back. Drop the ladders. Archers to the top platform. Storming party, after me."

One pair of ladders took the heavily armed and armored men up twelve feet, all of them gasping now with exertion but swept along with excitement. More ladders, another twelve feet. A hand passed Shef his halberd, forgotten in the rush. He seized it, watched the men jamming close together on the top platform. Were they level with the wall?

Yes! He could see the battlements below him, not much more than knee height. There was an Englishman shooting upward. The point found a gap between the planks, whirred through till the shaft caught and snapped, ended an inch from his good eye. Shef broke it off and dropped it. The men were ready now, all waiting for the signal.

Shef laid the razor edge of his halberd to the rope and cut.

Immediately the drawbridge began to fall forward, slowly for a moment, then hurtling forward like a great hammer, its front edge weighted with sandbags. A thump, a cloud of sand blowing in the wind as a bag burst, bowstrings twanging just above him as the archer tried to keep the battlements clear.

Then a great grunt as Brand propelled his massive frame onto the drawbridge and hurled himself across, beard-axe raised. As Shef leapt to follow, arms closed round him from behind. He found himself staring over his shoulder at Ulf, the ship's cook, the biggest man in three crews, after Brand.

"Brand said not you. He said keep you out of trouble for a few minutes."

The men poured by, first the detailed storming party, then the rest of the machine's crew, flinging themselves up the ladders and across the drawbridge without a pause. Then the men from the pick-and-shovel teams followed the rest of Brand's crew. Shef struggled in Ulf's grip, feet off the ground, hearing the clash of weapons, the screaming and shouting of the battle.

As complete strangers from other crews began to haul themselves up the ladder, Ulf released his grip. Shef leapt out onto the drawbridge, out into the open air, and for the first time could see how his plan had worked.

In the gray light, the cleared ground between wall and outer city was dotted with immense bulks, giant animals of some unknown species that had crawled there to die. That one must have shed a wheel or broken an axle on a bit of uneven ground, maybe an old cesspit. The one beyond them, the Hebridean one, seemed to have reached the wall successfully. The drawbridge was still in place from tower to battlements, and as he watched, another group of men trotted over it. Another, not as successful. They had cut the rope and then the drawbridge had fallen just feet short of the wall. It hung limply, like an enormous tongue from an eyeless face. Mailed bodies lay at the base of the wall beneath it.

Shef stepped off the drawbridge to let another wave of stormers pass by, then began to count. Three towers had not reached the wall, two had failed to get their men over the wall once they had reached it. That meant at most, five successful breaches. That had been enough. But they would have lost more if they had been slower, Shef thought. Or if they had not all come at once.

There must be a rule there. How would you say it? Maybe, in Norse, *"Höggva ekki hyggiask."* Hit 'em, don't think about it. One heavy blow, not a string of little ones. Brand would think that a good rule, once it was explained to him.

He looked up and saw in the sky what for weeks he had seen in his dreams, in his nightmares: the gigantic boulder rising with superhuman ease, still rising after all sense demanded that it must stop, reaching a peak. Starting to come down. Not on him. On the tower.

Shef cringed in terror—not for his own skin but for the appalling crash that must come, the ripping and rending as all the timbers and wheels and axles he had sweated over sprang apart. The Viking on the bridge cringed too and threw up a useless shield.

A thud, a ripple of loose earth. Hardly believing, Shef gaped at the boulder now embedded in the earth twenty feet from the side of his tower, looking as if it had been there since the dawn of creation. They had missed. Missed by yards. He had not thought they could.

The man in front of him, a burly figure in mail, was hurled aside.

Blood in the air, a thrum like the bottom note of a giant's

harp, a line in the air that came too fast to be seen and drove in and through the warrior's body.

The bolt-machine as well as the boulder-machine. Shef stepped to the edge of the wall and looked down at the broken body now sprawled at its foot. Well, they might be in action now—but one had missed and both were too late. They must still be captured.

"Come on, don't stand there like young maidens who've just seen the bull!" Shef gestured angrily at the men clustered in the tower's exit. "It will take them an hour to wind their machines again. Follow me now and we'll see they don't get the chance."

He turned and loped along the walkway behind the battlements, Ulf striding like an enormous nursemaid a pace behind.

They found Brand just inside the now-opened gates, in an open space scattered with the familiar debris of battle: split shields, bent weapons, bodies, incongruously, a torn shoe somehow parted from its owner. Brand was breathing hard, and sucking a scratch on his bare arm above his gauntlets, but otherwise was unhurt. Men were still pushing through the gates, being hailed and directed by the skippers according to some plan already agreed upon, all done with an air of frantic haste. As they approached, Brand called two senior warriors over to him and gave brief instructions.

"Sumarrfugl, take six men, go round all the bodies here, strip all the Englishmen and pile what you find over by that house there. Mail, weapons, chains, jewelry, purses. Don't forget to check under their armpits. Thorstein, take another six and go do the same job up along the walls. Don't get cut off and don't take any risks. Bring back all the stuff you find and pile it with Sumarrfugl's. When you've done that you can sort out our own dead and wounded. Now—you there, Thorvin!"

The priest appeared through the gates, leading a laden pack-horse.

"You've got your gear? I want you to stay here till we've

secured the Minster and then come right along as soon as I send a squad for you. Then you can set your forge up and start melting down the take.

"The take!" Brand's eyes gleamed with delight. "I can smell that farm in Halogaland already. Estate! County! All right, let's get going."

Shef stepped forward as he swung on his heel and grabbed an elbow.

"Brand, I need twenty men."

"What for?"

"To secure the shooting-machine up in the corner tower, and then go on to the throwing one."

The champion turned, still eying the confusion around him. He grasped Shef's shoulder in enormous metal fingers, squeezed gently.

"Young madman. Young snotnose. You have done great things today. But remember—men fight to rake together money. Money!" He used the Norse word *fe*, which meant every form of property together, money and metal and goods and livestock. "So forget your machines for a day, young hammerer, and let's all go get rich!"

"But if we have—"

Shef felt the fingers tighten crushingly on his collarbone.

"Now I have told you. And remember, you are still a carl in the Army, like all of us. We fight together, we share together. And by the shining tits of Gerth the Maiden, we are going to loot together. Now get in the ranks!"

Moments later, five hundred men were tramping in dense column into the mouth of one of the streets of the inner city, heading firmly in the direction of the minster. Shef, at the rear, stared at a mail-clad back, hefted his halberd, looked longingly over his shoulder at the little groups left behind.

"Come along," urged Ulf. "Don't worry, Brand left enough men there to guard the loot. It's share and share alike in the Army, and everyone knows it. They're only there to keep off any stragglers from the English."

The advancing column had speeded up almost to a trot and at the same time had shaken out into the familiar

wedge-shape Shef remembered from his first skirmish.
Twice it met resistance; makeshift barricades across the narrow street, desperate Northumbrian thanes hacking at their
enemies across the war-linden while their churls and followers hurled javelins and stones from the houses above them.
The Vikings stormed up, exchanged blows, poured into the
houses, dislodged the archers and spear-throwers, broke
down interior walls to take the English from flank and rear,
acting all the time without orders and without pause, with a
dreadful killing urgency. Each time there was a check, Shef
seized his chance to struggle closer to the front, aiming for
the broad back of Brand. He had to let them take the minster, he realized. But maybe once the loot had been secured,
the precious relics of centuries, he could be spared some
men to seize the machines. And above all, he must be near
the leaders to save prisoners' lives—the lives of the skilled
men, the number-workers.

The Vikings were up to a trot again, Brand only a couple
of ranks in front of him. A turn in the narrow street, the
men on the inside slowing fractionally to let their mates on
the outside keep up—and there was the minster, looming
suddenly above them like the work of giants, not sixty paces
off, set back in its own precinct from the lesser buildings
huddled round it.

And there too were the Northumbrians again, coming on
one last time with the valor of desperation and the house of
their God behind them.

The Vikings checked their rush, heaved shields high
again. Shef, still thrusting forward, found himself suddenly
level with Brand, saw a Northumbrian broadsword swinging
like a meteor at his neck.

Without thought he parried, felt the familiar clang of a
breaking blade, stabbed forward with the lance-head of the
halberd, twisted and jerked to tear his enemy's shield aside.
His back to Brand's, he lashed out blindly with a full-armed
sweep. Space round him, enemies to all sides. He swung
again, the axe-blade of the halberd hissing in the air, changed
grip, and swept back as his enemies tried to dart in beneath

the blows. A miss and another miss, but in those instants the Vikings had re-formed. Their wedge surged forward, the broadswords cutting from all angles, Brand leading them, swinging his axe with a joiner's precision.

As one wave the storming column broke over the English defenders, trampling them down. Shef found himself propelled forward at a run into open space, clear ground all around him, the minster in front, whoops of exultation in his ears.

Dazzled by the sudden gleam of sunshine he saw in front of him—saffron cloaks. Unbelievably, the familiar grinning face of Muirtach, driving a spike into the ground. A line of spikes, roped together, like the rowan-berry line that guarded Thorvin's forge. The whoops died uncertainly.

"Well-run, boys. But ye're off limits here. No one over the rope, d'ye hear?"

Muirtach backed away, spreading his arms, as Brand stepped forward. "Now take it easy, lads. Ye'll get yer share, I make no doubt. But it's all been fixed over yer heads. Ye'd have got yer share even if yer attack had failed, now."

"They came in the back," shouted Shef. "They never followed us this morning at all. They broke in the west gate while we attacked the north!"

"Broke in, nothing," snarled a furious voice. "They were let in. Look!"

Out from the minster door, as composed as ever, still dressed in scarlet and grass-green, strolled Ivar. By his side paced a figure in a garb Shef had not seen since the death of Ragnar a year before: a man in purple and white, a strange, tall hat on his head, a gold-decorated crook of ivory in his hand. As if automatically, he raised his other hand in benediction. The Archbishop of the Metropolitan Province of Eoforwich himself, Wulfhere *Eboracensis*.

"We've done a deal," said Ivar. "The Christ-folk offered to let us into the town on condition the minster itself was spared. I gave my word on it. We can have everything else: the town, the shire, the king's property, everything. But not

the minster or the belongings of the Church. And the Christ-
folk will be our friends and show us just how to wring this
land dry."

"But you are a jarl of the Army," bellowed Brand. "You
have no right to make deals for yourself and leave the rest
of us out."

Theatrically, Ivar moved one shoulder, rotating it and grimacing with exaggerated pain.

"I see your hand is recovered, Brand. When I too am fit
we will have several matters to talk over. But keep your
side of the rope! And keep your men in hand or they'll suffer for it.

"Boys too," he added, his eyes falling on Shef.

From behind the minster men had been pouring, the
Ragnarssons' personal followers in hundreds—fully armed,
fresh, confident, eyeing their scattered and weary comrades
coldly. The Snakeeye stepped out from among them, his
two other brothers flanking him—Halvdan looking grim,
Ubbi for once shamefaced, eyes on the ground as he spoke.

"You did well to get here. Sorry you got a surprise. It will
all be explained in full meeting. But what Ivar says is right.
Stay outside this rope. Keep away from the minster. Apart
from that you can get as rich as you like."

"Small chance of that," shouted an anonymous voice.
"What gold do the Christ-priests leave for anyone else?"

The Snakeeye made no reply. His brother Ivar turned,
gestured. Behind the Ragnarssons a pole rose into the sky,
was driven firmly into the packed earth in front of the minster doors. A jerk on a rope and from it spread—fluttering
limply in the damp wind—the famous Raven Banner, the
brothers' personal ensign, wings spread wide for victory.

Slowly, the once-united group who had stormed the wall
and fought their way through the city lost cohesion, began
to break up, mutter among themselves, count their losses.

"Well, they may have the minster," muttered Shef to himself. "But we can still get at the machines."

"Brand," he called. "Brand. *Now* can I have those twenty
men?"

Chapter Five

A group of men sat together in pale winter sunlight in a
leafless copse outside the walls of York. Cords encircled them, rowan berries dangling scarlet between the
spears. It was a conclave of priests, all the priests of the
Asgarth Way who had accompanied the Army of the Ragnarssons: Thorvin for Thor, Ingulf for Ithun, but others
too—Vestmund the navigator, charter of the stars, priest of
Njörth the sea-god; Geirulf the chronicler of battles, priest
of Tyr; Skaldfinn the interpreter, priest of Heimdall. Most
respected of all for his visions and his travels in the other
worlds, Farman, priest of Frey.

Within their circle was planted the silver spear of Othin,
next to it the sacred fire of Loki. But no priest in the Army
cared to take the great responsibility of the spear of Othin.
There had never been a priest of Loki—though that he ex-
isted was never forgotten.

Inside the roped circle, but sitting apart and silent, were
two laymen, Brand the champion and Hund the apprentice
of Ithun. There to give evidence and, if asked, advice.

Farman spoke, looking round the group. "It is time to
consider our position."

Silent nods of agreement. These were not men to talk
without need.

"We all know that the history of the world, *heimsins
kringla*, the circle of the earth, is not foreordained. But

many of us have seen for many years a vision of the world as it seems it must be.

"A world where the Christ-god is supreme. Where for a thousand years and more men are subject to him alone and to his priests. Then, at the end of that thousand years—the burning and the famine. And all through the thousand years, the fight to keep men as they are, to tell them to forget this world and think only of the next. As if Ragnarök—the battle of gods and men and giants—were already decided and men were sure of victory." His face was as stern as stone as he looked at the circle of priests.

"It is against that world that we have set our faces, and it is that future which we mean to avert. You will remember that by chance I heard in London of the death of Ragnar Hairy-Breeks. Then it came to me in my sleep that this was one of those moments when the history of the world may take a different turn. And so I called on Brand"—he waved a hand at the massive figure hunkered down a few feet away—"to take the news to the sons of Ragnar, and to take it in such a way that they could not refuse the challenge. Few men might have survived that errand. Yet Brand did it, as a duty to us, in the name of the one who will come from the North. Come from the North, we believe, to set the world on its true path."

The men in the circle touched their pendants respectfully.

Farman went on. "It was in my mind that the sons of Ragnar, falling on the Christian kingdoms of England, might break their power and be a mighty force for us, for the Way. I was a fool to guess at the meaning of the gods. A fool, too, to think that good might come from the evil of the Ragnarssons. They are not Christians, but what they do gives the Christians strength. Torture. Violation. The making of *heimnars*."

Ingulf, Hund's master, cut in. "Ivar—he is of the brood of Loki, sent to afflict the earth. He has been seen on the other side—and not as man. He is not one to be used for any good purpose."

"As now we see," replied Farman. "For far from breaking the power of the Christ-god church, he has made alliance with it. For his own ends—and only that fool of an archbishop would trust him. Yet for the moment both are stronger."

"And we are poorer!" growled Brand, driven beyond respect.

"But is Ivar richer?" asked Vestmund. "I cannot see what Ivar and his brothers have from this deal they have made. Except entry into York."

"I can tell you that," said Thorvin. "For I have looked well into this matter. We have all seen how poor their money is here. Little silver, much lead, much copper. Where has all the silver gone? Even the English ask each other that. I can tell you. The Church has taken it.

"We do not understand—even Ivar cannot know—how rich the Church in Northumbria is. They have been here two hundred years and all that time they have taken gifts of silver, and of gold, and of land. And from the land they wring more silver, and from the land they do not own they wring yet more. To splash a child with water, to make her wedding holy, in the end to bury them in holy soil and take away the threat of eternal torment—not for their sins, but for failure to pay the toll."

"But what do they do with this silver?" Farman asked.

"They make ornaments for their god. It all lies now in the minster, as useless as when it was first in the soil. The silver and the gold in their chalices, in their great roods and rood-screens, in the plates for the altar and the boxes for the bodies of their saints—it comes out of the money. The richer the Church, the poorer the coinage." He shook his head in disgust.

"The Church will hand nothing over—and Ivar does not even know what lies in his hand. The priests have told him that they will call in all the coins of the realm and melt them down. Purge out the base metal and leave him only the silver. And then with that they will make him a new coinage. A coinage for Ivar the Victorious, king of York. And Dublin too.

"The Ragnarssons may not be richer. They will be more powerful."

"And Brand, son of Barn, will be poorer!" snarled an angry voice.

"So what we have done," summed up Skaldfinn, "is to bring the Ragnarssons and the Christ-priests together. How sure are you now of your dream, Farman? And what of the world's history and of its future?"

"There is one thing I did not dream then," replied Farman. "But I have dreamed him since. And that is the boy Skjef."

"His name is Shef," put in Hund.

Farman nodded agreement. "Think of it. He defied Ivar. He fought the *holmgang*. He broke the walls of York. And he walked up to Thorvin's meeting months ago and said he was one who came from the North."

"He only meant he came from the north part of the kingdom, from the Northfolk," protested Hund.

"What he meant is one thing, what the gods mean is another," said Farman. "Do not forget also: I saw him on the other side. In the home of the gods itself.

"And there is another strange thing about him. Who is his father? Sigvarth Jarl thinks he is. But for that we have only his mother's word. It comes to me that perhaps this boy is the beginning of the great change, the center of the circle, though no one could have guessed it. And so I have to ask his friends and those who know him a question:

"Is the boy mad?"

Slowly, eyes turned to Ingulf. He raised his eyebrows.

"Mad? That is not a word to be used by a leech. But since you put it to me in that way, I will tell you. Yes, of course the boy Shef is mad. Consider . . ."

Hund found his friend, as he had known he would, standing amid a litter of charred wood and iron at the northeast tower, above the Aldwark, surrounded by a knot of interested pendant-wearers. He slipped between them like an eel.

"Have you worked it out yet?" he asked.

Shef looked up. "I think I have the answer now. There was a monk with each machine, whose duty was to see it destroyed instead of captured. They started the job, then scuttled back to the Minster. The men they left behind had no great desire to see the burning finished. This slave was captured," he nodded at a collared Englishman inside the ring of Vikings. "He told me how it worked. I haven't tried to rebuild the machine, but I understand it now."

He indicated the pile of charred timbers and iron devices.

"This is the machine that fires the bolts."

Shef pointed. "See, the spring is not in the wood, it is in the rope. Twisted rope. This axle is turned and twists the rope which puts more and more force on each bow-arm and the bowstring. Then, at the right moment, you release the bowstring . . ."

"Wham," said one of the Vikings. "And there goes old Tonni."

A grunt of laughter. Shef pointed at the toothed wheels on the frame. "See the rust on them? They are as old as time. I do not know how long it is since the Rome-folk left, or if these things have been lying round in some armory ever since. But anyway, they were not made by the minster-folk. It is all they can do to use them."

"What of the great boulder-machine?"

"They burnt that better. But I already knew how they

were made before we got over the wall. The minster-folk
had all that in a book, and the parts of the machine also, left
over from olden times, so the slave says. I am sorry they
burnt it all, for that alone. And I should like to see the book
that tells how to build machines. That and the book of
numbercraft!"

"Erkenbert has the numbercraft," said the slave suddenly,
catching the Norse word in Shef's still faintly English pronunciation. "He is the *arithmeticus*."

Several Vikings clutched their pendants protectively. Shef
laughed.

"*Arithmeticus* or no *arithmeticus*, I can build a better machine than him. Many machines. The thrall says he heard a
minster-man say once, of themselves and the Rome-folk,
that the Christians now are as dwarves on the shoulders of
giants. Well, they may have the giants to ride on, with their
books and their old machines and old walls left over from
time past. But they are dwarves just the same. And we, we
are—"

"Do not say it," cut in a Viking, stepping forward. "Do
not say the ill-luck word, Skjef Sigvarthsson. We are not
giants, and the giants—the *iötnar*—are the foes of gods and
men. I think you know that. Have you not seen them?"

Shef nodded slowly, thinking of his dream of the uncom-
pleted walls and the gigantic, clumsy stallion-master. His
audience stirred again, looking at each other.

Shef threw the iron parts he was holding onto the floor.
"Let the slave go, Steinulf, in payment for what he has told
us. Show him how to get well away from here, so the
Ragnarssons do not catch him. We can make our own machine without him now."

"Have we time to do it?" asked a Viking.

"All we need is wood. And a little work in the forge.
There are still two days till the Army meeting."

"It is new knowledge," added one of the listeners.
"Thorvin would tell us to do it."

"Meet here tomorrow, in the morning," said Shef decisively.

As they turned away, one of the Vikings said, "They will be a long two days for King Ella. It was a dog's deed of the Christian archbishop to hand him over to Ivar. Ivar has much in store for him."

Shef stared at the departing backs and turned again to his friend.

"What is that you have there?"

"A potion from Ingulf. For you."

"I need no potion. What is it for?"

Hund hesitated. "He says it is to ease your mind. And—and to bring back your memory."

"What is wrong with my memory?"

"Shef, Ingulf and Thorvin say—they say you have forgotten even that we blinded your eye. That Thorvin held you and Ingulf heated the needle, and I, I held it in position. We only did it so it would not be done by some butcher of Ivar's. But they say that it is not natural for you never to speak of it. They believe you have forgotten your blinding. And forgotten Godive, for whom you went into the camp."

Shef stared down at the little leech with his silver apple pendant.

"You can tell them, I have never forgotten either for a moment.

"But still." He stretched out his hand. "I will take your potion."

"He took the potion," Ingulf said.

"Shef is like the bird in the old story," Thorvin said. "The one the Christians tell of how the English in the North became Christian. They say that when the king Edwin called a council to debate whether he and his kingdom should leave the faith of their fathers and take a new one, a priest of the Aesir had said they might as well, for following the old gods had brought him no profit. But then another councillor said, and this is a truer tale, that to him the world seemed like a king's hall on a winter evening—warm and brightly lit inside, but outside dark and cold, and a world no one could see. 'And into that hall,' said the councillor, 'flies a bird, and for a moment it is in the light and the warm, and then flies out into the dark and cold again. If the Christ-god can tell us more surely about what happens before man's life and after man's life,' said the councillor, 'we should seek to learn more of his teaching.' "

"A good story, with some truth," Ingulf said. "I see why you think Shef could be like that bird."

"He could—or he could be something else. When Farman saw him in his vision, in Asgarth, he says he had taken the place of the smith of the gods, Völund. You do not know that story, Hund. Völund was caught and enslaved by the wicked king Nithhad, and hamstrung so that he could work, but not run away. But Völund enticed the king's sons to his forge, killed them, made brooches of their eyeballs and necklaces of their teeth, gave them to their father, his master. Enticed the king's daughter to his forge, stupefied her with beer, raped her."

"Why would he do that if he was still a prisoner?" asked Hund. "If he was too lame to run away?"

"He was the master-smith," said Thorvin. "When the king's daughter awoke, and ran to her father and told him the tale, and he came to kill the slave-smith with torments— then Völund put on the wings he had made secretly in his forge. And flew away, laughing at those who thought him crippled."

"So why is Shef like Völund?"

"He can see up and down. In a direction other men cannot see. It is a great gift, but I fear it is the gift of Othin. Othin Allfather. Othin Bölverk, Othin Bale-worker. Your potion will make him dream, Ingulf. But what will be in those dreams?"

Shef's sinking mind was brooding on taste. The potion Ingulf had sent him had tasted of honey, which was a change from the foul brews he and Hund usually concocted. Yet beneath the sweetness there had been another taste: of mold? of fungus? He did not know, but something dry and rotten beneath the mask. He had known as soon as he drank it that there would be something to be endured.

And yet his dream started sweetly, like one he had had many times before any of his troubles began, before even he had known that they meant him for a thrall.

He was swimming, in the fen. But as he swam on and on the power of his strokes doubled and redoubled, so that the bank seemed to fall away behind him and he was swimming faster than a horse could run. Now his strokes took him clear from the water and he was lifting in the air, no longer striking with his arms, but first climbing, and then, as fear left him, sweeping forward again, rising higher and higher in the air, like a bird. The country beneath him was green and sunny, with the new leaves of spring breaking out everywhere, and meadow rolling higher and higher to sunlit uplands. Suddenly dark. In front of him now there was an immense column of darkness. He had, he knew, been there before. But then he had been in the column, or on the column, looking out: he did not want to see again what he had seen then. The king, the king Edmund, with his sad and tortured face and his backbone in his hand. If he flew in carefully, and did not look out or back, he might not see him this time.

Slowly, cautiously, the wandering soul closed on the enormous darkened tree-trunk. To it was nailed, as he had known there would be, a figure with a spike projecting from its eye. He looked at the face with care—was it his own?

It was not. Its one whole eye was closed. It appeared to take no interest in him.

By the figure's head there hovered two black birds, with black beaks: ravens. They turned bright eyes on him, cocking their heads curiously. The flight pinions of their wings ruffled and shifted slightly as they maintained their positions without strain or effort. The figure was Othin, or Woden, and the ravens were his constant companions.

What were their names? That was the important thing. He had heard them somewhere. In Norse they were—That was right, Hugin and Munin. In English that would be Hyge and Myne. Hugin/Hyge. That meant "mind." That was not the one he wanted. As if dismissed, the one raven spiraled down, perched on its master's shoulder.

Munin/Myne. That meant "memory." That was what he wanted. But he would have to pay for it. He had a friend, a protector among the gods, so much he realized already. But it was not Othin, whatever Brand might think. So a price must be paid. He knew what the price must be. Again unbidden, another scrap of verse came to him, again in English. It described the hanged man, on the gallows, who swayed there creaking for the birds, unable to raise a hand to protect himself, while the black ravens came . . .

Came for his eyes. For his eye. The bird was there suddenly, so close that it blocked out all other sight, its black beak like an arrow only an inch from his eye. Not his good eye, though. His bad eye. The one he had already lost. But this was memory, back in a time when he still had it. His hands were down, he could not move them. That was because Thorvin was holding them. No, he could move them this time, but he must not. He would not.

The bird realized he would not move. It came forward with a shriek of triumph, driving its nail of a beak deep through his eye and into his brain. As the white-hot pain stabbed through him, the words shot into his head: the words of the doomed king.

*In willow ford, by woody bridge
The old kings lie, keels beneath them.
On down they sleep, deep home guarding.
Four fingers push in flattest line,
From underground. Grave the northmost.
There lies Wuffa, Wehha's offspring,
On secret hoard. Seek who dares it.*

He had done his duty. The bird released him. He fell instantly from the tree-trunk, tumbling without control, hands still locked, toward the ground miles below. Plenty of time

*to think what to do. No need for hands. He could just turn
his body whichever way was needed, turn and roll till he
was heading out into the sun once more, turn and dip till he
was spiraling down gently to the place where he should be,
where his body lay on straw.*

*Strange to see the land from here, and the people and the
armies and the merchants coming and going, many of them
spurring furiously, but not moving at all beneath his enormous twenty-mile circuits. He could see the fen, he could
see the sea, he could see the great tumuli, the barrows
swelling up beneath green turf. He would remember that,
think of it another time. Now he had only one duty, and he
would carry it out as soon as his spirit was back in its right
place, in the body he could now see on its mattress, in the
body he was entering. . . .*

Shef jerked from sleep in one motion. "I must remember,
but I cannot write," he called in dismay.

"I can," said Thorvin, on his stool six feet away, dimly
visible by the banked fire.

"Can you? Write like a Christian?"

"I can write like a Christian. But I can write like a Norseman too, or a priest of the Way. I can write in runes. What
do you want me to write?"

"Write it quickly," said Shef. "I bought this from Munin
with pain."

Thorvin kept his eyes down as he took a beech board and
a knife and prepared to cut.

> " *'In willow ford, by woody bridge*
> *The old kings lie, keels beneath them. . . .' "*

"It is hard to write English in runes," Thorvin muttered.
But he muttered it beneath his breath.

The Army mustered—in distrust and ill humor, three weeks
before the day the Christians celebrated the birth of their
God—on the open space outside the city's east wall. Seven

thousand men take up a good deal of space, especially when all are both fully armed and heavily wrapped against the wind and intermittent sleet. But since Shef had fired the remaining houses on that side there was room enough to spread everyone in a rough half-circle from wall to wall.

In the midst of the semicircle stood the Ragnarssons and their supporters, the Raven Banner behind them. A few paces away, gripped and encircled by a flutter of saffron plaids, waited the black-haired figure of the king—of the ex-king Ella. His face was as white, Shef reflected from his place in the semicircle thirty yards away, as white as the white of a cooked egg.

For Ella was doomed. The Army had not pronounced yet, but it was certain as fate. Soon Ella would hear the clash of weapons by which the Army signaled assent. And then they would start on him, as they had on Shef, as they had on King Edmund, on King Maelguala and all the other Irish kinglets on whom Ivar had sharpened his teeth and his techniques. There was no hope for Ella. He had put Ragnar in the orm-garth. Even Brand, even Thorvin accepted that a man's sons had a right to take revenge in kind. More than a right, a duty. The Army watched judiciously, to see that the job was done well and warriorlike.

But it sat, or rather stood, also in judgement on its own leaders. It was not only Ella who was at risk here. Not even Ivar Ragnarsson, not even Sigurth the Snakeeye himself, could this time be absolutely sure of walking from the meeting with a whole skin, or with an undamaged reputation. There was tension in the air.

As the sun reached what passed for midday in the English winter, Sigurth called the Army to business.

"We are the Great Army," he called out. "We are met to talk over what has been done and what should be done next. I have things to say. But first I heard that there are men in the Army who are not content with how this city was taken. Will one of them speak openly before us all?"

A man stepped forward from the ring, walked into the open space in the middle, and turned so that both his own supporters and the Ragnarssons could hear him. It was Skuli the Bald, who had led the second tower up to the wall, but had wrecked it without getting over.

"Put-up job," muttered Brand. "Been paid to speak, but not too hard."

"I am not content," called out Skuli. "I led my crews to attack the wall of this city. I lost a dozen men, including my brother-in-law, a good man. We got over the wall just the same and fought our way up to the minster. But then we were prevented from sacking the minster, as was our right. And we found that we did not need to lose the men, because the city was already taken. We got neither plunder nor compensation. Why did you let us attack the wall like fools, Sigurth, when you knew we had no need to?"

A rumble of agreement, some catcalls from Ragnarsson crews. Sigurth stepped forward in his turn, silencing the noise with a wave.

"I thank Skuli for saying this, and I admit that he has right on his side. But I want to say two things. First, I did not know he had no need to. We could not be sure that we would get in. The priests could have been lying to us. Or if the king had found it, he might have put his own men on the gate that was opened. If we had told the whole Army about it, some slave might have heard and passed the news. So we kept it to ourselves.

"The other thing I have to say is this: I did not think Skuli and his men would get over the wall. I did not think they would even get to the wall. These machines, these towers, they are something we have never seen before. I thought they were a toy, and that everything would be finished with just some arrowshot and wasted sweat. If I had known different I would have told Skuli not to risk his life and waste his men. I was wrong, and I am sorry."

Skuli nodded in a dignified way and walked back to his place.

"Not enough!" yelled a voice from the crowd. "What about compensation? Wergild for our losses!"

"How much did you get from the priests?" yelled another. "And why don't we all share?"

Sigurth raised a hand again. "That's more like it. I ask the Army: what are we here for?"

Brand stepped out, waving his axe, back of his neck purpling instantly with the effort in his shout. "Money!"

But even his voice was drowned in the chorus: "Money! Wealth! Gold and silver! Tribute!"

As the tumult died down, Sigurth shouted back. He had the meeting well in hand, Shef realized. All this was going according to a plan, and even Brand was going along with it.

"And what do you want the money *for*?" called Sigurth. Confusion, doubt, shouts of different answers—some ribald.

The Snakeeye drove on over them. "I'll tell you. You want to buy a place back home, with people to till it for you, and to never touch a plough again. Now I'm telling you this: there's not enough money here to get you what you want. Not good money." He threw a handful of coins derisively on the ground. The men recognized the useless low-alloy coinage they had found so often already.

"But that isn't to say we can't get it. Just that it's going to take time."

"Time for what, Sigurth? Time for you to hide your take?"

The Snakeeye stepped a little forward, his strange white-rimmed eyes searching the crowd for the man who had accused him. His hand reached for his sword-pommel.

"I know this is open meeting," he called, "where all may speak freely. But if anyone accuses me or my brothers of not acting like warriors, then we will call him to account for it outside the meeting!

"Now I tell you. We took a ransom from the minster, right enough. Those of you who stormed the wall took loot as well, from the dead and from the houses inside the wall. All of us profited from what was taken outside the minster."

"But all the gold was inside the minster!" That was

Brand shouting, still incensed, and well forward so that he could not be mistaken.

A cold look from Sigurth, but no check. "I tell you. We will all pool all that we took—ransom, loot, whatever—and divide it up crew by crew as has always been the custom of the Army.

"And then we will lay a further tribute on this shire and this kingdom, to be delivered before the end of the winter. They will pay in bad metal, sure enough. But we will take that metal and melt the silver out of it and coin it again ourselves. And *that* we will divide up so that everyone gets his share.

"Only one thing. To do that we need the mint." A buzz as the unfamiliar word was repeated. "We need the men to make the coins and the tools to make them with. And they are in the minster. They are the Christian priests. I have never said this before, but I say it now.

"We have to make the priests work with us."

This time the dissension in the Army went on a long time, with many men stepping forward and speaking confusedly. Shef realized slowly that Sigurth's point was being carried, had a certain appeal to men tired of profitless harrying. yet there was determined resistance—from adherents of the Way, from men who simply disliked and distrusted Christians, from those whose still resented losing the sack of the minster.

And the resistance was not dying down. Violence at a meeting was almost unheard-of, for the penalties were so severe. Yet the crowd was fully armed, even to mail, shields and helmets, and every man in it used to striking out. There was always the chance of an outburst. The Snakeeye was going to have to do something, Shef thought, to get the crowd back under control. Just at the moment one man—it was Egil from Skaane, who had taken a tower to the wall—had got the attention of the Army with a furious diatribe about the treachery of the Christians.

"And one more thing," he shouted. "We know the Christians never keep their word to us, because they think that only the followers of their god will live after death. But I tell you what is more dangerous. They make other men start to forget their word as well. Start to think a man may say one thing one day and another another, and tell the priest and ask for forgiveness, and wipe away the past like a housewife wiping shit off a baby's bottom. And I say this for you! For you, the sons of Ragnar!"

He turned to face the cluster of brothers, stepping closer to them in defiance—a brave man, thought Shef, and an angry one. He threw back his cloak deliberately to reveal the silver horn of Heimdall gleaming on his tunic.

"How have you remembered your father, who went to his death in the orm-garth here, inside this city? How have you remembered the boasts you made in the hall at Roskilde, when you stood on the stock and made your vows to Bragi?

"What happens to the oath-breakers in the world we believe in? Have you forgotten?

A voice supported him from the throng: a deep voice, a solemn one. Thorvin's, Shef realized, quoting the holy poems.

> *"There men writhe in woe and anguish,*
> *Murder-wolves and men forsworn.*
> *Nithhögg sucks blood from naked bodies,*
> *The wolf tears them. Do you wish more?"*

"Men forsworn!" shouted Egil. He turned and walked to his place, showing the Ragnarssons his back. Yet they seemed pleased, almost relieved. They had known someone would say it.

"We have been challenged," called Halvdan Ragnarsson, speaking for the first time. "Let us reply. We know well what we said in the hall at Roskilde, and this was it: I swore that I would invade England in vengeance for my father . . ." All four brothers, bunching together, began to call out the words in unison.

"And so I have. And Sigurth, he swore . . ."

"... to defeat all the kings of the English and bring them into subjection to us."

"Two I have defeated, and the rest will follow."

Yells of approval from the Ragnarsson followers.

"And Ivar, he swore ..."

"... to wreak vengeance on the black crows, the Christ-priests who counseled the orm-garth."

Dead silence, for Ivar to speak.

"And this I have not done. But it is unfinished, not forgotten. Remember: the black crows are now in my hand. I shall decide when to close it."

Still dead silence. Ivar went on. "But Ubbi, my brother, he swore ..."

The brothers in unison again. "... to capture King Ella and kill him with torments for Ragnar's death."

"And this we shall do," called Ivar. "So two of our boasts will be completed, and two of us free before Bragi, the oath-god. And the other two we shall yet complete."

"Bring out the prisoner."

Muirtach and his gang were hustling him forward instantly. The Ragnarssons were counting on this, Shef realized, to alter the mood of the crowd. He remembered the youth who had shown him round the slave-pens back at the camp on the Stour, with his tales of the cruelty of Ivar. There were always some who would be impressed. Yet it was not clear that this crowd was.

They had Ella well out in front now, and were hammering a thick pole into the earth. The king was even whiter than before, the black hair and beard showing it even more clearly. He was not gagged, his mouth was open, but no sound came out. There was blood on the side of his neck.

"Ivar's cut his voice-cords," said Brand suddenly. "They do it with pigs so they can't squeal. What's the brazier for?"

The Gaddgedlar, hands padded, were lifting forward a brazier full of glowing coal. Irons projected from it ominously, already shining red-hot. The crowd surged and muttered, some pushing forward for a closer look, others

sensing, apparently, that this was a distraction from their
real business, but unsure how to reject it.

Muirtach whisked the cloak suddenly from the doomed
man so that he stood naked before them, not even a loin-
cloth to cover him. Some laughter, some jeers, some groans
of disapproval. Four Gaddgedlar gripped him and spread-
eagled him upright between them. Ivar stepped in front, a
knife glinting in his hand. He bent towards Ella's belly, between the king and Shef's horrified gaze, not a dozen yards
off. A mighty contortion, a thrashing of limbs, held mercilessly by the four apostates.

Ivar stepped back, a coil of something blue-gray and slippery in his hand.

"He's opened his belly and pulled his gut out," commented
Brand.

Ivar stepped over to the pole, pulling gently but remorse-
lessly on the uncoiling intestine, watching the look of despair and agony on the king's face with a half-smile. He
reached the pole, took a hammer, nailed in the free end
he had extracted.

"Now," he called out. "King Ella will walk round the
pole till he pulls his own heart out and dies. Come, Englishman. The quicker you walk, the quicker it will be over. But
it may take a few turns before you reach that. You have ten
yards to walk, by my count. Is that so much to ask? Start
him, Muirtach."

The henchman stepped forward, brand glowing, thrust it
against the doomed king's buttock. A convulsive start, a
face turning gray, a slow shuffle.

This was the worst death a man could face, thought Shef.
No pride, no dignity. The only way out, to do what your enemies wanted, and to be jeered for it. Knowing you must do
it and come to an end, and yet not able to do it quickly. The
hot irons behind so you could not even choose your own
pace. Not even a voice to scream. And all the time your
bowels pulling out from inside.

He passed his halberd silently to Brand, and slipped back
through the shoving, craning crowd. There were faces look-

ing down from the tower where he had left his helpers to keep an eye on their machine. A rope snaking down as they realized what he wanted. A scramble up the wall to the familiar clean smell of new-sawn wood and new-forged iron.

"He has walked round the pole three times," said one of the Vikings on the tower, a man with the phallus of Frey round his neck. "That is no way for any man to go."

Bolt in place, the machine swiveled round—they had thought, yesterday, to rest the bottom frame on a pair of stout wheels. Barb upright between the vanes, three hundred yards, it would still shoot a little high.

Shef aimed the tip of the barb on the wound at the base of the king's belly as he hobbled round to face the wall a fourth time, red-hot brands urging him on. Shef squeezed the release slowly.

The thump, the line rising and falling—clear through the center of Ella's chest and straining heart, and on into the ground behind him, almost between Muirtach's feet. As the king was hurled backward by the force of the blow, Shef saw his face change. Relax in peace.

Slowly the crowd rippled, every face in it turning to face the tower from which the shot had come. Ivar bent over the corpse, but then straightened, turning too, hands clenched.

Shef took one of the new halberds and went down the wall toward the throng, wanting to be recognized. At the edge of the semicircle he stopped, vaulted onto the battlement.

"I am only a carl," he called out, "not a jarl. But I have three things to say to the Army:

"First, the sons of Ragnar fulfilled this bit of their Bragi boast because they had no heart to fulfill the rest.

"And second, whatever the Snakeeye says, when he sneaked into York by the back door with the priest holding it open for him, he was not thinking of the Army's good, but of his own and of his brothers'. He had no mind to fight and no mind to share."

Shouts of anger, the Gaddgedlar whirling, looking for the gate into the city and the steps up to where Shef stood. Oth-

ers obstructing them, grabbing at their plaids. Shef raised
his voice even more above the din.

"And third: to treat a man and a warrior the way they
treated King Ella has no *drengskapr*. I call it *nithingsverk*."

The work of a *nithing*, a man beneath honor, a man with
no legal rights, worse than an outlaw. To be proclaimed
nithing before the Army was the worst shame a carl—or a
jarl—could endure. If the Army agreed.

Some people were shouting agreement. Shef could see
Brand down there, axe raised now and ready to strike, his men
clustering behind him, thrusting off Ragnarsson followers with
their shields. A stream of men coming from the other side of
the circle to join him—Egil the Heimdall-worshipper at their
head. Who was that moving out? Sigvarth, face flushed as he
shouted reply to some insult. Skuli the Bald wavering by
Ella's corpse as Ubbi bellowed something at him.

The whole Army was moving. Dividing. After a hundred
heartbeats there was space between the two groups and both
were edging further away from each other. The Ragnarssons
in front of the furthest group; in front of the nearer one,
Brand, Thorvin, a handful of others.

"It is the Way against the rest," muttered the Frey-
worshipper behind Shef. "And some of your friends thrown
in. Two to one against us, I reckon."

"You have split the Army," said a Hebridean, one of
Magnus's crew. "It is a great deed, but a rash one."

"The machine was wound," replied Shef. "All I had to do
was shoot it."

Chapter Six

A s the army marched away from the walls of York,
snowflakes started to drift out of the windless sky. Not
the Great Army. The Great Army would never exist again.

That part of the once-great army which now refused the command of the Ragnarssons and could no longer live in fellowship with them—perhaps twenty long hundreds of men, two thousand four hundred by the Roman count. With them were a host of horses, pack-horses, pack-mules and fifty wooden carts creaking along with their burden of heavy loot: bronze and iron, smith-tools and grindstones—along with the chests of poor coinage and a meager handful of true silver from the division. Their burden, too, of wounded men not fit to march or straddle a pony.

From the city walls, the rest of the army watched them go. Some of the younger and wilder members had whooped and jeered, even launched a few arrows at the ground behind their former messmates. But the silence of the marching column, and of their own leaders on the wall, cast down their spirits. They pulled their cloaks tighter about them, and looked up at the sky, the lowering horizon, the frostbitten grass on the slopes outside the city. Grateful for their own billets, stored firewood, shuttered windows and draftless walls.

"It will snow harder before tomorrow's dawn," muttered Brand from his position at the rear of the column, the main point of danger till they were well past the Ragnarssons' reach.

"You are Norsemen," replied Shef. "I thought snow would not bother you."

"All right while the frost stays hard," said Brand. "If it snows and then thaws, like it does in this country, we'll be marching through mud. Tires the men out, tires the beasts out, slows the carts even more. And when you're marching in those conditions, you need food. You know how long it takes an ox-team to eat its own weight? But we must put some distance between us and those behind. No telling what they'll do now."

"Where are we making for?" asked Shef.

"I don't know. Who's leading this army anyway? Everybody else thinks you are."

Shef fell silent, in consternation.

* * *

As the last bundled figures of the rear-guard disappeared from view among the ruined houses of outer York, the Ragnarssons on the wall turned and looked at each other.

"Good riddance," said Ubbi. "Fewer mouths to feed, fewer hands to share. What are a few hundred Way-folk anyway? Soft hands, weak stomachs."

"No one ever called Viga-Brand soft-handed," replied Halvdan. Since the holmgang he had been slow to join in his brothers' attacks on Shef and his faction. "They're not all Way-folk, either."

"It doesn't matter what they are," said Sigurth. "They're enemies now. That's all you ever need to know about anyone. But we can't afford to fight them just yet. We have to keep our hold on . . ."

He jerked his thumb at the little cluster a few yards away from them on the wall: Wulfhere the archbishop with a knot of black monks, among them the scrawny pallor of Erkenbert the deacon, now master of the mint.

Ivar laughed, suddenly. His three brothers looked at him with unease.

"We don't need to fight them," he said. "Their own bane marches with them. For some it does."

Wulfhere too scowled at the retreating column. "Some of the blood-wolves gone," he said. "If they had gone earlier we might never have needed to treat with the rest. But now they are within our gates." He spoke in Latin, to make sure hostile ears did not overhear.

"We must, in these days of strife, live by the wisdom of the serpent," replied Erkenbert in the same language, "and by the cunning of the dove. But both our foes without the gates and those within may yet be overcome."

"Those within I understand. There are fewer of them now, and they may be fought again. Not by us in Northumbria. But by the kinds of the South—Burgred of Mercia, Ethelred of Wessex. That is why we sent south the crippled thane of East Anglia, slung between his ponies. He will show the southern kings the nature of the Vikings and wake their drowsy spirits to war.

"But what, Erkenbert, is your plan for those now marching away? What can we do in dead of winter?"

The little deacon smiled. "Those marching in winter need food, and the ravagers of the North are accustomed to take it. But every mouthful they steal now is one less for a man's children before spring comes. Even churls will fight with that incentive.

"I have seen to it that the word of their coming will run before them."

The attacks began as the short winter daylight seeped from the sky. At first they were little more than scuffles: a churl appearing from behind a tree, launching a stone or an arrow downwind, and then fleeing hastily, not even waiting to see if he hit the mark. Then a little knot of them coming in closer. The marching Vikings unslung bows if they had them, tried to keep the bowstrings dry, shot back. Otherwise they ducked heads behind shields, let the missiles bounce off, shouted derisively to their foes to stand and fight. Then one, irritated, launched a spear at a darting figure who seemed to come too close, missed and plunged off the track with a curse to recover it. For an instant a snow-flurry hid him. When it cleared he was nowhere to be seen. With difficulty his crewmates halted the column, plodding, head-down, and set off grimly to rescue him, a group thirty strong. As they lurched back with the body, already stripped and mutilated, the arrows came whipping from behind them again, out of the murk of the dying day.

The column was now spread over almost a mile of road. Skippers and helmsmen pushed and cursed the men into a thicker, shorter line, bowmen on both flanks, carts in the center. "They can't hurt you," Brand bellowed repeatedly. "Not with hunting bows. Just shout and bang your shields; they'll wet themselves and run. Anyone gets hit in the leg, sling him on a packhorse. Dump some of that junk in the carts if you have to. But keep moving forward."

Soon the English churls began to recognize what they could do. Their enemies were laden with gear, heavily wrapped and muffled. They did not know the country. The churls knew every tree, bush, path and patch of mud. They could strip to tunics and hose, rush in light-footed, strike and slash and be away before an arm was free of its cloak. No Viking would pursue more than a few feet into the gloom.

After a while some village war-leader organized the growing number of men. Forty or fifty of the churls came in together on the west flank of the column, beat down the few men they faced with clubs and billhooks, started to drag off the bodies like wolves with their prey. Furious, the Vikings rallied and charged after them, shields up, axes raised. As they straggled back, snarling, having caught no one, they saw the halted carts, the ox-teams poleaxed where they stood. The wagon tilts pulled open, their cargo of wounded men a burden no longer, the snow already blotting out the stains.

Prowling up and down the column like an ice-troll, Brand turned to Shef at his side. "They think they've got us now," he snarled. "But come daylight I'll teach them a lesson for this if it's the last thing I ever do."

Shef stared at him, blinking the snow from his eyes. "No," he said. "You are thinking like a carl, a carl of the Army. There is no Army anymore. So now we must forget to think like carls. Instead we must think as you say I do, like a follower of Othin, orderer of battle."

"And what are your orders, little man? Little man who has never stood in the battle-line?"

"Call over the skippers, as many as are within earshot." Shef began to draw swiftly in the snow.

"We marched through Eskrick, here, before the snow got bad. We must be a short mile north of Riccall." Nods, understanding. The area around York was well known from much foraging.

"I want one hundred picked men, young men, quick on their feet, not yet tired, to push ahead now and secure

Riccall. Take some prisoners—we'll need them—chase the others out. We will stay there the night. Not much, fifty huts and a church of wattles. But they will shelter a lot of us if we pack in close.

"Another long hundred in four small groups to keep moving up and down on our flanks. The English won't rush in if they even think there might be someone out there to cut them off. Without their cloaks they'll keep warm running. Everyone else, just keep going and keep the carts going. As soon as we reach Riccall, use the carts to block all the gaps between the huts. Oxen and all of us on the inside of the ring. We'll make fires and rig up shelters. Brand, pick the man, get everyone moving."

Two crowded hours later, Shef sat on a stool in the thane's longhouse of Riccall, staring at a grizzled elderly Englishman. The house was packed with Vikings, stretched out or squatting on their heels, already steaming as massed body heat dried the sodden clothes on their backs. As ordered, none paid any attention to what was going on.

Between the two men, on the rough table, stood a leather mug of beer. Shef took a pull at it, looked closely at the man facing him; he seemed to still have his wits about him. There was an iron collar round his neck.

Shef pushed the mug toward him. "You saw me drink, you know there is no poison. Go on, drink. If I wanted to harm you there are easier ways."

The thrall's eyes widened at the fluent English. He took the mug, drank deeply.

"Who is the lord you pay your rents to?"

The man finished the beer before he spoke. "Thane Ednoth holds much of the land, from King Ella. Killed in the battle. The rest belongs to the black monks."

"Did you pay your rents last Michaelmas? If you did not, I hope you hid the money. The monks are severe with defaulters."

A flash of fear when Shef spoke of the monks and their retribution.

"If you wear a collar, you know what the monks do with runaways. Hund, show him your neck."

Silently Hund unslung his Ithun pendant and handed it to Shef, pulled back his tunic to reveal the calluses and weals worn into his neck by years of the collar.

"Have any runaways been here? Men who spoke to you of these." Shef bounced the Ithun pendant in his hand, passed it back to Hund. "Or those." He pointed to Thorvin, Vestmund, Farman and the other priest, clustered nearby. Following the gesture, they too silently displayed their insignia.

"If they did, maybe they told you such men might be trusted."

The slave lowered his eyes, trembled. "I'm a good Christian. I don't know about no pagan things. . . ."

"I'm talking about trust—not pagan or Christian."

"You Vikings are men who take slaves, not men who set them free."

Shef reached forward and tapped the iron collar. "It was not the Vikings who put that on you. Anyway, I am an Englishman. Can you not tell from my speech? Now listen closely. I am going to let you go. Tell those out there in the night to stop the attacks, because we are not their enemies—they are still in York. If your fellows let us pass, no one will get hurt. Then tell your friends about this banner."

Shef pointed across the smoky, steaming room to a clutch of the army's drabs, who rose from the floor and stretched out the great banner at which they had been frantically stitching. There, on a background of red silk, taken from the carts of plunder, a double-headed smith's hammer in white linen was picked out with silver thread.

"The other army, the one we have left, marches behind the black raven, the carrion bird. I say that the sign of the Christians is for torture and death. Our sign is the sign of a maker. Tell them that. And I will give you an earnest of what the hammer can do for you. We're taking off your collar."

The slave was shaking with fear. "No, the black monks, when they return . . ."

"They will kill you most horribly. Remember this and tell the others. We offered to free you, we pagans. But fear of the Christians is keeping you a slave. Now go."

"One thing I ask. In fear. Do not kill me for speaking of it but—your men are emptying the meal-bins, taking our winter store. There'll be empty bellies and dead bairns before spring comes if you do that."

Shef sighed. This was going to be the hard bit. "Brand. Pay the thrall. Pay him something. Pay him in good silver, mind, not the archbishop's dross."

"Me pay him! He should pay me. What about the wergild for the men we have lost? And since when did the Army pay for its supplies?"

"There is no Army now. And he owes you no wergild. You trespassed on his land. Pay him. I'll see you don't lose by it."

Brand muttered under his breath as he untied his purse and began to count out six silver Wessex pennies.

The slave could scarcely believe what was happening, staring at the shining coins as though he had never seen money like this before; perhaps he hadn't.

"I will tell them," he said, almost shouting the words. "About the banner too."

"If you do that, and return here tonight, I will pay you six more—for you alone, not to share."

Brand, Thorvin and the others looked doubtfully at Shef as the slave went out, with an escort to see him outside the sentry-fires.

"You'll never see money nor slave again," Brand said.

"We'll see. Now I want two long hundreds of men, with our best horses, all with a good meal inside them, ready to move as soon as the slave returns."

Brand pushed a shutter open a crack and looked at the night and the whirling snow. "What for?" he grunted.

"I need to get your twelve pennies back. And I have another idea." Slowly, intense concentration furrowing his

brow, Shef began to scratch lines into the table in front of
him with the point of his knife.

The black monks of St. John's Minster at Beverley, unlike
those of St. Peter's at York, did not have the safe walls of
a legionary fortress round them. Instead, their tenants and
the men of the flatlands east of the Yorkshire Wolds could
easily put two thousand stout warriors into the field, with
many more half-armed spearmen and bowmen to back
them. All through the autumn of raids of York, they had
known themselves safe against anything but a move by a
major detachment of the Great Army. They had known it
must come. The sacristan had disappeared months since
with all the minster's most precious relics, reappearing days
later with word only for the abbot himself. They had kept
half their fighting force mobilized, the rest dispersed among
their holdings to oversee the harvest and the preparations for
winter. Tonight they felt secure. Their watchers had seen the
Great Army split, one detachment even marching away to
the South.

But a midwinter night in England is sixteen hours long
between sunset and dawn: more than time enough for determined men to ride forty miles. Guided on their way through
muddy, meandering farm-tracks for the first few miles, then
picking up speed as they walked or trotted their horses
along the better roads of the Wolds. They had lost a little
time circumventing each village they came to. The slave,
Tida, had guided them well, abandoning them only as the
first paling sky had shown them the steeple of Beverley
Minster itself. The guard-huts just beginning to disgorge
sleepy female quern-slaves, to light the fires and grind the
grain for the breakfast porridge. At the sight of the Vikings
they ran shrieking and wailing, to drag incredulous warriors
from their blankets. To be called fools for their pains and to
become part of the utter confusion which was the English
way of taking surprise.

Shef pushed open the great wooden doors of the minster
and walked in, his companions jostling behind.

From inside the minster came the antiphonal song of the choirmonks, facing each other across the nave and singing sweetly the anthems which called the Christ-child to be born. There were no other worshippers, though the doors were unbolted for them. The monks sang lauds every day, whether they were joined or not. At dawn on a winter morning they would not expect to be.

As the Vikings paced down the aisle which led to the high altar—still wrapped in sodden cloaks, no weapons showing except for the halberd over Shef's shoulder—the abbot looked at them in shocked horror from his great seat in the choir. For a moment Shef's nerve and wit faltered in the face of the majesty of the Church he had grown up in, worshipped in.

He cleared his throat, unsure how to begin.

Guthmund behind him, a skipper from the Swedish shore of the Kattegat, had no such doubts or scruples. All his life he had wanted to be at the sack of a really first-class church or abbey, and he had no intention of letting a beginner's nerves spoil it. Courteously he picked his young leader up and put him to one side, seized the nearest choir-monk by his black robe and hurled him into the aisle, dragged his axe from under his cloak and embedded it with a thunk into the altar-rail.

"Grab the blackrobes," he bellowed. "Search 'em, put 'em in that corner there. Tofi, get those candlesticks. Frani, I want all that plate. Snok and Uggi, you're lightweights, see that statue there . . ." He waved at the great crucifix, high above the altar, looking down at them with sorrowing eyes. "Shin up it and see if you can get that crown off, looks genuine from here. The rest of you, turn everything over and shake it, grab everything that looks as if it might gleam. I want this place clear before those bastards behind us have got their boots on. Now, you . . ." He advanced on the abbot shrinking back in his throne.

Shef forced his way between them. "Now, father," he began, speaking again in English. The familiar language drew a basilisk stare from the abbot, terrified but at the same time mortally offended. Shef wavered a moment—then remembered the inside of the minster door, covered, like many, with skin on the inside. Human skin, flayed from a living body for the sin of sacrilege, of laying hands on Church property. He hardened his heart.

"Your guards will be here soon. If you want to stay alive you will have to keep your men off."

"No!"

"Then you die now." The point of his halberd pushed at the priest's throat.

"For how long?" The abbot's shaking hands were on the halberd, could not move it back.

"Not long. Then you may hunt us, recover your stolen goods. So do as I say . . ."

Crashes of destruction behind, a monk being dragged forward by Guthmund. "I think this is the sacristan. He says the hoard is empty."

"True," the abbot admitted. "All was hidden months ago."

"What's hidden can be found again," said Guthmund. "I'll start on the youngest, just to show I mean it. One, two dead, the hoard-keeper will speak."

"You will not," Shef ordered. "We'll take them with us. There will be no torture among those who follow the Way. The Asa-gods forbid it. And we have taken a fair haul. Now get them out where the minster-guards can see them. We still have a long ride ahead."

In the growing light, Shef noticed something hanging on the wall: a flattened roll of vellum with no image on it that he could recognize.

"What's that?" he asked the abbot.

"It has no value to one like you. No gold, no silver on the frame. It is a *mappamundi*. A map of the world."

Shef tore it down, rolled it, thrust it deep inside his tunic as they hustled the abbot and the choirmonks out to face the ragged battle-line of Englishmen at last roused from bed.

"We'll never make it back," muttered Guthmund again as he clutched a clanking sack.

"Not going back," answered Shef. "You'll see."

Chapter Seven

Burgred, king of Mercia, one of the two great kingdoms of England still unconquered by the Vikings, paused at the entrance to his private chambers, dismissed the crowd of attendants and hangers-on, doffed his mantle of martenfur, allowed his snow-soaked boots to be removed and replaced by slippers of soft whittawed leather, and prepared to enjoy the moment. By command, the young man and his father were waiting for him, as was the atheling Alfred, there to represent his brother Ethelred, king of Wessex—the other surviving great English kingdom.

The issue before them was the fate of East Anglia. Its king dead with no successor, its people demoralized and uncertain. Yet Burgred knew well that if he marched an army to take it over, to add it to Mercia by force, the East Angles might well fight, Englishmen against Englishmen, as they had so often before. But if he sent them a man of their own, he calculated—one of noble blood, one who nevertheless owed absolutely everything, including the army he led with him, to King Burgred—well, that they might swallow.

Especially as this particular noble and grateful young man had such a very useful father. One who, so to speak— Burgred allowed himself a grim smile—carried his anti-Viking credentials with him. Who could fail to rally to such a figurehead? A figure-head and -trunk, indeed. Burgred blessed, silently, the day the two ponies with their leaders and their slung stretcher had brought him in from York.

And the beautiful young woman too. How affecting it had been. The young man, fair hair swept back, kneeling at his father's feet before ever they had unstrapped him from his litter, and begging forgiveness for having married without his father's consent. The pair might have been forgiven for more than that after all they had been through, but no, young Alfgar had been the essence of propriety all through. It was the spirit that would one day make the English the greatest of all nations. Decency, mused Burgred: *gedafenlicnis.*

What Alfgar had really muttered as he knelt at his father's feet had been: "I married Godive, father. I know she's my half sister, but don't say anything of it, or I'll tell everyone you're mad. And then an accident could happen to you. Men with no arms smother easily. And don't forget, we're both your children. If we succeed, your grandsons could still be princes. Or better."

And after the first shock, it had seemed well enough to Wulfgar. True, they had committed incest, "sibb-laying," as the English called it. But what did a trifle like that matter? Thryth, his own lady, had committed fornication with a heathen Viking, and who had done anything about that? If Alfgar and Godive had an incest child like Sigemund and his sister in the legends, it could be no worse than that gadderling brat he, Wulfgar, had been fool enough to rear.

As the king of the Mercians strode into the room, the men in it rose and bowed. The one woman, the East Anglian beauty with the sad face and the brilliant eyes, rose and made her courtesy in the new style of the Franks. Two attendants—they had been arguing quietly about the right thing to do—lifted Wulfgar's padded box to the vertical before leaning it back against the wall. At a gesture they resumed their seats: stools for all but the king and the heimnar. Wulfgar too was lifted into a highseat with wooden arms. He could not have balanced himself to sit on a stool.

"I have news from Eoforwich," began the king. "Later news than you brought," with a nod to Wulfgar. "And better news. Still, it has decided me to act.

"It seems that after the surrender by the Church of the town and of King Ella—"

"Say, rather," cut in the young atheling from Wessex, "the disgraceful betrayal of King Ella by those he had protected."

Burgred frowned. The young man, he had noticed, had little sense of respect to kings, and none at all for senior members of the Church.

"After the surrender of King Ella, he was unhappily put to death in vile manner by the heathen Ragnarssons, and especially the one called the Boneless. Just as happened to your master, the noble Edmund," he added, nodding again to Wulfgar.

"But it seems that this caused dissension among the heathens. Indeed there is a strange story that the execution was put to an end by a *machine* of some kind. Everything at Eoforwich seems to have something about machines attached to it.

"Yet the important news is the dissension. For after it the Viking army split."

Mutters of surprise and pleasure.

"Some of them have now left Eoforwich and are marching south. A lesser part of the Army, but still formidable. Where, I must ask myself, are they heading? And I say, they are heading back to East Anglia, from where they came."

"Back to their ships," snapped Alfgar.

"That could well be. Now, I do not think the East Anglians will fight them again. They lost their king and too many leaders, thanes and warriors in the battle by the Stour, from which you, young man, so valiantly fought your way. Yet, as you have all been telling me," Burgred glanced sarcastically at Alfred, "the Vikings must be fought.

"So I shall send East Anglia a war-leader, with a strong force of my men to support him till he can rally his own.

"You, young man. Alfgar, son of Wulfgar. You are of the North-folk. Your father was a thane of King Edmund. Your family has lost more, suffered more and dared more than any other. You will put the kingdom back on its feet.

"Only it can no longer be a kingdom."

Burgred locked eyes with the young atheling, Alfred of Wessex: eyes as blue and hair as blond as Alfgar's, a true prince of a royal line. But something queer, cross-grained about him. A clever look. They both knew that this was the sticking point. Burgred of Mercia had no more claim to East Anglia than Ethelred of Wessex. Yet the one who filled the gap would clearly become the mightier of the two.

"What would my title be?" asked Alfgar carefully.

"Alderman. Of the North-folk and the South-folk."

"Those are two shires," objected Alfred. "A man cannot be alderman of two shires at once."

"New times, new things," replied Burgred. "But what you say is true. In time, Alfgar, you may win a new title. You may be what the priests call *subregulus*. You may be my under-king. Say, will you be loyal to me and to Mercia? to the Mark?"

Alfgar knelt silently at the king's feet and put his hands between the king's knees in token of subjection. The king patted his shoulder and lifted him up.

"We will do this more formally by and by. I just wanted to know we are all agreed." He turned to Alfred. "And yes, young atheling, I know you have not agreed. But tell your king and brother the way of it is now this. Let him stay his side of the Thames and I'll stay mine. But north of the Thames and south of the Humber: that belongs to me. All of it."

Burgred let the tense silence hang a moment and then thought to disperse it. "One strange piece of news they told me. The Ragnarssons have always led the Great Army, but they have all stayed in Eoforwich. Those who marched away are said to have no leaders, or many. But one report is that among their leaders, or their main leader, is an Englishman. A man of the East Angles by his speech, the messenger said. But he could only give me what the Vikings call him, and they speak English so badly I could not make it out as a man's name at all. They call him Skjef Sigvarthsson. Now what could that be in English? Even in East Anglian?"

"Shef!" It was the silent woman who had spoken. Or gasped. Her eyes, her brilliant liquid eyes, blazed with life. Her husband stared at her like one who measures a back for the birch, while her father-in-law goggled and reddened.

"I thought you saw him dead," snarled the heimnar accusingly at his son.

"I will yet," muttered Alfgar. "Just give me the men."

Nearly two hundred miles to the north, Shef turned once again in his saddle to see if the rear-guard was keeping up. Important to have everyone well closed up, all within earshot of each other. Shef knew that four times his own number were pounding the filthy road behind him, unable to attack while Shef held his thirty hostages, the choirmonks of St. John's and their abbot Saxwulf. It was important too to keep up the pace, even after their long night's ride, to outrun the news of their coming and prevent any arrangement being made for their reception.

The smell of the sea led them on—and there, as they came trampling over a slight rise, there as an unmistakable landmark was Flamborough Head itself. Shef urged the vanguard on with a yell and a wave.

Guthmund dropped back a yard or two, hand still clutching the bridle of the abbot's horse. Shef waved him over. "Keep up—and keep the abbot close to me."

With a whoop he spurred his tiring gelding forward, catching up just as the whole cavalcade, a hundred and twenty raiders and thirty hostages, stormed down the long slope into the squalid huddle of Bridlington.

Instant confusion. Women running, snatching up bluelegged ragged children, men seizing spears, dropping them again, some racing for shelter down to the beach and the boats drawn up on the dirty snow-covered sand. Shef wheeled his horse and thrust the abbot forward like a trophy, instantly recognizable in his black robes.

"Peace," he shouted, "Peace. I want Ordlaf."

But Ordlaf was already there, the reeve of Bridlington, the capturer—though no one had ever credited him with it—of Ragnar. He stepped forward from his people, eyeing the Vikings and the monks with amazement, reluctantly taking responsibility.

"Show them the abbot," Shef snapped to Guthmund. "Make those behind keep their distance." He pointed at Ordlaf the reeve. "You and I have met before. The day you netted Ragnar."

Dismounting, he drove his halberd-spike deep into the sandy soil. Putting his hand on the reeve's shoulder, he drew him a little away, out of earshot of the wrathfully glaring abbot, began to speak in urgent tones.

"It's impossible," said Ordlaf a minute later. "Can't be done."

"Why not? It's a high sea, and cold, but the wind is from the west."

"Southwest a point west," corrected Ordlaf automatically.

"You can run downcoast with it on your beam. To the Spurn. Twenty-five miles, no more. Be there by dark. Never out of sight of land. I'm not asking for a sea-crossing. If the weather changes we can drop sea-anchor and ride it out."

"We'd be pulling into the teeth of it once we got to the Spurn."

Shef jerked a thumb over his shoulder. "Best rowers in the world, right with you. You can set them to it and stand back at the steering oar like lords."

"Well . . . What happens when I get back and the abbot sends his men down to burn me out?"

"You did it to save the abbot's life."

"I doubt he'll be grateful."

"You can take your time coming back. Time enough to hide what we'll pay you. Silver from the minster. Your silver. Your rents for many a year. Hide it, melt it down. They'll never trace it."

"Well . . . How do I know you won't just cut my throat? And my men's?"

"You don't—but you have little choice. Decide."

The reeve hesitated a moment longer. Remembered Merla, his wife's cousin, whom the abbot behind him had enslaved for debt. Thought of Merla's own wife and bairns, living still on charity with their man fled in terror.

"All right. But make it look as if you're treating me rough."

Shef exploded with feigned rage, swung a blow at the reeve's head, whipped a dirk from its scabbard. The reeve turned away, shouting orders at the little knot of men who had collected at a few yards' distance. Slowly men began to push beached fishing boats towards the tide, to step masts, haul sailcloth from sheds. In a tight huddle the Vikings pressed down to the water's edge, hustling their captives. Fifty yards away, five hundred English riders pressed forward, ready to charge sooner than see the hostages taken off, held back by the bright weapons waving over tonsured heads.

"Keep them back," snapped Shef to the abbot. "I'll let half your men go when we board. You and the rest go in a dinghy once we're afloat."

"I suppose you realize this means we lose the horses," said Guthmund gloomily.

"You stole them in the first place. You can steal some more."

"So we pulled into the mouth of the Humber under oars just at dusk, beached for the night when we were sure no one could see us, then rowed upriver in the morning to meet the rest of you. With the take."

"How much is it?" asked Brand, sitting with the other members of the impromptu council.

"I've weighed it out," said Thorvin. "Altar-plate, candlesticks, those little boxes the Christians keep saints' finger-bones in, box for the holy wafers, those things for burning incense, some coins—a lot of coins. I thought monks weren't supposed to have property of their own, but Guthmund says they all had purses if you shook them hard enough. Well, after what he gave the fishermen we still have ninety-two pounds weight of silver.

"Better than that is the gold. The crown you took off the Christ-image was pure gold, and heavy. So was some of the plate. That's another fourteen pounds. And we reckon gold as outvaluing silver eight for one. So that counts as eight stone of silver: a hundredweight to add to your ninety-two pounds."

"Two hundred pounds, all told," said Brand thoughtfully. "We will have to divide it all between crews and let the crews make their own division."

"No," said Shef.

"You say that a lot these days," Brand said.

"That is because I know what to do—others don't. The money is not to be divided. It is the war chest of the army. That was why I went for it. If we divide it up everyone will be a little richer. I want to use it so that everyone becomes a lot richer."

"If it's put like that," said Thorvin, "I think the army will accept it. You got it. You have a right to say how you think it should be used. But how are we all going to get a lot richer?"

Shef pulled from the front of his tunic the *mappamundi* he had taken from the minster wall. "Look at this," he said. A dozen heads bent over the vast vellum sheet, faces wearing different degrees of puzzlement at the scrawled, inked marks.

"Can you read the writing?" asked Shef.

"In the middle there," said Skaldfinn the Heimdall-priest. "Where the little picture is. It says 'Hierusalem.' That is the holy city of the Christians."

"Lies, as usual," commented Thorvin. "That black border is supposed to be Ocean, the great sea that runs round Mithgarth, the world. They are saying their holy city is the center of everything, just as you would expect."

"Look round the edges," rumbled Brand. "See what it has to tell us of places we know. If it lying about them, then we can guess it is all lies, as Thorvin says."

" 'Dacia et Gothis'," read Skaldfinn. " 'Gothia.' That must be the land of the Gautar, south of the Swedes. Unless they mean Gotland. But Gotland is an island, and this is marked as being mainland. Next to it—next to it they have 'Bulgaria.' "

The council broke into laughter. "The Bulgars are the enemies of the emperor of the Greeks, in Miklagarth," said Brand. "It is two months' travel from the nearest of the Gautar to the Bulgars."

"On the other side of Gothia they have 'Slesvic.' Well, at least that is clear enough. We all know Slesvik of the Danes. There is some more writing by it. *'Hic abundant leones.'* That means 'There are many lions here.' "

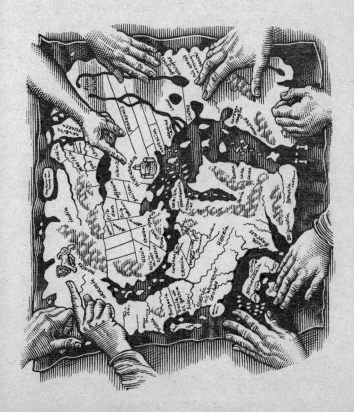

Again a roar of laughter. "I have been to Slesvik market a dozen times," said Brand. "And I have met men who have spoken of lions. They are like very large cats, and they live in the hot country south of Sarkland. But there has never been one lion in Slesvik, let alone many. You wasted your time bringing back this—what do you call it?—this *mappa*. It is just nonsense, like everything the Christians count as wisdom."

Shef's finger continued to trace lettering, while he muttered to himself the letters that Father Andreas had half-successfully taught him.

"There is some English writing here," he said. "In a different hand from the rest. It says 'Suth-Bryttas,' that is, 'South British.' "

"He means the Bretons," Brand said. "They live on a large peninsula the other side of the English Sea."

"So that is not so far wrong. You can find truth on a *mappa*. If you put it there."

"I still don't see how it is going to make us rich," replied Brand. "That is what you said it was going to do."

"This won't." Shef rolled the vellum up, thrust it aside. "But the idea of it may. We need to know more important things. Remember—if we had not known where Riccall was, that day in the snow, we might have been cut off and destroyed in the end by the churls. When I set off for Beverley, I knew the direction, but I would never have found the minster if we had not had a guide who knew the roads. The only way I found Bridlington and the man who could sail us out of a trap was because I had traveled the road already.

"You see what I mean? We have plenty of knowledge, but it all depends on people. But no one person knows enough for all the things we need. What a *mappa* should be is a store of knowledge from many people. Now if we had that we could find our way to places we had not been before. We could tell directions, work out distances."

"So we make a knowledge *mappa*," said Brand firmly. "Now tell me about rich."

"We have one other precious possession," said Shef. "And this we did not get from the Christians. Thorvin will tell you. I bought it myself. From Munin, the raven of Othin. I bought it with pain. Show them, Thorvin."

From inside his tunic Thorvin pulled a thin square board. On it were lines of small runic letters, each one scratched with a knife and then marked out with red dye.

"It is a riddle. The one who solves the riddle will find the hoard of Raedwald, king of the East Angles. That is what Ivar was searching for last autumn. But the secret died with King Edmund."

"A *royal* hoard," said Brand. "Now that could be worth something, all right. But first we have to solve the riddle."

"That is what a *mappa* can do," said Shef firmly. "If we write down every piece of knowledge we can find, in the end we will have the right number of pieces to solve the riddle. But if we do not write them down, by the time we come on the last piece we need we will have forgotten the first.

"And there is another thing." Shef struggled with an image in his mind, a trace of memory from somewhere, of looking down—down on the land in a way no man could ever in reality see it. "Even this *mappa*. It has one idea. It is as if we were looking down on the world from above. Seeing it all spread out below us. Like an eagle would see it. Now that is the way to find things."

Guthmund the skipper broke the considering silence. "But before we see or find anything, we have to decide where we go now."

"More important even than that," said Brand, "we must decide how this army is led, and under what law it shall live. While we were men of the Great Army we lived under the old *hermanna lög* of our ancestors—the warriors' law. But Ivar the Boneless broke that and I have no wish to return to it. Now I know that not everyone in this army wears the pendant." He looked significantly at Shef and Guthmund in the group around the table. "But it is in my mind that we should now agree to live under a new law. *Vegmanna lög*,

I would call it. The law of the Way-folk. The first stage to that, though, is for the army to agree in open assembly to whom it will give the powers to make the laws."

While they worked it out, Shef's mind drifted away, as it often did, from the wrangling debate that immediately broke out. He knew what the army would now have to do. March out of Northumbria to get away from the Ragnarssons, cross the shires of Burgred, the powerful king of the Mark, as fast as possible. Establish themselves in the kingless realm of the East Angles, and take toll of the population in return for protection. Protection from kings, protection from abbots and bishops. In a short while, toll on that scale would make even Brand feel contented.

Meanwhile he would work on the *mappa*. And on the riddle. And most important of all, if the Army of the Way was to protect its shires from other predators, he would have to give them new weapons. New machines.

As he began to draw, in his mind's eye, the lines of the new catapult, a voice broke through to his half-attention, arguing violently for a place in the council for all hereditary jarls.

That would include Sigvarth, his father, whose crews had joined the column leaving York almost at the last moment. He wished Sigvarth had remained behind. And his horse-toothed son, Hjörvarth. Still, maybe they need not meet. Maybe the Army would not make the rule about jarls.

Shef went back to wondering how he could replace the power of the slow and clumsy counterweight. His fingers itched again to hold a hammer.

Chapter Eight

Four weeks later the itch in Shef's fingers had been eased. Outside the makeshift camp where the Wayman army had halted for the winter, he stood on the catapult range. But the machine he stood behind was not one the Rome-folk would have recognized.

"Lower away," he shouted to his eight-man team.

The long boom creaked down towards his waiting hands, the ten-pound rock in its leather sling dangling from two hooks, one fixed, one free.

"Take the strain." The eight brawny Vikings on the other end of the catapult's arm put their weight on the ropes and braced themselves for a pull. Shef felt the arm—it was the top sixteen feet of a longship's mast, sawn off a little above deck level—flex between their weight and his, felt himself beginning to lift off the sodden ground.

"Pull!" The Vikings heaved as one, each man putting his full body-weight and back strength into it, as beautifully co-ordinated as if they had been heaving up a longship's yard in an Atlantic swell. The short arm of the catapult jerked down. The long arm whipped up. The sling, whirling round with sudden, vicious force, reached the point where the free hook was pulled off its ring, and swung loose.

Up into the murky sky soared the boulder. For a long moment it seemed to pause at the top of its arc, then began the long descent to splash into the Fenland soil two hundred and fifty paces off. Already a half-score of ragged figures were racing forward at the other end of the practice range, jealously competing to seize the ball and run back with it.

"Lower away!" bellowed Shef at the top of his lungs. His crew, as always, took not the slightest notice. They whooped and cheered, beating each other on the back, watching for the fall of the shot.

"A furlong if it's an inch!" shouted Steinulf, Brand's helmsman.

"Lower away! This is a speed test!" bellowed Shef again. His team slowly remembered his existence. One of them, Ulf the cook, ambled round and patted Shef tenderly on the back.

"Speed test be buggered," he said companionably. "If we ever have to shoot it fast, we will. Now—it's time to get the food on."

His mates nodded agreement, picked up their jackets from where they had draped them over the catapult's gallowslike frame.

"Good fun, good shooting," said Kolbein the Hebridean, newly sporting his Wayman pendant, the phallus of Frey. "We'll come down again tomorrow. Time to eat."

Shef watched them trail back toward the palisade, the cluster of tents and roughly roofed booths which were the winter camp of the Wayman army, wrath and frustration at his heart.

He had got the idea for this new-model catapult while watching Ordlaf's fishermen hauling on their mast-ropes. The giant boulder-thrower of the monks at York, the machine that had destroyed the Ragnarssons' ram three months before, had got its power from a counterweight. The counterweight itself was hauled into the air by men heaving at a windlass. All the counterweight really did was to store up the power the men had put into heaving on the windlass handles.

So why store the power? he had asked himself. Why not just have men attach ropes to the short arm and heave down on it directly? For small stones, like those they had roughly chipped into spheres, the new machine, the "pull-thrower" as the Vikings called it, was magnificent.

It threw in a perfectly straight line and could be aimed for direction within a couple of feet. The effect of the missile it hurled was literally pulverizing, turning rock to powder and smashing through shields like paper. As they learned how to shoot the weapon with maximum efficiency, its range steadily increased out to an eighth of a mile. And he was sure, if only they would do as they were told, that he could launch ten rocks while a man counted to a hundred.

But his team had no notion of the catapult as a weapon. To them, it was just a toy. Maybe useful one day against a stockade or a wall. Otherwise, a diversion during the tedium of a winter camp in the Fens, with even the traditional Viking amusements of raiding the surrounding countryside for girls and money severely forbidden.

But these throwers would work against anything, Shef thought. Ships. Armies. How would a drawn-up battle-line fare against a rain of boulders from men well out of bowshot, each one sure to kill or cripple?

He became aware that a cluster of excited, grinning faces was staring at him. The slaves. Runaways from the Northfolk or from the lands of the king of the Mark, drawn to the camp here in the flat, soggy borderland between the streams of Nene and Welland by the astonishing rumor that here their collars would be removed. That food was to be had in return for services. They had been told, though they didn't believe it yet, that they would not be re-enslaved once their masters moved on.

Each of the ragged figures was clutching one of the ten-

pound stones, which they had spent the last day or so chipping into shape with a couple of Thorvin's least-valued
chisels.

"All right," said Shef. "Take the pegs out, dismantle the
machine, take the beams back and wrap them in their tar-
paulins."

The men shuffled and looked at each other. One of them,
nudged forward by the rest, spoke haltingly, eyes on the
ground.

"We was thinking, master. You being from Emneth and
that. And talking like us and all. So . . ."

"Get on with it."

"We was wondering, you being one of us and all, if you
would let us have a shot."

"We know how to do it!" cried one of his supporters.
"We watched. We ain't got the beef they got, but we can
pull."

Shef stared at the excited faces. The scrawny, underfed
physiques. Why not? he thought. He had always assumed
that what you needed most for this task was raw strength
and weight. But coordination was even more important.
Maybe twelve lightweight Englishmen would be as good as
eight heavyweight Vikings. It would never have been true
with swords or axes. But at least these ex-slaves would do
what they were told.

"All right," he said. "We'll shoot five for practice. Then
we'll see how many you can loose while I count fivescore."

The freedmen cheered and capered, pushing for the ropes.

"Hold on. This is going to be a speed test. So, first thing.
Put the stones close there in a pile so you won't have to
move more than a step to get them. Now, pay attention . . ."

An hour later, his new team dismissed to store what they now
called their machine, Shef walked thoughtfully towards the
booth of Hund and Ingulf, where the sick and injured lay.
Hund met him coming out of the booth, wiping bloody hands.

"How are they?" Shef asked. He meant the casualties
from his other machine, the torsion-catapult or "twist-

shooter" as the Vikings called it, the dart-machine which had released King Ella into death.

"They'll live. One lost three fingers. Could as easily have been his hand, or arm for that matter. The other has most of his rib cage stove in. Ingulf had to cut him to get a piece out of his lung. But it's healing well. I've just smelt his stitches. No sign of the flesh-rot. That's two men badly hurt by that machine in four days. What's the matter with it?"

"Nothing wrong with the machine. It's these Norsemen. Strong men, proud of their strength. They twist the cog-wheels tight—then one of them will throw his weight on the lever just to wring an extra turn out of it. The bow-arm snaps—and someone gets hurt."

"Then it's not the machine at fault, but the men who use it?"

"Exactly. What I need are men who will take so many counted turns and no more, who will do what they're told."

"Not many of those in this camp."

Shef stared at his friend. "Not speaking Norse, certainly." The seed of an idea had been planted.

The winter dark upon them now, he would take a candle and continue to work on the new *mappa*—the map of England as it really was.

"Nothing left to eat, I suppose, but the rye porridge?"

Silently Hund passed him his bowl.

Sigvarth looked round with a trace of uncertainty. The priests of the Way had formed the holy circle, within the rowan-hung cords, spear planted and fire burning. Once again the laymen of the Way were excluded: no one was present in the dim, sail-roofed shed except the six white-clad priests and Sigvarth Jarl of the Small Isles.

"It is time we came to a clear understanding, Sigvarth," said Farman the priest, "and that is, how sure are you that you are the father of the boy Shef?"

"He says so," replied Sigvarth. "Everyone thinks he is. And his mother claims him—and she should know. Of course she might have done anything once she escaped from me—a girl on the loose for the first time. She might have enjoyed herself." Yellow teeth flashed. "But I don't think so. She was a lady."

"I think I know the main story," said Farman. "You took her from her husband. But a thing I cannot understand is this: She escaped from you, or so we hear. Are you usually as careless as that with your captives? How did she escape? And how could she have got back to her husband?"

Sigvarth rubbed his jaw reflectively. "This is twenty years back now. Still, it was funny. I remember pretty well.

"What happened was this: We were coming back from a trip down South. Hadn't gone very well. As we came back I decided, just for luck, to look into the Wash and see what we could find. Usual stuff. Pushed ashore. English all over the place, as always. Came down on this little village, Emneth, grabbed everyone we could. One of them was the thane's lady—I forget her name now.

"But I don't forget her. She was good. I took her for myself. I was thirty then, she was maybe twenty. That's often a good combination. She'd had a child, she was broken in all right. But I got the impression she had not had much joy from her husband. She fought me fiercely to start with, but I'm used to that—they have to do it to show they aren't whores. Once she knew there was no choice, though, she buckled down to it. Had a trick, a way to her—she used to lift herself right off the ground, me too, when she reached her moment."

Thorvin grunted disapprovingly. Farman, one hand clutching the dried stallion-penis that was his badge of office, as the hammer was Thorvin's, hushed him with a gesture.

"But it's not so much fun in a rolling longship. After we pushed up the coast a bit, I looked out for a good place. Bit of *strandhögg*, I thought. Light fires, warm up, roast some beef, get out a couple of barrels of ale, have some sport for an evening. Put the boys in good heart for the ocean crossing. But not take any risks, mind, not even with the English.

"So, I picked a spot. Stretch of beach backed by good, high cliffs. One stream leading down to it through a gully.

I put half a dozen men there just to make sure none of the girls we'd caught escaped. I put one man on each of the cliffs to either side, with a horn to blow if he saw any sign of a rescue party turning up. And because of the cliffs, I gave each of them a rope tied to a stake. If we were surprised, they blew the horns, the party in the gully ran back, and the ones on the cliffs slid down the ropes. We had the boats, three of them, tethered bow and stern—bow to the beach, stern to an anchor well out to sea. In a hurry all we had to do was pile in, loose the bow-ropes, haul ourselves off on the stern-rope and set sail. But the main thing is, I had the beach sealed off tight as a nun."

"You would know," said Thorvin.

Sigvarth's teeth flashed again. "None better, unless he's a bishop."

"But she got away," Farman prompted.

"Right. We had our fun. I did it with her, on the sand, twice. It got dark. Now, I wasn't passing her round, but the men had a dozen girls they were sharing, and I felt like joining in—hah, I was thirty then! So I hauled in my boat, I left my clothes on the sand and got in it with her. I pulled out on the stern-rope, maybe thirty yards out, and made fast. I left her there, dived in the sea and swam back. Fine, big blonde girl there I fancied. She'd been making a lot of noise.

"But after a while—I'd got a roast rib in one hand and a mug of ale in the other—the men started shouting. Just outside the light of our fires there was a shape on the sand, a big shape. Beached whale, we thought, but when we ran over, it wheezed and came at the first man there. He backed off, we looked for our weapons. I thought it might be a hrosswhale. *Whaleross*, some say.

"And right that moment there was a lot of shouting from the top of one cliff. The lad up there, Stig was his name, shouting for help. Not blowing his horn, mind, but wanting help. Sounded as if he was fighting something. So I climbed up the rope to see what it was."

"And what was it?"

"Nothing, when I got there. But he said, near in tears, he'd been attacked by a skoffin."

"A skoffin?" said Vigleik. "What's that?"

Skaldfinn laughed. "You must talk more to old wives, Vigleik. A skoffin is the opposite of a skuggabaldur. The one is the get of a male fox and a she-cat, the other of a tom and a vixen."

"Well," Sigvarth concluded, "by this time everyone was getting unsettled. So I left Stig up there, told him not to be a fool, slid back down the rope and told everyone to get back on board.

"But when we hauled the boat in, the woman was gone. We searched the beach. I checked the party in the gully—they hadn't moved an inch while we were getting ready, swore no one had passed. I went up both ropes to both cliffs. No one had seen anything. In the end I was so angry, what with one thing and another, that I threw Stig down the cliff for sniveling. He broke his neck and died. I had to pay wergild for him when I got home. But I never saw the woman again till last year. And then I was too busy to ask for her story."

"Aye. We know what you were busy with," said Thorvin. "The business of the Boneless One."

"Are you a Christian to whine about it?"

"What it comes to," said Farman, "is that she could have swum away in the confusion. You swam to shore."

"She would have had to do it fully dressed, for her clothes were gone too. And not just to shore. A long way, in the dark sea, to get round the cliffs. For she was not on the beach, I am sure of that."

"A whaleross. A skoffin. A woman who vanishes and reappears carrying a child," mused Farman. "All this could be explained. Yet there are more ways than one of explaining it."

"You think he is not my son," challenged Sigvarth. "You think he is the son of one of your gods. Well, I tell you: I honor no god save Ran the goddess who lives in the deep, whom drowned sailors go to. And the other world you talk of, the visions you boast of—I have heard them speak of it in camp about this Way of yours—I think them all born of

drink and sour food, and one man's blather infecting another, till everyone must tell his tale of visions to keep in
with the rest. There is no more sense in it than there is in
skoffins. The boy is my son. He looks like me. He acts like
me—like I did when I was young."

"He acts like a man," snarled Thorvin. "You act like a rut-
ting beast. I tell you that though you have gone many years
without regret and without punishment; still there is fate for
such as you. Our poet said it when he saw the Hel-world:

> " 'Many men I saw moan in pain,
> Walk in woe the ways of Hel.
> Streaming red their wretched faces,
> Punishment for the pain of women.' "

Sigvarth rose to his feet, left hand on sword. "And I will
tell you a better poem. The Boneless One's skald made it
last year, of the death of Ragnar:

> " 'We struck with the sword. I say it is good
> For swain to meet swain in the sway of brands.
> Not flinch from fighting. The friend of warriors
> Shall earn women by war, by the way of the drengr.

"That is poetry for a warrior. For one who knows how to
live and how to die. There will be a place for such a one
among the halls of Othin, no matter how many women he
has made weep. Poetry for a Viking. Not a milksop."

In the silence Farman said mildly, "Well, Sigvarth. We
thank you for your tale. We will remember you are a jarl and
one of our council. You will remember you live by the law of
the Waymen now, no matter what you think of our beliefs."

He pulled open the ropes of the precinct, to let Sigvarth
out. As the jarl left, the priests began to talk in low tones.

*Shef-who-was-not-Shef knew that the darkness round him
had not been breached by light for twice a hundred years.
For a while the stone chamber and the earth round it had*

glowed with the phosphorescence of corruption, lighting up the silent, heaving struggle of the maggots as they consumed the bodies, the eyes and livers and flesh and marrow of all that had been placed there. But the maggots were gone now, the many corpses reduced to white bone, as hard and inert as the whetstone lying under his own fleshless hand. They were nothing but possessions now, without life of their own, as unchallengeably his as the chests and coffers round his feet and under his chair, as the chair itself— the massive wooden high seat in which he had settled himself seven generations ago, for eternity. The chair had rotted underground with the owner—the two had grown into one another. Yet still the figure sat unmoving, the empty eye-sockets staring out into the earth and beyond.

He, the figure in the chair, remembered how they had placed him there. The men had dug the great trench, slid into it the longship on its rollers, placed the high seat as he had directed on the poop, by the steering oar. He had settled himself in it, placed the whetstone with its carved savage faces on one armrest, laid his long broadsword on the other. He had nodded to the men to continue. First they brought in his war-stallion, held it facing him, and poleaxed it where it stood. Then his four best hounds, each one pierced to the heart. He watched carefully to see that each one was quite dead. He had no mind to share his everlasting tomb with a trapped meat-eater. Then the hawks, each one quickly strangled. Then the women, a pair of beauties, weeping and calling out in spite of the poppy forced upon them; the men strangled them quickly.

Then they brought in the chests, two men to each one, grunting with the weight of them. He watched carefully again to see there was no delay, no reluctance. They would have kept his wealth if they dared. They would dig it up again if they dared. They would not dare. For a year to come the barrow would glow blue with the light of corruption beneath it; a man with a torch would ignite the bale-fires of the reek coming out of the ground. Tales would spread, till all feared and dreaded the grave-mound of Kar the Old. If grave it was for Kar.

The chests stacked, the men began to deck over the belly of the longship with its freight of corpses. Others piled stones around and behind him till they reached the height of the top of his seat with its silken canopy. Over them they laid stout beams, and over them in turn a sheet of lead. Around his feet and over his chests they tucked tarred canvas. In time the wood would rot, the earth fall in on the longship's hold, the dead women and beasts would lie mingled in confusion. Still he would sit here, looking out over them, the earth held at bay. They had been buried dead. He would not be.

When all was done a man came to stand in front of the seat: Kol the Niggard, men would call him, son of Kar the Old. "It is done, Father," he said, face twisting between fear and hate.

Kar nodded, eyes unblinking. He would not wish his son luck or farewell. If he had had the black blood of his ancestors, he would have joined his father in the mound, preferring to sit with his treasures for eternity than to hand them over to the new king pushing up from the South, to enjoy life with dishonor, to be an under-king.

The trusted warriors, six of them, began to slaughter the slave-laborers and stack them round the ship. Then they and his son scrambled out. A few moments later the loose earth of the digging began to fall in clods on the deck, covering it quickly, mounting up over the planks and the canvas and the sheet of lead. Slowly he saw it rise, to his knees, to his chest. He sat unmoving, even when earth began to trickle into the stone chamber itself, to cover his hand on the whetstone.

Still a glimmer of light. More earth raining down. The glimmer gone, the dark deepening. Kar settled back finally, sighing with relief and contentment. Now he had things as they should be. And so they would stay forever. His.

He wondered if he would die down here. What could kill him? It did not matter. Whether he died or lived he would always be the same. The hogboy, the haugbui. The dweller in the mound.

* * *

Shef woke with a start and a gasp. Underneath the coarse blankets his body streamed sweat. Reluctantly he pulled them back, rolled with a grunt from the string-bed to the wet, tramped-earth floor. He seized his hemp shirt as the freezing air hit him, pulled it on, groped for the heavy wool tunic and trousers.

Thorvin says these visions are sent by the gods for my instruction. But what did that tell me? There was no machine in it this time.

The canvas flap over the booth-door pulled back and Padda the freedman shuffled in. Outside, the late January dawn showed only thick mist rising from the waterlogged ground. The Army would frowst late in its blankets today.

The names of the men in the dream: Kar and Kol. They did not sound English. Nor Norse, altogether. But then the Norsemen were great ones for shortening names. Guthmund was Gummi to his friends, Thormoth became Tommi. The English did it too. Those names in King Edmund's riddle: ". . . Wuffa, Wehha's offspring . . ."

"What's your long name, Padda?" he asked.

"Paldriht, master. Haven't been called that since my mother died."

"What would Wuffa be short for?"

"Don't know. Wulfstan, maybe. Could be anything. I knew a man once called Wiglaf. Very noble name. We called him Wuffa."

Shef pondered as Padda began to blow carefully on the embers of last night's fire.

Wuffa, son of Wehha. Wulfstan or Wiglaf, son of—Weohstan, it might be, or Weohward. He did not know those names—he must find out more.

As Padda fiddled with wood and water, his pans and the everlasting porridge, Shef unrolled the vellum *mappamundi* from its waxcloth wrapping, spread it out, corners weighted, on his trestle table. He no longer looked at the completed side, the side with the map of Christian learning. On the reverse he had begun to draw a different map. A map of England, putting down all the information he could uncover.

He would sketch in rough outlines, names, distances, on birchbark. Only after information had been checked and proved consistent with what he knew already would he ink it in on the vellum itself. Yet the map still grew with every day, dense and accurate for Norfolk and the Fens, doubtful and patchy for Northumbria away from York, completely blank down in the South, apart from London on the Thames and the vague mention of Wessex to the west of it.

Padda had found a Suffolk man among the freedmen, though. In return for his breakfast he would tell Shef all he knew about the shire.

"Call him in," said Shef, unrolling fresh birchbark and testing the point of his scratching-tool as the man entered.

"I want you to tell me all you can about places in your shire. Begin with the rivers. I know already of the Yare and the Waverly."

"Ah," said the Suffolk man reflectively. "Well, below that you've got the Alde, which reaches the coast at Aldeburgh. The Deben next. That comes into the coast ten mile south of Aldeburgh at Woodbridge, near where they say the old kings lie. We had our own kings in Suffolk once, you know, before the Christians came. . . ."

Minutes later Shef pounded into the forge where Thorvin was preparing for another day of forging iron cogwheels for the twist-shooters.

"I want you to call the army council together," he demanded. "Why?"

"I think I know how to make Brand rich."

Chapter Nine

The expedition set out a week later, under a lowering sky, an hour after dawn. The council of the Wayman army had refused to sanction abandoning the base and

marching out in full force. There were still the ships to be
guarded, hauled up on the banks of the Welland. The camp
held not only warmth for the remaining weeks and months
of the winter but also a laboriously gathered food supply.
And it could not be denied that many of the councillors
were reluctant to believe Shef's passionate conviction that
his *mappa* held the secret of generations of wealth.

Yet it was obvious that more than a few crews were
needed. The kingdom of the East Angles was a kingdom no
more, and all its mightiest warriors and noblest thanes were
dead. Still, there was the chance that they might rally if pro-
voked. A small party of Vikings could be cut off and massacred by overwhelming numbers. Brand had rumbled that
foolish as he thought the whole expedition might be, he had
no wish to be woken one morning by the heads of his messmates being thrown into the camp. In the end Shef had been
allowed to call for volunteers. In the tedium of winter encampment, there had been no trouble in finding them.

A thousand Vikings rode out on their ponies, eight long
hundreds and forty, riding crew by crew as was their custom. Hundreds of pack-ponies carried tents and bedding,
food and ale, led in strings by English thralls. At the center
of the column, though, was something new: a string of carts,
carrying ropes and beams, wheels and levers—all the beams
carefully notched and marked for reassembly. A dozen pull-
throwers, eight twist-shooters. Every machine Shef and
Thorvin had been able to construct in their weeks at the
base was here. If he had left them behind they would have
been forgotten, dispersed, used for firewood. Too much
work had gone into them for that to happen.

Round the carts there clustered a mob of thralls, the runaways of the region, each catapult crew stepping by its cart
and its machine, each crew captained by one of Shef's orig-
inal dozen. The Vikings did not like this. Yes, every army
needed a gang of thralls to dig latrines, light fires, groom
horses. But gangs this size? All eating their share of the
supplies? And starting to think they might not be thralls after all? Even the followers of the Way had never considered

admitting men who did not speak Norse to full fellowship.
Nor did Shef dare to suggest it.

He had made clear to Padda and the rest of the machine-
captains that they had better tell their men to keep their
heads down. "If someone wants you to grind his meal or
pitch his tent, just do it," he had told them. "Otherwise keep
out of the way."

Yet he wanted his recruits to feel different. To take pride
in the speed and dexterity with which they leapt to their
places, turned the levers or whirled the beams.

To mark them out, every catapult-man now wore an identical jerkin, made only of rough sackcloth, hodden gray,
over the rags they had been wearing when they arrived. On
it each man had carefully stitched a white linen double-
headed hammer, front and back. Each man, too, had a belt
or at least a rope round his middle, and all those who owned
them bore knives.

Maybe it would work, thought Shef, watching the carts
creak forward, Vikings in front and behind, jerkined
freedmen in the middle. Certainly they were much better
already with the catapults than the Vikings they had replaced. And even on a winter day in the raw cold, they
looked cheerful.

A strange noise split the sky. At the front of the train of
carts, Cwicca, a thrall who had come in a few days before,
escaped from the shrine of St. Guthlac at Crowland, had
brought with him his treasured bagpipe. Now he led the
carts along, cheeks puffed, fingers skipping briskly on the
bone pipe. His mates cheered and stepped out harder, some
of them whistling in unison.

A Viking from the vanguard turned his horse, scowling
angrily, front teeth sticking out. It was Hjörvarth Sigvarthsson, Shef saw. His half brother. Sigvarth had volunteered instantly to join the expedition with all his crews, too quickly
to be turned down, quicker even than Thorvin or the Hebrideans or the still-doubting Brand. Now Hjörvarth trotted
back menacingly towards the piper, sword half-drawn. The
music wailed discordantly and died.

Shef turned his pony between them, slipped off it and handed the reins to Padda.

"Walking keeps you warm," he said to Hjörvarth, staring up at the angry face. "Music makes the miles go faster. Let him play."

Hjörvarth hesitated, jerked his pony's head round. "Suit yourself," he flung over one shoulder. "But harps are for warriors. Only a *hornung* would listen to a pipe."

Hornung, gadderling, thought Shef. How many words there are for bastard. It doesn't stop men putting them in women's bellies. Maybe Godive has one by now.

"Keep playing," he shouted to the bagpiper. "Play 'The Quickbeam Dance.' Play it for Thunor, son of Woden, and to Hell with the monks."

The piper started again to play the jerky quickstep tune, louder this time, backed by united defiant whistling. The carts rolled forward behind the patient oxen.

"You're sure King Burgred means to take over the East Angles?" King Ethelred asked. His question ended in a fit of coughing—sharp, high-pitched, going on again after it had seemed to stop.

Ethelred's younger brother, Alfred the atheling, looked at him with concern. Also, a reluctant calculation. Alfred's father, Ethelwulf—king of Wessex, conqueror of the Vikings at Oakley—had had four strong sons: Ethelstan, Ethelbald, Ethelbert, Ethelred. By the time the fifth came along it had seemed so unlikely that he would ever be called upon to rule that the royal mark of the house of Wessex, the Ethel-name, had seemed unnecessary. He had been called Alfred after his mother's people.

By now the father and three of the strong sons were dead. None killed in battle, but all killed by the Vikings. For years they had marched in all weathers, lain in damp cloaks, drunk water from streams that flowed through the camps of armies careless of where they dumped their waste or relieved themselves. They died of the bowel-cramps, of the lung-sickness. Now Ethelred had contracted the wasting-cough. How long might it be, Alfred thought, till he was the last atheling of the royal house of Wessex? Till then, though, he must serve.

"Quite sure," he replied. "He said so openly. He was mustering his men when I left. But he's not making it too obvious. He has an under-king, an East Angle, to put in charge. That will make it easier for the East Angles to accept his rule. Especially as he has a totem. The man with no limbs, the one I told you of."

"Does it matter?" Ethelred dabbed wearily at spittle-slimed lips.

"The East Angles have twenty thousand hides. That, added to what Burgred has already, will make him stronger than us, far stronger than the Northumbrians. If we could trust him to fight the heathens only . . . But he may prefer easier prey. He could say it was his duty to unite all the kingdoms of the English. Ours included."

"So?"

"We must put in a claim. See, Essex is ours already. Now the border of Essex and the South-folk runs . . ."

The two men, the king and the prince, began slowly to thrash out a claim to territory, a likely dividing line. They had no image of the territory they were discussing, only knowledge that this river was north of that one, this town in this or that shire. The debate took even more toll of Ethelred's waning strength.

"You're sure they've split?" said Ivar Ragnarsson sharply.

The messenger nodded. "Almost half of them marched south. Maybe twelve long hundreds left behind."

"But no quarrel?"

"No. The word in the camp was they had some scheme for getting the wealth of King Jatmund, whom you killed with the blood-eagle."

"Nonsense," snarled Ivar.

"You heard what they got from the raid on the minster at Beverley?" asked Halvdan Ragnarsson. "A hundred pounds of silver and the same again in gold. That's more than we've taken anywhere. The boy is good at new schemes. You should have settled with him after the holmgang. He is a better friend than enemy."

Ivar turned on his brother, eyes pale, face whitening in one of his celebrated rages. Halvdan stared back at him placidly. The Ragnarssons never fought each other. This was the secret of their power, even Ivar in his madness knew it. He would take his rage out on someone else in some other way. Another matter to keep secret. But they had done it before."

"Only now he is an enemy," said Sigurth decisively. "We have to decide if he is our main one at this moment. And if he is . . . Messenger, you can go."

The brothers put their heads together in the little room off the drafty hall of King Ella in Eoforwich, and began to reckon numbers, rations, distances, possibilities.

"The wisdom of the serpent, the cunning of the dove," said Erkenbert the archdeacon with satisfaction. "Already our enemies destroy themselves and each other."

"Indeed," agreed Wulfhere. "The heathen make much ado and the kingdoms are moved. But God hath showed his voice and the earth shall melt away."

They spoke over the clanging of the dies, as each of the lay brothers in the monastic mint put his silver blank in place, struck it firmly with his hammer to drive the embossed design into one side. Moved it to the other die, struck again. First the spread-winged raven for the Ragnarssons. Then the letters *S.P.M.—Sancti Petri Moneta.* Collared slaves shuffled by, carrying man-loads of charcoal, rolling out carts of rejected lead, copper, slag. Only choirmonks touched the silver. They shared in the wealth of the minster. And any who thought for a moment of his own advantage could reflect on the Rule of Saint Benedict and the archbishop's power of chastisement written into it. It was long since a choirmonk had been flogged to death in chapter, or bricked alive into the vaults. But such cases had been known.

"They are in God's hand," concluded the archbishop. "Surely a divine vengeance will fall upon those who stole the goods of St. John's at Beverley."

"But God's hand shows itself through the hands of others," said Erkenbert. "And we must call for help from those."

"The kings of the Mark and of Wessex?"

"A mightier power than they."

Wulfhere looked down with surprise, doubt, comprehension. Erkenbert nodded.

"I have drafted a letter, for your seal. To Rome."

Pleasure showed on Wulfhere's face, perhaps anticipation of the much-rumored pleasures of the Holy City. "A vital matter," he announced. "I shall take the letter to Rome myself. In person."

Shef stared thoughtfully at the reverse side of his *mappa*, the map of England. Halfway through his work he had discovered the concept of scale, too late to apply consistently. Suffolk now bulked incongruously large, taking up a whole quadrant of the vellum. At one edge was his detailed drawing of all the information he had been able to wring out about the north bank of the Deben.

It fits, he thought. There is the town Woodbridge. That is in the first line of the poem, and the line must mean the town, because otherwise it would make no sense: all bridges are wood bridges. But more important is what the thrall says about the place, with no name, downstream of the bridge and the ford. That is where the barrows are, the resting place of the old kings. And who are the old kings? The slave knew no names, but the thane of Helmingham, who sold us mead, listed the ancestors of Raedwald the Great, and among them were Wiglaf and his father Weohstan: Wuffa, then, Wehha's offspring.

If the slave had remembered well, then there were four barrows together in a line running roughly south to north. The northmost of those. That was the place of the hoard.

Why had it not been plundered? If King Edmund had

known it was the secret hiding place of the treasures of his realm, why was it not guarded?

Or maybe it was guarded. But not by men. That was what the slave had thought. When he had realized what Shef intended to do he had grown silent. Now no one could find him. He had preferred to take his chances of recapture than go to rob the grave.

Shef turned his attention to practicalities. Diggers, guards. Spades, robes, boxes and slings for hauling up earth from deep down. Lights—he had no intention of digging in daylight with an interested county watching.

"Tell me, Thorvin," he said. "What do you think we might find inside this barrow? Other than gold, we hope."

"A ship," said Thorvin briefly.

"Close on a mile from the water?"

"See on your map. You could carry it up the slope there. The barrows are ship-shaped. And the thane told us Wiglaf was a sea-king, from the shores of Sweden, if he told us true. In my country even rich farmers, if they can afford it, will have themselves buried sitting upright in their boats. They think that this way they can sail over the seas to Odainsakr—to the Undying Shore—where they will join their ancestors and the Asa-gods. I do not say they are wrong."

"Well, we will soon know." Shef looked at the setting sun, glanced through the tent flap at the picked men—fifty Viking guards, a score of English diggers—quietly making ready. They would move only after dark.

As he rose to make his own preparations, Thorvin caught his arm. "Do not take this too lightly, young man. I do not believe—much—in *draugar* or in hogboys, the living dead or dragons made from corpses' backbones. Yet you are going to rob the dead. There are many tales of that, and all say the same. The dead will give up their goods, but only after a struggle. And only for a price. You should let a priest come with you. Or Brand."

Shef shook his head. They had argued this out before. He had made excuses, given reasons. None of them true. In his heart Shef felt he alone had the right to the hoard, bequeathed him by the dying king. He went out into the falling dusk.

Many, many hours later, Shef heard a mattock strike on wood. He straightened from his crouch over the black hole. It had been a night to forget so far. They had found the site without trouble, guided by the map. They had encountered no one. But where to begin digging? The guards and the diggers had clustered together in silence, waiting for orders. He had had torches lit, to see if he could discover signs of soil disturbance. But the moment the first resinous bundle had crackled to life a sudden blue flare of flame had run up the barrow and into the sky. Shef had lost half his diggers in that moment; they had simply bolted into the night. The Viking escort had held together much better, instantly drawing weapons and facing about them as if expecting to be attacked any moment by the vengeful dead. Yet even Guthmund the Greedy, keenest treasure-hunter of all, had suddenly lost enthusiasm. "We'll spread out a bit," he had muttered. "Not let anyone get too close." Since then no Viking had been seen. They must be out there in the dark somewhere, in little knots, backs together. Shef had been left with ten English freedmen, teeth chattering with fear. Lacking knowledge or plan he had simply taken them all to the top of the barrow and told them to dig straight down, as near to the center as he could measure.

At last they had hit something. "Is it a box?" he called hopefully down the shaft.

The only response was frantic tugs on the ropes that led down into the eight-foot-deep hole. "They want to come up," muttered one of the men standing round it.

"Haul away, then."

Slowly the mud-stained men were dragged up out of the earth. Shef waited with what patience he could for a report.

"Not a box, master. It's a boat. The bottom of a boat. They must have buried 'un upside down."

"So break through it."

Heads shook. Silently, one of the ex-slaves held out his mattock. Another passed a faintly glowing fir-brand. Shef took both. There was no point now, he realized, in asking for further volunteers. He drove the halberd in his hand deep into the ground by its spike, took a rope, tested its anchor-stake, glanced round at the dark figures, only their eyeballs showing in the night.

"Stay by the rope." Heads nodded. He lowered himself awkwardly, torch and mattock in one hand, into the dark.

At the bottom he found himself standing on gently sloping wood, obviously near the keel. He ran his hand over the planks in the faint torchlight. Overlapping, clinker-built. And, he could feel, heavily tarred. How long might that have lasted in this dry, sandy soil? He lifted the mattock and struck—struck again more firmly, heard the sound of splintering wood.

A rush of air and a foul stench enveloped him. His torch glowed with sudden force. Cries of alarm and scamperings from above. Yet this was not a stench of corruption. More, he felt, like the smell of a cow-byre at winter's end. He struck again and again, widening the hole. Beneath it, he realized, there was vacancy, not earth. The barrow-builders had succeeded in creating a chamber for the dead, and for the hoard, had not merely left it buried in the ground for him to sift through a shovel at a time.

Shef dropped the rope through the hole he had made and swung himself after it, torch in hand.

His feet crunched on bones. Human bones. He looked down, and felt a wave of pity. The ribs he had snapped were not those of the master of the hoard. They were a woman's bones. He could see her cloak-brooch glinting below the skull. But she lay facedown, one of a pair, stretched out lengthwise along the floor of the burial chamber. Both women's spines, he could see now, were snapped, by the great quernstones that must have been hurled down upon them. Their hands had been tied, they had been lowered into the tomb, their backs had been broken and then they had been left to die in the dark. The quernstones showed what they had been and what they were there for: they were the master's grinding slaves. Here to grind his meal and prepare his porridge into eternity.

Where the slaves were, there the master would be. He lifted his torch and turned toward the stern of the ship.

There, on his high seat, sat the king. Gazing out over hounds and horse and women. His teeth grinning out through shriveled skin. A gold circlet still lay on the bald skull. Stepping closer, Shef stared into the half-preserved face, as if looking for the secret of majesty. He remembered the urge of Kar the Old, to keep things his, to have them under his hand forever rather than live without them. Beneath this king's hand there was a regal whetstone, the ensign of the warrior-king who lived by sharpened weapons alone. Shef's torch suddenly went out.

Shef stood stock-still, skin crawling. In front of him there was a creak, a shifting of weight. The old king lifting himself out of his chair to settle with the invader who had come to take what he had hoarded. Shef braced for the touch of bony fingers, the awful teeth in the dried leather face.

He turned from his place and in the pitch-black walked back four, five, six paces, hopefully to the point where he had first descended. Was the blackness just perceptibly reduced? Why was he shaking like a common slave? He had faced death above—he would face death here in the darkness.

"You have no right to the gold now," he said into the blackness, groping his way back to the high seat. "Your children's children's child gave it to me. For a purpose."

He groped till his fingers found the torch, then bent over while he worked his flint and steel and tinder out of their pouch, strove to catch a spark.

"Anyway, Old Bones, you should be glad to give your wealth to an Englishman. There are worse than me who would take it from you."

Torch alight again, he propped it against a rotting timber, stepped up to the seat with its grisly occupant, put his arms round the body and lifted it carefully, hoping the remains of

flesh and skin and cloth would hold the crumbling bones together. Turning, he laid it down to face the women's bodies
in the well of the boat.

"Now you three must fight your own battles down here."

He took the gold circlet from the skull and pressed it
down on his own head. Turning back to the empty chair, he
picked up the whetstone, the scepter that had lain under the
king's right hand and tapped its solid two-foot weight meditatively into one palm.

"One thing I will give you for your gold," he added.
"And that is vengeance for your descendant. Vengeance on
the Boneless One."

As he spoke, something rustled in the dim darkness behind
him. For the first time Shef recoiled with shock. Had the
Boneless One heard his name and come? Was he trapped in
the tomb with some monstrous serpent?

Mastering himself, Shef stepped towards the noise, torch
high. It was the rope by which he had climbed down. The
end of it had been cut.

From above, dimly, he heard grunts of effort. Earth began, as it had done in his dream of Kar the Old, to patter
down through the hole.

It took all his effort of will to reason this out. It was not a
nightmare, not something to destroy one's wits. Call it a
puzzle, something to work out and solve.

There are enemies up there. Padda and his men might
have become frightened and run off, but they would not
have cut the rope or thrown earth down on me. Nor would
Guthmund. So someone has driven them off while I was
down here, maybe the English, come to defend their king's
mound. But they do not seem to want to come down after
me. Still, I will never get out this way.

But is there another way? King Edmund had spoken of
this as Raedwald's hoard, but this is the mound of Wuffa.
Could he and his ancestors have been using this as a hiding
place for wealth? If so, there might be a way to add to
it—or to withdraw it. But the mound was solid above. Is

there another way? If there is, it will be close to the gold. And the gold will be as close as it can be to the guardian.

Stepping over the bodies he walked to the chair and pulled it to one side to reveal four stout wooden boxes with leather handles. Sound leather handles, he noted, fingering one. Behind them, cut neatly out of the planking where the bow of the boat curved down, a square black hole, hardly bigger than a man's shoulders.

That is the tunnel! He felt immense relief, an invisible weight lifted from him. It was possible. A man from outside could crawl along that, open a box, close a box, do what he needed. He would not even have to face the old king he knew was there.

The tunnel must be faced. He pushed the circlet down on his head again, gripped the torch, now burned almost to its end. Should he take whetstone or mattock? I could dig myself out with the mattock, he thought. But now I have taken his scepter from the old king, I have no right to put it down.

Torch in one hand, whetstone in the other, he stooped and crawled into the blackness.

As he inched forward the tunnel narrowed. He had to thrust first with one shoulder, then with the other. The torch burned down, scorching his hand. He crushed it out against the earth wall and crawled on, trying to believe that the walls were not closing on him. Sweat sprang out on his head and ran into his eyes; he could not free a hand to wipe them. Nor could he crawl back now; the tunnel was too low for him to raise his hips and edge backward.

His hand before him met not earth floor but vacancy. A push and his head and shoulders were over a gap. Cautiously, he reached forward again. Solid earth, two feet ahead, leading only downward. The builders did not want to make this too easy, he thought.

But I know what must be there. I know this is not a trap, but an entrance. So I must crawl down, round the bend. My face will be in the soil for a foot or two, but I can hold my breath for long enough.

If I am wrong, I will die smothered, face down. The

worst thing will be if I struggle. That I will not do. If I cannot get through I will push my face in the earth and die.

Shef crawled over the edge and twisted his body down. For a moment he could not make his muscles force him on, as his legs retained a lingering grip on the level floor he had left. Then he pushed himself down, slid a foot or two, and stuck. He was jammed upside down in the tunnel in the pitch-black.

Not a nightmare, no panic. I must think of this as a puzzle. This cannot be a blind alley, no sense to it. Thorvin always said that no man bears a better burden than sense.

Shef groped round him. A gap. Behind his neck. Like a snake he slid into it. And there was level floor again, with this time a gap leading upward. He heaved himself into it, and for the first time in what seemed an age, stood upright. Beneath his fingers he found a wooden ladder.

He climbed unsteadily upward. His head bumped against a trapdoor. But a door designed to be approached from outside would not open so readily from within. There could be feet of earth heaped on top of it.

Pulling the whetstone from his belt he braced himself against the shaft-wall and stabbed upward with the sharpened end. The wood splintered, creaked. He struck again and again. When he could get a hand through broken wood he wrenched more free. Sandy soil began to patter down into the tunnel, rushing faster and faster as the hole widened and the pale sky of dawn appeared above.

Shef hauled himself exhaustedly from the tunnel, emerging inside a copse of dense hawthorns, no more than a hundred paces from the barrow he had entered so long ago. On the barrow-top stood a knot of figures, staring down. He would not hide nor crawl away from them. He straightened up, settled the circlet, hefted the whetstone and walked quietly over toward them.

It was Hjörvarth, his half brother, as he had almost expected. Someone saw him in the growing light, cried out, fell back. The clump of men drew away from him, leaving Hjörvarth in the middle, by the still-unfilled hole. Shef stepped over the body of one of his English diggers, cut from shoulder to chest by a broadsword. He was aware now that Guthmund had a group of men drawn up fifty yards off, weapons drawn but unready to interfere.

Shef looked wearily at the horse-toothed face of his half brother.

"Well, brother," he said. "It seems you want more than your share. Or are you maybe doing this for someone who is not here?"

The face in front of him tightened. Hjörvarth pulled his broadsword free, thrust his shield forward and paced down the slope of the barrow.

"You are no son to my father," he snarled, and swung his broadsword.

Shef lifted the wrist-thick whetstone into its path. "Stone blunts scissors," he said as the sword snapped. "And stone crushes skull." He whipped the stone round backhand and felt the crunch as one of the carved, savage faces at one end sank into Hjörvarth's temple.

The Viking staggered, fell on one knee, propping himself for a moment with his broken sword. Shef stepped sideways, measured the blow and swung with all his strength. Another crunch of bone, and his brother toppled forward, blood streaming from mouth and ears. Slowly, Shef wiped the gray matter from the stone and looked round at the gaping men from Hjörvarth's crew.

"Family business," he said. "None of you need be concerned."

Chapter Ten

His appeal to the Viking council was not going Sigvarth's way. His face, white and strained, stared across the table.

"He killed my son—and for that I demand compensation."

Brand lifted a great hand to silence him. "We will hear Guthmund out. Continue."

"My men were spread out in the darkness around the mound. Hjörvarth's men came on us suddenly. We heard their voices, knew they weren't Englishmen, but were not sure what to do. They pushed aside those who challenged them. No lives lost. Then Hjörvarth tried to kill his brother Skjef, first by burying him alive in the barrow, then by attacking him with a sword. We all saw it. Skjef was armed only with a stone rod."

"He killed Padda and five of my diggers," said Shef. The council ignored him.

Brand's voice rumbled gently but decisively. "As I see it there can be no claim for compensation, Sigvarth. Not even for a son. He tried to kill a fellow member of the Army, protected under our Wayman-law. If he had succeeded I would have hanged him. He tried, too, to bury his brother in the barrow. And if he had succeeded in that, think what we would have lost!" He shook his head with disbelieving wonder.

At least two hundred pounds' weight of gold. Much of it of workmanship far exceeding the value of the raw metal. Carved bowls from the Rome-folk. Great torques of pale gold from the land of the Irish. Coins with the heads of unknown Rome-folk rulers. Work of Córdoba and Miklagarth, of Rome and Germany. And added to it, sackloads of silver wedged into the tunnel mouth where the kings' depositors had put them over the generations. Enough there, all told, for every man of the whole Wayman army to be rich for life. If they lived to spend it. Secrecy had vanished with the dawn.

Sigvarth shook his head, his expression unchanging. "They were brothers," he muttered. "One man's sons."

"So there must be no question of vengeance," Brand said. "You cannot avenge one son on another, Sigvarth. You must swear to that." He paused. "It was the doom of the Norns. An ill doom, maybe. But not to be averted by mortals."

Sigvarth nodded this time. "Aye. The Norns. I will swear, Brand. Hjörvarth will lie unavenged. For me."

"Good. Because I tell you all," Brand looked round the table, "with all this wealth in hand I have grown nervous as a virgin at an orgy. The countryside must be buzzing with tales of what we have found. Shef's freedmen talk to the churls and the thralls. News goes both ways. They have heard that a new army has marched into this kingdom. An English army, from the Mark, come to reestablish the kingdom. You can be sure they have already heard of us. If they have any sense they will be marching already to cut us off from our ships, or to pursue us there if they are too late.

"I want camp struck and the men marching before the sun sets. March through the night and the next day. No halt before sunset tomorrow. Tell the skippers, get the beasts fed and the men in ranks."

As the group broke up and Shef moved to see to his carts, Brand caught him by the shoulder.

"Not you," he said. "If I had polished steel I would make you look in it. Do you know you have white hairs on your temples? Guthmund will take care of the carts. You travel in the back of a cart, with my cloak over you as well as your own." He passed over a flask.

"Drink this. I saved it. Call it a gift from Othin, for the man who found the greatest hoard since Gunnar hid the gold of the Niflungs." Shef caught the odor of fermented honey: Othin's mead.

Brand looked down at the ghastly, ruined face—one eye sunk and shriveled, cheekbones standing out over tight-drawn muscles. I wonder, he thought. What price did the *draugr* in the mound take for his treasure? He clapped Shef again on the shoulder and hurried away, shouting for Steinulf and his skippers.

They marched with Shef in the back of a cart, flask drained now, lulled to half-sleep by the rocking motion. Wedged in between two treasure-chests and a catapult-

beam. Close beside each treasure-cart marched a dozen men
of Brand's own crews, now detailed as close escort. Round
them clustered the freedmen catapulteers, spurred on by the
rumor that they too might earn a small share, hold money
for the first time in their lives. To front and rear and on the
flanks rode strong squads of Vikings, alert for ambush or
pursuit. Brand rode the length of the column, changing
horses as often as one flagged beneath his weight, continually cursing all to greater effort.

Someone else's job now, thought Shef. He slid again into
a deeper slumber.

*He was riding across a plain. More than riding—spurring
frantically. His horse groaned under him as he raked the
rowels again across its bleeding ribs, fought against the bit,
was mastered and driven on. Shef rose in his saddle and
looked behind. Over the brow of a low hill, a horde of riders pouring after him, one well out in front on a mighty
gray. Athils, king of Sweden.*

*And who was he, the rider? The Shef-mind could not tell
what body it occupied. But it was a man strikingly tall, so
tall that even from the great horse he rode his long legs
brushed the ground. The tall man had companions, the Shef-
mind noted. Strange ones too. Nearest him was a man so
broad in the shoulder that it seemed he had a milkmaid's
yoke under his leather jacket. His face was broad also, his
nose snub, his expression one of animal resource. His horse,
too, was laboring, unable to bear the weight at the speed
they were traveling. By him was a man unusually handsome—tall, fair, eyelashes like a girl's. Nine or ten other
riders pounded along at the same killing pace in front of the
tall man and his two nearest companions.*

*"They will catch us!" called the broad man. He detached
a short axe from his saddle-bow and shook it cheerfully.*

*"Not yet, Böthvar," said the tall one. He halted his horse,
pulled a sack from his own saddlebag, reached inside,
pulled out handfuls of gold. He scattered them on the
ground, wheeled the horse again, rode on. Minutes later,*

turning on the brow of a hill again, he saw the pursuing horde check, fragment, break into a cluster of men pushing and thrusting their horses against each other while they groped on the ground. The gray horse detached itself, came on, other riders spurring to catch up in its wake.

Twice more the tall man did the same thing as the pursuit continued, each time losing more of the pursuers. But the spurs were having no effect now, the ridden horses moving at hardly a walk. Yet there was not far to go, to reach safety—what the safety was the Shef-mind did not know. A ship? A boundary? It did not matter. All that had to be done was reach it.

Böthvar's horse collapsed suddenly, rolling over in a flurry of foam and blood from its nostrils. The broad man leapt nimbly free, clutched his axe, turned eagerly to face the riders now a bare hundred yards off. Still too many riders, and the king in front—Athils of Sweden on the gray horse Hrafn.

"Drag him, Hjalti," said the tall man. He reached in the sack once again. Nothing there for his fingers to draw out. Except one thing. The ring Sviagris. Even as death rode toward him, with safety a final spurt away, the tall man hesitated. Then, with an effort, he raised it and flung it far back down the muddy trail toward Athils, slipping instantly from his horse and running with all his might towards the safe haven across the ridge.

At the ridge, he turned. Athils had reached the ring. He slowed his horse, reached down with a spear, trying to pick the ring off the ground with its point and ride on without check. Failure. He wheeled his horse, confusing the men behind him, tried again. Again a miss.

In hatred and indecision Athils looked at his enemy there on the brink of escape, looked down again at the ring sinking in the muck. Suddenly he lunged from his horse, bent down, groped for his treasure. Lost his chance.

The tall man cawed with laughter, ran on after his fellows. As the broad one, Böthvar, turned questioningly to-

*wards him, he cried out in triumph: "Now I have made he
who is greatest among the Swedes root like a swine!"*

Shef sat up violently in the cart, mouthing the word
svinbeygt. He found himself staring into Thorvin's face.

" 'Swine-bowed,' is it? That is the word that King Hrolf
spoke on Fyrisvellir Plain. I am glad to see you rested. But
now I think it is time you stepped out like all of us."

He helped Shef scramble over the side of the cart, jumped
down beside him. Spoke in a low whisper. "There is an
army behind us. At every hamlet your thralls manage to get
more news. They say there are three thousand men behind
us, the army of the Mark. They left Ipswich as we left
Woodbridge, and they have heard now about the gold.
Brand has sent riders ahead to the camp at Crowland and
told the rest of our army to meet us ready for battle—at
March. If we join with them we are safe. Twenty long hundreds of Vikings, twenty-five of Englishmen. But they will
break as usual. If they catch us before March it will be another story.

"They say a strange thing, too. The army, they say, is led
by a heimnar. A heimnar and his son."

Shef felt a chill sweep through him. A volley of shouted
orders rang out from ahead, with carts pulling aside and
men suddenly unslinging packs.

"Brand halts the column every two hours to water the
beasts and feed the men," said Thorvin. "Even in haste he
says it saves time."

An army behind us, thought Shef. And us marching in
haste for safety. That is what I saw in my dream. I was
meant to learn from the ring, the ring Sviagris.

But *who* meant it? One of the gods, but not Thor, not
Othin. Thor is against me, and Othin only watches. How
many gods are there? I wish I could ask Thorvin. But I do
not think my protector—the one who sends the warnings—I
do not think he likes inquiries.

As Shef strode toward the head of the column, brooding
on Sviagris, he saw Sigvarth by the side of the road,

slumped on a folding canvas stool his men had placed for him. His father's eyes followed him as he passed.

It was just dawn when Shef's weary eyes picked out through the February murk the bulk of Ely Minster, to the right of their line of march. It had been gutted already by the Great Army, but the spire was still there.

"Are we safe now?" he asked Thorvin.

"The thralls seem to think so. Look at them laughing. But why? It is a day's tramp yet to March, and the Mark-men are close behind."

"It is the fens beyond Ely," said Shef. "This time of year, the road to March is a causeway for many miles, built up above the mud and water. If we needed to, we could turn and block the road with a few men and a barricade. There is no way round. Not for strangers."

There was a stillness spreading down the column, a stillness in the wake of Brand. He suddenly stood before Shef and Thorvin, his cloak black with mud, face white and shocked.

"Halt!" he yelled. "All of you. Feed, water, loosen girths." In a much lower voice he muttered to the two councillors, "Bad trouble. Meeting up ahead. Don't let it show on your face."

Shef and Thorvin looked at each other. Silently they followed him.

A dozen men, the Viking leaders, stood to one side of the track, boots already sinking in the mire. Unspeaking in the midst of them, left hand always on sword-pommel, was Sigvarth Jarl.

"It's Ivar," said Brand without preamble. "He hit the main camp at Crowland last night. Killed some, scattered the rest. Certainly caught some of our people. They must have talked by now. He'll know where we're supposed to meet. He'll know about the gold.

"We have to figure that he's already marching to intercept us. So we've got him to the north and the English a couple of miles to the south."

"How many men?" asked Guthmund.

"They thought—the ones who escaped and rode to meet us—about two thousand. Not the whole York army. None of the other Ragnarssons there. Only Ivar and his lot."

"We could take them if we were at full strength," said Guthmund. "Bunch of criminals. Gaddgedlar. Broken men." He spat.

"We aren't at full strength."

"But we will be soon," went on Guthmund. "If Ivar knows about the gold, I bet everyone in that camp knew about it first. They were probably all pissed drunk celebrating when he turned up. As soon as their heads clear, the ones who got away will head straight for the meeting ground at March. We meet them there, we're at full strength, or damn near. Then we'll settle Ivar's lot. You can have Ivar yourself, Brand. You have a score to pay."

Brand grinned. It was hard, Shef reflected, to scare these people. They had to be killed, one at a time, till they were all dead, to defeat them. Unfortunately that was what was likely to happen.

"What about the English behind us?" he asked.

Brand sobered again, drawn from his dream of single combat.

"They should be a lot less of a problem. We've always beaten them. But if they come up on us from behind while we're engaged with Ivar . . . We need time. Time to pick up the rest of the army at March. Time to settle Ivar's hash."

Shef thought of his vision. We have to throw them something they want, he reflected. Not treasure. Brand would never let go of it.

The old king's whetstone from the barrow was still in his belt. He pulled it out, stared at the bearded, crowned faces carved on each end. Savage faces, full of the awareness of power. Kings have to do things other men would not. So do leaders. So do jarls. They had said there would be a price to be paid for the hoard. Maybe this was it. When he looked up he saw Sigvarth was staring round-eyed at the weapon that had beaten out the brains of his son.

"The causeway," said Shef hoarsely. "A few men can block it against the English for a long time."

"They could," Brand agreed. "But they will have to be led by one of us. A leader. One who is used to independent command. One who can rely on his own men. Maybe a long hundred of them."

For long moments the silence was unbroken. Whoever stayed behind was as good as dead. This was asking a lot—even of these Vikings.

Sigvarth stared at Shef coldly, waiting for him to speak. But it was Brand's voice that broke the silence.

"There is one here who has a full crew to back him. One who made the heimnar that now is carried toward us by the English. . . ."

"Do you speak of me, Brand? Do you ask me to set my feet and those of my men on the path to Hell?"

"Yes, Sigvarth, I speak of you."

Sigvarth started to answer, then turned and looked towards Shef. "Yes, I will do it. I feel that the runes are already cut that tell of this. You said my son's death was the will of the Norns. I think the Norns are weaving fates together on this causeway too. And not the Norns alone."

He raised his eyes to meet his son's.

The front ranks of the army of the Mark, hurrying on through the night in pursuit of their fleeing enemies, fell into Sigvarth's trap an hour after sunset. In twenty heartbeats of slaughter the Englishmen, packed ten abreast on the narrow causeway through the marsh, lost half a hundred picked champions. The rest—weary, wet, hungry, furious with their leaders—fell back in confusion, not even coming on again to recover the bodies and their armor. For an hour Sigvarth's men, standing tensely ready, heard them shouting and haranguing each other. Then, slowly, the noise of men retreating. Not frightened. Unsure. Wondering if there was a way round. Waiting for orders. Leaving it to the next man. Ready for a night's sleep, even in a sodden blanket on the ground, before risking precious life against something unknown.

Twelve hours gained already, thought Sigvarth, standing his men down. Though not for me. I may as well watch as anything else. I shall not sleep again after the death of my son. My one son. I wonder if the other *is* my son. If he is, he is his father's bane.

With dawn, the English returned, three thousand men, to see the nature of the barrier that blocked their way.

The Vikings had dug into the sodden February soil on both sides of the track through the fens. A foot down they had reached water. Two feet down and only mud came up. Instead of their normal earthwork they had dug a water-filled ditch ten feet broad. On their side of it they had jammed into the ground such bits of timber as they could break up from the cart Shef had left behind. A flimsy obstacle to be cleared in a few moments by a gang of churls. If there had been no men behind it.

There was room on the causeway for only ten to stand. For only five to wield weapons. The warriors of the Mark, coming forward cautiously, shields raised, found themselves floundering thigh-deep in freezing water before they were in sword-range of an enemy. Their leather shoes skidded on the bottom. As they edged on, bearded faces glared at them, two-handed axes resting on shoulders. Strike at the men? A man had to struggle up a muddy slope to get in a blow. While he did, the axemen could pick their spot.

Strike at the timbers then, at the breastwork. But take your eyes off the man above you and he would cut arm from shoulder or head from neck.

Gingerly, striving desperately for balance, the Mercian champions probed crabwise into battle, urged on by cries of encouragement from those not yet engaged.

As the short day drew on, the fighting gathered momentum. Cwichelm, the Mercian captain, deputed by his king to advise and support the new alderman, lost patience with the tentative assaults, pulled his men back, ordered forward a score of bowmen with unlimited arrows to line the track. "Shoot at head level," he told them. "Doesn't matter if you miss. Just keep them down."

Other men kept up a barrage with javelins, just over the heads of their fighting fellows. Cwichelm's best swordsmen, spurred on with appeals to their pride, were told to go forward and fence—to not rush forward. Tire them out for a while, then change places with the next rank. Meanwhile a thousand men had been sent miles to the rear, to cut brushwood, bring it forward, throw it under the feet of the fighters, let them trample it under to make, in time, a solid platform.

Alfgar, watching from twenty paces back, pulled his fair beard with vexation.

"How many men do you need?" he asked. "It's only a ditch and a fence. One good push and we'll be through it. It doesn't matter if we lose a few."

The captain eyed his master-by-title sardonically. "Try telling that to the few," he said. "Or maybe you'd care to try it yourself? Just take out that big fellow in the middle. The one laughing. With the yellow teeth."

In the dim light, Alfgar stared across the cold water and the struggling men at Sigvarth, padding from side to side as he beat aside sword-strokes, sparred to get in a blow. Alfgar thrust his hand into his belt as it began to tremble.

"Bring my father forward," he muttered to his attendants. "There is something for him to see."

"The English are bringing up a coffin," observed one of the Viking front-rankers to Sigvarth. "I would have thought they needed more than just one by now."

Sigvarth stared at the padded box, held almost upright by its bearers, its occupant held in place by chest- and waist-straps. Across the water, his eyes met those of the man he had maimed. After a moment, he threw his head back in a wild cry of laughter, raised his shield, shook his axe, called out in Norse.

"What does he say?" muttered Alfgar.

"He is calling to your father," translated Cwichelm. "Does he recognize the axe? Does he think it forgot something? Drop his breeches and he will do his best to remember."

Wulfgar's mouth moved. His son bent to hear the hoarse mumble.

"He says he will give his whole estate to the man who takes that one alive."

Cwichelm pursed his lips. "Easier said than done. One thing about these devils. You can beat them, sometimes. But it's never easy. Never, never easy."

From the sky above them came a shrill whistling, dropping closer.

"Lower away!" barked the leader of catapult team one. The twelve freed thralls on the ropes thrust right hand over left hand over right hand, shouting hoarsely as they did so. "One—two—three." The sling dropped into the leader's hands. As it came down, the loader sprang from his kneeling position, shoved a ten-pound rock into position, leapt instantly back into his place, reaching for the next one.

"Take the strain!" Backs bent, the machine's arm flexed, the leader felt himself pulled up on to his toes.

"Pull!" A simultaneous grunt, the lash of the sling, a rock whirling into the air. As it went, it span, the chipped grooves on its surface setting up an ominous whistling. In the same moment, the crew heard the cry from behind them of the leader of catapult two.

"Take the strain!"

Traction-catapults were strange beasts in that they had most power at maximum range. They lobbed their missiles up in the sky. The higher they went, the harder they hit. The two teams of ex-slaves Shef had left behind with their cart and their machines had accordingly set up their pull-throwers a carefully paced two hundred yards behind Sigvarth's breastwork on the causeway; their missiles would strike twenty-five yards further on.

The narrow causeway was the ideal killing-ground for the machines. They threw perfectly straight, never deviating more than a few feet either side of the center. The English freedmen had perfected a drill designed to ensure that everyone did everything exactly the same way every time, and as fast as possible. For three minutes they shot. Then stood easy, panting.

The boulders dropped death from the sky on the Mercian column. The first one struck a tall warrior on the head as he stood unmoving, beating his skull almost into his shoulders. The second hit an automatically raised shield, shattering the arm behind it, caroming off to smash in a rib cage. The third hit a turned back, crushing the spine. In instants the causeway was jammed with struggling men, attempting to get back and away from a death they still could not see or understand. On the packed mass the stones continued to fall, varying a few yards forward or back as the launchers' heaves fluctuated, but never missing the causeway itself. Only those who crowded forward into the ditch closest to the Vikings remained safe.

At the end of the three minutes the warriors leading the attack saw only chaos and ruin behind them. Those who fled to the rear saw now that at a certain distance they were safe.

Cwichelm, in the fore, waved his broadsword, yelled out in rage to Sigvarth, "Come out! Come out from your ditch and fight like men. With swords, not stones."

Sigvarth's yellow teeth showed again in a grin. "Come and make me," he called, in an approximation of English. "You so brave. How many of you you need?"

More hours gained, he thought. How long does it take an Englishman to learn sense?

Not quite long enough, he reflected as the short February day drew toward its end in rain and sleet. The ditch and the stone-throwers had shocked them. But very, very slowly, maybe not quite slowly enough, they had got over their shock and worked out what they should have done in the first place.

Which was everything—and all at once. Frontal assault to keep Sigvarth busy. Spears and arrows launched overhead, to harass. Brushwood under the feet of the fighters, to build up a platform. Men coming up in thin lines, eyes alert, to

give poor targets for the stone-throwers. Others floundering
through the marsh in small bodies, to try to climb the causeway behind his block, splitting his meager force. Comman-
deered boats poling along to get behind him and threaten to
cut off his retreat. Sigvarth's men were looking behind them
now. One solid push by the English, regardless of casualties,
and they really would be through.

One of the slaves from the stone-throwers was tugging at
Sigvarth's sleeve, talking in broken Norse.

"We go now," he said. "No more rocks. Master Shef, he
said, shoot till rocks gone, then go. Cut ropes, throw machines in swamp. Go now!"

Sigvarth nodded, watching the puny figure scamper away.
Now he had his own honor to think of. His own destiny to
fulfill. He walked forward toward the front line of the fighters, clapping men on the shoulder. "Move," he said to each
one. "Get your horse. Get out of this now. Ride straight for
March and they won't catch you."

His helmsman Vestlithi hesitated as Sigvarth tapped him.
"Who's bringing your horse, jarl? You'll have to move
quick."

"I have something to do yet. Go, Vestlithi. This is my
fate, not yours."

As the feet splashed away behind him, Sigvarth faced the
five leading champions of the Mark, probing suspiciously
forward, made wary of every opportunity by a long day of
slaughter.

"Come on," he called to them. "Only me!"

As the foot of the center man slipped, he leapt forward
with appalling speed, slashed, countered, thrust sword
through beard, leapt back again, feinting from one side to
the other as the enraged Englishmen closed in.

"Come on!" he shouted, yelling again the words of Ragnar's death-song, which Ivar Ragnarsson's skald had made:

" 'We struck with the sword. Sixty times and one
I have fought in the front when foemen clashed.
Never yet have I met—young though I started

To mar the mailcoats—my match in battle.
The gods will greet me. I grieve not for death.' "

Over the clash of combat, one man against an army,
Wulfgar's deep tones carried.

"Take him alive! Pin him with shields! Take him alive!"

I must let them do it, thought Sigvarth as he whirled and
slashed. I have not bought my son quite enough time. But
there is a way to buy him yet one more night.

It will be a long one for me.

Chapter Eleven

Shef and Brand, standing close together, watched the
battleline, two-hundred-men wide, tramping slowly toward them across the level meadowland turf. Over the advancing line battle-standards waved, the personal flags of
jarls and champions. Not the Raven Banner of the Ragnarssons, which flew only when all four brothers consented to
it. But above the central reserve a gust puffed out one long
ensign: the Coiling Worm of Ivar Ragnarsson himself. Even
at this distance Shef thought he could catch the glint of the
silver helmet, the scarlet cloak.

"Going to be a killing-ground today. We're too evenly
matched," Brand muttered. "Even the side that wins is going to take very heavy losses. Takes guts to walk forward in
the front rank, knowing that. Ivar's not in the front, pity. I
was hoping he would be; I could have a go at him myself.
The only cheap way for us to win this will be to kill a
leader and take the heart out of the rest."

"Is there a cheap way for them?"

"I doubt it. Our lads have seen the money. They've only
heard about it."

"But you still think we're going to lose?"

Brand patted Shef reassuringly. "Heroes never think things like that. But everybody loses some time. And we're outnumbered."

"You haven't counted my thralls."

"I've never known thralls to win battles."

"Wait and see."

Shef ran back a few paces from where he and Brand had been standing, beneath the Flag of the Hammer, at the rear center of their own—the Wayman line. It was drawn up in exactly the same style as Ivar's force, but only five-deep, with fewer reserves. Shef had placed his wheeled torsion-catapults—the dart-shooters—in the line, screened only by a single rank of men and shields. Well back behind the line stood the traction-catapults—the stone-throwers—all of them except for the pair he had left with Sigvarth, their half-crews clutching the flapping ropes.

But it was the twist-shooters that would do the work now. Using his halberd, Shef vaulted onto the central cart of the nine he had left, still drawn up, oxen still hitched. He looked up and down the line of men, seeing the faces of his catapult-crews turned toward him.

"Clear your line!"

The Vikings masking the line of fire shuffled sideways. The ropes were wound tight; loader stood ready with bundles of javelins; they were aimed and ready. The slowly advancing line of men was a target impossible to miss. Over the turf came the hoarse chanting of the Ragnarsson army: *"Ver thik,"* they shouted again and again. *"Ver thik, her ek kom."*—"Guard yourself, here I come."

Shef dropped the head of his halberd forward as he shouted, "Shoot!"

Black streaks, rising at the launch, falling as they flashed through the air. Plunging into the lines of advancing men.

The lever-men were rewinding furiously, javelins dropped into place. Shef waited until the last one was reloaded, the last hand up to signal readiness.

"Shoot!"

Again the thrums, the streaks, the swirls. A hum of excitement rose from the Wayman army. And there was something happening with the Ragnarsson line as well. They had abandoned their steady walk, their chanting wavered and died. Now they were trotting forward, anxious to close before they were impaled like roast pigs—without a blow struck. Running half a mile in armor would tire them nicely. The shooters had done one job already.

But they could not shoot much longer. Shef calculated that he could shoot twice more before the attackers reached the line. Kill a few more men, unsettle the rest.

As the machines leapt back on their wheels for the last time he ordered them back.

The crews lifted the trails, ran their machines back out of the line toward the carts, calling out with triumph.

"Shut up! Man the throwers."

In seconds the ex-thralls were loading and aiming the machines. Vikings would never have done that, thought Shef. They would have needed time to tell each other what deeds they had done. He raised his halberd up and ten boulders were hurled simultaneously into the air.

They reloaded as quickly as they could, inched the clumsy frames round as the captains lined them up. A rain of boulders whistled out of the sky, no longer in volleys, each machine shooting as fast as its crew could lower and load.

Harassed and shaken, the Ragnarsson line broke into all-out charge. Already stones were flying high, landing behind the charging men. Still Shef saw with satisfaction a long trail of smashed bodies and writhing injured, like a snailtrack behind the oncoming army.

The two battle-lines met with a roar and a crash of metal, instantly swaying back and then forward as the impetus of the Ragnarsson rush was felt, held, returned. In moments the battle had become a line of single combats, men beating swords and axes on shields, trying to drag an arm down, stab under a guard, crush face or rib with shield-boss.

In unison the white-clad priests of the Way, grouped behind their men round the sacred silver spear of Othin, god of battles, began a deep chant.

Shef hefted his halberd in indecision. He had done the job he meant to do. Should he now thrust forward to stand amid the fighters? One man amid four thousand?

No. There was still a way to bring his machines to bear. He ran to the thralls round their throwers, shouting and gesturing. Slowly, they took his meaning, ran back to the dart-shooters, began to run the wheeled machines up onto the waiting carts.

"Around their flank—follow me! They battle face-to-face. We can get behind them."

As the ox-carts creaked with agonizing slowness round behind the Wayman position, Shef saw faces turning. Wondering whether he was fleeing from battle. Fleeing in ox-carts? Some of them he recognized: Magnus, Kolbein and other Hebrideans, clustered at the rear in reserve. Brand had put them there, saying their weapons would be difficult to fence with in a packed mass.

"Magnus! I want six of your men with each cart for close defense."

"If we do that there'll be no reserve left."

"Do it and we won't need a reserve."

Halberdiers closed round the carts as Shef led them in a long sweep round the flanks of both battling armies, first the Waymen, then the Ragnarsson troops gaping in surprise. But with battle joined, unable to see the lumbering carts as anything but a distraction. At last they were in a position well to the rear right flank of the Ragnarsson army.

"Stop. Wheel the carts left. Chock the wheels. No! Don't unload the machines. We'll shoot from inside the carts.

"Now. Drop the tilts." Halberdiers whipped out the pins, let the wagon tilts fall forward. The wound and loaded catapults trained round.

Shef stared carefully at the scene in front of him. The two battle-lines were locked along a two-hundred-yard front, making no attempt to outmaneuver each other. But at the center of the Ragnarsson line Ivar had bunched a mass of men, twenty-deep, pushing steadily forward, aiming to break their outnumbered enemy by sheer weight. Above the central mass flew his standard. There was the place to aim—not at the front, where Shef might hit his own men.

"Aim for the center. Aim for the Coiling Worm. Shoot!"

The catapults leapt in the air as they shot, their recoil on hard planks instead of soft ground sending them skidding. The thralls seized them and ran them back again, lever-men struggling to fit the winders back in place.

Round the Worm Standard of Ivar there was chaos. In the throng of milling men Shef saw for an instant a long spike with two bodies threaded on it like larks on a spit. There was another man threshing desperately to free a snapped javelin-head from his arm. Faces were turning, and not just faces. He could see shields as well, as men realized the attack had come somehow from their rear and turned bodily to meet it. The Worm Standard still waved, its bearer still protected by the ranks of bodies that had been behind it. Reloading complete, Shef screamed the command.

"Shoot!"

This time the Worm went down, to a roar of delight from the Wayman center. Someone seized it, heaved it defiantly up once more, but the Ragnarsson center had yielded five blood-soaked yards, the men in it trying to keep their footing as they stumbled back over wet soil and their own dead. But there were men running now toward the carts.

"Change target?" shouted a captain, pointing at the advancing men.

"No! The Worm again! Shoot."

Another hail of darts into the tight-packed throng, and again the Worm went down. No time to see if it would come up again, or if Brand would now finish the job. The lever-men were still winding desperately but they would not get in another shot.

Shef reached down with his armored gloves, seized "Thrall's-Wreak" and the helmet he had never yet worn in battle.

"Halberdiers in the carts," he shouted. "Just fend them off. Catapulteers, use your levers, use your mattocks."

"What about us, master?" Fifty unarmed freedmen still

clustered behind the carts, hammer-emblems on their jerkins. "Shall us run?"

"Get under the carts. Use your knives."

Moments later the Ragnarsson wave reached them in a turmoil of glaring faces and slashing blades. Shef felt a weight roll from him. There was no need for thought now. No responsibility for others. The battle would be won or lost elsewhere. All he had to do now was swing his halberd as if he were still beating out metal at the forge: ward and cut, lunge overhand and stab downward.

On level ground the Ragnarsson followers would have rolled over Shef's outnumbered and half-armed force in instants. But they had no idea of how to fight men in farm wagons. Their enemies were feet higher than themselves, behind oak planks. The halberds Shef had made for them gave Magnus and his Hebrideans extra feet of reach. Vikings lunging under the halberds and trying to haul themselves into the carts were simple targets for the clubs and mattocks of the English thralls. Knives in skinny hands ripped upward at thigh and groin from behind sheltering wheels.

After a few desperate trials the Vikings fell back. Orders barked from the more level-headed among them. Men slashed the oxen free, seized the drag-poles, prepared to haul the carts off the thralls underneath. Javelins poised, ready for a united volley against the exposed halberdiers.

Shef found himself staring suddenly into the eyes of Muirtach. The big man paced forward, his own ranks parting for him, like a great wolf. He wore no mail, only the saffron plaid which left his right arm and torso bare. He had thrown away his targe, and carried only the dagger-pointed longsword of the Gaddgedlar in two hands.

"You and me now, boy," he said. "I'm going to keep yer scalp and use it for a bum-wipe."

In answer Shef jerked the pin free and kicked the wagon tilt down once more.

Muirtach charged before he could straighten up, faster than Shef had ever seen a human being move. Reflex alone hurled Shef backward, stumbling on the wheel of the machine behind him. But Muirtach was already in the cart, swordpoint down for the thrust. Shef leapt back again, cannoning off Magnus, unable to drop his halberd enough to stab or guard.

Muirtach was swinging already. A lunging lever from Cwicca deflected his stroke, guided it onto the bowstring of the fully wound but unloosed catapult.

A deep twang, a thwack louder than a whale-fluke on water.

"Son of the Virgin," said Muirtach, staring down.

One arm of the catapult, released, had slammed forward the six inches which were all that it could travel. In those six inches it had expended all the stored energy that could drive a barb a mile. The whole side of Muirtach's bare chest was crushed in as if from the hammer-blow of a giant. Blood ran from the Irishman's mouth. He stepped back, sat down, slumped back against the wagon wall.

"I see you have turned Christian again," said Shef. "So you will remember, 'an eye for an eye.'" Reversing his halberd, he drove its butt-spike deep through Muirtach's eye and into the brain.

In the brief seconds of the confrontation everything had changed. Shef looked up and saw only backs. The Ragnarsson attackers had turned away, were throwing down their weapons, unbuckling their shields. "Brother," they shouted, "fellow, messmate." One, incongruously, was pulling open his tunic, hauling out a silver emblem. A Wayman, maybe, who had decided to stay with a father or a chief rather than march out of York. Behind them hundreds of men were moving forward in a bristling wedge, the giant figure of Brand at its apex. In front of the wedge the plain was covered only with men running, men limping, men standing in knots with their hands raised. The Ragnarsson army had broken. Its survivors had the choice only of running for their lives in heavy mail or hoping for immediate mercy.

Shef lowered "Thrall's-Wreak," suddenly weary. As he started to clamber from the wagon a flash of movement caught his eye. Two horses, one a rider with a scarlet cloak, grass-green trousers.

For an instant Ivar Ragnarsson stared from his saddle across the lost battlefield at Shef standing on the cart. Then he and his horse-swain were away, clods flying in the air from the trampling hooves.

Brand strode over, clasped Shef's hand.

"You had me worried there, thought you were running away. But toward battle, not from it. A good day's work done."

"The day's not done yet. There is still an army behind us," said Shef. "And Sigvarth. The Mercians should have been at our backs this dawn. He has held them twelve hours longer than I thought possible."

"But maybe not long enough," said Magnus Gaptooth from his place on the wagon. He stretched out an arm, pointed. Far away across the level plain, a stray shaft of winter sunlight sent up a prickle of darting reflections: the spear-points of an army, deployed and advancing.

"I need more time," said Brand gruffly in Shef's ear. "Go talk, bargain, buy me some."

He had no choice. Thorvin and Guthmund joined him as he walked toward the advancing Mercian battle-line, different from the one they had just broken, only—to outward appearance—by the three great crosses towering above it.

Behind them the Wayman army struggled to regroup. Perhaps a third of them were dead or gravely injured. Now even the walking wounded were furiously busy: stripping the surrendered Ragnarsson warriors of weapons and armor, scavenging the battlefield for whatever was usable or valuable—with the enthusiastic assistance of Shef's freedmen—herding the enemy wounded off in the direction of their ships still under guard by the Wash, carrying such few as had survived the attentions of the body-strippers off to the leeches.

The "army" was a mere front. A few hundreds of the fittest men in line to make a show. Behind them, rank on rank of captives, hands loosely roped, told to stand there and be counted in return for their lives. Half a mile behind them, thralls and warriors were hastily digging a ditch, setting up the machines—and rounding up horses and wagons ready for the next retreat. The Wayman army was not yet fit to fight—the heart had not gone out of it, not yet. But all tradition dictated a pause for celebration and relief after surviving a pitched battle against superior forces. Being asked to do the same again immediately was too much.

The next few minutes, Shef thought, would be very dangerous. Men were coming to meet him and his small party: three men walking together, one a priest. Two more pushing a strange, upright box on wheels. The thing in it, he realized an instant later, could only be his stepfather Wulfgar.

The two groups halted ten paces apart, surveyed each other. Shef broke the deep, hating silence.

"Well, Alfgar," he said to his half brother, "I see you have risen in the world. Is our mother pleased?"

"Our mother never recovered from what your father did. Your late father. He told us much about you before he died. He had plenty of time."

"Did you capture him, then? Or did you stand back as you did in the fight by the Stour?"

Alfgar stepped forward, hand reaching for his sword. The grim-faced man beside him, the one who was not a priest, caught his arm quickly.

"I am Cwichelm, marshal of King Burgred of the Mark," he said, "charged to restore the shires of Norfolk and Suffolk to their new alderman and to make them subject to my kind. And who are you?"

Slowly, mindful of the frantic preparations still going on behind, Shef introduced the others on his side, let Cwichelm do the same. Disclaimed hostile intention. Declared intention to withdraw. Hinted at compensation for damage.

"You're fencing with me, young man," broke in Cwichelm. "If you were strong enough to fight, you wouldn't be talking. So I'll tell you what you have to do if you want to see tomorrow's dawn. First, we know you took treasure from the mound by Woodbridge. I must have it all, for my king. It comes from his realm."

"Second," cut in the black-robed priest, staring fixedly at Thorvin, "there are Christians among you who have deserted their faith and betrayed their masters. They must be handed over for punishment."

"You included," said Alfgar. "Whatever happens to the others, my father and I will not see you march away. I will put the collar on you with my own hands. Think yourself lucky we do not treat you as we did your father."

Shef did not bother to translate for Guthmund.

"What did you to my father?"

Wulfgar had not spoken till then. He sprawled in his box, held by the straps. Shef remembered the yellow, pain-racked face he had last seen in the trough. Now Wulfgar's face was ruddy, his lips showing red in the white-streaked beard.

"What he did to me," he said, "I did to him. Only more skillfully. First we took the fingers, then the toes. Ears, lips. Not his eyes, so he could see what we did, nor his tongue, so he could still call out. Hands, feet. Knees and elbows. And never allowed to bleed. I whittled him like a boy whittling a stick. In the end there was nothing left but the core.

"Here, boy. A memorial of your father."

He nodded and a servant threw a leather pouch in Shef's direction. Shef loosed the strings, glanced inside, hurled it at Cwichelm's feet.

"You are in poor company, warrior," he remarked.

"Time to go," said Guthmund.

The two sides backed away from each other, turned at safe distance. As they stepped briskly toward their own lines, Shef heard the Mercian warhorns bellow, heard a roar and a clash of mail as the English army came on.

Instantly, as prearranged, the Wayman line turned tail and ran. The first stage of its long, planned retreat.

Hours later, as the long winter twilight faded into dark, Brand muttered dry-throated to Shef, "I think we may have done it."

"For the day," Shef agreed. "I see no hope for the morning."

Brand shrugged massively, called the orders to stand down, light fires, heat water, make food.

All day the Waymen had fallen back, screening Shef's machines, shooting as the Mercians deployed, making them check, loading the carts and pack-horses hastily and then falling back in sections to another line. The Mercians had followed them like men anxious to tether a savage dog, closing in, drawing back from the snarls and snaps, pressing forward again. At least three times the two armies had clashed hand to hand, each time when the Waymen had had some obstacle to defend: the ditch they had cut, a dyke along the edge of the fen, the shallow muddy stream of the Nene. Each time, after half an hour's slashing and hewing, the Mercians had fallen sullenly back, unable to force the crossing—and in doing so, exposed themselves again to the lash of the boulders and the barbs.

The Waymen had fought better as their spirits rose, thought Shef. The trouble was, the Mercians were learning too. At the start they had flinched from the first whistle in the sky, the first displayed twist-shooter in a battle-line. Each ditch in the boggy soil made them hesitate. Sigvarth must have taught them a bitter lesson in the fen.

But as the day wore on they grew bolder, seeing the true weakness of the Wayman numbers.

Still holding a half-eaten bowl of porridge, Shef sank back on a pack-saddle and fell into instant sleep.

He woke, stiff, clammy and bitterly cold, as the horns blew for first light. All round him men clambered to their feet, drank water or the last hoarded remains of ale or mead. They shuffled to the crude breastwork they had made in the hamlet Brand had selected for their last stand.

As the light grew they looked out on a sight to daunt the boldest. The army they had fought the day before, like themselves, had grown steadily more ragged—clothes sodden, shields defaced with muck, its men grimed up to their eyebrows, weakened by a steady trickle of casualties and deserters—down to the point where it was barely half again their own size.

It had gone. In its place, drawn up in front of them, rank on rank, horns blasting a continual challenge, stood a new army, as fresh as if it had never marched a mile. Shields blazed with new paint, mail and weapons glinted red in the dawn. Crosses towered over the ranks, but the banners—the banners were different. Next to the crosses, a golden dragon.

From the line in front of them trotted a rider on a gray horse, his saddle and trappings bright scarlet, shield turned outward in sign of truce.

"He wants a parley," Shef said.

Silently the Waymen shifted an upturned cart to one side, allowed their leaders to edge out: Brand, Shef, Thorvin and Farman, Guthmund and Steinulf. Still silent, they tramped behind the horsemen to a long trestle-table, set up incongruously in the midst of the standing men.

To one side of it sat Cwichelm and Alfgar, faces set. Wulfgar in his vertical box a pace behind them. The herald waved the six councillors of the Way to stools opposite.

Between the two groups sat one man—young, fair-haired, blue-eyed, a golden circle on his head like the old king in the mound. He had a strange, intense look, thought Shef. As he sat down, their eyes met. The young man smiled.

"I am Alfred, atheling of Wessex, brother of King Ethelred," he said. "I understand that my brother's fellow-king, Burgred of the Mark, has appointed an alderman for the shires once belonging to the king of the East Angles." He paused. "That cannot be allowed." Sour looks, silence from Alfgar and Cwichelm. They must have heard this already.

"At the same time I will not allow any Viking army from the North to base itself within any English shire, to rob and kill as has been your custom. Rather than do that I will destroy you all."

Another pause. "But I do not know what to do with you. From what I hear, you fought and beat Ivar Ragnarsson yesterday. Him, I will have no peace with, for he killed my brother's fellow-king Edmund. Who killed King Ella?"

"I did," said Shef. "But he would have thanked me for it if he could. I told Ivar that what he did to the king was *nithingsverk*."

"On so much we agree, then. The thing is, can I have peace with you? Or must we fight?"

"Have you asked your priests?" said Thorvin in his slow, careful English.

The young man smiled. "My brother and I have found that whenever we ask them anything, they demand money. Nor will they aid us even to keep off the likes of Ivar. But I am a Christian still. I believe in the faith of my fathers. I hope one day even you warriors of the North will take baptism and submit to our law. But I am not a Churchman."

"Some of us are Christians," said Shef. "Some of us are English."

"Are they full fellows of your army? With full rights to share?"

Brand, Guthmund and Steinulf looked at each other as they grasped the sense of the question.

"If you say they must be, then they are," said Shef.

"So. You are English and Norse. You are Christian and heathen."

"Not heathen," said Thorvin. "Wayman."

"But you can get along together. Maybe that is a model for us all. Listen, all of you. We can work out a treaty: shares and taxation, rights and duties, rules about wergilds and freedmen. All details. But the center of it must be this:

"I will give you Norfolk, to rule under your own law. But you must rule fairly. Never let in invaders. And the one who becomes alderman, he must swear on my relics and on your holy things to be the good friend of King Ethelred and his brother. Now, if that is to happen, who shall the alderman be?"

Brand's scarred hand reached out, tapped Shef. "He it must be, king's brother. He speaks two languages. He lives in two worlds. See, he has not the mark of the Way on him. He has been baptized. But he is our friend. Choose him."

"He is a runaway," yelled Alfgar suddenly. "He is a thrall. He has the marks of the whip on his back!"

"And of the torturer on his face," said Alfred. "Maybe he will see to it there is less of both in England. But console yourself, young man. I shall not send you back to King Burgred alone."

He waved a hand. From somewhere behind them came a flutter of skirts. A group of women were led into view.

"I found this party left behind and wandering, so I brought them along lest worse befall. I hear one of them is your wife, young noble. Take her back to King Burgred and be grateful."

His wife, thought Shef, staring deeply into Godive's gray eyes. She looked more beautiful than ever. What could she possibly think of him, covered in mire, stinking of sweat and worse, eye sunk in its socket? Her face showed utter horror. He felt a cold fist close round his heart.

Then she was in his arms, weeping. He held her tight with one hand, looked round. Alfgar was on his feet, struggling in the grip of two guards, Wulfgar bellowing from his box, Alfred rising with alarm on his face.

As the tumult ceased, Shef spoke. "She is mine."

"She is my wife," shouted Alfgar.

She is his half sister too, thought Shef. If I said that the Church would intervene, take her away from him. But then I would be letting the rule of the Church shape me and the law of the Way. The land of the Way.

This is the price the old *draugr* demands for his gold. Last time it was an eye. This time it is a heart.

He stood still as the attendants pulled Godive from him, drew her back to incest—her husband—and the blood-stained birch.

To be a king, to be a leader, demands things that cannot be asked of an ordinary man.

"If you are prepared to return the woman as a sign of good faith," said Alfred clearly, "I will take Suffolk into my brother's realm, but recognize you, Shef Sigwardsson, as alderman of Norfolk. What do you say?"

"Do not say 'alderman,'" said Brand, cutting in. "Use our word. Say he will be our jarl."

Jarl

Chapter One

Shef sat facing the crowd of supplicants on a plain, three-legged stool. He still wore a hemp tunic and woolen breeches, with no signs of rank. But in the crook of his left arm rested the whetstone-scepter taken from the mound of the old king. From time to time Shef ran a thumb gently over one of its cruel carved, bearded faces as he listened to the witnesses.

". . . and so we took the case to King Edmund at Norwich. And he judged it in his private chamber—he had just returned from hunting and was washing his hands, God strike me blind if I lie—and he decided that the land should come to me for ten years and then be returned."

The speaker, a middle-aged thane of Norfolk, years of good living swelling his gold-mounted belt, hesitated for a moment in his tirade, unsure whether the mention of God might not count against him in a Wayman court of doom.

"Have you any witnesses to this agreement?" Shef asked.

The thane, Leofwin, puffed out his cheeks with grotesque pomposity. Not used to being questioned, or contradicted, evidently.

"Yes, certainly. Many men were in the king's chamber then. Wulfhun and Wihthelm. And Edrich the king's thane. But Edrich was killed by the pagan—was killed in the great battle, and so was Wulfhun. And Wihthelm has since died of the lung-sickness. Nevertheless, things are as I say!" Leofwin ended defiantly, glaring round him at the others in the court: guards, attendants, his accuser, others waiting for their cases to be heard and decided.

Shef closed his one eye for a moment, remembering a far-off evening of peace in the fen with Edrich, not so very far from here in space. So that was what had happened to him. It might have been guessed.

He opened it again and stared fixedly at Leofwin's accuser. "Why," he said gently, "why does what King Edmund decided seem to you unjust in this case? Or do you deny that what this man says is what the king decided?"

The accuser, another middle-aged thane of the same stamp as his opponent, blanched visibly as the jarl's piercing gaze fell on him. This was the man, all Norfolk knew, who had begun as a thrall in Emneth. Who had been the last Englishman ever to speak to the martyred king. Who had appeared—God only knew how—as leader of the pagans. Had dug up the hoard of Raedwald. Defeated the Boneless One himself. And somehow had gained the friendship and support of Wessex as well. Who could tell how all that had come about? Dog's name or no, he was a man too strange to lie to.

"No," said the second thane. "I do not deny that was what the king decided, and I agreed to it as well. But when it was agreed, the understanding behind the decision was this: That after ten years' time the land in question should revert from Leofwin to my grandson, whose father was also killed by the pagans. That is to say, by the—by the men from the North. In the state in which it was in the beginning! But what this man has done"—indignation replaced caution in his voice—"what Leofwin has done ever since is to ruin it! He has cut the timber and planted no more, he has let the dykes and the drains go to ruin, he has turned ploughland into a watermeadow for hay. The land will be worth nothing at the end of his lease."

"Nothing?"

The complainant hesitated. "Not as much as before, lord jarl."

Somewhere outside a bell rang, a sign that the dooms-giving was over for the day. But this case must be decided. It was a hard one, as the court had heard already at tedious length, with debts and evasions of them going back for generations, and all the parties in the case related to each other. Neither of the men present today was of much consequence. Neither had seemed of special note to King Edmund, which was why they had been allowed to live on their estates when better men, like Edrich, had been called to service and to death. Still, they were Englishmen of rank, whose families had lived in Norfolk for generations: the sort of people who had to be won over. It was a good sign that they had come to the new jarl's court for judgement.

"This is my doom," said Shef. "The land shall remain with Leofwin for the rest of his ten-year lease." Leofwin's red face brightened into a beam of triumph.

"But he shall render an account of his gains each year to my thane at Lynn, whose name is—"

"Bald," said a black-robed figure standing by a writing-desk to Shef's right.

"Whose name is Bald. At the end of the ten years, if the gain on the property seems more than is reasonable to Bald, Leofwin shall either pay the extra gain for the whole ten years to the grandson in this case, or else he shall pay a sum to be fixed by Bald, equal in value to the worth the land has lost during his stewardship. And the choice shall be made by the grandfather, here present today."

One face lost its beam, the other brightened. Then both faces took on an identical expression of anxious calculation. Good, thought Shef. Neither is altogether happy. So they will respect my decision.

He rose. "The bell has struck. The dooms-giving is over for today." A babble of protest, men and women pushing forward from the waiting ranks.

"It will begin again tomorrow. You have your tally-sticks? Show them as you enter and cases will be heard in proper order." Shef's voice rose strongly above the babble.

"And all mark this! In the court of the Way there is neither Christian nor pagan, neither Wayman nor Englishman.

See—I bear no pendant. And Father Boniface here"—he pointed to the black-robed scribe—"priest though he is, he bears no cross. Justice here does not depend on faith. Mark it and tell it. Now go. The hearing is over."

The doors at the back of the room swung open. Attendants began to urge the disappointed litigants outside into the spring sunshine. Another, the hammer-sign stitched neatly onto his gray tunic, waved the two disputants of the last case over toward Father Boniface, to see the jarl's doom written out twice and witnessed, one copy to remain in the jarl's scriptorium, the other to be torn carefully in two and divided between the litigants, so that neither could present a forgery at some future court.

Through the rear doors there stalked a massive figure, head and shoulders above the people pushing out, in mail and cloak, but unarmed. Shef felt the lonely gloom of judgement suddenly lighten.

"Brand! You are back! You come just at the right moment, when I am free to talk."

Shef felt his hand gripped in one the size of a quart tankard, saw his own beaming smile answered.

"Not quite, lord jarl. I came two good hours ago. Your guards would not let me through, and with all those halberds waving and never a word of Norse among the lot of them I had not the heart to argue."

"Hah! They should—No. My orders are to let no one interrupt court of doom except for news of war. They did right. But I am sorry I did not think to make an exception for you. I would have liked you to attend the court and say what you thought of it."

"I heard." Brand jerked a thumb behind him. "The head of your guards there was a catapulteer and knew me, though I did not know him. He brought me good ale—excellent ale, after a sea-voyage, to wash out the salt—and told me to listen through the door."

"And what did you think?" Shef turned Brand about and strolled with him through the now-cleared doorway into the courtyard outside. "What did you think of the jarl's assembly?"

"I am impressed. When I think of what this place was like four months ago—mud everywhere, warriors snoring on the floor for lack of beds, never a kitchen in sight and no food to cook in it. And now. Guards. Chamberlains. Bakeries and brewhouses. Woodwrights fixing shutters and gangs painting everything that doesn't move. Men to ask your name and business. And *writing it down* when you tell them."

Then Brand frowned and looked about, lowered his enormous voice to an unpracticed whisper. "Shef—lord jarl, I should say. One thing. Why all these blackrobes? Can you trust them? And what in the name of Thor is a jarl doing, a lord of warriors, listening to a couple of muttonheads arguing about drains? You'd be better off shooting catapults. Or in the forge even."

Shef laughed, looking across at the massive silver buckle holding together his friend's cloak, the bulging purse on his sword-belt, the ornamental waist-chain of linked silver coins.

"Tell me, Brand, how did your trip home go? Were you able to buy all you meant to?"

Brand's face took on a hucksterish look of caution. "I put some money in safe hands. Prices are high in Halogaland, and folk are mean. Still, when I hang up my axe for good, it may be there is some small farm for me to retire to in my old age."

Shef laughed again. "With your share of all our winnings, in good silver, you must have bought up half the county for your relatives to look after."

This time Brand grinned too. "I did pretty well, I admit. Better than ever in my life before."

"Well, let me tell you about the blackrobes. What none of us has ever realized is the money the stay-at-homes have. The wealth in a whole county, a rich county of England, not a poor stony one in Norway where you come from. Tens of thousands of men, all tilling the soil and raising sheep and trimming wool and keeping bees and cutting timber and smelting iron and raising horses. More than a thousand square miles. Maybe a thousand thousand acres. All those acres must pay something to me, to the jarl, if it is only the war-tax, or bridge-and-road money.

"Some of them pay everything. I took all Church land into my own possession. Some of it I gave at once to the freed slaves who fought for us, twenty acres a man. Wealth to them—but a fleabite compared to the whole. Much I leased out straightaway, to the rich men of Norfolk, at low rates, for ready money. Those who got it will not want to see the Church come back. Much I kept in my own hand, for the jarldom. In future it will make money for me, to hire workers and warriors.

"But I could not have done it without the blackrobes, as you call them. Who could keep all this land, all these goods, all these leases, in his head? Thorvin knows how to write in our letters, but few others. Suddenly there were many lettered men, men of the Church, with no land and no income all of a sudden. Some now work for me."

"But can you trust them, Shef?"

"The ones who hate me and will never forgive me, or you, or the Way—they have gone off to King Burgred, or to Wulfhere the Archbishop, to stir up war."

"You should have just killed them all."

Shef hefted his stone scepter. "They say, the Christians, that the blood of martyrs is the seed of the Church. I believe them. I make no martyrs. But I made sure that the angriest of those who left knew the names of those who stayed. The ones who work for me will never be forgiven. Like the rich thanes, their fate now depends on mine."

They had come to a low building within the stockade that ran round the jarl's *burg*, its shutters open to the sun. Shef pointed inside to the writing-desks, the men conferring quietly, writing on parchment. On one wall Brand could see hung a great *mappa*: a newly made one, devoid of ornament, full of detail.

"By the winter I shall have a book of every piece of land

in Norfolk, and a picture of the whole shire on my wall. By next summer not a penny will be paid for land without my knowledge. And then there will be wealth such as even the Church has never seen. We can do things with it that have never been done before."

"If the silver is good," said Brand dubiously.

"It is better than up North. I have been thinking this: It seems to me that there is only so much silver in this country, in all the kingdoms of the English put together. And there is always the same amount of work for it to do—land to buy, things to trade. Now, the more that there is locked up in the coffers of the Church, or traded for gold, or made into precious things that do not move, the more the less that is left— No, the harder the less that is left . . ."

Shef floundered to a halt, neither English nor Norse adequate to explain what he meant.

"What I mean is, the Church took too much out of the Northern kingdom and put nothing back. That is why their coins were so bad. King Edmund was less kind to the Church, and so money here was better. Soon it will be the best.

"And not only the money will be the best, Brand." The young man turned to face his massive colleague, his one eye glittering. "I mean this shire of Norfolk to be the best and the happiest land in the whole of the Northern world. A place where everyone can grow from child to graybeard in safety. Where we can live like people, not like animals scratching for a living. Where we can help each other.

"Because I have learned another thing, Brand, from Ordlaf the reeve of Bridlington, from the slaves who made my *mappa* and led us to the riddle of Edmund. It is something the Way needs to know. What is the most precious thing to the Way, the Way of Asgarth?"

"New knowledge," said Brand, automatically clutching his hammer-pendant.

"New knowledge is good. Not everyone has it. But this is just as good, and it can come from anywhere: *old knowledge that no one has recognized*. It is something I have seen more clearly since I became the jarl. There is always some-

one who knows the answer to your question, the cure for
your need. But usually no one has asked him. Or her. It may
be a slave, a poor miner. An old woman, a fisher-reeve, a
priest.

"When I have all the knowledge in the county written
down, as well as all the land and the silver, then we shall
show the world a new thing!"

Brand, on Shef's blind side, glanced down at the taut ten-
dons in the neck, the young man's trimmed beard now
sprinkled with gray.

What he needs, he thought, is a fine, active woman to
keep him busy. But even I, Brand the Champion, even I
dare not offer to buy him one.

That evening, as the woodsmoke from the chimneys began
to mix with the gray twilight, the priests of the Way met
within their corded circle. They sat in the wort-yard, the
garden of a cottage outside the jarl's stockade, in a pleasant
smell of apple-sap and green growth. Thrushes and black-
birds trilled vigorously about them.

"He has no idea of the real purpose of your sea-trip?"
asked Thorvin.

Brand shook his head. "None."

"But you passed the news?"

"I passed the news and I got the news. The word of what
has happened here has gone to every Way-priest in the
Northern lands, and they will tell their followers. It has
gone to Birko and to Kaupang, to Skiringssal and to the
Tronds."

"So, we can expect reinforcements," said Geirulf, Tyr's
priest.

"With the money that has been taken home, and the tales
every skald is telling, you can be sure that every warrior of
the Way who can raise a ship will be here looking for work.
And every priest who can free himself as well. There will
be many who take the pendant in hope, also. Liars, some of
them. Not believers. But they can be dealt with. There is
more important matter."

Brand paused, looking round the circle of intent faces. "In Kaupang, as I came home, I met the priest Vigleik."

"Vigleik of the many visions?" asked Farman tensely.

"Even so. He had called a conclave of priests from Norway and from the South Swedes. He told them—and me—that he was disturbed."

"What about?"

"Many things. He is sure now, as we are, that the boy Shef is the center of the change. He has even thought, as we have, that he may be what he said he was when first he met you, Thorvin: the one who will come from the North."

Brand looked round the table to meet the eyes fixed on him. "And yet, if that is true, the story is not what any of us expected, not even the wisest. Vigleik says, for one thing, he is not a Norseman. He has an English mother."

Shrugs. "Who hasn't?" asked Vestmund. "English, Irish. My grandmother was a Lapp."

"He was brought up a Christian, too. He has been baptized."

This time, grunts of amusement. "We've all seen the scars on his back," said Thorvin. "He hates the Christians, just as we do. No. He doesn't even hate them. He thinks they are fools."

"All right. But this is the sticking point: He has not taken the pendant. He has no belief in us. He sees the visions, Thorvin, or so he has told you. But he does not think they are visions of another world. He is not a believer."

This time the men sat silent, eyes turning slowly to Thorvin. The Thor-priest rubbed his beard.

"Well. He is not an unbeliever, either. If we asked him, he would say that a man with a pendant of a heathen god, as the Christians call them, could not rule Christians, not even for as long as it will take for them to stop being Christians. He would say that wearing a pendant is not a matter of belief, it would just be a mistake, like starting to hammer before the iron was hot. And he does not know which pendant he should wear."

"I do," said Brand. "I saw it and said it last year, when
he killed his first man."

"I think so too," agreed Thorvin. "He should wear the
spear of Othin, God of the Hanged, Betrayer of Warriors.
Only such a one would have sent his own father to death.
But he would say, if he were here, that it was the only thing
to do at that time."

"Is Vigleik only talking of probabilities?" asked Farman
suddenly. "Or did he have some particular message? Some
message a god sent him?"

Silently Brand pulled a packet of thin boards wrapped
round with sealskin from inside his tunic and passed it over.
Runes were cut on the wood, and inked in. Slowly Thorvin
scanned them, Geirulf and Skaldfinn leaning close to look
also. The faces of all three darkened as they read on.

"Vigleik has seen something," said Thorvin at length.
"Brand, do you know the tale of Frodi's mill?"

The champion shook his head.

"Three hundred years ago there was a king in Denmark
called Frodi. He had, they say, a magic mill, which did not
grind corn, but instead ground out peace and wealth and fer-
tility. We believe it was the mill of new knowledge. To
grind the mill he had two slaves, two giant-maidens called
Fenja and Menja. But so anxious was Frodi to have continuing peace and wealth for his people that no matter how
much the giantesses begged for rest, he denied it to them."

Thorvin's deep voice broke into sonorous chant:

" 'You shall not sleep,' said Frodi the king,
'Longer than the time it takes a cuckoo
To answer another, or an errand-lad
To sing a song as he steps on his way.'

"So the slaves grew angry and remembered their giant-
blood, and instead of grinding peace and wealth and fertil-
ity, they began to grind out flame and blood and warriors.
And his enemies came on Frodi in the night and destroyed
him and his kingdom, and the magic mill was lost forever.

"That is what Vigleik has seen. He means one can go too far, even in hunting new knowledge, if the world is not ready for it. One must strike while the iron is hot. But one can also blow the bellows too long and too furiously."

A long pause. Reluctantly, Brand got ready to reply. "I had better tell you," he said, "what the jarl, what Skjef Sigvarthsson told me this morning of his intentions. Then you must decide how this fits Vigleik's visions."

A few days later, Brand stood staring at the great stone now sunk into the meadow, near the spot where the muddy causeway from Ely debouched into the fields outside March.

On it was carved a curling ribbon of runes, their edges still sharp from the chisel. Shef touched them lightly with his fingertips.

"What they say is this. I composed it myself, in verse in your language as Geirulf taught me. The runes read:

" *'Well he left life, though ill he lived it.*
All scores are settled by death.'

At the top is his name: *'Sigvarth Jarl.'* "

Brand grunted doubtfully. He had not liked Sigvarth. And yet the man had taken the death of his one son well. And there was no doubt he had saved his other son, and the Army of the Way, by enduring his last night of torture.

"Well," he said at last. "He has his *bautasteinn*, right enough. It is an old saying: 'Few stones would stand by the way, if sons did not set them up.' But this is not where he was killed?"

"No," said Shef. "They killed him back in the mire. It seems my other father, Wulfgar, could not wait even till he reached firm ground." His mouth twisted, and he spat on the grass. "But if we had set it up there it would have been out of sight in the marsh in six weeks.

"Besides, I wanted you here to see this."

He grinned, turned, and waved an arm in the direction of

the almost imperceptible rise that led toward March. From somewhere out of sight there came a noise like the squealing of a dozen pigs being butchered simultaneously. Brand's axe flicked from the ground as his eyes darted round for a lurking enemy, an attacker.

Into sight, from down the deeply rutted track, came a column of bagpipers, four abreast, cheeks puffed. As his alarm receded Brand recognized the familiar face of Cwicca, the former slave of St. Guthlac's at Crowland, in the front rank.

"They are all playing the same tune," he bellowed over the din. "Was that your idea?"

Shef shook his head and jerked a thumb at the pipers. "Theirs. It's a tune they made up. They call it 'The Boneless Boned.' "

Brand shook his head in disbelief. English slaves mocking the champion of the North himself. He had never thought . . .

Behind the pipers, a score of them, stepped a longer column of men clutching halberds, their heads hidden in shining, sharp-rimmed helmets, each man wearing a leather coat with metal plates stitched onto it, and a small round targe strapped to his left forearm. They must be English too, Brand thought as they marched on. How could he tell? Mainly, it was their size—not a man much above five and a half feet. And yet many of the English ran to size and strength as well, to look at the hulks whom Brand had seen fighting to the last round their lord King Edmund. No, these were not only Englishmen, but poor Englishmen. Not thanes of the English, not carls of the Army, but churls. Or slaves. Slaves with arms and armor.

Brand looked at them in skepticism and disbelief. All his life he had known the weight of mail, known the effort needed to swing an axe or a broadsword. A fully armed warrior might need to carry—and not just to carry, to wield—forty of fifty pounds' weight of metal. How long could a man do that? For the first man whose arm weakened in a battle-line would be dead. In Brand's language, to call a man "the stout" was a valued compliment. He knew seventeen words for "man of small size," and all of them were insults.

He watched the pygmies tramp by, two hundred of them. All held their halberds the same way, he noticed, straight up above the right shoulder. Men marching close together could not afford the luxury of individual decision. But a Viking army would have straggled and held its weapons any way that seemed good, to show proper independence of spirit.

Behind the halberdiers came team after team of horses, he noticed with surprise. Not the slow, dogged ox-teams that had dragged Shef's catapults round the flank of Ivar's army. The first ten pairs of horses dragged the carts with the disassembled beams he had seen before, the pull-throwers, the traction-catapults that lobbed stones. By each cart walked its crew, a dozen men with the same gray jerkins and white hammer-insignia as the pipers and halberdiers. In each crew, a familiar face. Shef's paid-off veterans of the winter campaign had seen their land, had left men to till it, and had returned to their master, the wealth-giver. Each one now captained a crew of his own, recruited from the slaves of the vanished Church.

The next ten pairs were something new again. Behind the horses came a thing on broad cart-wheels, a long trail on each lifted high so that the other end bowed like a chicken scratching for worms in the mud. A twist-shooter, the torsion-catapults that shot the great darts. Not disassembled, but ready for action, the high wheels marking the only difference from the one that had killed King Ella: the ones that had brought down the Coiling Worm standard of Ivar. Again, a dozen men crewed each, marching with their winding-levers sloped and bundles of darts over their shoulders.

As they too tramped by, Brand realized that the bagpipe music, though changed, had not moved into the distance. The five hundred men he had seen already were filing past and then turning back on themselves, lining up in ranks behind him.

But here at last was something like an army approaching, scores and scores of men, not in ranks, not marching, but slouched on ponies and flooding forward down the track like a gray tide. Mail-shirts, broadswords, helmets, familiar faces. Brand waved cheerfully as he recognized Guthmund—still known as the Greedy—in front of his ship's crew. Others waved back, calling out as the English had not done: Magnus Gaptooth and his friend Kolbein, clutching halberds as well as the rest of their armament, Vestlithi, who had been the helmsman of Sigvarth Jarl; and a dozen others he knew for followers of the Way.

"Some went off to spend their winnings, like you," said Shef in Brand's ear. "Others sent the money off or kept it, and stayed on here. Many have bought land. It is their own country they are defending now."

The pipers ceased their din simultaneously, and Brand realized he was surrounded by a ring of men. He stared round, counting, calculating.

"Ten long hundreds?" he said at last. "Half English, half Norse?"

Shef nodded. "What do you think of them?"

Brand shook his head. "The horses to pull the teams," he said. "Twice the speed of ox-teams. But I did not know the English knew how to harness them properly. I have seen them try, and they harness them as if they were oxen, pushing against a pole. Cuts their wind off and they cannot use their strength. How did you realize that?"

"I told you," said Shef. "There is always someone who knows better. This time it was one of your men, one of your own crew—Gauti, who walks with a limp. The first time I tried to harness horses he walked by and told me what a fool I was. Then he showed me how you do it in Halogaland, where you always plough with horses. Not new knowledge—old knowledge. Old knowledge not everyone knows. But we worked out how to hitch up the catapults ourselves."

"Well and good," said Brand. "But answer me this: Catapults or no catapults, horse-teams or no horse-teams: how many of your English are fit to stand in a battle-line against trained warriors? Warriors half their weight again and twice their strength? You cannot make front-fighters out of kitchen boys. Better to recruit some of those well-fed thanes we saw. Or their sons."

Shef crooked a finger and two halberdiers hustled a prisoner forward. A Norseman—bearded, pale-faced beneath windburn, a head taller than his two escorts. He held his left wrist awkwardly in his right hand, like a man whose collarbone is broken. The face was half-familiar: a man whom Brand had seen once at some forgotten campfire when the Viking army had still been as one.

"His three crews tried their luck raiding our lands near the Yare two weeks ago," Shef remarked. "Tell them how you got on."

The man stared at Brand with a kind of plea. "Cowards. Wouldn't fight us fair," he snarled. "They caught us coming out of our first village. A dozen of my men down with great darts through them before we could see where they were coming from. When we charged the machines they held us off with the big axes. Then more of them came round from behind. After they had dealt with us they took me along—my arm was broken so I could not lift shield—to see them attack the ships we had left offshore. They sank one with the stone-throwers. Two got away."

He grimaced. "My name is Snaekolf, from Raumariki. I did not know you men of the Way had taught the English so much, or I would not have raided here. Will you speak for me?"

Shef shook his head before Brand could reply. "His men behaved like beasts in that village," he said. "We will have no more of it. I kept him to say his piece and he has said it. Hang him when you can find a tree."

Hoofbeats came from behind them as the halberdiers hustled the silent Viking away. Shef turned without haste or alarm to meet the rider cantering down the muddy track. The man reached them, dismounted, bowed briefly and spoke. The men of the Wayland army, English and Norse together, stretched their ears to listen.

"News from your *burg*, lord jarl. A rider came in yesterday, from Winchester. King Ethelred of the West Saxons is dead, of the coughing-sickness. His brother, your friend Alfred the atheling, is expected to succeed him and take power."

"Good news," said Brand thoughtfully. "A friend in power is always good."

"You said 'expected'?" said Shef. "Who could oppose him? There is no other of that royal house left."

Chapter Two

The young man stared out from a narrow window in the stone. Behind him, very faintly, he could hear the sound of the monks of the Old Minster singing yet another of the many masses he had paid for, masses for the soul of his last brother, King Ethelred. In front of him, all was activity. The wide street that ran east to west through Winchester was crowded with traders, stalls, customers. Through them pushed carts laden with timber. Three separate gangs of men were working on houses either side of the street, digging foundations, driving beams into the soil, fitting planks over timber frames. If he lifted his eyes he could see, round the edge of the town, many more men strengthening the rampart his brother had ordered, driving in the logs and fitting the fighting-platforms. From all directions came the sound of saws and hammers.

The young man, Alfred the atheling, felt a fierce satisfaction. This was his town: Winchester. The town of his family for centuries, for as long as the English had been on their island, and longer even than that, for he could number ancestors among the British and the Romans too. This Minster was his. His many greats-grandfather King Cenwalh had given the land on which it was to be built to the Church two hundred years before, as well as the land to support it and provide its revenues. Not only his brother Ethelred was buried here, but his father Ethelwulf as well, and his other brothers, and uncles and great-uncles in number more than a man could count. They had lived, they had died, they had gone back to the earth. But it was the same earth. Last of his line, the young atheling did not feel alone.

Strengthened, he turned to face the saw-edged voice that had been grating away behind him in competition with the sounds from outside. The voice of the bishop of Winchester, Bishop Daniel.

"What was that you said?" demanded the atheling. "*If* I come to be king? I *am* the king. I am the last of the house of Cerdic, whose line goes back to Woden. The *witenagemot*, the meeting of the councillors, elected me without debate. The warriors raised me on my shield. I am the king."

The bishop's face set mulishly. "What is this talk of Woden, the god of the pagans? That is no qualification for a Christian king. And what the *witan* do—what the warriors do—that has no meaning in the eyes of God.

"You cannot be king till you have been anointed with the holy oil, like Saul or David. Only I and the other bishops of the realm can do that. And I tell you—we will not. Not unless you satisfy us you are a true king for a Christian land. To prove this you must cease your alliance with the Church-despoilers. Remove your protection from the one they call the Sheaf. Make war on the pagans. The pagans of the Way!"

Alfred sighed. Slowly he walked across the room. He rubbed with his fingers at a dark stain on the wall, a mark of burning.

"Father," he said patiently. "You were here two years ago. It was the pagans then who sacked this town. Burned every house in it, stripped this minster itself of all the gifts my ancestors had put in it, drove off all the town-folk and priests they could catch to their slave-marts.

"Those were true pagans. And it was not even the Great Army that did it, the army of the sons of Ragnar, of Sigurth the Snakeeye and Ivar Boneless. It was just a troop of marauders.

"That is how weak we are. Or were. What I mean to do"—his voice rose suddenly and challengingly—"is see to it that bane never comes on Winchester again, so that my long fathers can rest in peace in their graves. To do that I must have strength. And support. The men of the Way will not challenge us, they will live in fellowship, pagans or no pagans. They are not our enemies. A true Christian king cares for his people. That is what I am doing. Why will you not consecrate me?"

"A true Christian king," said the bishop, slowly, carefully, "A true Christian king cares first and above all for the Church. The pagans may have burned the roof from this minster. But they did not take its land and revenues forever. No pagan, not the Boneless One himself, has taken all the Church land for his own, and given it to slaves and hirelings."

That was the reality, thought Alfred. Gangs of marauders, the Great Army itself, might come down on minster or monastery and strip it of its goods, its treasures and relics. Bishop Daniel would resent it bitterly, torture to death every last stray Viking he caught. But it was not yet to him a matter of survival. The Church could re-roof its minsters, restock its lands, breed new parishioners and even ransom back its books and holy bones. Pillage was survivable.

Taking away the land that was the basis of permanent wealth, land the Church had booked to itself from death-bed donations over many centuries, that was more dangerous. That was what the new alderman, no, the jarl of the Way-folk had done. That had taught Bishop Daniel a new fear. Daniel feared for the Church. He himself, Alfred realized: he feared for Winchester. Rebuilding or no, ransoms or no, long view or short view—he would never see it ravaged and burned again. Church was less important than city.

"I do not need your holy oil," he said peremptorily. "I

can rule without you. The aldermen and the reeves, the thanes and the councillors and the warriors. They will follow me as king whether I am consecrated or not."

The bishop stared unwinkingly at the set young face before him, shook his head with cold anger. "It will not be. The scribes, the priests, the men who write your royal writs and book your leases: they will not aid you. They will do as I tell them. In all your kingdom—if king you call yourself—there is not one man who can read and write who is not a member of the Church. What is more—you cannot read yourself! Much though your holy and pious mother wished you to learn the craft!"

The young atheling's cheeks flushed with rage and shame as he remembered the day he had deceived his mother. Had had the priest read one of her much-loved English poems over and over until he had learned it by heart. Then had stood in front of her reciting it and pretending to read from the book he had coveted. Where was the book now? Some priest had taken it. Probably had scraped the writing from it so he could inscribe on it some saintly text.

The bishop's voice rasped on. "So, young man, you do need me. And not only for the power of my subordinates, the power I lend you. For I have allies, too, yes, and superiors. You are not the only Christian king in England. The pious Burgred of Mercia, he knows his duty. The young man you dispossessed of Norfolk, Alfgar the alderman, and his worthy father Wulfgar, whom the pagans mutilated—they know their duty too. Tell me, are there none of your thanes and aldermen who might not follow one of them? As king?"

"The thanes of Wessex will only follow a man of Wessex."

"Even if they are told different? If the order comes—from Rome?"

The name hung in the air. Alfred paused, contemptuous reply checked on his lips. Once before in his lifetime Wessex had challenged Rome: when his brother Ethelbald had married his father's widow against all the rules of the

Church. The word had come, the threats had been made.
Ethelbald had died soon after—no one knew what of—the
bride had been returned to her father, king of the Franks.
They had not let Ethelbald's body lie in Winchester.

The bishop smiled, knowing his words struck home.
"You see, lord king, you have no choice. And what you do
does not matter in any case. It is only a test of your loyalty.
The man you supported—Sheaf the son of the heathen jarl,
the Englishman who was brought up as a Christian and then
turned his back on it, the apostate, worse than any pagan,
worse than the Boneless One himself—he has no more than
weeks to live. His enemies ring him round. Believe me! I
hear news that you do not.

"Sever your bond with him at once. Show your obedience
to the Church your Mother."

The bishop leaned back in his new-carved chair, sure of
his power, anxious to mark an ascendancy which would last
as long as the young man in front of him might live.

"King though you may yet be," he said, "you are in our
minster now. You have our leave to go. Go. And issue the
orders I demand."

The poem he had learned for his mother years ago came
back suddenly to the young atheling's mind. It had been a
poem of wise advice for warriors, a poem from before
Christian times.

"Answer lie with lie," it had said, *"and let your enemy,
the man who mocks you, miss your thought. He will be unaware, when your wrath shall fall."* Good advice, thought
Alfred. Maybe my mother sent it.

"I will obey your words," he said, rising humbly. "And I
must beg you to forgive the errors of my youth, while I
thank you for your prudent direction."

Weakling! thought the bishop.

He hears news that I do not? wondered the king.

To anyone who knew him—and to the many who did not—
the marks of defeat and shame and ignominious flight in the
depths of winter, all were visible on Ivar Ragnarsson's face.

The terrible eyes were still there, the eyes under frozen
lashes that never blinked. But there was something in them
that had not been there before: an absence, a withdrawal.
Ivar walked like a man with something forever on his mind,
slowly, absently, almost painfully, shorn of the lithe grace
that had once marked him out.

It was still there when needed. The long flight from the
fields of Norfolk across England to his brothers' base at
York had not been an easy one. Men who had slipped out
of sight when the Great Army passed that way before now
emerged from every lane and byroad as a mere pair of exhausted men cantered back. Ivar and the faithful horse-
swain Hamal, who had ridden to save him from the Way. At
least six times the pair had been ambushed by angry peasants, local thanes, and the border-guards of king Burgred.

Ivar had dealt contemptuously with them all. Before the
pair were out of Norfolk he had slashed the heads from two
churls driving a farm-cart, taken their leather jackets and
blanket coats, handed them to Hamal without a word. By
the time they reached York his kills had been beyond count.

Three trained warriors at once could not stand against
him, reported Hamal to a curious, fascinated audience. He
means to prove he is still the Champion of the North.

Takes a lot of proving now, his audience muttered, the
carls of the Army talking freely as was their right. Go with
twenty long hundreds, come back with one man. He can be
beaten.

That was what Ivar could not forget. His brothers, plying
him with hot mead in front of the fire in their quarters by
the minster, they had seen it. Seen too that their brother,
never safe, now could not be trusted at all in any matter that
required calculation. It had not broken their famous unity—
nothing ever would—but now, whenever they talked among
themselves, there were three and one, where once there had
been four.

They had seen the change the first night. Silently, their
eyes had met, silently they did what they had done before,
telling none of their men, not admitting it even to each

other. They had chosen a slave-girl from the Dales, wrapped her in a sail, gagged and bound her, thrust her into Ivar's quarters at dead of night while he lay, unsleeping and expectant.

In the morning they had come and taken away, in the wooden chest they had used before, what remained. Ivar would not run mad for a while, not fall into the berserk mood. Yet no sensible man felt anything but fear in his presence.

"He's coming," called a monk, poised at the entrance to the great workshop where the minster-men of York toiled for their allies-turned-masters. The slaves sweating at forge, vice or rope-walk redoubled their efforts. Ivar would kill the man he saw standing still.

The scarlet cloak and silver helmet stalked through the doorway, stood glaring round. Erkenbert the deacon, the only man whose behavior did not change, turned to meet him.

Ivar jerked a thumb at the workmen. "All ready? Ready now?" He spoke the jargon mixed of English and Norse that the Army and the churchmen had learned that winter.

"Enough of both to try."

"The dart-throwers? The stone-throwers?"

"See."

Erkenbert clapped his hands. Immediately the monks shouted orders, their slaves began to wheel and tug at a line of machines. Ivar watched them, his face blank. After his brothers had taken the chest away, he had lain without moving for a day and a night, his cloak over his face. Then, as every man in the army knew, he had stood up, walked to the door of his room, and screamed to the sky: "Sigvarthsson did not beat me! It was the machines!"

Since then, since he had called for Erkenbert and the learned ones of York to obey his wishes, the forge-din had not ceased.

Outside the workshop, the slaves set up the dart-thrower, identical to the one that had broken the first assault on York, inside the minster-precinct itself, training across a furlong of

open space to the far wall. There a dozen churls hung a
great straw target. Others wound feverishly on the new-
forged cogs.

"Enough!" Erkenbert himself stepped across, checked the
alignment of the barbed javelin, fixed Ivar with his eye,
handed him the thong attached to its iron toggle.

Ivar jerked it. The toggle flew sideways, clanging unnoticed from his helmet, the line rising and falling in the air,
a monstrous thump. Before the eye could follow it, the dart
was buried deep—quivering in its straw bed.

Ivar dropped the string, turned. "The other."

This time the slaves tugged forward a strange machine.
Like the twist-shooter, it had a wooden frame of stout
beams. This time the cogwheels were not on top but at the
side. They twisted a single rope, embedded in its strands, a
wooden rod. At the end of the rod, a heavy sling, its pouch
just clearing the ground. The rod quivered against its
retaining-bolt as the slaves turned the levers.

"This is the stone-thrower," declared Erkenbert.

"Not like the one that broke my ram?"

The deacon smiled with satisfaction. "No. That was a
great machine that threw a boulder. But many men were

needed to move it, and it could shoot only once. This throws smaller stones. No man has made such a machine since the days of the Romans. But I, Erkenbert, the humble servant of God, I have read the words in our Vegetius. And have built this machine. The *onager* it is named: that is, in your tongue, 'the wild ass.' "

A slave placed a ten-pound rock in the sling, signed to Erkenbert.

Again the deacon passed a thong to Ivar. "Pull the bolt," he said.

Ivar jerked the string. Faster than sight the great rod leapt forward like a great swinging arm.

Stopping with a crash against a padded beam, the entire weighted frame jumped from the ground. The sling whirled round far faster than Shef's self-designed stone-throwers. Like a streak the rock flashed across the minster-yard, never rising—not lobbed but hurled. The straw target billowed into the air, slowly collapsed on its slings. The slaves cheered once in triumph.

Slowly Ivar turned to Erkenbert. "That is not it," he said. "The machines that rained death on my army, they threw high in the sky." He lobbed a pebble upward. "Not like this." He hurled another at a pecking sparrow.

"You have made the wrong machine."

"Impossible," said Erkenbert. "There is the great machine for sieges. And this one for men. None other is described in Vegetius."

"Then those bastards of the Way have made a new thing. One not described in—in your book."

Erkenbert shrugged his shoulders, unconvinced. Who cared what this pirate said? He could not even read, still less read Latin.

"And how fast does it shoot?" Ivar glared at the slaves twirling their levers. "I tell you, I saw the stone-throwers hurl another while the first was still in the air. This one is too slow."

"But it strikes hard. No man can resist it."

Ivar stared thoughtfully at the fallen target. Suddenly he

whirled, yelled orders in Norse. Hamal and a handful of companions sprang forward, pushed the slaves out of the way, and heaved the cumbrous, tense-wound machine round.

"No," shouted Erkenbert, pushing forward. Ivar's arm clamped irresistibly round his throat, a wire-muscled hand forced his mouth shut.

Ivar's men pushed the machine round another foot, hauled it back a trifle as their leader ordered. One hand still effortlessly holding the limp deacon off the ground, Ivar jerked the string a third time.

The giant door of the minster—oak beams nailed across each other in double-ply, held fast over all with iron bands—exploded in all directions, splinters flying in slow arcs across the yard. From inside came a chorus of wails, monks leaping out, darting back, shrieking in terror.

They all stared in fascination at the great hole the boulder had smashed.

"You see," said Erkenbert. "This is the true stone-thrower. It strikes hard. No man can resist it."

Ivar turned, eyes fixed on the little monk in contempt. "It is not the true stone-thrower. There is another kind in the world of which you know nothing. But strike hard it does. You must make me many."

Across the narrow sea to the land of the Franks beyond, a thousand miles away in the land of the Romans, there within the gates of a minster greater than Winchester, greater even than York, deep silence lay. Popes had had many troubles, many failures, since the time of their great founder. Some had met martyrdom, some been forced to flee for their lives. Not thirty years before, Saracen pirates had made their way to the very gates of Rome, and had sacked the holy basilica of St. Peter himself which was then outside the wall.

It would not happen again. He who was now the equal of the Apostles, the successor of Peter, the holder of the keys of Heaven, he had set his face above all toward power. Vir-

tue was great: humility, chastity, poverty. But without power
none of those could survive. It was his duty to the humble,
the chaste and the poor, to seek power. In pursuit of it he
had put down many mighty ones from their high seats on
their thrones—he, Nicholas I, Pope of Rome, Servant of the
servants of God.

Slowly the hawk-faced old man stroked his cat, his secretaries and attendants sitting round him in silence. The foolish archbishop from the town in England, the town with the
strange outlandish name—*Eboracum*, evidently, though hard
to tell with his barbarous pronunciation—he had been dismissed with courtesy, and a cardinal deputed to show him
all honor and provide him with amusement. What he had
said had been nonsense: a new religion, a challenge to the
authority of the Church, the barbarians of the North developing intellect. Panic and terror-stories.

Yet it corroborated his other information from England:
Robbery of the Church. Alienation of land. Willing apostasy. There was a word for it. *Dispossession*. That was striking at the base of power itself. If that were to become
known, there might be too many ready to imitate, yes, even
in the lands of the Empire. Even here in Italy. Something
would have to be done.

And yet the Pope and the Church had other problems,
many more pressing ones, more immediate than this matter
of English barbarians and Northern barbarians fighting over
land and silver in a country he would never see. At their
heart lay the partition of the Empire, the great Empire
founded by Charlemagne, king of the Franks, crowned emperor in this very cathedral on Christmas Day 800, a lifetime before. For twenty years now, that Empire had been in
pieces, and its enemies ever encouraged. First the grandsons
of Charlemagne had fought against each other, till they had
hacked out peace and partition. Germany to one, France to
another, the great, long, ungovernable strip from Italy to the
Rhine to a third. And now that third was dead and his third
of the Empire divided once again among three, the emperor
himself, eldest son of the eldest son, holding a bare ninth of

what his grandfather had ruled. And what did that emperor, Louis II, care about it? Nothing. He could not even drive back the Saracens. What about his brother Lothar? Whose only interest in life was to divorce his barren wife and marry his fertile mistress—a thing he, Nicholas, would never permit.

Lothar, Louis, Charles. The Saracens and the Norsemen. Land, power, dispossession. The Pope stroked his cat and considered them all. Something told him that here, here in this trivial, far-off squabble brought by a foolish archbishop running from his duty, might be the solution to all his problems at once.

Or was the prickle he felt one of fear? An alert to the tiny black cloud that would grow and grow?

The Pope cleared his dry old throat with a noise like a cricket creaking. The first of his secretaries dipped his pen instantly.

" 'To our servants Charles the Bald, king of the Franks. To Louis, king of the Germans. Louis, emperor of the Holy Roman Empire. Lothar, king of Lotharingia. Charles, king of Provence'—you know their titles, Theophanus. To all these Christian kings, then, we write in the same way . . .

" 'Know, beloved, that we, Pope Nicholas, have taken thought for the greater security and the greater prosperity of all our Christian people. And therefore we direct you, as you will have our love in the future, to work together with your brothers and your kinsmen the Christian kings of this Empire, to this effect . . .' "

Slowly the Pope outlined his plans. Plans for common action. For unity. For a distraction from civil war and the tearing apart of the Empire. For the salvation of the Church and the destruction of its enemies, even—if what Archbishop Wulfhere had said were true—its rivals.

" '. . . and it is our wish,' " the dry, creaky voice concluded, " 'that in recognition of their service to Mother Church, each man of your armies who shall join this blessed and sanctified expedition shall wear the sign of the Cross upon his clothing over his armor.

"Finish the letters in proper form, Theophanus. I'll sign and seal them tomorrow. Pick appropriate messengers."

The old man rose, clutching his cat, and left the office without haste for his private quarters.

"Nice touch about the cross," remarked one of the secretaries busily drafting copies in the Pope's own purple ink.

"Yes. He got it from what the Englishman said, about the pagans wearing a hammer in mockery of the cross."

"The touch they'll really like," said the senior secretary, sanding vigorously, "is the bit about prosperity. He's telling them if they do what they're told they can loot all Anglia. Or Britannia. Whatever it's called."

"Alfred wants *missionaries*?" said Shef incredulously.

"His very word. *Missionarii*." In his excitement Thorvin betrayed what Shef had come to suspect, that for all his scorn of Christian learning he knew something of their sacred tongue, the Latin. "It is the word they have long used for the men they send to us, to turn us to the worship of their God. I have never before heard of a Christian king asking for men to be sent to his country, to turn them to the worship of our gods."

"And that is what Alfred wants now?"

Shef was dubious. Thorvin, he could see, for all his belief in calm and self-control, was carried away by the thoughts of the glory this would bring him and his friends among the followers of the Way.

Yet it did mean something, he was sure, and not what it seemed. The atheling Alfred whom he had met took no interest in pagan gods, and had, as far as he could tell, a deep belief in the Christian one. If he was calling now for missionaries of the Way to be sent into Wessex it was for a deeper reason. A move against the Church, that was certain. You could believe in the Christian God and hate the Church that His followers had set up. But what did Alfred think he had to gain? And how would that Church react?

"My fellow priests and I must decide which of us, which of our friends are to go on this mission."

"No," said Shef.

"His favorite word again," observed Brand from his chair.

"Do not send any of your own college. Do not send Norsemen. There are Englishmen now who know well enough what you believe. Give them pendants. Instruct them in what must be said. Send them into Wessex. They will speak the language better and will be more easily believed."

As Shef spoke he stroked the carved faces on his scepter.

Brand had noted this before—that Shef did this now when he was lying. Shall I tell Thorvin? he thought. Or shall I tell Shef, so that he can lie better when need be?

Thorvin rose from his stool, too excited to sit. "There is a holy song," he said, "that the Christians sing. It is called the *nunc dimittis*, a song that says 'Lord, You may let Your servant die, for he has seen his purpose fulfilled.' I have a mind to sing it myself. For more hundreds of years than I can count this Church of theirs has spread, has spread, across first the Southern and then the Northern lands. They think they can conquer all of us. Never before have I heard of the Church giving up what once it won."

"They have not given up yet," said Shef. "The king asks you to send missionaries. He cannot say they will get a hearing, or make the folk believe."

"They have their Book, we have our visions!" cried Thorvin. "We shall see which is the stronger."

From his chair, Brand's bass joined in. "The jarl is right, Thorvin. Send freed slaves of the English to do this task."

"They do not know the legends," protested Thorvin. "What do they know of Thor or Njörth, of the legends of Frey and Loki? They do not know the sacred stories or the hidden meanings within them."

"They don't need to," said Brand. "We're sending them to talk about money."

Chapter Three

That fine Sunday morning, as every Sunday morning, the villagers of Sutton in the county of Berkshire in the kingdom of the West Saxons drew together, as directed, before the hall of Hereswith their lord, thane of King Ethelred-that-was. Thane now, so they said, of King Alfred. Or was he still only atheling? They would be told. Their eyes roved as they counted each other, assessing who was present, whether any had dared to test the orders of Hereswith that all should be present, to attend the church three miles off and learn the law of God which stood behind the laws of men.

Slowly the eyes turned the same way. There were strangers in the little cleared space before the lord's timber house. Not foreigners, or not obvious foreigners. They looked exactly like the forty or fifty other men present, churls and slaves and churls' sons: short, ill-dressed in grubby wool tunics, unspeaking—six of them together. Yet these were men who had never been seen in or near Sutton before— something unprecedented in the heart of the untraveled English countryside. Each leaned on a long stout stave of wood guarded with strips of iron, like the handle of a war-axe, but twice the length.

Without seeming to, the villagers drew away from them. They did not know what this novelty meant, but long years had taught them that what was new was dangerous—till their lord had seen and approved, or disapproved.

The door of the timber house opened and Hereswith marched out, followed by his wife and their gaggle of sons and daughters. As he saw the lowered eyes, the cleared space, the strangers, Hereswith stopped short, left hand dropping automatically to the handle of his broadsword.

"Why are you going to the church?" called out one of the strangers suddenly, his voice sending the pigeons pecking in the dirt into flight. "It's a fine day. Wouldn't you rather sit in the sun? Or work in the fields if you need to? Why walk three miles to Drayton and three miles back? And listen to a man tell you you must pay your tithes in between?"

"Who the hell are you?" snarled Hereswith, striding forward.

The stranger stood his ground, called out loudly so all could hear. His accent was strange, the villagers noticed. English, sure enough. But not from here, not from Berkshire. Not from Wessex?

"We are Alfred's men. We have the king's word and leave to speak here. Whose men are you? The bishop's?"

"The hell you're Alfred's men," grunted Hereswith, freeing his sword. "You're foreigners. I can hear it."

The strangers remained braced on their staves, unmoving.

"Foreigners we are. But we have come with leave, to bring a gift. The gift we bring is freedom: from the Church, from slavery."

"You'll not free my slaves without my leave," said Hereswith, his mind made up. He swung his sword backhand in a horizontal cut at the nearer stranger's neck.

The stranger moved instantly, hurling his strange metal-ribbed staff straight up. The sword clanged on the metal, rebounded out of Hereswith's unpracticed hands. The thane crouched, groping for the hilt, eyes darting from one stranger to the other.

"Easy, lord," said the man. "We mean you no harm either. If you'll listen, we'll tell you why your king has asked us to come here, and how we can be his men and foreigners at once."

Nothing in Hereswith's makeup urged him to listen or to

compromise. He straightened, the sword again in his hand, and lashed out forehand at the knee. Again the staff blocked it, blocked it easily. As the thane recovered his blade, the man he had attacked stepped forward and pushed him back with the staff across his chest.

"Help me, you men," bellowed Hereswith at the silent watchers, and charged forward, shoulder dropped and sword ready this time for a disemboweling thrust.

"Enough," said one of the other men he faced, thrusting a staff between his legs. The thane crashed down, started to scramble again to his feet. From his sleeve the first man jerked a short, limp canvas cylinder: the slave-taker's sandbag. He swung once, to the temple, crouched, ready to swing again. As Hereswith fell forward on his face, to lie unmoving, he nodded, straightened, tucked the sandbag away, beckoned to the thane's wife to come and treat him.

"Now," said the stranger, turning to his fascinated but still unmoving audience. "Let me tell you who we are, and who we were.

"We are men of the Way, from the North-folk. But this time last year we were slaves of the Church. Slaves to the great minster of Ely. Let me tell you how we became free."

The slaves in the crowd, maybe a dozen of the fifty men there and the same proportion of women, exchanged frightened glances.

"And to the freemen here," went on Sibba, once slave of the minster of Ely, then catapulteer in the Army of the Way, veteran of the victory over Ivar the Boneless himself, "to the freemen here we will say how we were given our own land. Twenty acres each," he added. "Free of toll to any lord, except the service we owe to Shef Jarl. And the service we give freely—freely, mark you—to the Way. Twenty acres. Unburdened. Is there any freeman here who can claim as much?"

This time the freemen in the crowd looked at each other, a low growl of interest rising. As Hereswith was dragged away, head lolling, his tenants edged closer to the new arrivals, ignoring the broadsword left forgotten in the dirt.

"How much does it cost you to follow Christ?" began Sibba. "Cost you in money? Listen and I will tell you . . ."

"They're everywhere," the bishop's bailiff reported. "Thick as fleas on an old dog."

Bishop Daniel's brows knitted at his servant's levity, but he held his tongue: he needed the information.

"Yes," the bailiff went on, "all men from Norfolk, it seems, and all claiming to be freed slaves. It makes sense. See, your grace, we have a thousand slaves just on our own estates here round Winchester and in the minsters and shires. The man you speak of, the new *jarl* as the heathens call him—he could have sent three thousand slaves in here to spread his word from Norfolk alone, if he sent them all."

"They must be caught," Daniel grated. "Rooted out like corn-cockle from amid the wheat."

"Not so easy. The slaves won't hand them over, nor the churls, from what I hear. The thanes can't catch 'em. If they do, they defend themselves. They never travel in less than pairs. Sometimes they group together to be a dozen, or a score, no light matter for a small village to deal with. And besides . . ."

"Besides what?"

The bailiff picked his words with care. "What these incomers say—lies it may be, but what they say—is that they have been summoned in by the King Alfred . . ."

"The *atheling* Alfred! He has never been crowned."

"Your pardon, lord. By the atheling Alfred. But even some of the thanes would be loath to hand over men sent by the king to the Church. They say—they say this is a quarrel among the great ones and they will not interfere." And many would side with the atheling, last of the great line of Cerdic, against the Church anyway, thought the bailiff. But he knew better than to say it.

Liar and deceiver, thought the bishop. Not a month ago and the young prince had sat in that very room, eyes down like a maiden, apologizing and begging for direction. And he had left the room to call instantly for help from the unbelievers! And now he was gone, no one knew where, except that rumors came of his appearance in this part or that of Wessex, appealing to his thanes to deny the Church: to follow the example of the North-folk and the creed they called the Way. It did not help that he continued to protest that he remained a believer in Christ. How long would belief last without the land and the money to support it? And if things continued as they were, how long would it be before some messenger, or some army appeared at the very gates of the minster, ordering the bishop to surrender his rights and his leases?

"So," Daniel said at last, half to himself. "We cannot cope with this thing in Wessex. We must send outside. And indeed there is force coming from outside which will cure this evil so that it never raises its head again.

"Yet I cannot afford to wait. It is my Christian duty to act." And also, he added silently, my duty to myself. A bishop who sits quiet and does nothing—how will he seem to the Holy Father in Rome, when the moment comes to decide who shall bear rule for the Church in England?

"No," the bishop went on, "the heart of the trouble comes from the North-folk. Well, what the North-folk caused, the North-folk must cure. There are some who still know their Christian duty."

"In Norfolk, lord?" asked the bailiff doubtfully.

"No. In exile. Wulfgar the cripple, and his son. The one lost his limbs to the Vikings. The other lost his shire. And King Burgred too, of Mercia. It was nothing to me, I thought, who should rule East Anglia, Mercia or Wessex. But I see now. Better that the pious Burgred should have the kingdom of Edmund the Martyr than it should go to Alfred. Alfred the Ingrate, I name him.

"Send in my secretaries. I will write to them all, and to my brothers of Lichfield and Worcester. What the Church has lost, the Church will win back."

"Will they come, lord?" asked the bailiff. "Will they not fear to invade Wessex?"

"It is I who speaks for Wessex now. And there are greater

forces than either Wessex or Mercia astir. All I offer
Burgred and the others is the chance to join the winning
side before it has won. And to punish insolence: the insolence of the heathens and the slaves. We must make an example of them."

The bishop's fist clenched convulsively. "I will not root
out this rot, like a weed. I shall burn it out, like a canker."

"Sibba. I think we've got trouble." The whisper ran across
the dark room where a dozen missionaries lay sleeping,
wrapped in their blankets.

Silently Sibba joined his companion at the tiny, glassless
window. Outside, the village of Stanford-in-the-Vale, ten
miles and as many preachings from Sutton, lay silent, lit by
a strong moon. Clouds scudding before the wind cast shadows round the low wattle-and-daub houses that clustered
round the thane's timber one, in which the missionaries of
the Way now slept.

"What did you see?"

"Something flashing."

"A fire not dowsed?"

"I don't think so."

Sibba moved without speaking towards the little room
that opened off the main central hall. In there the thane
Elfstan, their host, a man who protested his loyalty to King
Alfred, should be sleeping with his wife and family. After a
few moments he drifted back.

"They're still there. I can hear them breathing."

"So they're not in on it. Doesn't mean I didn't see anything. Look! There it is again."

Outside, a shadow slipped from one patch of darkness to
another, coming closer. In the moonlight something flashed:
something metal.

Sibba turned to the men still sleeping. "On your feet,
boys. Get your stuff together."

"Run for it?" asked the watchman.

Sibba shook his head. "They must know how many of us
there are. They wouldn't attack if they weren't confident

they could deal with us. Easier to do that outside than dig us out of here. We must try to break their teeth first."

Men were scrambling to their feet behind him, groping for their breeches, buckling belts. One man undid a pack, began to haul from it strange, metallic shapes. The others queued in front of him, clutching the long pilgrim-staves all had carried openly.

"Force them down hard," grunted the packman, struggling to push the first halberd-head on its socket over the carefully designed shaft.

"Move fast," said Sibba. "Then, Berti, you take two men to face the door, one either side of it. Wilfi, you at the other door. The rest, stay with me, see where we're needed."

The movement and the clanking of metal had brought the thane, Elfstan, from his bed. He stared, wonderingly.

"Men outside," said Sibba. "Not friendly."

"Nothing to do with me."

"We know. Look, lord, they'll let you out. If you go now."

The thane hesitated. He called to his wife and children, dressing hastily, spoke to them in a low voice.

"Can I open the door?"

Sibba looked round. His men were ready, weapons prepared. "Yes."

The thane lifted the heavy bar that held closed the main double doors, and pushed them both open together. As he did so a groan came from outside, almost a sigh. There were many men out there, poised for a rush. But now they knew they had been seen.

"My wife and children—coming out!" shouted Elfstan. Quickly the children slipped through the door, his wife scurrying after them. A few feet beyond she turned, beckoned frantically to him. Her husband shook his head.

"They are my guests," he said. His voice rose to a shout, addressing the ambushers outside. "My guests and the guests of King Alfred. I do not know who are these thieves in the night, within the bounds of Wessex, but they will hang when the king's reeve catches them."

"There is no king in Wessex," shouted a voice from outside. "And we are men of King Burgred. Burgred and the Church. Your guests are vagabonds and heretics. Slaves from outside! We have come to collar and brand them."

Suddenly the moonlight shone on dark shapes, moving together out of the cover of houses and fences.

They did not hesitate. It would have been easier to catch their enemies sleeping, but they had been told what their enemies were: released slaves, lowest of the low. Men who had never been taught swordplay, who had not been conditioned from birth to war. Who had not felt the bite of edges over the linden-shield. A dozen Mercian warriors swarmed together at the dark doors of the hall. Behind them, now that concealment was gone, horns blew for the assault.

The double doors of the hall were six feet across, a man's full arm-span. Room only for two armed men to enter at once. Two champions rushed in together, shields up, faces glaring.

Neither saw the blows that killed them. As they peered into the gloom for men to face them, faces to hack at, the halberds swept from both sides, at thigh level, below shield and mail-shirt. The halberd-heads, axe one side, spike the other, were twice the weight of a broadsword. One shore through a warrior's leg and deep into the facing thigh. The other sliced upward from the bone, deep into the pelvis. As one man lay in the flow of blood that would kill him in seconds, the other flapped and twisted, shrieking, trying to tear free the great blade lodged in bone.

More men pushed over them. This time spearpoints met them from in front, driving through wooden shields and metal rings, hurling men back into the confusion of the doorway, groaning from belly wounds. Now the long blades, sweeping in six-foot arcs, chopped down the mailed warriors like cattle before the poleaxe. For a few seconds it seemed as if the sheer weight and numbers of the first rush would break through the defenders.

But against the dim-seen menace, nerves failed. The Mercians scrambled back, those in front weaving desperately behind their shields, trying to drag their dead and wounded with them.

"So far so good," muttered one of the Waymen.

"They'll come again," said Sibba.

Four more times the Mercians came on, each time more warily, trying now, as they realized the tactics and the weapons against them, to draw the blow and evade it, to leap forward before the halberdiers could recover their cumbrous weapons. The Norfolk freedmen used their advantage of numbers, two men to face each door, a man striking from each side. Slowly the casualties on both sides grew.

"They're trying to cut through the walls," muttered Elfstan to Sibba, still on his feet as the sky began to pale.

"Makes no difference," replied Sibba. "They still have to climb in. As long as there's enough of us to block each gap."

Outside, a fair angry face stared at a bleeding exhausted one. Alfgar had come with the attackers to watch the destruction of the Waymen. He was not pleased.

"You can't break in?" he shouted. "Against a handful of slaves?"

"We've lost too many good men to this handful of slaves. Eight dead, a dozen hurt and all of them badly. I'm going to do what we should have done first."

Turning to his men, he waved a group forward to the undamaged gable end of the hall. With them they carried thorn fencing. They piled it against the wall, stamped it into a pile of thick brush. Steel struck flint, sparks dropping onto dried straw. The fire flared up.

"I want prisoners," Alfgar said.

"If we can get them," said the Mercian. "Anyway, now they have to come to us."

As the smoke began to pour into the drafty hall, Sibba and Elfstan exchanged glances. They could see each other now in the growing dawn.

"They might still take you prisoner, if you went out," said

Sibba. "Hand you over to your own king. You being a thane, who knows?"

"I doubt that strongly."

"What are we going to do?"

"What is always done. We will wait in here for every breath we can draw, until the smoke is thickest. Then we will run out and hope one or two of us may get away in the confusion."

The smoke poured in more thickly, followed by the red gleams of fire eating at planking. Elfstan moved to draw a wounded man lying on the floor out of the smoke, but Sibba waved him back.

"Breathing smoke is the easy death," he said. "Better than feeling the fire in your flesh."

One by one, as their endurance waned, the halberdiers ran out in the smoke, trying to run downwind for a few yards of screen. Gleefully their enemies pounced, blocking their path, making them strike or lunge, leaping in behind with sword and dagger, and a long night of loss and frustration to avenge. Last and unluckiest ran Sibba. As he came out two Mercians, realizing by now which way their prey would go, stretched a rawhide rope across the path. Before he could rise or draw his short knife, there was a knee on his back, brawny arms on his wrists.

The last man left in the shell of his home, Elfstan stepped slowly forward, not running downwind like the others, but taking three long strides out of the smoke, shield raised, broadsword drawn. The Mercians running in hesitated. Here at last was a man like themselves. At a safe distance Elfstan's serfs and tenants watched, to see how their lord faced death.

Huskily Elfstan snarled a challenge, gesturing to the Mercians to come on. One detached himself, stepped forward, swinging backhand, forehand, clubbing upward with his iron shield-boss. Elfstan parried, edge to edge with the skill of a lifetime's practice, chopping with his own shield, circling one way then the other as he tried to detect a weakness in his enemy's wrist or balance or technique. For minutes the grave ballet of the sword-duel, the thing thanes were bred for, went on. Then the Mercian sensed the Wessex thane's exhaustion. As the shield-arm facing him drooped, he feinted a low cut, turned it into sudden short thrust. The blade drove in below the ear. As he fell, Elfstan stuck one last failing blow. His enemy staggered, looked unbelievingly at the arterial blood spouting from his thigh, and fell also, struggling to cover the flow with his hands.

A groan rose from the men of Stanford-in-the-Vale. Elfstan had been a hard master, and many had felt the weight of his fist if slaves, or the power of his wealth if free. Yet he had been their neighbor. He had fought the invaders of the village.

"Good death," the Mercian captain said professionally. "He lost, but maybe he took his man with him."

Alfgar moaned with disgust. Behind him, men rolled the traveling cart of his father forward. Through the shattered palisade of the village, a further cortege advanced, black-robed priests in the van. In the midst of it the rising sun glittered on the bishop's gilded crozier.

"At least we have *some* prisoners," he said.

"Two?" asked Bishop Daniel disbelievingly. "You killed nine and caught two?"

No one bothered to answer him.

"We must make the best of it," said Wulfgar. "Now, how are you going to deal with them? 'Make an example,' you said."

The two freedmen stood in front of them, each held by two warriors. Daniel paced forward, stretched his hand out, pulled a thong from round one captive's neck, broke it with a jerk. He stared at what lay in his hand, did the same to the other prisoner. A silver hammer, for Thor, a silver sword, for Tyr. He tucked them into his pouch. For the archbishop, he thought. No, Ceolnoth is too much a weakling, feeble as the weathercock Wulfhere of York.

These are for Pope Nicholas. With this silver in his hand

he may reflect that the Church in England cannot afford weakling archbishops any longer.

"I swore to burn the canker out," he said. "And so I will."

An hour later Wilfi of Ely stood tethered to the stake, legs tightly bound to prevent him kicking out. The brushwood burned brightly, caught at his woolen breeches. As the fire blistered his skin he began to twist in his bonds, gasps of agony forced from him despite his efforts. The Mercian warriors stared at him judgementally, interested to see how a slave-born bore pain. The villagers watched more fearfully. Many had seen executions. But even the wickedest, secret murderers and housebreakers, faced no more than the noose. To kill a man slowly was outside English law. Though not outside Church law.

"Breathe the smoke," yelled Sibba suddenly. "Breathe the smoke!"

Through the pain Wilfi heard him, ducked his head, breathed in great gasps. As his tormentors hesitated to approach, he began to fall forward in his bonds. As unconsciousness came on him, he rallied for an instant, looked upward.

"Tyr," he called, "Tyr aid me!" The smoke billowed up round him as if in reply. When it cleared he hung limp. A rumble of talk rose from the watchers.

"Not much of an example there," observed Wulfgar to the bishop. "Why don't you let me show you how to do it?"

As they dragged Sibba forward to the second stake, men went running at Wulfgar's word to the nearest house, came out moments later trundling the beer-barrel which even the meanest home could boast. At a gesture they stove in one end, tipped the barrel over, stove in the other to create a short stout cylinder. The barrel's owner watched unspeaking as his summer ale ran into the dirt.

"I've thought about this," said Wulfgar. "What else have I to do? What you need for this is draft. Like a clay chimney in a fireplace."

They tied Sibba, pale and glaring, next to the stake where

his comrade had died. As they piled the brushwood deeply round him, Daniel stepped forward.

"Abjure your pagan gods," he said. "Return to Christ. I will shrive and absolve you myself, and you will be stabbed mercifully before you burn."

Sibba shook his head.

"Apostate," yelled the bishop. "What you feel now will only be the start of everlasting burning. Mark this!" He turned and shook a fist at the villagers. "His pain is what you will all suffer forever. What all men must suffer forever, if not for Christ. Christ and the Church that keeps the keys of heaven and hell!"

At Wulfgar's direction, they lowered the barrel over stake and condemned man together, struck sparks to the brush and fanned the blaze. The tongues of flame reached in, were sucked upward as the air burned out above them, leapt savagely at the body and face of the man inside. After a few moments the shrieking began. Continued, growing louder. A slow smile began to spread across the face of the limbless trunk that watched from its padded upright box.

"He's saying something," snapped Daniel suddenly. "He's saying something. He wants to recant. Put the fire out! Pull the brush away."

Slowly the burners raked back the blaze. Approaching cautiously, they wrapped cloths round their hands and lifted the smoldering barrel high over the stake.

Beneath it lay charred flesh, teeth showing white against blackened face and scorched lips. Flame had shriveled Sibba's eyeballs and was forced deep into his lungs as his body gasped for breath. He was still conscious.

His face lifted as the bishop approached, aware through its blindness that it was again in open air.

"Recant now," shouted Daniel for all to hear. "Make a sign, any sign, and I will cross you and send your soul without pain to Doomsday."

He bent forward under his miter to catch any word that burned lungs could pronounce.

Sibba coughed twice and spat the charred lining of his throat into the bishop's face.

Daniel stepped back, wiping the black mucus with disgust onto his embroidered robe, shaking involuntarily.

"Back," he gasped. "Put it back. Put it over him again. Restart the fire. And this time," he shouted, "he can call on his pagan gods till the devil has him."

But Sibba did not call out again. As Daniel raved and Wulfgar grinned at his confusion, as the warriors slowly moved in to pull the fire in on the bodies and spare the need for burial pit, two men slipped away from the back of the crowd, unseen by any except their silent neighbors. One was Elfstan's sister's son. The other had seen his home destroyed in a battle not of his concern. The rumor of the shire had told them where to take their news.

Chapter Four

Shef's face did not change as the messenger, staggering with fatigue after his long ride, poured out his news: a Mercian army in Wessex. King Alfred vanished, no one knew where. The emissaries of the Way mercilessly hunted down wherever they could be found. The Church proclaiming King Alfred and all allies of the Way anathema, stripped of all rights, to be neither helped nor harbored.

And everywhere, the burnings; or, by order of the bishop of Winchester, where the dreaded living corpse Wulfgar was not present, the crucifixions. Long lists of names of those caught: catapulteers, comrades, veterans of the battle against Ivar. Thorvin moaned, shocked, as the list ran on and on, moved even though those caught and killed were not of his race or blood and were only for a few short weeks of his faith. Shef remained seated on his camp-stool, thumb running again and again across the cruel faces of his whetstone.

He knew, thought Brand, watching, and remembering the sudden veto Shef had imposed on Thorvin's eager readiness to spread the word himself. He knew this would happen, or something like it. That means that he had sent his own folk, Englishmen, men he raised from the dirt himself, to what he must have known would be death by torture. He did the same for his own father. I must be very sure, very, very sure that he never looks at me in quite that same considering fashion. If I had not known before that he was a son of Othin I would know it now.

And yet if he had not done it I would be grieving for the death of Thorvin by now, not for a bunch of gangrel churls.

The messenger ran down, news and horror finally exhausted. With a word Shef dismissed him to food and rest, turned to his inner council sitting round him in the sunlit upper hall: Thorvin and Brand, Farman the visionary, Boniface the former priest with his ever-ready ink and paper.

"You heard the news," he said. "What must we do?"

"Is there any doubt?" asked Thorvin. "Our ally called us in. Now he is being robbed of his rights by the Church. We must march at once to his assistance."

"More than that," added Farman. "If there is a moment for lasting change, surely it is this. We have a kingdom divided within itself. A true king—Christian though he may be—to speak for us, for the Way. How often have the Christians spread their word through converting the king, and having him convert his people? Not only will the slaves be with us, but the freemen and half the thanes. Now is our chance to turn the Christian tide. Not only in Norfolk, but in a great kingdom."

Shef's lips set stubbornly. "What do you say, Brand?"

Brand shrugged massive shoulders. "We have comrades to avenge. None of us are Christians—your pardon, Father. But the rest of us are not Christians to forgive our enemies. I say march."

"But I am the jarl. It is my decision."

Slowly, heads nodded.

"What I think is this. When we sent the missionaries we

stirred up the wasps' nest. And now we are stung. We should have foreseen it."

You did foresee it, thought Brand to himself.

"And I stirred up another when I took the Church's land. I have not been stung for that yet, but I expect it. I foresee it. I say let us see where our enemies are before we strike. Let them come to us."

"And let our comrades lie unavenged?" growled Brand.

"We will miss our chance of a kingdom, a kingdom for the Way," cried Farman.

"What of your ally Alfred?" demanded Thorvin.

Slowly Shef wore them down. Repeated his conviction. Countered their arguments. Persuaded them, in the end, to wait a week, for further news.

"I only hope," said Brand in the end, "that good living has not made you soft. Made us all soft. You should spend more time with the army, and less with the muttonheads in your doom-court."

That at least is good advice, thought Shef. In order to cool feelings, he turned to Father Boniface, who had taken no part, waiting only to record decisions or write down orders.

"Father, send out for wine, will you? Our throats are dry. At least we can drink the memorial for our dead comrades in something better than ale."

The priest, still stubbornly black-gowned, paused on his way to the door.

"There is no wine, lord jarl. The men said they were looking for a cargo from the Rhine, but it has not come. There have been no ships from the South for four weeks, not even into London. I will broach a barrel of the finest hydromel instead. Maybe the wind is wrong."

Quietly Brand rose from the table, stalked to the open window, stared at the clouds and the horizon. Why, he thought, I could sail from Rhinemouth to the Yare in my mother's old washtub in weather like this. And he says the wind is wrong! Something is wrong, but it is not the wind.

* * *

That dawn, the crews and captains of a hundred impounded trading vessels—half-decked single-masters, round-bellied cogs, English, Frankish and Frisian longships—all rolled unhappily from their blankets to stare at the sky above the port of Dunkerque, as they had done every day for a month and more. To see if the conditions were right. To wonder whether their masters would deign to make a move.

They saw the light that had come from the east, that had raced already across the tangled forests and huddled settlements of Europe, across river and toll-gate, *Schloss* and *chastel* and earthwork. Everywhere on the continent it had lit soldiers gathering, provision-carts mustering, horse-boys leading remounts.

As it swept towards the English Channel—though at this time men called it still the Frankish Sea—it touched the topmost banderole on the stone *donjon* within the wooden keep that guarded the port of Dunkerque. The guard-commander looked at it, nodded. The trumpeter wetted his lips, pursed them, sent a defiant bray down his metal tube. Immediately the quarter-guards answered from each wall, men began to roll from their blankets inside the keep. And outside, in the camp and the port, and along all the horse-lines that trailed off into the open fields, the soldiers stirred and checked their gear and began the day with the same thought as the sailors who were trapped in the port: this time, would their master stir? Would King Charles, with his levies, with the levies sent him by his pious and Pope-fearing brothers and nephews, give the sign for the short trip to England?

In the harbor, the skippers looked at their weathervanes, stared towards the eastern and western horizons. The master of the cog *Dieu Aide*, the cog which would carry not only the king but the archbishop of York and the Pope's legate himself, nudged his chief mate, jerked a thumb at the flag standing out stiffly from the mast. High tide in four hours, both knew. Current would be with them then and for a while. Wind in the right quarter and not dropping.

Could the landsmen get themselves down and embarked in time? Neither bothered to speculate. Things would be as they would be. But if the king of the Franks, Charles, nick-named the Bald—if the king seriously wanted to obey the instructions of his spiritual lord the Pope, unite the old dominions of his grandfather Charlemagne, and plunder the wealth of England in the name of holiness, then he would never get a better chance.

As they watched the flag and the wind they heard, half a mile off in the *donjon* trumpets blaring again. Not for dawn, but for something else. And then, faintly, carried on the southwest wind, the noise of cheering. Soldiers acclaiming a decision. Without wasting words, the captain of the *Dieu Aide* jerked a thumb at the derricks and the canvas slings, tapped the hatches of the cog's one hold. Get the hatches off. Get the derricks over the side. We'll need them for the horses. The war-horses, the *destriers* of France.

The same wind, that dawn, blew across the bows of the forty dragon-boats cruising down the English coast from the Humber, almost in their teeth, making it impossible to rig sail. Ivar Ragnarsson, in the prow of the first boat, did not care. His oarsmen were rowing at their paddling-stroke, which they could keep up for eight hours a day if need be, grunting in unison as they heaved their oars through the water, feathering with the ease of long practice, continuing their conversations with a word or two as they swept them back, dipping and heaving again.

Only in the first six boats was there extra work for the men. In each, a ton and a half of dead weight squatted, carefully stowed before the mast: the onagers of Erkenbert, all the forges of York Minster had been able to turn out in the weeks Ivar had given them. Ivar had raged furiously about the weight, demanded that they be lightened. Impossible, the black archdeacon had replied. This is the way they are drawn in Vegetius. More convincingly, lighter models had knocked themselves to pieces in a dozen shots. The kick of the wild ass that gave these machines their name came when the throwing-arm struck the crossbeam. If there were no crossbeam the stone would not be hurled out with its astonishing force and velocity. A light crossbeam, however padded, would crack.

Ivar's meditations were interrupted by loud retching from behind him. Each onager was served by a dozen slaves from the minster; in command of them all, torn deeply against his will from the studies and library of the minster, Erkenbert himself. Now one of the lubbers had succumbed to the long, North Sea swell and was vomiting his heart out over the side. The wrong side, naturally, so that the meager contents of his stomach blew back over the nearest rowers, provoking shouts and curses, disruption of the long, automatic rowing-stroke.

As Ivar stepped toward the disturbance, hand dropping to the gutting-knife at his belt, Hamal the horse-swain, the man who had saved Ivar from the lost battle at March, moved quickly. The slave grasped the man by the scruff of his neck. A violent blow across the side of the head, repeated as Hamal heaved the wretched man off his feet and flung him across the thwarts to the lee side, there to retch in peace.

"We'll have the hide off him tonight," said Hamal. Ivar stared unblinkingly for a moment, knowing well what Hamal was doing. Decided to leave it for the moment. Turned back to his thoughts in the prow.

Hamal caught the eye of one of the rowers, mimed wiping sweat from his brow. Ivar killed a man a day now on average, mostly from the valueless slaves of the minster. At that rate they would have no one left to wind a machine at all by the time they met the enemy. And no one could be sure who Ivar would turn on next. He could be diverted, sometimes, by sufficient cruelty.

Thor send that we meet the enemy soon, thought Hamal. The only thing that will cool Ivar's temper for good is the head and balls of the man who bested him—Skjef Sigvarthsson. Without that, he will destroy everyone around him. That is why his brothers have sent him out this time on his own. With me as his nursemaid, and the Snakeeye's foster father to report.

If we don't meet the enemy soon, thought Hamal, I am going to desert the first chance I get. Ivar owes me his life. But he is too mad to pay. And yet if he takes his rage out in the right quarter, something tells me there are fortunes yet to be gained, here in the rich kingdoms of the South. Rich and ripe to fall.

"It's a bugger," said Oswi, once slave to St. Aethelthryth's of Ely, now captain of a catapult-team in the Army of Norfolk and the Way. There were nods of agreement from his crew as they looked thoughtfully at their much-loved but not-quite-trusted artillery piece. It was one of the torsion-catapults, the wheeled twist-shooters. Every man in the crew was desperately proud of it. They had given it a name weeks before: "Dead Level." They had polished every wooden part of it many times over. Yet they were afraid of it.

"You can count the turns you give to the cogwheels," said Oswi, "so it don't tighten too much."

"And I put my head right down on the ropes every time and listen to 'em," said one of his mates, "till I can hear they're in tune like a harper's harp-strings."

"But she'll still bloody well break one day when you don't expect it; they always do. Break one or two of us for breakfast."

A dozen heads nodded gloomily.

"What we need are stronger wooden arms," said Oswi. "They're what goes."

"Wrap 'em with rope?"

"No, that would work loose."

"I used to work in the forge at my village," the newest member of the team said hesitatingly. "Maybe if they had iron supports . . ."

"No, those wooden arms bend a bit," said Oswi firmly. "They have to. Anything iron would stop them doing that."

"Depends on the iron. If you heat and reheat and hammer it the right way the iron turns into what my old master called *steel*. But it's steel that bends a bit, not soft, like bad iron, but with spring in it. Now if we put a strip of that along the inside of each of the arms it would bend with the wood—and stop them flying apart if the wood broke."

Thoughtful silence.

"What about the jarl?" asked a questioning voice.

"Yes, what about the jarl?" came another voice from behind the half-circle. Shef, strolling round the camp in response to Brand's advice, had seen the cluster of intent faces and had walked silently up to overhear.

Consternation and alarm. Swiftly the group of catapulteers rearranged itself so that their newest member was left in the center, to face the unpredictable.

"Er, Udd here's got an idea," said Oswi, also shifting responsibility.

"Let's hear it."

As the new recruit, first hesitatingly, then fluently and with confidence, began to describe the procedure of making mild steel, Shef watched him. An insignificant little man, even smaller than the others, with weak eyes and a stoop. Any one of Brand's Vikings would have dismissed him immediately as useless to an army, not worth his rations even as a latrine-digger. Yet he knew something. Was it new knowledge? Or was it old knowledge, something many smiths had always known, given the right conditions, but had been unable to pass on except to an apprentice?

"This steel bends, you say," said Shef. "And springs back? Not like my sword"—he drew from its sheath the fine Baltic sword Brand had given him, made like his own self-forged and long-lost weapon of mixed strips of soft iron and hard steel—"but made in one piece? Springy all the way through?"

Udd, the little man, nodded firmly.

"All right." Shef thought a moment. "Oswi, tell the camp marshal you and your team are off all duties. Udd, tomorrow morning go to Thorvin's forge with as many men as you need to help, and start making strips the way you say. Fit the first pair to 'Dead Level' and see if they work. If they do, fit them to all the machines.

"And Udd: When it's done I want to see some of this new metal. Make some extra strips for me."

Shef walked away as the horns blew to dowse fires and to mount the night-guard. Something there, he thought. Something he could use. And he needed something to use. For in spite of the newfound confidence of Thorvin and his friends, he knew that if they just repeated what they had done before, they would be destroyed. Every stroke teaches its own counter. And he had enemies everywhere, in the South and in the North, in the Church and among the pagans. Bishop Daniel. Ivar. Wulfgar and Alfgar. King Burgred. They would not stand up to be shot at a second time.

He did not know what would come, but it would be unpredictable. It was vital to be unpredictable in reply.

The dream, or vision, came this time almost as a relief. Shef felt himself surrounded by difficulties. He knew he did not know the way through them. If some greater agency did, he would welcome the knowledge. He did not think it was Othin in his guise as Bölverk, Bale-Worker, who was guiding him, for all that Thorvin continued to urge him to accept the spear-pendant, the sign of Othin. But who else would help him? If he knew, Shef reflected, he would wear that one's sign.

In his sleep, he found himself suddenly looking down. Down from what seemed a great height, at what he realized, as his eyes cleared, was a great board. A chessboard, with the pieces on it. In the middle of a game. And the players of the game were the mighty figures he had seen before: the gods of Asgarth, so Thorvin said, here playing at chess on their sacred board with squares of gold and silver.

But there were more than two playing. So gigantic were the shapes round the board that Shef could not bring them into focus all at once, any more than he could a mountain range, but he could see one of the players. Not the ruddy, Brand-shaped figure he had seen before, who was Thor, not the one with the axe for a face and a voice like a calving glacier, who was Othin. This one seemed somehow sharper, slighter, his eyes not level. An expression of intense glee crossed his face as he shifted a piece. Loki the Trickster perhaps. Loki, whose fire burned always in the holy circle, but whose followers went unknown.

No, Shef reflected. Tricky this god might be, but he did not have the Loki-look. The look of Ivar. As his vision cleared, Shef realized he had seen him before. It was the god who had looked at him as if he were a horse to be bought. And the expression on his face—surely this too was the owner of the ever-amused voice which twice had given him warnings. That is my protector, thought Shef. It is not a god I know. I wonder, what are his attributes, his purpose? What is his sign?

The board they were playing on, Shef saw suddenly, was not a board but a mappa. Not a mappamundi, but a map of England. He strained forward to see, sure now that the gods knew where his enemies were and what they planned. As he did so he realized that he was up on a mantelpiece, like a mouse in a king's hall. But like a mouse, though he could see, he could not understand. The faces were moving their pieces, laughing in voices like rumbles of thunder. None of it made any sense to him. And yet he was here, he had been brought here, he was sure, to see and understand.

The gleeful face had turned up toward him. Shef stood transfixed, unsure whether to duck back or to freeze. But the face knew he was there. It held a piece up to him, the other gods remaining intent on the game.

It was telling him, Shef realized, that this was the piece he had to take.

What was it? It was a queen, his eyes made out at last. A queen. With the face of . . .

The unknown god looked down, waved an arm dismissively. As if caught by a gale, Shef was toppling away, away back toward his camp, his bed, his blankets. As he fell he recognized in an instant whose the face was on the chess-queen.

* * *

Shef sat up suddenly with a gasp. Godive, he thought slowly, his heart thumping. It must be my own wish that sent me that vision. How could a girl affect the map of the contending enemies?

Outside Shef's sleeping-chamber, noise and upheaval, horses stamping, booted feet striding toward him past the cries of his bower-thanes. Pulling on a tunic, Shef opened the door before the boots reached him.

Facing him was a familiar figure: the young Alfred, still crowned with a golden circle, still as fresh-faced and full of nervous energy as before, but with a new grimness in his eyes.

"I gave you this shire," he said without preamble. "I think now I should have given it to the other one, your enemy. Alfgar. Alfgar and his cripple-father. For between the two of them, and my traitor-bishops and King Burgred my brother-in-law, they have hounded me out of my kingdom."

Alfred's expression changed, showed a sudden weariness and defeat. "I am here as a suppliant. Driven out of Wessex. No time to rally my loyal thanes. The army of Mercia marching on my heels. I saved you. Will you, now, save me?"

As Shef collected his thoughts to reply, he heard more running feet, coming from outside the circle of torches round Alfred. A messenger, too anxious and hasty to remember protocol. As soon as the man saw Shef standing in the doorway, he poured out his alarm.

"Beacons, lord jarl! Beacons for a fleet at sea. Forty ships at least. The men on watch, they say it can only be—it can only be Ivar."

As Shef watched the consternation on the face of King Alfred, something cold inside him drew a conclusion. Alfgar on one side. Ivar on the other. And what have they in common? I took a woman from one. The other took the same woman from me. At least I can be sure now that it was a true dream the god sent me, whoever he may be. Godive is the key to this. Someone is telling me to use her.

Chapter Five

Early in his experience of being jarl, Shef had discovered that news was never quite as good or quite as bad as it was made to seem on first hearing. So it proved again. Beacons were a good way of signaling danger, and direction, and even—with care—number. They said nothing about distance. The beacon-chain started far up the coast, in Lincolnshire. It could mean only that Ivar—if Ivar it was—had left the Humber with, as Brand had immediately pointed out, the wind dead in his teeth. He could be three days off, or even more.

As for King Burgred, with Alfgar and Wulfgar in his train, Alfred was sure that he was in pursuit and that he meant, on the urgings of his bishops, nothing less than the entire destruction of the land of the Way, and the submission of the whole of England south of the Humber to his rule. But Alfred was a young man who rode hard, and who had only his personal bodyguard with him. Burgred was famous for the splendor of his camp-furniture and the number of ox-wagons needed to carry it. Forty miles to him was four days' march.

Shef might expect a heavy stroke from each of his enemies. Not a sudden one.

It would have made no difference in any case. As Shef dealt with the immediate necessities of the situation, he thought only of what he knew he must do—and who he could trust in this situation to help him. There was only one answer to the latter. As soon as he could get rid of all his council-members on one errand or another, he slipped through the gates of his *burg*, sent back the troubled guards who had tried to accompany him, and made his way as unobserved as possible through the crowded streets surrounding it.

Hund was, as he expected, busy in his booth, treating a woman whose evident terror at the sight of the jarl suggested a guilty conscience: a drab or a hedge-witch. Hund continued to treat her as if she were a thane's lady. Only after she had gone did he sit down by his friend, unspeaking as usual.

"We saved Godive once," said Shef. "Now I am going to do it again. I need your help. I cannot tell anyone else what I am doing. Will you help?"

Hund nodded. Hesitated. "I'll help you any time, Shef. But I have to ask. Why have you decided to do this now? You could have tried to get Godive back any time the last few months, when there was far less on your mind."

Shef coldly wondered once more how much he could safely say. Already he knew what he needed Godive for: as bait. Nothing could enrage Alfgar more than knowing Shef had stolen her away. If he made it seem like an insult from the Way, Alfgar's allies would be drawn in. He wanted them to pursue Godive like a great fish striking. Onto the hook of Ivar. And Ivar too could be baited. By a reminder of the woman he had lost, and the man who had taken her.

But he dared say none of this to Hund, not even to his childhood friend. Hund had been a friend of Godive too.

Shef allowed concern and confusion to show on his face. "I know," he said. "I should have done it before. But now, suddenly, I am afraid for her."

Hund looked his friend steadily in the eye. "All right," he said. "I dare say you have good reason for what you do. Now, how are we going to work it?"

"I'll get out at dusk. Meet me where we used to shoot the catapults. During the day I want you to collect half a dozen men. But listen. They must not be Norse. All English. All freedmen. And they must all look like freedmen, understand. Like you." Undersized and underfed, Shef meant. "With horses and rations for a week. But dressed shabby, not in the clothes we've given them.

"And there's another thing, Hund, and this is why I need you. I am too easy to recognize with this one eye"—the one eye you left me with, Shef did not say. "When we went into the Ragnarsson camp that did not matter. Now, if I am to go into a camp with my half brother and stepfather in it, I need a disguise. Now, what I thought was . . ."

Shef poured out his plan, Hund occasionally altering or improving on it. At the end the little leech slowly tucked his apple-pendant, for Ithun, out of sight, adjusting his tunic so nothing showed.

"We can do it," he remarked, "if the gods are with us. Have you thought what will happen here in the camp when they wake up and find you gone?"

They will think I have deserted them, Shef realized. I will leave a message, to let them think I have done it for a woman. And yet it will not be true.

He felt the old king's whetstone dragging at his belt, where he had tucked it. Strange, he thought, when I went into the camp of Ivar, the only thought I had in my head was to rescue Godive, to take her away with me and find happiness together. Now I mean to do the same again. But this time—this time I am not doing it for her. I am not even doing it for me. I am doing it because it must be done. It is the answer. And she and I: we are just parts of the answer.

We are like the little cogs that turn the ropes that wind the catapults. They cannot say they do not want to turn anymore, and neither can we.

He thought of the strange tale of Frothi's mill which Thorvin had told him, about the giant-maidens, and the king who would not let them rest. I would like to give them rest, he told himself, and the others who are caught up in this mill of war. But I do not know how to release them. Or myself.

When I was a thrall, then I was free, he thought.

* * *

Godive came through the women's door at the back of King Burgred's immense camp-pavilion and began to edge down the long rows of trestle-tables, at the moment unfilled. She had a task, in case anyone questioned her—a message for King Burgred's brewer to broach extra barrels, and instructions from Alfgar to stand over him while he did it. Actually, she had had to get out of the stifling atmosphere of the women's quarters before her heart burst with fear and grief.

She was no longer the beauty she had been. The other women, she knew, had noticed, were talking among themselves about what had happened to her, talking with malicious pleasure at the fall of a favorite. They did not know what the causes were. They must know that Alfgar beat her, beat her with increasing fury and frenzy as the weeks went by, beat her with the birch on her bare body till the blood ran and her shift stuck to her morning after morning. Such things could not be done quietly. Even in the timber hall of Tamworth, Burgred's capital, some noise carried through the planks and panels. In the tents where kings spent the summer, the campaigning months . . .

But though they heard, and though they knew, there was no one who would help her. Men would hide their smiles the day after a thrashing; women, to begin with, spoke quietly and consolingly. They all thought that it was the way of the world, however they speculated on how she had failed to please her man.

None of them—except Wulfgar, and he no longer cared—knew the weight of despair and dismay that came upon her whenever she thought of the sin that she and Alfgar committed every time they lay together, the sin of incest that must surely mark their souls and bodies forever. No one at all knew that she was a murderess as well. Twice in the winter she had felt the life swell within her, though—thank God—she had never felt it quicken. If she had, she might not have had the strength to go into the woods, find the dog's mercury, the birthwort, and drink the bitter drench that she made from it to kill the child of shame in her own womb.

And even that was not what had made her face drawn and lined beyond its years, her walk stooped and shuffling like that of an old woman. It was the memory of pleasure that she hugged to herself. That hot morning in the woods, the leaves above her head, the warm skin and thrusting flesh in her arms: the sense of release and freedom.

An hour, it had lasted. The memory of it blotted out the rest of her young life. How strange he had looked when she had seen him again. The one eye, the fierce face, the air of pain mastered. The moment he handed her back . . .

Godive's eyes dropped lower and she half ran across the space kept clear outside the pavilion, crowded now with Burgred's personal guard, his hearth-band, and with the hundred officers and errand-runners of the Mercian army marching stolidly on Norfolk at their king's command. Her skirts brushed past the group standing idly listening to a blind minstrel and his attendant. Dimly, without thinking of it, she heard that they were listening to a lay of Sigemund the Dragon-slayer: She had heard it before in her father's hall.

Shef watched her go with a curious chill at his heart. Good, she was there, with her husband, in the camp. Very good; she had failed completely to recognize him, though not six feet away. Bad that she looked so ill and frail. Worse that when he saw her his heart had not turned over as he expected, as it had done every time he had seen her since the day he had known she was a woman. Something was missing in himself. Not his eye. Something in his heart.

Shef dismissed the thought as he finished his song and Hund, his attendant, pushed forward quickly, bag outstretched in appeal. The listening warriors pushed the little man from one to the other as he moved round the ring, but in little more than good nature. His bag filled a little with bread, a lump of hard cheese, half an apple, whatever they had about them. This was no way to work, of course. What a sensible pair would have done was to wait till evening, approach the lord after dinner and ask permission to entertain the company. Then there would be a chance of proper food afterward, a bed for the night, maybe even a gift of money or a bag filled with breakfast.

But their own ineptitude fitted their cover. Shef knew he could never have passed for a professional minstrel. He meant instead to look like a part of the debris of war that covered all England: a younger son crippled in battle, cast out by his lord, turned away as useless by his family, and now trying to keep from starvation by singing memories of glory. Hund's skill had created a story on Shef's body that anyone could read by looking at him. First he had carefully and artistically painted a great scar on Shef's face, the slash-mark of an axe or a sword across the eyes. Then he had bandaged the fake scar with the filthy rags of an English army-leech, letting only the edges of it hint at what lay underneath. Then he had splinted and strapped Shef's legs beneath his wide breeches so that it was impossible for him to bend a knee; and finally, as a refinement of torment, strapped a metal bar to his back to prevent any free movement.

"You dropped your guard," he had said. "A Viking hit you across the face. As you fell forward you got the back of an axe, or a war-hammer, that crushed your spine. Now your legs can only trail behind you as you hobble on crutches. That's your story."

But no one had ever asked Shef his story. No experienced warrior needed to. Another reason that the Mercian companions did not bother to interrogate the cripple and his meager attendant was that they were afraid. Every warrior knew that such a fate one day might be his own. Kings and lords might keep a few cripples, pensioners, as signs of their own generosity or out of some family feeling. But gratitude or care for the useless were too expensive luxuries for a land at war.

The ring of listeners turned to other interests. Hund emptied the bag, passed half of the bits to Shef, squatted by him as they both devoured their gifts, heads down. Their hunger was not an act. For two days now they had worked closer and closer into the center of Burgred's camp, trailing behind it for ten miles each day, Shef slumped on a stolen donkey, living only on what they could pick up, sleeping each night in their clothes in the cold dew.

"You saw her," muttered Shef.

"When she comes back I will throw her the sign," replied Hund. Neither spoke again. They knew this was a moment of critical danger.

Eventually Godive could prolong her errand no further. Back in the women's quarters, she knew, the old woman Alfgar had set to watch over her would be growing suspicious, fearful: Alfgar had told her that if his whore of a wife found a lover, he would sell her to the slave-market in Bristol, where the Welsh chiefs bought cheap lives.

She began to make her way back across the still-crowded courtyard. There were the minstrel and his boy still. Poor folk. A blind cripple and a starveling. Even the Welsh would not buy such. How long would they live? Till the winter, maybe. They might outlive her at that.

The minstrel had raised his coarse brown hood against the slow drizzle that was turning the dust into mud. Or maybe it was against the cruel stares of the world, for his face was in his hands. As she came level with them, the attendant bent forward and dropped something onto the ground at her feet. Instinctively, she stooped for it.

It was gold. A gold harp, a tiny brooch for a child's dress. Small as it was, it would buy food for two men for a year. How could a wandering beggar have such a thing? Tied to it with a thread was—

It was a sheaf. Just a few cornstalks threaded together, but tied to make the shape unmistakable. But if the harp meant the minstrel, then the sheaf was—

She turned convulsively to the blind man. His hands came away from his face, bandage in them; she saw the one eye staring deep into her own. Gravely, slowly, the eye winked. As Shef dropped his face into his hands once more he said four words, low but clear. "The privy. At midnight."

"But it's guarded," said Godive. "And there's Alfgar . . ."

Hund stretched out his bag towards her, as if begging in desperation. As the bag touched her, he slipped a small flask from his hand to hers.

"Put it in the ale," he whispered. "Whoever drinks it will sleep."

Godive jerked back convulsively. As if rejected, Hund sank back, the minstrel dropped his face once more into his hands, as if too far gone in despair to look up. A few yards away, Godive saw old Polga hobbling towards her, reproaches already forming. She turned away, fighting an urge as she did so to leap, fighting an urge to run and embrace the old woman as if she was a young virgin with never a care or a fear. The lacerations on the backs of her thighs caught her woolen dress and slowed her to a cramped shuffle.

Shef had not expected to sleep on the edge of the abduction, but it had come upon him irresistibly. Too irresistibly to be natural, he feared. As he fell asleep, a voice was speaking. Not the now-recognized, amused voice of his unknown patron. The cold voice of Othin, fosterer of battle, betrayer of warriors, the god who took the sacrifices offered to Dead Man's Strand.

"Be very careful, mannikin," said the voice. "You are free to act, you and your father, but never forget to pay me my due. I will show you what happens to those who do."

In his dream, Shef found himself at the very edge of a circle of light, in the dark but looking in. Within the light, a harper sang. He sang to a man, an old man with gray hair, but with a forbidding, cruel beaked face like the ones on his whetstone. The harper sang to this man. But he sang, Shef knew, for the woman who sat at her father's feet. He was singing a lay of love, a lay from the Southlands about a woman who heard the nightingale sing in an orchard and pined away helplessly for her lover. The old king's face relaxed in pleasure, his eyes closing, remembering his youth and the wooing of his dead wife. As he did so the harper, never missing a note, placed a runakefli—*a stick carved with runes—by the woman's skirt: the message from her lover. He himself was the lover, Shef knew, and his name was Heoden. The harper was Heorrenda the peerless singer, sent by his lord to woo the woman Hild away from her jealous father, Hagena the remorseless.*

Another time, another scene. This time two armies faced each other by a restless strand, the sea hurling in rollers over the kelp. One man stepped forward from the ranks, went toward the other. It was Heoden this time, Shef knew, come to offer bride-price for the stolen bride. He would not have done it if Hagena's men had not caught up with him. He showed the bags of gold, the precious jewels. But the other man, the old man was speaking. Shef knew he was rejecting the offer: for he had drawn the sword Dainslaf, which the dwarves had made, and which could never be sheathed till it had taken a life. The old man was saying he would be satisfied with nothing less than Heoden's life, for the insult put upon him.

Haste and pressure, pressure from somewhere. He must see this last scene. Dark, and a moon shining through scattered clouds. Many men lay dead on the field, their shields cloven, their hearts pierced. Heoden and Hagena lay close together in a death-grapple, each the other's bane. But one figure was still alive, still moving. It was Hild, the woman, who now had lost both husband-abductor and father. She moved among the corpses, singing a song, a galdorleoth which her Finnish nurse had taught her. And the corpses began to move. Began to rise. Stared at each other in the moonlight. Lifted their weapons and began again to strike. As Hild shrieked in rage and frustration her lover and her father ignored her, faced each other, began again to hack, to chop at the splintered shields. So it would go till Doomsday, Shef knew, on the strand of Hoy in the far-off Orkney isles. For this was the Everlasting Battle.

The pressure grew till he woke with a start. Hund was pressing a thumb under his left ear, to bring him awake silently. Around them the night was quiet, broken only by the stirring and coughing of hundreds of sleepers in their tents and shelters, the army of Burgred. The noise of revelry from the great pavilion had finally stopped. A glance at the moon told Shef it was midnight. Time to move.

Rising from their places, the six freed slaves Shef had brought with him, led by Cwicca the bagpipe-player of Crowland, went silently to a cart standing a few yards away. They clustered round it, seized the push-handles and set off. Immediately a great squeaking of ungreased wheels filled the night, provoking immediate complaints. The gang of freedmen took no notice, marched doggedly on. No longer strapped and bandaged, but still dragging himself on his crutches, Shef followed thirty paces behind. Hund stood watching them for a moment, then slipped away in the moonlight toward the edge of camp and the waiting horses.

As the cart shrieked its way toward the pavilion, a thane of Burgred's guard stepped across. Shef heard his snarl of challenge, heard his spear-shaft crack across some unfortunate's shoulder. Wails of complaint, expostulation. As the thane stepped closer to find out what the men were doing he caught the reek of the cart and stepped back again, gagging and waving a hand in front of his face. Dropping his crutches, Shef slid past behind his back and into the maze of the pavilion guy-ropes. From there he could see again the thane ordering Cwicca's gang back, Cwicca cringing but sticking to his litany of explanation: "Clean out them pots now, they said. Chamberlain said he don't want no shit-shoveling in daylight. Nor no shit-shovelers disturbing no ladies. We don't want to do it, lord, we'd sooner be in bed, but we got to do it, it's our hides if it ain't done by morning; chamberlain told me he'd have the skin off me for sure."

The whine of the slave was unmistakable. As he spoke he kept pushing the cart forward, making sure the aged reek of twenty years of human dung got well to the thane's nostrils. The thane gave up, walked away still waving a hand in front of his face.

It would be hard to make this a story for poets, Shef reflected. No poet had ever found a place for the likes of

Cwicca. yet the plan could never work without him. Slaves, freemen, and warriors looked different from each other, walked and talked differently. No thane could ever doubt that Cwicca was a slave on an errand. How could an enemy warrior be so undersized?

The gang reached the door of the women's privy, at the rear of the great quarter-acre pavilion. In front of it stood the permanent sentry, one of Burgred's hearth-companions, six feet tall and fully armed from helmet to studded boots. From his place in the shadows Shef watched intently. It was a critical moment, he knew. Cwicca had blocked as much of the view as possible with his cart, but just the same a watchful eye might be there in the darkness.

The gang surrounded the companion-sentry, pressing round him, deferential but determined, pawing at his sleeve as they tried to explain. Catching his sleeve, catching his arm, pulling him down as a skinny arm shut off his throat. A momentary heave, a strangled half-cry. Then a spurt of blood black in the moonlight as Cwicca passed a razor-sharp knife across vein and artery and windpipe, cutting down to the neckbone with the force of one slash.

As the sentry fell forward, was seized by six pairs of hands and upended into the cart, Shef reached them, grabbing the helmet, spear and shield. In a moment he too was out in the moonlight, waving the dung-cart impatiently on. Now any watchful eye would see only what was normal: the armed six-footer waving forward a gang of dwarvish toilers. As Cwicca's gang got the door open, pressed round it with their shovels and buckets, Shef stood for a moment in full view. Then stepped back into the shadow as if to watch the slaves more closely.

A moment later and he was through the door. And Godive was in his arms, naked beneath her shift.

"I couldn't get my clothes," she whispered. "He locks them away every night. And Alfgar—Alfgar took the drink. But Wulfgar sleeps also within our booth, and he would drink no ale because it is a fast-day. He saw me leave. He may cry out if I do not return."

Good, thought Shef, his brain cold as ice in spite of the warmth in his arms. Now what I meant to do all along will seem natural to her. So much less to explain. Maybe she will never know that I did not come for her.

Behind him, Cwicca's men were pressing in, still giving the impression of men trying to work quietly but openly.

"I am going into the sleeping-chamber," Shef whispered to them. "The lady will show me. If you hear an alarm, flee at once."

As they stepped into the unlit passage between the little individual sleeping-places of Burgred's most trusted courtiers—Godive moving with the sureness of one who had walked it a hundred times—Shef heard Cwicca's voice behind him. "Well, since we're here we might as well do the job. What's a few buckets of shit in a day's work?"

Godive paused as they reached the lowered canvas flap, pointed, spoke almost soundlessly. "Wulfgar. To the left. He sleeps in our room many nights, so I can turn him. He is in his box."

I have no gag, thought Shef. I expected him to be asleep. Silently he caught the hem of Godive's shift, began to lift it up over her body. For a moment she caught at the material with automatic modesty, then gave way, let him strip her naked. The first time I have done that, thought Shef. I never imagined it would be no pleasure. But if she enters naked, Wulfgar, will be confused. It may give me an extra moment.

He pushed her bare back forward, felt the wince and the familiar feel of dried blood. Rage filled him, rage at Alfgar, rage too at himself. Why had he not thought, not once these long months, what they must be doing to her?

Moonlight through the canvas showed Godive walking naked across the room to the bed where her husband lay in drugged sleep. A grunt of surprise, anger from the short, padded box to the left. In an instant Shef was standing over it, looking down into his stepfather's face. He saw the recognition, saw the mouth open in horror. Stuffed the bloody shift firmly between Wulfgar's teeth.

Instant resistance, a furious twisting like a giant trapped

snake. Though Wulfgar had neither arms nor legs, he still struggled desperately with all the force of his back and belly muscles to get a stump over the edge of the box, maybe roll to the floor. Too much noise, Shef knew, and the privileged couples sleeping in the little canvas boxes around him would wake as well, perhaps decide to intervene.

Perhaps not. Even noble couples learned to turn a deaf ear to the sounds of love. The sounds of punishment too. Shef thought of Godive's scarred back, thought of his own, conquered the momentary repugnance. A knee in the belly. Hands forcing the shift deep down into the throat. Twisting the ends behind the head and knotting them, knotting them again. And then Godive was with him, still naked, thrusting forward the rawhide ropes Alfgar's men used to fasten their trunks of belongings onto the pack-mules. Quickly they ran the ropes round the sleeping-box, not tying Wulfgar down, but making sure he could not climb out, crawl across the floor. As they finished, Shef waved Godive to the other end of the box. Carefully they lifted it from its stand, placed it on the floor. Now he could not even tip the box over, make a noise.

The short struggle over, Shef took two paces across to the big bed, looked down at Alfgar, asleep in drugged slumber in the moonlight. His mouth hung open, a steady snore coming from his throat. Still a handsome man, Shef recognized. He had had Godive these twelve months and more. He felt no urge to cut his throat. He needed Alfgar still. For the plan. And yet a gesture. A gesture would make the plan work better.

Godive was coming forward, in gown and mantle now, recovered from the box where Alfgar had locked them. In her hand she held her little seamstress's scissors, a look of set determination on her face. Quietly Shef blocked her, forced the hand down. He touched her back, looked inquiringly.

She pointed to a corner. There it was, the bundle of birch-twigs, fresh ones, without blood. He must have been planning to use them later. Shef straightened Alfgar on his

bed, folded his hands on his chest, placed the birch-bundle
between them.

He moved over to where Wulfgar lay in the rays of the
moon, eyes bulging, staring up with an unreadable expression: terror? disbelief? could it be remorse? A memory
came to Shef from somewhere: the three of them, Shef and
Godive and Alfgar, small children, playing excitedly at
something—bulliers maybe, the game with the plantain-
shoots, where each child took it in turn to cut at the other's
shoot with their own, till the head of one or the other came
off. And Wulfgar watching, laughing, taking a turn himself.
It was not his fault he was a heimnar. He had kept Shef's
mother, not repudiated her as he might.

He had watched his son flog his daughter half to death.
Slowly, making certain Wulfgar saw every movement, Shef
took the borrowed silver pendant from his pouch, breathed
on it, polished it. Laid it on Wulfgar's chest.

The hammer of Thor.

Silently the two slipped from the room, headed through
the darkness for the door to the privy, guided by the muffled
sounds of scraping and clanking. A problem occurred to
Shef suddenly. He had not thought of this in advance. A noble lady, gently bred and brought up. There was only one
way out for her. Cwicca and his gang could walk out, protected by the obviously shameful nature of their task and
their own size and gait, the unmistakable marks of the
slave-born. He could seize the spear and shield again and
walk with them, complaining loudly if need be about the
shame of a noble thane escorting a shit-cart to see the slaves
did not steal or loiter. But Godive. She must needs go in the
cart. In her gown. With a dead body and twenty buckets of
human dung.

As he got ready to explain to her, to speak of necessity,
apologize, to promise a bright future, she stepped ahead of
him.

"Get the lid off," she snapped to Cwicca. She put her
hand on the fouled edge of the cart, vaulted into the dark,
stomach-gagging reek inside. "Now move," came her voice

from the depths. "This is fresh air compared with King Burgred's court."

Slowly the cart squeaked its way across the courtyard, Shef striding ahead, spear-shaft sloped.

Chapter Six

Shef looked along the row of faces confronting him: all hostile, all disapproving.

"You took your time," said Alfred.

"I hope she was worth it," said Brand, looking with incredulity at the drawn and shabby figure of Godive in her borrowed churl-wife's gown, straddling the pony behind Shef's.

"This is not the behavior of a lord of warriors," said Thorvin. "To leave the Army threatened on two sides, and ride off on some private errand. I know you came to us first to save the girl, but to go now . . . Could she not have waited?"

"She had waited too long already," said Shef briefly. He swung from his horse, grimacing slightly from the pain in his thighs. It had been another long night and day of a ride, though the consolation was that even coming on hell-bent, with the fury of Wulfgar and the bishops to spur him, Burgred must still be two days behind.

Shef turned to Cwicca and his comrades. "Go back to your places in the camp," he said. "And remember. This was a great deed that we did. You will see in time that it meant even more than it seems. I will not forget to reward you all for it."

As the men trotted off, Hund among them, he turned back to his councillors. "Now," he said. "We know where Burgred is. Two days behind and coming toward us as fast as he can bring himself to march. We can expect him to reach our boundary the second night from this."

"But where is Ivar?"

"Bad news there," said Brand briefly. "He came down on the mouth of the Ouse two days ago with forty ships. The Norfolk Ouse, of course, not the Yorkshire Ouse. Attacked Lynn at the river mouth straight away. The town tried to resist him. He battered the stockade down in a few minutes and stamped the place flat. No survivors to say how he did it, but there's no doubt it happened."

"The mouth of the Ouse," muttered Shef. "Twenty miles off. And Burgred about the same."

Without orders Father Boniface had produced the great map of Norfolk and its borders which Shef had had made for the wall of his main chamber. Shef stood over it, estimating, looking from place to place.

"What we have to do . . ." he began.

"Before we do anything," Brand interrupted, "we have to discuss the matter of whether you are still fit to be trusted as our jarl."

For a long moment Shef stared at him, one eye against two. In the end it was Brand's eyes that dropped.

"All right, all right," he muttered. "You're up to something, no doubt, and one day you may consent to tell us what."

"Meanwhile," Alfred put in, "since you went to such trouble to fetch the lady, it might only be polite to have some thought for what she is to do now. Not just leave her standing outside our tents."

Shef looked again from face to hostile face, focusing finally on Godive's eyes—once more brimming with tears.

There is no time for all this! Something inside him shrieked. Persuading people. Lulling people. Pretending they are important. They are all wheels in the machine, and so am I! But if they thought that they might refuse to turn.

"I am sorry," he said. "Godive, forgive me. I was so sure we were safe that my mind turned to other things. Let me present to you my friends . . ."

* * *

The dragon-boats cruised down the shallow, muddy stream of the Great Ouse river, the western frontier of the Wayland jarldom they had come to destroy, forty in line ahead. Some of the crews were keeping up a song as they wound through the green, summer countryside, the masts and furled sails marking their passage over the flat levels. Ivar's men did not bother. They knew the time without a song or a shanty-man to mark it. Besides, wherever Ivar Ragnarsson stood there was now a cloud of strain and tension, even for veteran pirates who would boast and believe that they feared no man.

Not far ahead the helmsmen—the rower-reliefs and the cowed slaves who manned Ivar's machines, one to each of the front six vessels—could see a wooden bridge across the river: not much of a bridge, not part of a town, just the place where the road happened to cross the stream. Chance of ambush from it, none. Just the same, veteran pirates grew to be veterans by taking no unnecessary risks at all. Even Ivar, totally careless of his own safety as he was, did things the way his men expected. A furlong short of the bridge, the figure in the prow, resplendent in scarlet cloak and grass-green trousers, turned and gave one harsh call.

The rowers finished their stroke, recovered oars, and then dropped them in the water, blades reversed. Slowly the ship drifted to a stop, the rest of the fleet easing into close line behind. Ivar waved to the two clumps of riders on both banks, here easily visible in the flat meadowland round the city. They moved forward at a trot, to check the bridge. Behind them the crews began with the ease of long practice to unstep their masts.

No resistance. Not a man in view. Yet as the horsemen slid from their ponies and moved to meet each other on the wooden cart-bridge, they saw that men had been there. A box. Left clear in the middle of the track, where no one could fail to spot it.

Dolgfinn, captain of the mounted scouting party, eyed it without enthusiasm. He did not like the look of it. It had been left there for a purpose. It had been left there by someone who had a very good idea of how a Viking fleet approached. Such things invariably contained a message or a sign of defiance. Probably it was a head. And there was no doubt that it was meant to be delivered to Ivar. Just to confirm his opinion, there was a crude painting on the top, of a tall man in scarlet cloak, green breeches and silver helmet. Dolgfinn had no great fear for himself—he was Sigurth Ragnarsson's own foster father, sent by the Snakeeye himself to keep an eye on his insane relative, and if Ivar had any lingering concern for what any man thought, it was for his elder brother. Just the same, Dolgfinn had no particular relish for the scene that was likely to erupt. Someone would suffer for it, that was sure. Dolgfinn remembered the scene many months before, when Viga-Brand had dared and taunted the Ragnarssons together with the news of their father's death. Good material for a tale, he reflected. Yet things had not turned out so well afterward. Had Brand perhaps, plain man though he seemed to be, foreseen what would follow? And if so, what of this?

Dolgfinn put the thoughts from his mind. Trap it might be. If so, he had no choice but to test it. He picked up the box—not a head at least, too light—walked down to the edge of the water where the dragon-boat was edging in, leapt from shore to oar to thwart, and strolled toward Ivar standing on the half-decked prow, near the giant ton-and-a-half weight of his machine. Silently he put the box down, indicated the painting, whipped a knife from his belt and offered it to Ivar hilt-first, to pry up the nailed lid.

A king of the English would have waved forward a servant to do such a menial task. Chiefs of the pirates had no such dignity to stand on. In four brisk heaves Ivar had the nails out. His pale eyes looked up at Dolgfinn, while his face broke into an unexpected smile of pure pleasure and anticipation. Ivar knew insult or provocation was coming. He liked the thought of something to repay.

"Let's see what the Waymen have sent us," he said.

Hurling the box-lid aside, he reached in.

"First insult. A capon." He lifted the dead bird out, stroked its feathers. "A neutered cockerel. Now, I wonder who that might signify."

Ivar held the silence till it was quite clear that neither Dolgfinn nor anyone else had anything to say, then reached down again.

"Second insult. Tied to the capon, some straw. Some stalks."

"Not stalks," said Dolgfinn. "That is a sheaf. Do I need to tell you who that is for? His name was often in your mouth a few weeks ago."

Ivar nodded. "Thank you for the reminder. Have you heard it said, Dolgfinn, the old saying: 'A slave takes vengeance at once, a coward never'?"

I did not think you were a coward, thought Dolgfinn, but he did not say it. It would have sounded too much like an apology. If Ivar meant to take offense, he would.

"Have you heard another old saying, Ivar Ragnarsson?" he countered. " 'Often from a bloody bag come bad tidings.' Let us riddle this bag to the bottom."

Ivar reached again, pulled out a third and last object. This time he stared at it with genuine puzzlement. It was an eel. The snake-like fish of the marshes.

"What is this?" Silence.

"Can anyone tell me?" Still only headshakes from the warriors crowding round. A slight stir from one of the slaves of the monks of York, crouching by his machine. Ivar's eyes missed nothing.

"I grant a boon to whoever can tell me the meaning of this."

The slave straightened up doubtfully, realizing all eyes were now on him.

"One boon, lord, given freely?"

Ivar nodded.

"It is what we call in English an *eel*, lord. I think it may mean a place. Ely, down the Ouse, Eel-island, only a few miles from here. Perhaps what it means is that he, the Sheaf, that is, will meet you there."

"Because I must be the capon?" inquired Ivar.

The slave gulped. "You granted a boon, lord, to whoever would speak. I choose mine. I choose freedom."

"You are free to go," said Ivar, stepping back from the ship's thwart. The slave gulped again, looking round at the bearded, impassive faces. He stepped forward slowly, gained confidence as no one moved to hinder him, leapt to the side of the ship, and then, in two moves, to a trailing oar and to the side of the river. He was off like a flash, heading for the nearest cover, running in awkward bounds like a frog.

"Eight, nine, ten," said Ivar to himself. The silver-mounted spear was in his hand; he poised, took two paces sideways. The leaf-blade took the running slave neatly between shoulders and neck, hurling him forward.

"Would anyone else care to call me a capon?" inquired Ivar generally.

Someone already has, thought Dolgfinn.

Later that night, after the ships had moored a cautious two miles north of the challenge-ground, some of Ivar's most senior skippers were talking quietly, very quietly, round their campfire well away from Ivar's tent.

"They call him the Boneless," said one, "because he cannot take a woman."

"He can," said another. "He has sons and daughters."

"Only if he does strange things first. Not many women survive them. They say—"

"No," cut in a third man, "do not speak. I will tell you why he is the Boneless. It is because he is like the wind, which comes from anywhere. He could be behind us now."

"You are all wrong," said Dolgfinn. "I am not a Wayman, but I have friends who are. I had friends who were. They say this, and I believe them. He is the *Beinnlauss*, right enough. But that does not mean 'boneless.' " Dolgfinn held up a beef-rib to point out which of the two meanings of the Norse word he meant. "It means 'legless.' " He patted his own thigh.

"But he has legs," queried one of his listeners.

"On this side, he does. Those who have seen him in the Otherworld, the Waymen, say that there he crawls on his belly in the shape of a great worm, a dragon. He is not a man of one skin. And that is why it will take more than steel to kill him."

Experimentally, Shef flexed the two-foot-long, two-inch-wide strip of metal that Udd, the little freedman, had brought him. The muscles on his arms stood out as he did so: muscles strong enough to bend a soft iron slave-collar by main force alone. The mild steel gave an inch, two inches. Sprang back.

"It works on the shooters all right," offered Oswi, watching with interest a ring of catapulteers.

"I'm wondering if it would work for anything else," said Shef. "A bow?" He flexed the strip again, this time putting it over one knee and trying to get the weight of his body behind it. The metal resisted him, giving only a couple of inches. Too strong for a bow. Or too strong for a man's arms? Yet there were many things that were too strong for a man's arms alone. Catapults. Heavy weights. The yard of a longship. Shef hefted the metal once more. Somewhere in here there was a solution to his puzzle: a mixture of the new knowledge the Way sought and the old knowledge he kept on finding. Now was not the time for him to work the puzzle out.

"How many of these have you made, Udd?"

"Maybe a score. After we refitted the shooters, that is."

"Stay in the forge tomorrow. Make more. Take as many men and as much iron as you need. I want fivescore—tenscore—as many as you can make."

"Does that mean we'll miss the battle?" cried Oswi. "Never get a chance to shoot old 'Dead Level' once?"

"All right. Udd chooses just one man from each crew to help him. The rest of you get your chance at the battle."

If there is a battle, Shef added silently to himself. But that is not my plan. Not a battle for us, at any rate. If England is the gods' chessboard, and we are all pieces in their game, then to win the game I must clear some of the pieces off the board. No matter how it looks to the others.

In the early morning mist King Burgred's army, the army of the Mark—three thousand swordsmen and as many slaves, drivers, muleteers and whores—prepared to continue its march in the true English fashion: slowly, grumpily and in-efficiently, but for all that, with mounting expectation. Thanes wandered toward the latrines, or eased themselves onto any unoccupied spot. Slaves who had not done so the night before began to grind meal for the everlasting por-ridge. Fires began to burn, pots began to bubble, the voices of Burgred's guardsmen grew hoarse as they attempted to impose the king's will on his loyal but disorganized sub-jects: get the bastards fed, get their bowels emptied, and get them moving, as Cwichelm the marshal endlessly repeated. Because today we move into enemy territory. Cross the Ouse, advance on Ely. We can expect a battle any time.

Driven on by the fury of their king at the violation of his own pavilion, by the exhortations of their priests and the near-incoherent rage of Wulfgar the dreaded heimnar, the army of the Mark struck its tents and donned its armor.

In the dragon-boats, matters went differently. A shake from the ship-watch, a word from each skipper. The men were over the side in minutes, and every one dressed, booted, armed and ready to fight. Two riders trotted down from the advanced pickets half a mile away, reporting noise to the west and scouts sent out. Another word, this time from Ivar, and half the men in each crew stood down immediately, to prepare food for themselves and the others still formed up. Detachments swarmed round each of the ton-weight ma-chines in the six lead ships, attaching ropes and rigging pul-leys. When the word came they would sway them up from the strengthened yards, drop each one onto its waiting car-riage. But not yet. "Wait till the last moment and then move fast" was the pirates' watchword.

The Wayman camp, four miles off in dense beechwood,

made no sound and showed no lights. Shef, Brand, Thorvin
and all their lieutenants had been round again and again the
day before, impressing it on the most important Viking and
dullest ex-slave. No noise. No straggling. Stay in your blankets till you're called. Get some rest. Breakfast by units.
Then form up. Don't go outside the wood.

Obeying his own orders, Shef lay alert in his tent, listening to the muted bustle of the army waking. Today was a
day of crisis, he thought. But not the last crisis. Maybe the
last one he could plan. It was critically important, then, that
this day should go well, to provide him with the start, the
reserve of force that he would need before all was over.

On the pallet beside him lay Godive. They had been together four days now, and yet he had still not taken her, not
so much as stripped off her shift. It would be easy to do.
His flesh was hard, remembering the one time he had done
it. She would not resist. Not only did she expect it, he knew
she wondered why he had not. Was he another like the
Boneless? Or was he less of a man than Alfgar? Shef imagined the cry she would make as he penetrated her.

Who could blame her for crying? She still winced every
time she moved. Like his, her back must be scarred forever.

Yet she still had both eyes. She had never faced the
mercy of Ivar, the *vapna takr*. As he thought of the mercy
of Ivar, Shef's erected flesh began to shrink; the thoughts of
warm skin and soft resistance dwindled like a catapult-stone
going up into the sky.

Something else entered him instead, something cold and
fierce and longsighted. It was not today that mattered, nor
the fleeting good opinion of his men. Only the end.
Stretched out, relaxed, perfectly aware of himself from
crown to toe, Shef reflected on how the day might go.

Hund, he decided. Time for another call on Hund.

As the sun sucked up the morning mist, Ivar looked from
his place with the ridge-line pickets to the familiar chaos of
an English army advancing. Familiar chaos. An English
army.

"It's not them," said Dolgfinn beside him. "Not the Way-folk. Not Skjef Sigvarthsson. Look at all the Christ-stuff, the crosses and the black robes. You can hear them singing their morning *massa*, or whatever they call it. So either Sigvarthsson's challenge was just a lie, or else . . ."

"Or else there's another army hiding round here some-where, to finish off the winners," Ivar completed for him. The grin was back on his face, pinched and painful, like a fox nibbling meat from the wolf-trap.

"Back to the boats?"

"I think not," said Ivar. "The river's too narrow to turn forty boats in a hurry. And if we row on there's no certainty they won't mount and catch us. And if they do that they can take us out one boat at a time. Even the English might man-age that.

"No. At our Bragi boast in the Braethraborg, my brothers and I swore to invade England and conquer all its kingdoms in revenge for our father. Two we have conquered, and to-day is the day for the third."

"And Sigvarthsson?" prompted Dolgfinn.

The grin spread wider, teeth showing like a rictus. "He will have his chance. We will have to see he doesn't take it. Now, get down to the boats, Dolgfinn, and tell them to un-load the machines. But not this bank. The far bank, under-stand? A hundred paces back. And rig a sail over each one as if it was a tent. Have men ready to look as if they're tak-ing them down when the English come in sight. But take them down English-style—you know, as if you were ten old gammers comparing grandchildren. Have the slaves do it."

Dolgfinn laughed. "You have trained the slaves to work better than that these months, Ivar."

The mirth had drained completely from Ivar's face, the eyes gone as colorless as his skin. "Then untrain them," he said. "The machines on that bank. The men on this." He turned back to his survey of the army coming forward, six-deep, banners waving, great crosses on standard-carts behind its center. "And send up Hamal. He will lead the mounted patrol today. I have special orders for him."

* * *

From his vantage point beneath a great flowering hawthorn, Shef looked out at the developing battle. The Army of the Way lay in its ranks behind and to either side of him, well spread-out and under cover of wood or hedgerow. The bulky pull-throwers were still not assembled, the twist-shooters with their horse-teams well to the rear. English bagpipers and Viking horn-blowers had all alike been threatened with disgrace, torment and forfeiture of a week's ale ration if they sounded a note. Shef was sure they had remained undiscovered. And now, as the battle seemed likely to be joined, both sides' wandering scouts would have been called into the center. So far so good.

And yet already there was a surprise. Ivar's machines. Shef had watched them being swayed from the boats, had noted the way the yards dipped and the boats heeled: heavy objects, whatever they were, far heavier than his own. Was that how Ivar had taken Lynn? And they had been put on the wrong bank. Safer from attack, maybe, but unable to move forward if the battle shifted the other way. Nor could even Shef's keen sight see how the machines were constructed. How would they affect his plan to fight the battle?

Even more, his plan not to fight the battle.

Cwichelm the marshal, veteran of many battles, would have halted the army if he could, as soon as his advance-guard reported the dragon-boats on the river in front of him. A Viking fleet was not what he had expected to fight. Anything unexpected should be scouted first—especially when dealing with the folk of the Way, whose many traps he remembered from the fight in the marsh when Sigvarth had died.

He was not left to make the decision. Vikings and Waymen were all the same to his king: enemies of decency. To Wulfgar and the bishops, all were heathens. Dragon-boats spread out in line? So much the better! Destroy them before they could mass together. "And if they are not Way-folk," the young Alfgar had added with pointed insolence, "so much less to worry about. At least they will not have the machines you fear so much."

Stung by the insult, aware that complex maneuvering would not work with the untrained thanes who made up most of King Burgred's army, Cwichelm took his men over the slight ridge above the river at a brisk trot, he and his assistants well out in front, shouting their war-cries and waving their broadswords for the rest to come on.

The English army, seeing the hated dragon-boats in front of them, each crew clumped in a wedge before its boat, cheered and came on with enthusiasm. Just so long as they don't get disheartened, thought Cwichelm, dropping back till the ranks closed round him. Or get tired before the battle's even started. He settled his shield firmly on his shoulder, making no effort to lift it to guard-position. It weighed a stone—fourteen English pounds—the rest of his weapons and armor, three stone more. Not too much to carry. A lot to run with. Even more to wield. Through the sweat that ran into his eyes he noted dimly the men on the far bank struggling with canvas. Not often you catch Vikings napping, he thought. It's usually us that's up last.

The first volley from Erkenbert's onagers smashed six holes in the English battle-line, each stone driving clear through the six-deep ranks. The one aimed for the commanders in the center—conspicuous in gold and garnets and scarlet tunics—lifted a trifle high, at head height. Cwichelm never felt or saw the blow that drove his head straight back till the neckbone snapped, that reaped a file of men behind him and crashed on to bury itself in the earth just short of the cart from which Bishop Daniel was chanting an encouraging psalm. In an instant both he and the army were headless.

Most of the English warriors behind their visored helmets did not even see what had happened to their right or their left. They could see only the enemy in front of them, the enemy so tantalizingly gathered in isolated clumps and wedges, each one forty-strong in front of its ship, five or ten yards between them. In a yelling wave they ran forward to beat on the Viking wedges with spear and broadsword, hacking at the linden-shields, sweeping at head and leg. Braced and rested, Ivar Ragnarsson's outnumbered men strained every muscle to hold them for the five minutes their chief had demanded.

Through the carefully measured firing-lanes the catapults launched their irresistible missiles again and again.

"Something's happening already," grunted Brand.

Shef made no reply. For several minutes he had strained his one eye desperately to see what he could of the machines that were wreaking such havoc in Burgred's army. Then he fixed on one, counted his heartbeats carefully between one launch and the next. By now he had a good idea of what the weapons were. They must be torsion-machines—the slow rate of shot showed that, as did the smashing effect, the swirls of men bowled over as each missile struck. They were not on a bow principle. Little as he could see from a mile's distance, the square, high shape showed that. And the weight of them, the weight he could detect from the way they had to be slung on yards and pulleys—that showed they must be built stoutly to take some sort of impact. Yes. A little experiment, a closer look if he got the chance, and . . .

Time now to think more immediately. Shef turned his attention to the battle. Something happening, Brand said. And easy enough to guess what. After a few volleys, the men on the English side, nearest to where the stones were arriving, had started to edge sideways, realizing that safety lay in having wedges of their enemies between them and the machines. But as they edged sideways they hampered the efforts and the sword-arms of the champions trying to break through Ivar's crewmen. Many of those champions, half-blinded by their helmets, weighed down by their armor, had no idea what was going on, only that something strange was happening round them. Some of them were beginning to step back, to look for space to raise their visors, to shove off the men who should be backing them but were jostling them instead. If Ivar's men were concentrated they could use such a moment to break out. But they were not. They themselves were in small groups, each one liable to be swallowed instantly by superior numbers if they drove forward from their ships and the protecting riverbank. The battle hung in balance.

Brand grunted again, this time digging his fingers deep into Shef's arm. Someone by Ivar's machines had given an order to change targets, was enforcing it with kicks and blows. As the English swordsmen rushed forward, the clumsy standard-carts behind them were left exposed, each one with a waving banner on it—of king or alderman, or the giant cross of bishop or abbot. But now there was one fewer than there had been a moment ago. Splinters still flew in the air, turning end over end. A direct hit. And there again—a whole file of draft-oxen slumped onto their knees in a row and a wheel hurled itself sideways. From the Wayman army behind Shef and his group, all by now watching intently, there rose an exhalation, an exhalation that would have been a cheer without the instant kicks and curses of marshals and team-leaders. A cross held steady for a moment, then tipped inexorably over, crashed to the ground.

Something deep inside Shef clicked like a winding cog-wheel. Thoughtfully, unnoticed in the rising excitement around him, he took a deep pull at the flask he had held all day in one hand: good ale. But in it was the contents of the little leather sack he had taken from Hund that morning. He drank deep, forcing himself to ignore the gagging reflex, the vile taste of long-rotten meat. How do you give a man a vomit, for a purge? he had asked. "That is one thing we *can* do," Hund had said with somber pride. Shef felt no doubt, as the drench went down, that that was exactly true. He drank the flask to its end, leaving not a drop as evidence, then rose to his feet. A minute, maybe two, he thought. I need all eyes.

"Why are they riding forward?" he asked. "Is it a charge?"

"A cavalry charge like the Franks do?" replied Brand uncertainly. "I've heard of that. Don't know that the English—"

"No, no, no," snapped Alfred, also on his feet, almost dancing with impatience. "It's Burgred's horse-thanes. Oh, look at the fools! They've decided that the battle is lost, so they're riding forward to rescue their lord. But as soon as he mounts . . . Almighty God, he's done it!"

Far away across the battlefield, a gold-ringed head rose into view from a ruck of bodies—the king mounting. For a moment he seemed to be resisting, waving his sword forward. But someone else had hold of his bridle. A clot of riders began to walk, then canter from the fighting. As they did so, instantly men began to shred away from the fighting-lines, following their leader, at first casually. Then briskly, hastily. Realizing the movement behind them, others turned to look, to follow. The army of the Mark, still undestroyed, still unbeaten, many of its men still unafraid, began to stream to the rear. As it did so, the stones lashed out again. Men began to run.

The Wayman army was all on its feet now, all eyes turning expectantly toward the center. The moment, Shef thought. Sweep forward when both sides are fully engaged, take the machines before they can change target, board the ships, take Ivar in flank and rear . . .

"Give me some horsemen," Alfred begged. "Burgred's a fool, but he's my sister's husband. I have to save him. We'll pension him off, send him to the Pope . . ."

Yes, thought Shef. And that will be one piece still on the board. And Ivar—even if we beat him Ivar will get away, by boat or horse, like he did last time. And that will be another. But we must have fewer pieces now. In the end, one piece alone. I want the mills to stop.

Blessedly, as he stepped forward, he felt some dreadful thing rising inside him, his mouth filling with the terrible cold saliva he had felt only once before, the time he had eaten carrion one hard winter. Grimly he clamped it down. All eyes, all eyes.

He turned, looked at the men rising from bracken and

bush, eyes glaring, teeth showing with expectant rage. "Forward," he shouted, lifting his halberd from the ground and sweeping it toward the river. "Men of the Way . . ."

The vomit shot from his mouth so fiercely it caught Alfred high up on his enameled shield. The king gaped, uncomprehending. Shef doubled up, acting no more; his halberd dropped. Again the great retchings took him, again and again, lifting him off his feet.

As he rolled on the fouled earth the Wayman army hesitated, staring in horror. Alfred raised an arm to shout for his horse, for his companions, then dropped it, turned back to stare at the figure writhing on the ground. Thorvin was running forward from his place in the rear. A buzz of doubt ran along the ranks: What's the order? Are we going forward? Sigvarthsson is down? Who commands? Is it the Viking? Do we obey a pirate? An Englishman? The Wessex king?

As he sprawled in the grass, gasping for breath before the next upheaval, Shef heard the voice of Brand, looking down at him with stony disapproval.

"There is an old saying," it said. " 'When the army-leader weakens, then the whole army wavers.' What do you expect it to do when he spews his guts out?"

Stand fast, thought Shef, and wait till he's better. Please, Thor. Or God. Or whoever. Just do it.

Ivar, his eyes as pale as watered milk, stared out across the battlefield for the trap he knew must be there. At his feet—he had fought by choice at the tip of the wedge of his ship's crew—lay three champions of the Mark, each in turn eager for the fame that would ring through the whole of Christendom for the bane of Ivar, cruelest of the pirates of the North. Each discovering in turn that Ivar's slim height belied his extraordinary strength of arm and body, though not his snakelike speed. One of them, cut through mail and leather from collarbone to ribcage, moaned involuntarily as he waited for death. Quick as a snake's tongue Ivar's sword licked out, stabbing through Adam's apple and spine be-

neath. Ivar did not want sport, for the moment. He wanted
quiet, for consideration.

Nothing in the woods. Nothing to either flank. Nothing
behind him. If they did not spring the trap soon it would be
too late. It was almost too late already. Round Ivar his army,
without orders or briefing, was crying out one of its many
experienced battle-drills: securing a battlefield after victory.
It was one of the many strengths of Viking armies that their
leaders did not have to waste their energies in telling the
rank and file how to do anything that could be turned into
a routine. They could watch and plan instead. Now, some
men went forward in pairs, one to stab, one to guard, making doubly and triply sure that no Englishman was lying
still but conscious, ready to take a last enemy with him. Behind them came the loot-gatherers with their sacks, not
stripping the dead of everything, as would be done later, but
taking everything visible and valuable. In the ships, leeches
were splinting and binding.

And at the same time every man kept a tense eye on their
leader, for further orders. All knew that the moment of victory was a time to exploit advantage. They carried out their
immediate tasks with savage haste.

No, reflected Ivar. The trap had been set, he was sure of
that. But it had not been sprung. Probably the fools got up
too late. Or were stuck in a marsh somewhere.

He stepped forward, placed his helmet on a spear, waved
it in a circle. Immediately, from their concealment half a
mile on the downstream flank of the English army, there
broke a wave of riders, legs flapping as they kicked their
horses into speed, steel glinting in the morning sun on point
and edge and mail. The English swordsmen still shredding
to the rear pointed, yelled, ran faster. Fools, thought Ivar.
They still outnumber Hamal up there six to one. If they
stood fast, formed line, they could finish him off before we
got up to join in .And if we broke ranks to hurry they could
win this battle yet. But there was something about armed
riders that made scattered men run without even looking
over their shoulders.

In any case Hamal and the mounted patrol—three hundred men, every horse that Ivar's army had been able to lay bridle on—had targets other than single fugitives. Now, after battle, was the time to destroy leaders, to ensure that kingdoms could never recover their strength again. Ivar noted with approval the swerve as fifty men on the fastest horses aimed to head off the gold-coroneted figure now being urged over the skyline by his horse-thanes. Others pounded down on the straggle of carts and standards making laboriously for the rear. The main body was galloping hard along the ridge-line, obviously intent on the camp and the camp-followers that must be there, out of sight but only a few hundred yards the other side of the ridge.

Time to join them. Time to get rich. Time for sport. Ivar felt the excitement rise in his throat. They had balked him with Ella. Not with Edmund. They would not with Burgred. He enjoyed killing kings. And afterward—afterward there would be some one of the whores, maybe some one of the ladies, but anyway some soft, pale creature that no one would miss. And in the tumult of a sacked camp, with rape and death on every side, no one would notice. It would not be the girl that Sigvarthsson had taken from him. But there would be some other. Meanwhile.

Ivar turned, stepped carefully round the mess of entrails slowly spilling from the butchered man at his feet, replaced his helmet, waved his shield forward. The watching army, loot already stacked, men back in their ranks, gave a short, hoarse cheer and walked forward with him, up the hill, over the men they had killed themselves and the men the machines had slaughtered. As they tramped forward they shook out from their wedges to form a solid line four hundred yards across. Behind them the ship-guards already detailed watched them go.

So, from its concealment in the woods a mile upstream, did the Wayman army—confused, frustrated, already bickering over the limp shape of its leader.

Chapter Seven

"We cannot afford to wait any longer," said Thorvin. "We must settle this matter for good. And now."

"The army is divided," objected Geirulf, the priest of Tyr. "If the men see you too ride away, they will lose heart even more."

Thorvin brushed the objection aside with an impatient gesture. Round him ran the cords with their holy rowan berries; the spear of Othin stood in the ground beside him next to the burning fire of Loki. Just as the time before, only priests of the Way sat in the sacred circle, with no laymen present. They meant to speak of things no layman should hear.

"That is what we have told ourselves for too long," replied Thorvin. "Always there is something more important to think of than this central one. We should have solved the riddle long ago, as soon as we began to think the boy Shef might indeed be what he said: the one who will come from the North. We asked the question, we asked his friend, we asked Sigvarth Jarl—who thought he was his father. When we could find no answer we passed to other things.

"But now we must be sure. When he would not wear the pendant, I said, 'there is still time.' When he left the army and rode to find his woman, we thought, 'he is a boy.' Now he pretends to lead the army and leaves it in disorder. Next time what will he do? We have to know. Is he a child of Othin? And if he is, what will he be to us? Othin Allfather,

father of gods and men? Or Othin Bölverk, God of the Hanged, Betrayer of Warriors, who gathers the heroes to himself only for his own purposes?

"Not for nothing is there no priest of Othin with the army, and few within the Way. If that is his birth, we must know. And it may be that is not his birth. There are other gods than Allfather who walk in the world."

Thorvin looked meaningfully at the crackling fire to his left. "So: let me do what should have been done before. Ride to ask his mother. We know which village she comes from. It is not twenty miles off. If she is still there I will ask her—and if her answer is wrong, then I say we must cast him off before worse befalls us. Remember the warning of Vigleik!"

A long silence followed Thorvin's words. Finally Farman, the priest of Frey, broke it.

"I remember Vigleik's warning, Thorvin. And I too fear the treachery of Othin. Yet I ask you to think that Othin, and his followers, may be as they are for a reason. To keep off worse powers."

He too looked thoughtfully at the Loki-fire. "As you know, I have seen your former apprentice in the Otherworld, standing in the place of Völund the smith. But I have seen other things in that world. And I can tell you that not far from here there is far worse than your apprentice: one of the brood of Fenris himself, a grandchild of Loki. If you had seen them in the Otherworld, you would never again confuse the two, Othin and Loki, or think that the one might be the other."

"Very well," replied Thorvin. "But I ask you, Farman, to think this. If there is a war between two powers in this world, gods and giants, with Othin at the head of one and Loki at the other—how often do we see it even in this world, that as the war goes on, the one side begins to resemble the other?"

Slowly the heads nodded, even, in the end, Geirulf's, then Farman's.

"It is decided," said Farman. "Go to Emneth. Find the boy's mother and ask her whose son hers is."

Ingulf the healer, priest of Ithun, spoke for the first time. "A deed of kindness, Thorvin, that may come to good. When you go, take with you the English girl Godive. She has realized in her way what we have. She knows he did not rescue her for love. Only to use her as bait. That is no good thing for anyone to know."

Shef had been dimly aware, through first the racking cramps and then the paralyzing weakness that succeeded them, of the leaders of his army's factions arguing. At some point Alfred had threatened to draw sword on Brand, an action dismissed like some great dog brushing aside a puppy. He could remember Thorvin pleading passionately for something, some rescue or expedition. But most of the day he had been aware of nothing except hands lifting him, attempts made to get him to drink, hands holding him through the retchings that followed: Ingulf's hands sometimes, then Godive's. Never Hund's. With just a fragment of mind Shef realized that Hund feared his leech-detachment might suffer if he saw too closely what he had done. Now, as the dark came on, he felt recovered, weary, ready to sleep: to wake to action.

But first the sleep must come. It had the nauseous taste about it of Hund's mold-and-carrion draft.

He was in a gully, a rocky defile, in the dark. Slowly he clambered forward, unable to see more than a few feet, lit only by a last pale light in the sky—the sky visible only many yards above his head, where the gully's jagged outline showed black against gray. He moved with agonized care. No stumble, no dislodgement of stone. Or something would be on him. Something no human could fight against.

He had a sword in his hand, gleaming very faintly in the starlight. There was something about the sword: it had a will of its own, a fierce urge. It had already killed its creator and master, and would gladly do so again, even though he was its master now. It tugged at his hand, and from time to time it rang faintly, as if he had knocked it on stone. It seemed to know about the need for stealth, though. The sound would be inaudible to anyone or anything except himself. It was covered, too, by the rushing of the water at the bottom of the gully. The sword was anxious to kill, and ready to keep silent till its chance came.

As he moved into the dream, Shef realized, as he often did, what sort of person he himself was. This time, a man impossibly broad of hip and shoulder, with wrists so thick they bulged round the gold bracelets he wore. Their weight would have dragged a lesser man's arms down. He did not notice them.

The man he was, was frightened. His breath came short, not from the climbing, but from fear. There was a sense in his stomach of emptiness and chill. It was especially frightening to this man, Shef realized, because he had never felt such a feeling before. He did not even understand it, and could not name it. It was bothering him, but not affecting him, because this man did not know it was possible to turn back from an enterprise once begun. He had never done it before; he would never do so till the day he died. Now he was climbing beside the stream, holding his drawn sword carefully, to reach the position he had decided on and to do the thing he had planned, though his heart turned over inside him at the thought of what he must face.

Or not face. Even this man, Sigurth Sigmundsson, whose name would live till the end of the world, knew he could not face what he had to kill.

He came to a place where the gully wall on one side was broken down, falling into a jumble of scree and broken stone, as if some great metal creature had smashed it and rolled it flat so that it could get down to the water. And as he reached it, a sudden overwhelming reek stopped the hero in his tracks, a reek like a solid wall. It stank of dead things, of a battlefield two weeks old in the summer sun—but also of soot, of burning, with some extra tang about it that attacked the nostrils, as if the smell itself would catch fire if someone struck a spark.

It was the smell of the worm. The dragon. Dawn-ravager, venom-blower, the naked spite-creature that crawled on its belly. The legless one.

As the hero found, in the jumble of stone, a crack large enough to take his body and crawled inside it, he realized he had not been too early. For the dragon was not legless, and seemed so only to those who saw it crawling forward from a distance. Through the stone the hero could hear a heavy stumping, as one foot after another groped forward; in between and all the time, the heavy slither of the belly dragging on the ground. The leather belly, if reports were true. They had better be.

The hero tried to lie on his back, then hesitated, changing position rapidly. Now he lay on one side, facing the direction from which the dragon must come, propped on his left elbow, right elbow down and sword across his body. His eyes and the top of his head projected above the track. It would look like another stone, he told himself. The truth was that even this hero could not lie still and wait for the thing to appear above him, or he—even he—would be unmanned. He had to see.

And there it was, the great head silhouetted against the gray like some stone outcrop. But moving; its armored crest and skull-bones like a metal war-machine rotating. The bloated swag body behind it. Some trick of the starlight caught one foot planted on the stone, and the hero stared at it, shocked almost into paralysis. Four toes, sticking out from each other like the arms of a starfish, but each one the size of a man's thigh, warty and gnarled like a toad's back, dripping slime. The very touch of one of those would kill from horror. The hero had just enough self-command not to shrink back with fear. The slightest movement now would be deadly dangerous. His only hope was to be a stone.

Would it see him? It must. It was coming toward him, directly toward him, padding forward with great, slow steps. One forefoot was only ten yards from him, then the other was planted on the stone almost on the lip of his crack. He must let it walk right over him, the hero thought with his last vestige of sense, let it walk right down to the river where it drank. And when he heard the first noise of drinking, of the water gushing up as it must into the belly above him, then he must strike.

As he told himself this, the head reared up only a few feet above him, and the hero caught sight of a thing of which no man had spoken. The dragon's eyes. They were white, as white as those of an old woman with the film-disease, but light shone through them, a pale light from within.

The hero realized what it was that he feared the most. Not that the legless one, the boneless longserpent, would kill him. That would almost be a relief in this terrible place. But that it would see him. And stop. And speak, before it began its long sport with him.

The dragon halted, one foot in mid-stride. And looked down.

Shef came from his sleep with a shriek and a bound, landing in one movement, just feet from the bed where they had stretched him. Three pairs of eyes stared at him, alarmed, relieved, surprised. One pair, Ingulf's, looked suddenly knowing.

"You saw something?" he said.

Shef passed a hand over his sweat-soaked hair. "Ivar. The Boneless One. As he is on the other side."

The warriors around Ivar watched him out of the corners of their eyes, too proud to show alarm or even anxiety, yet conscious that at any time now he might break out, turn on anyone at all, even his most trusted followers or the emissaries of his brothers. He sat in a carved chair looted from one of King Burgred's baggage-carts, a horn of ale in his right hand, dipped from the great keg in front of him. In his left hand he swung the gold coronet they had taken from Burgred's head. The head itself was on a spike in the stark ring surrounding the Vikings' camp. That was why Ivar's mood was grim. He had been balked yet again.

"Sorry," Hamal had reported. "We tried to take him alive, as you ordered, to pin him between our shields. He fought like a black bear, from his horse and then on foot. Even then we might have taken him, but he tripped, fell forward on a sword." "Whose sword?" Ivar had demanded, his voice quiet. "Mine," Hamal had said, lying. If he had indicated the young man who had really killed Burgred, Ivar would have taken out his spite and frustration on him. Hamal had a chance of surviving. Not an especially strong one, for all his past services. But Ivar had only studied his face for a moment, remarked dispassionately that he was a liar, and not a pretty one, and had left the matter there.

It would break out some other way, they were sure. As Dolgfinn went on with the tale of victory—prisoners taken, loot from the field, loot from the camp, gold and silver, women and provisions—he wished deeply that some of his own men would turn up. "Go round everywhere," he had told them, "look at everything. Never mind the women for the moment; there'll be plenty left for you before the night's over. But in the name of old Hairy Breeks himself, find something to keep the Ragnarsson amused. Or it could be us he pegs out for the birds tomorrow."

Ivar's eyes had shifted past Dolgfinn's shoulder. He dared to follow them. So—Greppi and the boys had found something after all. But what in the name of Hel, goddess of the dead, could it be?

It was a box, a wheeled box that could be tipped forward and trundled along like an upright coffin. Too short for a coffin. And yet there was a body inside. A dozen grinning Vikings pushed the box forward and tipped it to stand in front of Ivar. The body inside looked out at them, and licked its lips.

Ivar rose, putting down the golden coronet for the first time that evening, and stood in front of Wulfgar.

"Well," he remarked at last. "Not such a bad job. But not

one of mine, I think. Or at least I don't remember the face. Who did this to you, heimnar?"

The pale face with its bright red, incongruous lips, stared back at him, made no reply. A Viking stepped forward, knife whipping clear, ready to slice or gouge on command, but Ivar's hand stopped him.

"Think a little, Kleggi," he urged. "It's not easy to frighten a man who's already lost so much. What's an eye or an ear now?

"So tell me, heimnar. You are a dead man already; you have been since they did this. Who did it to you? Maybe he was no friend of mine either."

Ivar spoke in Norse, but slowly, clearly, so an Englishman could pick out some of the words.

"It was Sigvarth Jarl," said Wulfgar. "Jarl of the Small Isles, they tell me. But I want you to know, what he did to me, I did to him. Only more. I caught him in the marsh by Ely—if you are the Ragnarsson, then you were not far away. I trimmed him finger by finger and toe by toe. He did not die till there was nothing left a knife could reach. Nothing you can do to me will equal what I did to him."

He spat suddenly, the spittle landing on Ivar's shoe. "And so may perish all you Godless heathen! And it is my comfort. As you die in torment, for you it is only the gateway to the eternal torment. I will look down from *Neorxnawang*, from the plain of the blessed dead, and see you blister in the heat. Then you will beg for the smallest drop from my ale-cup to cool your agony. But God and I will refuse."

The blue eyes stared up, jaw set in determination. Ivar laughed suddenly, throwing his head back, raised the horn in his right hand and drained it to the last drop.

"Well," he said. "Since you mean to be so niggard with me, I will do what your Christian books say and return you good for evil.

"Throw him in the keg!"

As the men gaped, Ivar stepped forward, slashing at the straps which held Wulfgar's trunk and stumps in place. Seizing him by belt and tunic he lifted him bodily out of the container, took three heavy paces to the side, and thrust the heimnar deep into the four-foot-high, hundred-gallon butt of ale. Wulfgar bobbed, thrashing with the stumps of his arms, truncated legs not quite reaching the bottom.

Ivar put one hand on Wulfgar's head, looked round like a teacher demonstrating.

"See, Kleggi," he pointed out. "What is a man maimed like this afraid of?"

"Of being helpless."

He pushed the head firmly down. "Now he can take a good drink," he remarked. "If what he says is true, he won't need it on the other side, but it's as well to be sure."

Many of the watching Vikings laughed, calling to their mates to come and see. Dolgfinn allowed himself a smile. There was no credit in this, no glory or *drengskapr*. But maybe it would keep Ivar happy.

"Let him up," he shouted. "Maybe he will offer us a drink from heaven after all."

Ivar seized the hair, heaved Wulfgar's head up out of the frothing brew. The mouth gaped wide, sucking in air by frantic reflex, the eyes bulged with terror and humiliation. Wulfgar threw the stump of one arm over the edge of the barrel, tried to lever himself up.

Carefully Ivar knocked it free, stared into the eyes of the drowning man as if searching for something. He nodded, thrust the head back down again.

"Now he is afraid," he said to Kleggi, standing by. "He would bargain for his life if he could. I do not like them to die defying me. They must give in."

"They all give in in the end," said Kleggi, laughing. "Like women."

Ivar thrust the head spasmodically deeper.

Shef hefted the object Udd had brought him. They stood in the center of an interested circle—all Englishmen, all freed-men, catapulteers and halberdiers together—near the front the gang Udd had collected to help him forge the strips of mild steel.

"See," Udd said, "we done what you told us. We made the strips, two-foot long. You said try and make bows out of them, so we filed notches in the ends and fitted strings. Had to use twisted gut. Nothing else strong enough."

Shef nodded. "But then you couldn't pull them."

"Right, lord. You couldn't, and we couldn't. But we thought about that for a bit, and then Saxa here"—Udd indicated another member of his gang—"said anyone who's ever carried loads for a living knows legs are stronger than arms.

"So: we took thick oak blocks. We cut slots for the metal near the front and slid the strips through, wedged 'em tight. We fitted triggers like we got already on the big shooters.

"And then we put these iron hoops, like, on the front of the wood. Try it, lord. Put your foot through the hoop."

Shef did so.

"Grip the string with both hands and pull back against your own leg. Pull till the string goes over the top of the trigger."

Shef heaved, felt the string coming back against strong resistance—but not impossibly strong. The puny Udd and his undersized colleagues had underestimated the force a big man trained in the forge could exert. The string clicked over the trigger. He was holding, Shef realized, a bow of sorts— but one that lay crosswise to the shooter, not up and down like a wooden handbow.

A grinning face from the crowd handed Shef a short arrow: short because the steel bow flexed only a few inches, not the half-arm's-length of a wooden bow. He fitted it in the rough gouge in the top of the wooden block. The circle parted in front of him, indicating a tree twenty yards off.

Shef leveled the bow, aimed automatically between the arrow-feathers, as he would have with a twist-shooter, squeezed the trigger. There was no violent thump of recoil as there would have been with the full-sized machine, no black streak rising and falling. Yet the bolt sped away, struck fair in the center of the oak-trunk.

Shef walked over, grasped the embedded arrow, worked it

backward and forward. After a dozen tugs, it came free. He
looked at it speculatively.

"Not bad," he said. "But not good, either. Although the
bow is steel, I do not think in the end it strikes harder than
the hunting bows we use already. And they are not strong
enough for war."

Udd's face fell, he started automatically to make the excuses of the slave with a hard master. Shef held up a hand
to stop him.

"Never mind, Udd. We are all learning something here.
This is a new thing that the world has never seen before, but
who made it? Saxa, for remembering that legs are stronger
than arms? You, for remembering how your master made
the steel? I, for telling you to make a bow? Or the Rome-
folk of old, for showing me how to make the twist-shooters
that started all this?

"None of us. What we have here is a new thing, but not
new knowledge. Just old knowledge put together, old
knowledge from many minds. Now, we need to make this
stronger. Not the bow, for that is strong enough. The pull.
How can we make it so that my pull up is double the
strength of what I can do now?"

The silence was broken by Oswi, leader of the catapult-
team.

"Well, if you put it like that, lord, answer's obvious. How
do you double a pull?

"You use a pulley. Or a windlass. A little one, not a great
big one like the Norse-folk use on their ships. Fix it to your
belt, wind on one end of the rope, hook the other end of the
rope over the bowstring, pull it up as far as you like."

Shef handed the primitive crossbow back to Udd.
"There's the answer, Udd. Set the trigger further back, so
the bow can flex as far as the steel will let it. Make a winding gear with a rope and a hook to go with every bow. And
make a bow out of every strip of steel you have. Take all
the men you need."

The Viking shouldering his way through the crowd
looked suspiciously at the jarl surrounded by a throng of

midgets. He had arrived only that summer, called from Denmark by incredible stories of success, wealth and profit, and of the Ragnarssons defeated. All he had seen so far was an army drawn up to fight that had then suddenly stopped in its tracks. And now here was the jarl himself, talking like a common man to a crowd of thralls. The Viking was six feet tall, weighed two hundred pounds, and could lift a Winchester bushel with either hand. What sort of a jarl is this? he wondered. Why does he talk to them and not to the warriors? *Skraelingjar* such as these will never win a battle.

Out loud he said, with a minimum of deference, "Lord. You are called to council."

His message delivered, he turned away, contempt in the set of his shoulders.

Greatly daring, Oswi asked what all had wondered: "Battle this time, lord? We got to stop that Ivar sometime. We wouldn't have minded if we'd done it sooner."

Shef felt the reproach, overrode it. "Battle always comes soon enough, Oswi. The thing is to be ready."

As soon as Shef stepped into the great meeting tent, he felt the hostility that faced him. The whole of the Wayman council was present, or seemed to be: Brand, Ingulf, Farman and the rest of the priests, Alfred, Guthmund, representatives from every group and unit of the joint army.

He sat down at his place, hand groping automatically for the whetstone-scepter left lying there for him. "Where is Thorvin?" he said, suddenly noting one absence.

Farman started to give a reply, but was immediately overridden by the angry voice of Alfred—the young king—speaking already in a fair approximation of the Anglo-Norse pidgin the Wayman army and council so often used with each other.

"One man here or there does not matter. What we have to decide on cannot wait. Already we have waited too long!"

"Yes," rumbled Brand in agreement. "We are like the

farmer who sits up all night to watch the hen-roost. Then in the morning he finds the fox has taken all his geese."

"So who is the fox?" asked Shef.

"Rome," said Alfred, rising to his feet to look down at the council. "We forgot the Church in Rome. When you took the land from the Church in this county, when I threatened to take the revenues from it in my kingdom, the Church took fright. The Pope in Rome took fright."

"So?" asked Shef.

"So now there are ten thousand men ashore. Mailed horsemen of the Franks. Led by their king Charles. They wear crosses on their arms and their surcoats, and say that they have come to establish the Church in England against the pagans.

"The pagans! For a hundred years we have fought against the pagans, we Englishmen. Every year we sent Peter's pence to Rome as a token of our loyalty. I myself"— Alfred's youthful voice rose in pitch with indignation—"I myself was sent by my father to the last Pope, to good Pope Leo, when I was a child. The Pope made me a consul of Rome! Yet never have we had a ship or a man or a silver penny sent into England in exchange. But the day Churchland is threatened, Pope Nicholas can find an army."

"But it is an army against the pagans," said Shef. "Maybe us. Not you."

Alfred's face flushed. "You forget. Daniel, my own bishop, declared me excommunicate. The messengers say these Cross-wearers, these Franks, announce on all sides that there is no king in Wessex and they demand submission to King Charles. Till that is done they will ravage every shire. They come against the pagans. But they rob and kill only Christians."

"What do you want us to do?" asked Shef.

"We must march at once and defeat this Frankish army before it destroys my kingdom. Bishop Daniel is dead or fleeing, and his Mercian backers with him. No Englishman will challenge my king-right again. My thanes and aldermen are already gathering to me, and I can raise the entire levy of Wessex, from every shire. If, as some say, the messengers have overcounted the strength of the enemy, then I can fight them on even terms. I will fight them on any terms. But your assistance would be greatly welcome."

He sat down, looking round tensely for support.

In the long silence, Brand said one word. "Ivar."

All eyes turned to Shef, sitting on his camp-stool, whetstone across his knees. He still seemed pale and gaunt after his sickness, cheekbones standing out, the flesh round his ruined eye pulled in so that it seemed a dark pit.

I do not know what he is thinking, reflected Brand. But he has not been with us these last days. If what Thorvin says is true, about the spirit leaving the body in these visions, then I wonder if it can be that you leave a little of it behind each time.

"Yes, Ivar," repeated Shef. "Ivar and his machines. We cannot leave him behind us while we march to the South. He would grow stronger. For one thing, now Burgred is dead it will be only a matter of time till the Mercians elect a king to make peace with Ivar and save them from ravaging. Then Ivar will have their men and money to draw on, as he has already drawn on the money and the skills of York. He did not make those machines himself.

"So we must fight him. I must fight him. I think he and I are bound together now so that we cannot part till this is finished.

"But you, lord king." The whetstone-scepter was cradled in Shef's left arm while he stroked its stern, implacable faces. "You have your own people to consider. Maybe it is best for you to march to your own place and fight your own battle, while we fight ours. Each in our own way. Christian against Christian and pagan against pagan. And then, if your God and our gods will, we shall meet again, and set this country on its feet."

"So be it," said Alfred, his face flushing again. "I will call my men and be on my way."

"Go with him, Lulla," said Shef to the leader of the halberdiers. "And you, Osmod," he added to the leader of the

catapult-teams, "see the king has his pick of horses and remounts for his journey south."

As the only Englishmen on the council left, Shef looked
round at those who remained, and broke into fluent, rapid
Norse, tinged with the thick Halogaland accent he had
learned from Brand.

"What are his chances? If he fights his way? Against
these Franks? What do you know of them, Brand?"

"A good chance, if he fights our way. Hit them when
they're not looking. Catch them when they're asleep. Didn't
old Ragnar himself—bad luck to his spirit—did he not sack
their great town back in our fathers' day, and make their
king pay tribute?

"But if the king fights in the English way, with the sun
high in the sky and everyone forewarned . . ."

Brand grunted doubtfully. "The Franks had a king in our
grandfather's day: King Karl, Karl the Great—Charlemagne
they call him. Even Guthfrith, king of the Danes, had to
submit to him. The Franks can beat anybody, given time.
You know why? It's the horses. They fight on horseback.
About once in a blue moon they'll be there, with their saddles on, and their girthstraps tight, and their fetlocks plaited,
or whatever it is they call them—I am a sailor, not a horse-
man, Thor be praised; at least ships never shit on your feet.

"But that day, that one day, you don't want to stand up to
them. And if King Alfred's like all the other Englishmen,
that's the day he'll choose."

"Horses on one side, devil-machines on the other," said
Guthmund. "Enough to make anyone sick."

Eyes scrutinized Shef's face, to see how he would take
the challenge.

"We will deal with Ivar and the machines first," he said.

Chapter Eight

Two figures dressed in the rags of incongruous finery cantered slowly down the green lanes of central England: Alfgar, thane's son, once favorite of a king; Daniel, a bishop without a retinue, still a king's deadly enemy. Both had escaped with difficulty from Ivar's riders by the Ouse, but had managed to end the day with a dozen guards between them, and money and rations enough to take them back in safety in Winchester. Then their troubles had begun.

First they woke one morning to find their guards had simply deserted in the night, perhaps blaming their masters for defeat, perhaps seeing no reason any longer to put up with Alfgar's caustic tongue, Daniel's outbursts of fury. They had taken the food, money and horses with them. Striding across the fields towards the nearest church-spire, Daniel had insisted that as soon as he reached a priest, his episcopal authority would provide them with mounts and supplies. They had never reached the spire. In the troubled countryside, the churls had abandoned their homes for the summer and had built themselves shelters in the greenwood. The village priest had indeed recognized Daniel's status, enough to persuade his parishioners not to kill the pair of wanderers, and even to leave Daniel his episcopal ring and cross, and the gold head of his crozier. They had taken everything else, including Alfgar's weapons and silver arm-rings. After that, for three nights in a row the fugitives had lain belly-pinched in the dew, cold and afraid.

Yet Alfgar, like his half brother and enemy Shef, was a child of the fen. He could make an eel-trap out of withies, could catch fish with a cloak-pin on twisted thread. Slowly the pair had ceased to hope for rescue, had learned to rely on themselves. The fifth day of their journey Alfgar had stolen two horses from an poorly guarded stud, and the herd-boy's knife and his flea-infested blanket as well. After that they had made better time. It had not improved their humor.

At the ford of the Lea they had heard the news of the Frankish landing from a merchant disposed to be respectful to Daniel's cross and ring. It had altered their plan.

"The Church does not fail her servants," Daniel had declared, eyes red with rage and weariness. "I knew the stroke would fall. I did not know where or when. Now, to the glory of God, the pious King Charles has come to restore the faith. We will go to him and make our report—our report of those he must punish: the pagans, the heretics, the slack in faith. Then the evil Way-folk and the graceless adherents of Alfred will find that the quernstones of God grind slow, but they grind to the last grain."

"Where do we have to go?" asked Alfgar sullenly, reluctant to follow Daniel's lead but anxious to contact once again the side that might win, that might bring him vengeance on the ravisher, the bride-stealer, the one who had stolen first his woman, then his shire, and then his woman again. Every day he remembered a dozen times, with a shiver of shame, waking with the birch-twigs in his hand and the curious faces staring down: Didn't you hear? He took your woman? Trussed up your father, with no arms or legs, but just left you to lie there? And you never woke?

"The Frankish fleet crossed the Narrow Sea and landed in Kent," Daniel replied. "Not far from the see of St. Augustine in Canterbury. They are camped at a place called Hastings."

Surveying the walls of Canterbury, his base at Hastings left for a careful, six-day foray, Charles the Bald, king of the Franks, sat on his horse and waited for the procession trailing from the open gates to reach him. He was sure enough what it was. In the lead he could see holy banners, choir-monks singing, censers waving. Behind them, carried in a chair of state, came a gray-bearded figure in purple and white, tall miter nodding: surely the archbishop of Canterbury, the primate of England. Though back at camp in Hastings, Charles reflected, he had Wulfhere, archbishop of York, who would probably dispute this archbishop's claim. Perhaps he should have brought him and let the two old fools fight it out.

"What's this one called?" he asked his constable, Godefroi, sitting his charger next to him.

Godefroi—like his king, sitting easily in a deep saddle, high pommel in front, high saddle-bow behind, feet braced in steel stirrups—raised his eyes to heaven. "Ceolnoth. Archbishop of Cantwarabyrig. God, what a language."

Finally the procession reached its goal, finished its anthem. The bearers lowered the chair; the old man stumbled out of it and stepped across to face the menacing silent figure in front of him, metal man on armored horse. Behind him the smoke of burning villages smudged the sky. He began to speak.

After a while the king raised a gauntlet, turned to the papal legate on his left, Astolfo of Lombardy: a cleric without a see—as yet.

"What is he saying?"

The legate shrugged. "I have no idea. He seems to be speaking English."

"Try him in Latin."

The legate began to talk, easily and fluently in the Latin of Rome—a Latin, of course, pronounced in exactly the same way as the inhabitants of that ancient city spoke their own, modern tongue. Ceolnoth, who had learned his Latin from books, listened without comprehension.

"Don't tell me he can't speak Latin either."

The legate shrugged again, ignoring Ceolnoth's faltering attempts to reply. "The English Church. We had not known things were so bad. The priests and the bishops. Their dress is not canonical. Their liturgy is out-of-date. Their priests preach in English because they know no Latin. They have even had the temerity to translate God's word into their own barbarous speech. And their saints! How can one venerate names like Willibrord? Cynehelm? Frideswide, even! I think it likely that when I make my report to His Holiness he will remove authority from all of them."

"And then?"

"This will have to become a new province, ruled from Rome. With its revenues going to Rome. I speak only, of course, of the spiritual revenues, the proceeds of tithing, of fees for baptism and burial, of payments for entry into sacred offices. As regards the land itself—the property of secular lords—that must fall to its secular rulers. And their servants."

The king, the legate and the constable exchanged looks of deep and satisfied understanding.

"All right," said Charles. "Look, the graybeard seems to have found a younger priest with some grasp of Latin. Tell him what we want."

As the list ran on and on—of indemnities, supplies to be provided, toll to be paid to protect the city from sack, hostages to be delivered and laborers to start work immediately on a fort for the Frankish garrison to be installed— Ceolnoth's eyes widened with horror.

"But he is treating us as defeated enemies," he stammered to the priest who translated for him. "We are not enemies. The pagans are his enemies. It was my colleague of York and the worthy bishop of Winchester who called him in. Tell the king who I am. Tell him he is mistaken."

Charles, about to turn away toward the hundreds of mailed horsemen waiting behind him, caught the tone of Ceolnoth's voice, though he did not follow the words. He was not an uneducated man by the low standards of Frankish military aristocracy. He had learned a trifle of Latin in his youth, learned too some of Titus Livius's stories of the history of Rome.

Smiling, he drew his long, double-edged sword from his scabbard, held it like a merchant's balance.

"This will not need translating," he said to Godefroi. Then, bending from the saddle to Ceolnoth, he said slowly and clearly, two words.

"*Vae victis.*"

Woe to the conquered.

Shef had considered all the possible plans he could use to attack Ivar's camp, weighed them like moves on a chessboard, rejected them one by one. These new ways of making war introduced complexities that could lead to confusion in battle, loss of lives, loss of everything.

It had been much easier when line had clashed with line, battled hand to hand until the stronger side won. He knew that his Vikings were becoming more and more displeased with these new things. Yearned for the certainty of the clash of arms. But the new ways had to be used if Ivar and his weapons were to be defeated. Old and new must blend.

Of course! He must weld the old and the new together like the soft iron and hard steel of a pattern-welded sword, like the sword he had forged and lost in the battle when Edmund was taken. A word formed in his mind.

"*Flugstrith!*" he cried, leaping to his feet.

"*Flugstrith?*" said Brand, turning from the fire. "I do not understand."

"That is how we will fight our battle. We will make it the *eldingflugstrith*."

Brand looked disbelieving. "The lightning-battle? I know Thor is with us, but I doubt you can convince him to hurl his thunderbolts to clear our way to victory."

"It is not the thunderbolts I want. What I want is a battle fast as lightning. The thought is there, Brand; I feel I know what must be done. But I must make it clearer—as clear in my head as if it had already happened."

Now, waiting in the mist in the dark hour before dawn, Shef felt sure his battle-plan would work. The Vikings had ap-

proved it—so had his machine-tending Englishmen. And it
had better work. Shef knew that after his rescue of Godive,
and then his collapse as the army waited to attack, his credit
with the council and the army too was almost exhausted.
Things were being kept secret from him. He did not know
where Thorvin had gone, nor why Godive had slipped away
with him.

As he had before the walls of York, he reflected that in
this new style of battle the fighting was the easiest part. Or
at least it promised to be so for him. Yet somewhere inside
himself his flesh still crawled with a kind of fear: not of
death or disgrace. Fear of the dragon he sensed in Ivar's
skin. He fought the fear and repulsion down, glanced at the
sky for the first pale streaks of dawn, strained his eyes
through the mist to see if he could see the outline of Ivar's
battlements.

Ivar had made his fortified camp in exactly the same style
as the one which King Edmund had stormed south of
Bedricsward by the Stour: a low ditch and bank with stakes
driven into it, forming three sides of a square with the river
Ouse as the fourth side, his ships drawn up along the muddy
bank. The sentry who paced the bank behind the stockade
had been at that battle too, and lived. He needed no urging
to keep alert. Yet to him the dark hours were the dangerous
ones, short enough at this time of year. As he saw the sky
beginning to pale, and felt the little wind that comes before
the dawn, he relaxed and began to think of the day that
might follow. He had no great desire to see Ivar Ragnarsson
at his butcher's work again among his prisoners. Why, he
wondered, did they not move on? If Ivar had been challenged to fight at Ely, he had met the challenge. It was
Sigvarthsson and the Way-folk who must feel disgrace.

The sentry halted, braced himself chest-high against the
wall of the stockade, fighting to keep alert. He brooded on
the sounds he had heard so often in the last few days, coming from under the bloody hands of Ivar. Out there two hundred corpses lay in fresh graves, the product of a week's
sacrifice and slaughter of Mercian prisoners taken after the

battle. An owl called, and the sentry started, thinking for an instant it was the shriek of a spirit come for vengeance.

It was his last thought. Before he heard the thrum of the bowstring the quarrel drove through his throat. From the ditch, the figures who had crept up in the mist caught him, eased him to the ground, waited. Knowing the other sentries on the wall had been dispatched in the same instant, on the cry of the owl.

Even the softest of shoes makes a sound moving through the grass. The hundreds of running feet sounded like small waves rushing down a pebbled strand. Dark bulks loomed, moving swiftly toward the western palisade of the camp, their moment carefully chosen. They were black shapes against a black sky behind them. But the lightening sky in the east would silhouette the defenders when they awoke and rushed to battle.

Shef stood to the side, watching the attack, fists clenched: the success or failure of everything depended on the next few seconds. Taking the camp would be like taking York—only simpler and quicker. No clumsy, moving towers, no slow development of the attack in stages. This was being done in a way even the Ragnarssons would understand—in explosive attack, win or lose in the first minute.

His eager men had shaped the bridges, stout planks pegged together. Twelve yards long and three wide. Iron bands clamped the oars beneath the structure, their handles projecting to either side. Each handle grasped by a Viking, secure in the feel of the familiar wood, proud of the strength needed to lift the structure and run forward with it at the stockade of the camp.

The tallest warriors were in front. As they ran they grunted with the effort, not only from carrying the dead weight—but at the last moment they lifted it over their heads until the front was more than seven feet off the ground. Enough to clear the six-foot-high stakes of the camp.

And clear it they did with a final explosive heave as they leaped over the ditch, slammed wood down on wood, the men in the front springing clear at the last second and rolling down into the ditch.

But not those that ran behind. The instant the bridge was in place they thundered up it and leapt into the enclosure behind. Ten, twenty, a hundred, two hundred were over before the bridge-carriers could unsheathe their weapons and join in the attack.

Shef smiled into the darkness. Six had been built, six had attacked—and only one had not succeeded in topping the wall. It lay half in, half out of the ditch, while cursing Vikings crawled out from under it and joined the rush to the other bridges.

Screams of pain, roars of anger over there as the sleeping men realized that the enemy was in among them. First the thud of axes into flesh, then the clang of metal as men woke, seized arms, defended themselves. Shef took one last look in the growing light, saw that the warriors were following instructions and advancing in a steady line, slaughtering as they went. But keeping position even after they had cut down the man they faced. Keeping pace with the murderous advance. Then Shef ran.

On the eastern side of the camp his English freedmen had waited in the darkness as they had been instructed, trotting forward to the attack only when they heard the first clash of battle. Shef hoped his timing had been correct. He had stationed them two hundred yards form the palisade. Estimated that if they ran forward when they heard the attack they would reach the camp when the armed struggle was joined and intense. All eyes should be on the Viking attack-force— all of Ivar's men rushing to the aid of their comrades. So he fervently hoped. He reached the corner of the camp just as the running men appeared.

Halberdiers led the way, each weighted with a great bundle of brushwood as well as his weapon. To be hurled into the ditch before the sharp blades were wielded against the stakes and the leather thongs that bound the palisade together.

The second wave of attackers approached, crossbowmen

who pushed between the halberdiers, used knives to sever
the last of the bindings, heaved stakes aside, climbed over
and through them.

Shef followed them, pushing forward through the jostling
ranks. No need to shout orders. The crossbowmen were following their long-rehearsed instructions, pacing forward ten
carefully counted steps, then stopping and forming a line.
Others halted behind them to make a double line that
stretched from wall to river-line. Swift runners dashed forward to cut the tent-ropes, fled back to safety as the archers
fitted bolts to cocked strings.

A few drabs and youths had seen them, had stood gape-
mouthed and fled. But incredibly, none of Ivar's men
seemed aware of their presence, totally taken up with the familiar clash of weapons coming from the other wall.

Shef stepped a pace beyond the double line, saw the faces
turning toward him for the prearranged signal. He raised his
arm, dropped it. The heads turned to their front, sighted for
an instant. Then the sharp snap of a hundred strings released
together.

The short, stout arrows shot across the camp, driving
through leather and mail and flesh.

Already the front rank had hooked onto their tackle to re-
load, while the second rank stepped forward between them,
looked to Shef, caught his signal, loosed their second volley.

Shouts of alarm and disbelief were now mingling with
cries of pain as the warriors saw men falling, all to the rear
of the battle. Heads turned, faces pale in the dawn's light, to
see the silent death that was striking them from the rear,
while the Vikings of the Way still kept up their violent pressure from the front, expending energy furiously in an assault
they had been promised would last only minutes.

The first row of bowmen was ready again. As each man
finished loading, he stepped through the line in front to re-
sume rank. Some faster than others. Shef waited impassively till the last had formed up—the lines must be kept
separate if this maneuver was to work—before he dropped
his arm again.

Four times the lines shot before the first of the defenders could turn, order themselves and race across the camp in a wavering line, hindered by collapsed tents and the embers of cooking fires. As they closed, the bowmen obeyed orders again. Shot if they had loaded, then turned and ran with the rest, through the ranks of halberdiers dressed behind them. The halberdiers shifted sideways to let their fellows pass, then closed ranks again in a solid line of points.

"Don't advance, just stand!" shouted Shef as he followed the last of the crossbows through. Few could hear him over the growing din of war-cries. Yet he knew this was the moment Brand had said would not work: the puny slave-born taking the full weight of a Viking charge.

The English obeyed their orders. Stood still, points leveled, second rank bracing the first. Even a man whose belly crawled with fear knew he had to do no more than he could. And the Viking charge did not come with full weight. Too many men shot down, and those the leaders; too many of the rest, uncertain, unprepared. The wave that came to hack at the wall of steel came piecemeal. Each man who ran in faced a point in front, blades chopping from either side. The blows they swung were caught by long shafts thrusting from the rear ranks. Slowly the Vikings drew back from the unshaken line, looking round for leadership.

As they did so a cry of triumph rang from behind them. Viga-Brand, seeing the battle-line in front of him thin and shred, had thrown his picked men through the center of what remained, to wheel instantly and to start to roll up the Ragnarsson line.

Beaten men began to throw their weapons down.

From the riverbank Ivar Ragnarsson stood and watched his men fall, then surrender. Sleeping in his ship, the *Lindormr*, he had rolled from his blankets too late to be more than an observer. Now he knew that he had lost this battle.

He knew why, too. The last few days of blood and slaughter had been a delight for him, a relief. The easing of some frenzy that had lain within him for many years, consoled only now and then and only for a time by the brief pleasures his brothers had arranged for him, or by the grand executions the Great Army had tolerated as appropriate. A delight for him; the army had slowly sickened of it. It had rotted their morale. Not much. Enough to make them put a little less than their best into the desperate defense they had needed.

He did not regret what he had done. What he regretted was that this attack could only come from one man, from the Sigvarthsson. The attack in the night, the instant breaching of his defenses. Then, when his warriors rallied for battle, the cowardly attack from the rear. The engagement was truly lost. He had fled a lost battle before—must he flee again? The victors were close on him, and on the other side of the river—moved across on clumsy punts and rafts five miles downstream—waited the ten torsion dart-throwers, lined up wheel to wheel, guided to their position by willing local churls. As the light strengthened, the twist-shooter teams lowered their sights on to the Ragnarsson ships.

On Ivar's ship, the *Lindormr*; the minster-slaves crouched round their machine. At the first noise of onset they had whipped the covers off it, wound and loaded. Now they hesitated, uncertain in which direction to shoot. Ivar stepped across and on to the gunwale.

"Boom off," he ordered. "Leave that. Push out from shore."

"Are you deserting your men already?" asked Dolgfinn, standing with a clutch of senior skippers a few feet away. "Without so much as a blow struck? That may sound bad when the story is told."

"Not deserting. Getting ready to fight. Come aboard if that's what you mean to do. If you mean to stand round like old whores waiting for trade, stay where you are."

Dolgfinn flushed at the insult, stepped forward with his hand on hilt. Feathers sprouted suddenly from his temple, and he fell. With the camp taken, the crossbowmen had fanned out again, shooting wherever they saw resistance. Ivar stepped behind the protecting bulk of the machine mounted on the prow of the ship. As the slaves clumsily poled the *Lindormr* out into the slow current, he pointed quickly to one man still on the bank.

"You. Jump. Over here."

Reluctantly Erkenbert the archdeacon gathered up his black robe, leapt the widening gap of water, landed staggering in Ivar's arms.

Ivar jerked a thumb at the crossbowmen growing ever more visible in the dawning light. "More machines you did not tell me of. I suppose you will tell me they cannot exist either. If I live past today I will cut your heart out and burn your minster to the ground."

To the slaves he shouted, "Stop pushing. Drop anchor. Drop the gangplank."

As the mystified slaves heaved the weighted, two-foot-wide plank from gunwale to shore, Ivar placed the stout protective beam of his machine behind him, took a firm grip on Erkenbert's right wrist, and leaned back to watch his army die. Unafraid, he had only one thought left: how to spoil his enemies' triumph, how to sour victory into failure.

Firmly escorted, Shef walked forward through the chaos of the camp. His helmet was strapped on, his halberd was over his shoulder. He had not yet struck a blow or dodged one. Ivar's army was no more. The Waymen were rounding up prisoners while a few survivors ran toward the river, running in twos and threes both ways along the bank to get away. There were not many of them, surely not enough to be a threat.

The battle was won, Shef told himself, and won easily, exactly according to plan. Yet something still chilled in his belly: too easy, he felt, too easy. The gods demand a price for favors. What was it to be? He began to run in earnest, heading for the helmet of Brand, now at the very tip of the Waymen's advance toward the river and the ships. As he did so, a flash of color came from the mast of one of the ships only a few yards ahead, gold catching the first direct rays of the rising sun. It was the Coiling Worm. Ivar had broken out his banner.

Brand slowed to a walk as he saw Ivar standing, one foot on the gunwale of the *Lindormr*, with six feet of water between the ship and the bank. Ivar was fully dressed, wearing his grass-green breeches and tunic, his mail-coat and silver helmet. He had thrown his scarlet cloak aside, but the polished boss of his shield caught the red light of morning. By his side stood a small man in the black robe of a Christian cleric, a look of horror on his face.

As men on both sides saw the confrontation, fighting finally stopped. The Vikings on both sides, Waymen and Ragnarssons, looked at each other, nodded, accepted that the battle was won and lost. As the English halberdiers, less businesslike in their attitudes, closed in, those Ragnarsson troops still resisting began hastily to throw their weapons down, put themselves under the protection of their former enemies. Then all, English and Norse, Waymen and pirates, faced inward, to see how their leaders would behave. At the rear of the watching ring, Shef struggled and cursed to get through.

Brand checked for a moment, breathing hard with the exertion of ten minutes' desperate struggle. Then he strolled forward toward the gangplank. He raised his right hand, split between two fingers in King Edmund's battle the previous year. He moved the fingers to show how they had healed.

"We had words a while back, Ivar," he remarked. "I told you you should look after your women better. You did not take my advice. Maybe you don't know how to. But you said when your shoulder was whole you would remember what I said. And I said when my hand was whole I would remind you of it. Well, I have kept my word. Will you keep yours? You look as if you are thinking of sailing away."

Ivar grinned, showing his even teeth. Deliberately, he drew his sword and threw the decorated scabbard into the Ouse.

"Come and try me," he said.

"Why don't you come to fight on firm ground? No one will help me. If you win, you will have free passage back to where you stand now."

Ivar shook his head. "If you are so bold, fight on my ground. Here"—Ivar leapt forward onto the gangplank, took two steps forward—"I will take no advantage. We will both stand on the same plank. Then all can see who gives way first."

A buzz of interested comment rose as the watching men grasped the situation. At first sight the outcome of the fight looked evident. Brand outweighed Ivar by seventy pounds at least, out-topped him by a head and more, was as skillful and experienced with his weapons. Yet everyone could see the plank flex with one man's weight on it. With two, and one as heavy as Brand, how would the footing feel? Would both men be awkward and clumsy? Or just one? Ivar stood braced, feet as far apart as the plank would allow, sword-arm forward like a fencer, not crouched behind his shield like a warrior in a battle-line.

Slowly Brand walked forward to the end of the plank. He had his great axe in one hand, a small round shield buckled to his forearm. Meditatively he unstrapped it, threw it to the ground, took his axe in both hands. As Shef finally wormed his way gasping to the front, Brand leapt onto the plank, took two paces forward, and lashed suddenly backhand and upward at Ivar's face.

Ivar swayed easily away, moving only the six inches necessary to avoid the blow. Instantly he was beneath the stroke, chopping at a thigh. The blow was beaten down with the metal-shod haft of Brand's axe, counterstroke slashing in the same movement at the wrist. For ten seconds the two men sent a rain of blows at each other, the cuts coming faster than the watchers could follow them: parrying, ducking, swaying their bodies to let thrust or slash go by. Neither man moved his feet.

Then Brand struck. Beating a blow from Ivar upward, he took half a pace forward, leapt high in the air, and came down with his full weight on the very center of the plank. It flexed, bounced upward, hurling both men off their feet. In the air, Brand swung the iron-shod butt of his axe at Ivar's head, connecting with a furious clang on his helmet's cheek-piece. In the same instant Ivar recovered blade and thrust with fierce dexterity through mail and leather, deep into Brand's belly.

Brand landed staggering, Ivar still in perfect balance. For a further instant both stood still, connected by the bar of iron between them. Then, just as Ivar tensed his grip for the savage twist that would rend gut and arteries forever, Brand hurled himself backward off the blade. He stood at the very end of the plank, groping with his left hand at the blood streaming through the torn steel.

With two hands Shef seized him by collar and waist and jerked him from the plank, thrust him staggering backward. The watchers roared disapproval, outrage, encouragement. Gripping his halberd in both hands, Shef stepped forward onto the plank. For the first time since the day he had been blinded, he looked full into Ivar's eyes. Tore his gaze away. If Ivar was a dragon, like the vision he had seen of Fafnir,

then he might yet put on him the dragon-spell of terror and
paralysis. A spell that could not be broken by steel.

Ivar's face split in a grin of triumph and contempt. "You
come late to our meeting, boy," he remarked. "Do you think
you can succeed where champions fail?"

Shef raised his eye again, stared deliberately into Ivar's
face. As he did so he filled his mind with the thought of
Godive—of what this man, this creature, had meant to do with
her. What he had done with so many slaves and captives. If
there was a protection against Ivar's spell, it lay in justice.

"I have succeeded where you failed," he said. "Most men
can do what you cannot. That is why I sent you the capon."

Ivar's grin had turned into a rictus, like the bared teeth of
a skull. He flicked the tip of his sword slightly. "Come on,"
he whispered. "Come on."

Shef has already decided what to do. He had no chance
at all toe to toe with Ivar. He must use other weapons. Drag
him down. Use Ivar's open contempt against him.

Shuffling gingerly forward along the gangplank, Shef
aimed a clumsy two-hand thrust with the spear-point on the
end of his shaft. Ivar batted it aside without moving eyes or
body, waiting for his incompetent enemy to move closer or
lay himself open.

Swinging the halberd way up over his head, Shef prepared for a mighty stroke, a stroke that would split an
armored man from nape to crotch. Ivar grinned more
broadly as he saw it, caught the moan of disbelief from the
bank. This was no holmgang, where the parties were bound
to stand still. Such a mighty stroke could be avoided by an
old grandfather. Who would then step over and stab for the
throat while the wielder was off balance. Only a thrall-bred
fool would try it: and that was what this Sigvarthsson was.

Shef swung down with all his force, aiming not at Ivar
but at the plank at his feet. The great blade, swung in a
drawing cut, slashed clean through the wood. As Ivar, surprised and off balance, tried to leap back the two steps to
his ship, Shef dropped the halberd, threw himself forward,

grappled Ivar round the body. Fell instantly with him down into the cold, muddy current of the Ouse.

As the two men hit the water Shef gasped reflexively. Instantly his mouth and windpipe filled. Choking, he struck out for the surface. Was held and forced below. He had dropped the halberd, but his loose-fitting helmet had filled with water, was dragging his head down. A hand like a strangling snake was crushing his throat, but the other hand was free, was groping toward the belt and the gutting-knife in it. Shef grasped Ivar's right wrist in his left hand with the force of desperation.

For an instant both men broke the surface, and Shef managed to blow his lungs clear. Then Ivar had him again, was forcing him down.

Suddenly the cold inner revulsion that had held Shef half-paralyzed since the fight had started—the dragon-fear—was gone. No scales, no armor, no dreadful eyes to look into. Just a man. Not even a man, shrilled some triumphant fragment of Shef's mind.

Twisting fiercely in the water like an eel, Shef grappled his enemy close. Ducked his head, butted forward with the rim of his helmet. The rim which he had filed again and again to razor-sharpness. A crunch, something giving way, Ivar trying for the first time to wrench back. From the bank above there came a great roar as the craning watchers saw blood spreading in the water. Shef butted again and again, realized suddenly that Ivar had shifted his grip, had caught him in a stranglehold, rolled him under. Now Ivar was on top, face in the air, grimly concentrating on holding his enemy under. And he was too strong, growing stronger with every breath.

Shef's right hand, thrashing wildly, caught Ivar's knee. There is no *drengskapr* in this, thought Shef. Brand would be ashamed of me. But he would have taken Godive and cut her in pieces like a hare.

He drove his right hand firmly under Ivar's tunic, seized him by the crotch. His convulsive, drowning grip closed round the roots of Ivar's manhood, squeezed and twisted with every ounce of the strength years at the forge had given him. Somewhere, he heard dimly, there was a scream of mortal agony resounding. But the Ouse drowned it, the muddy stream poured choking in. As Shef's straining lungs also gave way and let in the cold, rushing, heart-stopping water, he thought only the one thing: Crush. Crush. Never let go . . .

Chapter Nine

Hund was sitting by his bed. Shef stared at him for a moment, then felt the sudden bite of fear deep within him, sat up with a jerk.

"Ivar?"

"Easy, easy," said Hund, pushing him back on the bed. "Ivar's dead. Dead and burned to ashes."

Shef's tongue felt too big for him to control. With an effort he managed to gasp, "How?"

"A difficult question," replied Hund judiciously. "It could be that he drowned. Or he might have bled to death. You cut his face and neck to pieces with the edge of your helmet. But personally, I think he died of pain. You would not loose him, you know. In the end we had to cut him free. If he had not been dead before, he would have died then.

"Funny," Hund added reflectively. "He was quite normal, you know, in body. Whatever was the matter with him and women—and Ingulf had heard many tales of it—it was in his head, nowhere else."

Slowly Shef's muddled brain disentangled the questions he needed to ask.

"Who got me out?"

"Ah. That was Cwicca and his mates. The Vikings just stood and watched, both sides. Apparently men trying to drown each other is a sport in their homeland, and no one wanted to interfere till they could see who had won. It would have been very bad manners. Fortunately Cwicca has no manners."

Shef thought back to the moments before he had faced Ivar on the swaying plank. Remembered the sudden shocking sight of Brand jerking himself backward off Ivar's sword.

"And Brand?"

Hund's face changed to an expression of professional concern. "He may live. He is a man of great strength. But the sword went right into his guts. It was impossible for them not to be pierced. I gave him the garlic porridge to eat myself, and then bent down and sniffed the wound. It stank, right enough. Most times that means death."

"This time?"

"Ingulf did what he has done before. Cut him open, stitched the gut, put it back. But even with the poppy and henbane drink we gave to Alfgar, it was hard, very hard. He did not lose consciousness. His belly muscles are thick as cables. If the poison starts to work inside him . . ."

Shef levered his legs over the side of the bed, tried to stand up, felt an instant rush of faintness. With the relics of his strength he fended off Hund's attempts to push him back.

"I have to see Brand. Especially if he is going to die. He has to tell me—tell me things. Things about the Franks."

Many miles to the south, a weary and dispirited figure crouched over the fire in the hearth of a wretched hut. Few would have recognized it as the one-time atheling of Wessex, the king that was to be. His golden circlet had gone—knocked from his helmet by the stab of a lance. His mail and shield decorated with animal-patterns had gone, too, stripped off and dropped in the intervals of desperate flight. Even his weapons were missing. He had cut his sword-scabbard free to run when, finally, after a long day's slaughter there had been no final alternative but flight or death—or surrender to the Franks. He had carried his sword drawn for miles, fighting again and again with his last few bodyguards to get free of the pursuing Frankish light cavalry. Then, as his horse died under him he had dropped it, rolled over. When the running fight had moved past his body and he had staggered to his feet again, there was nothing there. He had run off into the welcome dusk and the deep, thick forest of the Kentish Weald as empty-handed as a beggar. He had been lucky to see a glimmer of light before the night came. To beg shelter in the poor, starve-acre cottage where he now crouched, watching the oatcakes on the griddle while his reluctant hosts secured their goats outside. Discussed, perhaps, who they should betray him to.

Alfred did not think they would betray him. Even the poorest folk of Kent and Sussex knew now that it was deadly dangerous to so much as approach the Cross-wearers from across the sea. They spoke even less English than Vikings, cared no more for the harm they did than pagans. It was not personal fear that bowed his shoulders, brought the tears prickling unmanfully to his eyes.

It was fear for something strange at work in the world. Twice now he had met the young man Shef with the one eye. The first time he had had him in the hollow of his hand: he, Alfred, atheling and commander of an undefeated army; the other, Shef, at the very last end of his resources, about to be overwhelmed by the army of the Mark. That time the atheling had rescued the carl, raised him to alderman, or *jarl* a the Way-folk said. The second time Shef the jarl had been the one with the undefeated army; he, Alfred, had been the fugitive and the suppliant. Yet even then not a suppliant without hope or without resources.

And now how did things stand? The one-eye had sent him south, said each should fight their own battle. Alfred had fought his, fought it with all the men he could gather to his banner from the eastern shires of his kingdom, men who had come willingly to fight an invader. And they had been scattered like leaves in a gale, unable to hold the terrible charge of the mailed horsemen. Alfred was sure in his heart that matters had not gone so in the battle his ally and rival had meant to fight. Shef would have won.

Christianity had not entirely driven from Alfred and his countrymen the belief in something older and deeper than any gods—pagan or Christian ones: luck. The luck of a person. The luck of a family. Something that did not change with the years, something you either had or did not have. The great prestige of Alfred's royal house, the descendants of Cerdic, depended silently on a deep belief in the family's luck, which had kept them in power for four hundred years.

To the fugitive sitting by the hearth it seemed that his luck and that of his family had run out. No. It had been cancelled by the luck of a stronger figure—the one-eyed man who had started as a slave, a thrall in the heathen language, who had fought his way up past the execution-ground to be a carl in the Great Army of the North, and then up yet again to be a jarl. What greater proof of luck could there be? With so much of it in one man, how could there be any left for his allies? His competitors? Alfred felt the heart-chilling despair of someone who has given away the advantage in a contest, lightheartedly and without thought of consequences, only to see the advantage grow and grow, the initiative pass forever into the other's hands. In that bleak moment he felt it was over for him, for his family, for his kingdom. For England. He sniffed back a tear.

Smelled as he did so the reek of charring bread. Guiltily his hand darted to the griddle, to flip the oatcakes over to cook on the other side. Too late. Burned through. Burned inedible. Simultaneously Alfred's belly cramped inside him at the realization that after sixteen hours of desperate exertion there was nothing, nothing at all left to eat. And the door of the hovel opened to let in the churl and his wife, to fill the air with rage and blame. Nothing left to eat for them either. Their last food wasted. Burned by a good-for-nothing. A vagrant, too cowardly to die in battle, too lazy to do the simplest task. Too proud to pay anything for the meal and shelter they had offered him.

As they loaded curses on him, the worst of Alfred's punishment was the feeling that what they said was true. He could not imagine, ever, the slightest recovery. This was the bottom from which no one could climb. Any future there was would not be for him and his like, the Christians of En-

gland. It would be decided between the Franks and the
Norse, the Cross-wearers and the Way-folk. Alfred walked
into the shelterless night, heart breaking with despair.

This time it was Shef who sat by the bed. Brand turned his
head very slightly to look at him, face gray under the beard.
Shef could see that even the tiny movements needed for that
caused agony, as the poison spread inside Brand's belly cavity
to fight against the strength still locked in his massive frame.

"I need to know about the Franks," said Shef. "We have
beaten everyone else. You were sure they would beat Alfred."

Brand's head nodded, very faintly.

"So what is dangerous about them? How can I fight
them? I have to ask you, for no one else in the army has
met them in the field and lived. Yet many say they have had
years of good plunder from the Frankish kingdom. How can
they let themselves be robbed and still be enemies even you
would rather not face?"

Shef could see Brand trying to work out not the answer,
but how to say the answer in fewest words. Finally he
spoke, in a gravelly whisper.

"They fight among themselves. That is what has always
let us in. They are no seamen. And they breed few warriors.
With us—a spear, a shield, an axe—you are a warrior. With
them, it takes a whole village to arm one man. Mail-shirt,
sword and lance and helmet. But most of all, the horse. Big
horses. Stallions a man can hardly control. Have to learn to
ride them with a shield on one arm and a lance in the other.
Start when you're a baby. Only way.

"One Frankish lancer, no problem. Get behind him, ham-
string horse. Fifty of 'em, problem. A thousand . . ."

"Ten thousand?" asked Shef.

"Never believed it. Aren't that many. Lot of light horsemen. Can be dangerous because they're quick, turn up when
you don't think they're near."

Brand summoned his failing energies. "They'll ride over

you if you let 'em. Or cut you up on the march. Stick to rivers is what we do. Or keep behind a stockade."

"To beat them in open field?"

Brand shook his head faintly. Shef could not tell whether he meant "Impossible," or "I don't know." After a moment Ingulf's hand fell on his shoulder, urged him out.

As he came blinking from the tent into daylight, Shef found himself once more besieged with problems. Guards to be detailed for the substantial plunder of Ivar's army, on its way to the treasury in Norwich. Prisoners' fate to be decided: some of them Ivar's torturers, some of them mere rank and file. Messages to be received and dispatched. At the back of Shef's mind there hung always the query: Godive. Why had she gone off with Thorvin? And what did Thorvin himself think was so important that it could not wait?

But now, immediately in front of him, Father Boniface, his own priest-turned-scribe, beside him another little man in clerical black with an expression of bitter, malignant spite on his face. Slowly Shef realized that he had seen him before, if only from a distance. In York.

"This is Deacon Erkenbert," said Boniface. "We took him from Ivar's own ship. He is the master of the machines. The slaves who wound the machines—slaves first to York Minster and then to Ivar—they say that he built the machines for Ivar. They say the whole Church in York now works night and day for the Ragnarssons." He looked down at Erkenbert with heartfelt contempt.

The master of the machines, thought Shef. There was a day when I would have given everything for a chance to talk with this man. Now, I wonder what he can tell me. I can guess how his machine works, and in any case I can go to see for myself. I know how slowly they shoot, how hard they hit. One thing I do not know: how much else is there in his head and in his books? But I do not think he will tell me that.

Yet I think I can use him. Dimly, Brand's words were working inside Shef's brain. Collecting into a plan.

"Keep close watch on him, Boniface," said Shef. "See the York slaves are well treated, and tell them they are free

from this moment. Then send Guthmund to me. After him,
Lulla and Osmod. And Cwicca, Udd and Oswi, too."

"We don't want to do that," said Guthmund flatly.

"But you could do it?" asked Shef.

Guthmund hesitated, not wanting to tell a lie, reluctant to
concede a point.

"Could do it. Still don't think it's a good idea. Take all the
Vikings out of the army, load them into Ivar's boats, press
Ivar's men into service as galley-slaves, and head round the
coast to some rendezvous near this Hastings place . . .

"Look, lord." Guthmund spoke pleadingly, as near to
wheedling as his character would go. "I know, me and the
boys, we haven't always been fair to the English you've
hauled in. Called them midgets. Called them *skraelingiar.*
Said they're no use and never will be. Well, they've proved
us wrong.

"But there was a reason for what we said, and it goes
double if you're going to fight these Franks and their
horses. Your English can shoot machines. One of them with
a halberd hits as good as one of our boys with a sword. But
there's still a lot of things they can't do, no matter how hard
they try. They aren't strong enough.

"Now these Franks. Why are they dangerous? Everyone
knows it's because of the horses. How much does a horse
weigh? A thousand pounds? That's what I'm telling you, lord.
To even get a few shots in at these Franks, you'll have to hold
them off for a while. Maybe our boys could do it, with the
halberds and all. Maybe. They've never done it before. But it's
dead sure they can't if you've sent them all off. What happens
if you get caught with just a line of your little fellows between
you and the Franks? They can't do it, lord. They haven't the
strength." Nor the training, Guthmund thought silently. Not to
watch armed men walk right up to you and start hacking
away. Or ride up to you. They've always had us to help them.

"You are forgetting King Alfred and his men," said Shef.
"He will have gathered his army by now. You know the En-

glish thanes are as strong and brave as your men—they just have no discipline. But I can supply that."

Guthmund nodded, grudgingly.

"So each group must do what it does best. Your men, sail. With the ship and the machines. My freedmen, wind their machines and shoot. Alfred and his Englishmen, stand still to do what they're told. Trust me, Guthmund. You did not believe me last time. Or the time before. Or when we raided the minster at Beverley."

Guthmund nodded again, slightly more willingly this time. As he turned to go he added one more remark.

"Lord jarl, you aren't a sailor. But don't forget another thing in all this. It's harvest now. When the night grows as long as the day, every sailor knows, the weather changes. Don't forget the weather."

The news of Alfred's total defeat reached Shef and his truncated army two days' march south. Shef listened to the exhausted, white-faced thane who brought the news in the center of an interested circle—he had abandoned the custom of council meetings in private as soon as the still-grumbling Guthmund and his Norse fellows had boarded their captured boats. The freedmen watched his face as he listened, marking that it changed expression only twice. The first time, when the thane cursed the Frankish archers—who had shot such a rain of arrows that twice Alfred's advancing army had been forced to stand and raise its shields, only to be caught motionless both times by the Frankish cavalry charge. The second time when the thane admitted that no one had seen or heard of Alfred the king since the day of the disaster.

In the silence that followed the story, Cwicca, presuming on his status as Shef's companion and rescuer, had asked what all thought. "What do we do now, lord? Turn back, or go on?"

Shef answered immediately. "Go on."

Opinion round the campfires that night was divided about the sense of that. Ever since the Viking Waymen had left with Guthmund, the army had seemed a different creature.

The freed English slaves had always secretly feared their allies—so like their former masters in strength and violence, superior to any English master in warlike reputation. With the Vikings gone, the army marched as if on holiday: pipes playing, laughter in the ranks, calling out to the harvesters in the fields, who no longer fled at the sight of the first scouts and advance-guard.

Yet the fear the army had felt had also been a guarantee. Proud as they were of their machines, their halberds and their crossbows, the ex-slaves did not have the self-belief that comes from a lifetime of winning battles.

"All right saying 'Go on,' " said one anonymous voice that night. "What happens when we get there? No Alfred. No Norse-folk. No Wessexers to help out like we were promised. Just us. Eh? What then?"

"We'll shoot 'em down," said Oswi confidently. "Like we did with Ivar and them Ragnarssons. 'Cos we got the machines and they haven't. And the crossbows and all."

A mutter of agreement greeted his statement. Yet every morning the camp marshals came to Shef with a new and growing figure: the number of men who had slipped away in the night, taking with them freedom and the silver pennies already paid to each man from the spoils of Ivar, but forfeiting the promise of land and stock in the future. Already, Shef knew, he had not enough men in the ranks both to man his fifty machines—pull-throwers and twist-shooters—and to use the two hundred pulley-wound crossbows that Udd's forges had produced.

"What will you do?" asked Farman, Frey's priest, the fourth morning of the march. He, Ingulf and Geirulf the priest of Tyr were the only Norsemen who had insisted on staying with Shef and the freedmen.

Shef shrugged.

"That is no answer."

"I will tell you the answer when you tell me where Thorvin and Godive have gone. And why. And when they will come back."

This time it was Farman's turn to give no answer.

* * *

Daniel and Alfgar had spent many angry days of frustration, first finding the base of the Frankish Cross-wearers, and then getting through its guards and outposts to see its leader. Their appearance had been against them: two men in soiled and sodden cloaks after nights in the open, riding bareback on the sorry nags that Alfgar had stolen. The first sentry they had approached had been amazed to see any Englishmen come near the camp of their own will: the local churls had fled long since, taking their wives and daughters with them if they were lucky. Yet he had not troubled to call an interpreter for Alfgar's English or Daniel's Latin. After several minutes of shouting up at him above the gate of the camp stockade, he had meditatively fitted arrow to bow and shot it into the ground at Daniel's feet. Alfgar had pulled Daniel away at once.

After that they had tried several times to approach the daily cavalcade of warriors streaming out from the Hastings base, to rob and forage while King Charles waited unhurriedly for the further challenge he was sure must come. The first time had cost them their horses, the second, Daniel's episcopal ring, which he had waved too eagerly. Eventually, and in despair, Alfgar had taken a hand. As Daniel shouted angrily at a Frankish priest they had discovered picking over the ruins of a ransacked church, he pushed him aside.

"*Machina*," he said clearly, in the fragment of Latin he possessed. "*Ballista. Catapulta. Nos videre*"—he pointed to his eyes. "*Nos dicere. Rex.*" He waved at the camp with its flying banners, two miles off, made speaking gestures.

The priest looked at him, nodded, turned back to the barely coherent bishop and began to talk to him in strangely accented Latin, cutting Daniel's furious complaints short, demanding information. After a while he had called to his guard of mounted archers and set off back toward the camp, taking the two Englishmen with him. After that they had been passed from hand to hand, with cleric after cleric coming in to extract more and more of Daniel's story.

But now at last the clerics had gone. It was Alfgar, his cloak brushed and a substantial meal inside him, who stood in front of Daniel, facing a trestle-table, behind it a group of men with the look of warriors: one of them wearing the gold circle of royalty over a bald head. At his side stood an Englishman, listening carefully to what the king said. Eventually he turned to Alfgar, speaking the first English they had heard since they arrived in the camp.

"The priests have told the king," he said, "that you have more sense than the bishop behind you. But the bishop says that you two alone know the truth of what has happened up there in the North. And that for some reason"—the Englishman smiled—"you are anxious to help the king and the Christian religion with information. Now the king takes no interest in your bishop's complaints and proposals. He wants to know, first about the army of Mercia, second about the army of the heathen Ragnarssons, and thirdly about this army of heretics which his own bishops are especially anxious for him to meet and fight. Tell him all that, behave yourself sensibly, and it will do you good. The king will have to have some Englishmen he can trust once his kingdom is established."

Putting on his sincerest expression of loyalty, and looking the Frankish king firmly in the eye, Alfgar began his account of the death of Burgred and the defeat by the Ouse. As he spoke on, his English translated phrase by phrase into French, he began to act out the workings of the machines with which Ivar had demoralized Burgred's army. He laid stress on the machines which the Way-folk also had, and which he had seen again and again in the previous winter's battles. His courage rising, he drew the hammer-sign in wine on the king's table, told of the freeing of Church-slaves.

Eventually the king stirred, threw a question over his shoulder. A cleric appeared from the shadows, took stylus and wax, began to draw on his tablets the picture of an onager. Then a torsion-catapult. Then a counterweight-machine.

"He says, are these what you have seen?" asked the translator.

Alfgar nodded.

"He says, interesting. His learned men know how to make them also, taking them from a book by one Vegetius.

He says he did not know the English were learned enough to make such things. But among the Franks these are used only for sieges. To use them against an army of horsemen would be foolish. Horsemen move too fast for them to be effective. But the king thanks you for your goodwill, and wishes you to ride with him when he takes the field. He believes your knowledge of his enemies will be useful. Your companion will be sent to Canterbury, to await the inquiry of the legate of the Pope." The English interpreter smiled again. "I think your chances will be better than his."

Alfgar straightened, bowed, and walked backward from the table as he would never have done for Burgred, firmly resolving to find a teacher of French before nightfall.

King Charles the Bald watched him go, turned again to his wine. "The first of the rats," he remarked to his constable Godefroi.

"Rats with siege-engines they use in the field. Do you not fear what he says?"

The king laughed. "Crossing the Narrow Sea is like going back to the time of our forefathers, when the kings rode to battle in ox-chariots. In all this country there is nothing to fight but the Norse brigands, harmless away from their ships, and the brave, stupid swordsmen we beat the other day. Long mustaches and slow feet. No horses, no lances, no stirrups, no generals.

"We must take our precautions now we know their way of fighting." He scratched his beard thoughtfully. "But it will take more than a few machines to beat the strongest army in Christendom."

Chapter Ten

This time Shef was anxious for the vision he knew would come. His mind buzzed with doubts, with possibilities.

Yet he had no certainty. Something must come, he knew, from outside to help him. It came usually when he was exhausted, or sleeping off a heavy meal. That day he had walked deliberately beside his pony, ignoring the chaff from the ranks. In the evening, had stuffed himself slowly with the porridge they had made from the last of the winter store, before the new grain came from the harvesters. He stretched out to sleep, fearful that his mysterious adviser would fail him.

"Yes," said the voice in the dream. Shef felt an instant surge of relief as he recognized it. The amused voice which had told him to seek the ground, which had sent him the dream of the wooden horse. The voice of the nameless god with the sly face who had shown him the chessqueen. This was the god who sent him answers. If he could recognize them.

"Yes," said the voice, "you will see what you need to know. But not what you think you need to know. Your questions are always 'What?' and 'How?' But I shall show you 'Why?' And 'Who?' "

Instantly he found himself on a cliff, so high up he could see the whole world stretched out before him, the dust-plumes rising, the armies marching, just as he had seen them the day they killed King Edmund. Again he felt that if he narrowed his eye exactly right, he would be able to pick out anything he needed to know: the words on the lips of the Frankish commander, the place where Alfred lurked—live or dead. Shef gazed round anxiously, trying to orient himself so he could see what he needed to.

Something turned his head away from the panorama below, made him stare into the far, far distance, remote from the real world in space and time.

What he saw was a man walking along a mountain road, a man with a dark, lively, humorous face, one not entirely to be trusted, the face of the unknown god of his dreams. Now that man, Shef thought, drifting into the vision, that man has more than one skin.

The man, if man he was, came to a hut, a hovel in fact, a grubby shelter of poles and bark reinforced with turf and inept handfuls of clay on the chinks. *That was the way men lived in the old time,* Shef thought. *They know better now. But who showed them better?*

By the hut a man and a woman stopped their tasks and stared at the newcomer: a stranger couple, both bent over from continuous work, short and squat in physique, brown haired and sallow, bow-legged, crooked-fingered. "Their names are Ai and Edda," the god's voice said.

They were welcoming the newcomer, showing him in. They offered him food, burnt porridge, full of husks, full too of stone particles from being hand-ground in a pestle and mortar, moistened only with goat's milk. The newcomer seemed undaunted by this welcome, talked cheerfully; when the time came, lay down on the heap of ill-cured skins between his host and his hostess.

In the middle of the night he turned to Edda, still dressed in her long black rags. Ai lay in a deep sleep, unmoving, stung perhaps by a sleep-thorn. The clever-looking man pulled up the rags, mounted upon her, thrust away without preliminaries.

The stranger in the vision rose next morning and went his way, leaving Edda behind him to swell, to moan, to bring forth children as squat and ugly as herself—but more active, more industrious. They carted dung, they carried brush-wood, they tended swine, they broke clods with wooden spades. *From them come,* the Shef-mind said, *the race of thralls. Once I too might have been a thrall. No longer.*

The traveler went on his way, walking briskly, along through the mountains. The next night he came to a log cabin, well-built, its ends fitted into each other in deep, axe-cut grooves, a window on one side with solid, well-fitting shutters, a privy outside over a deep ravine. Again a couple paused from their work as the traveler came up to them: a stout and powerful pair, ruddy-faced, thick-necked—the man bald, with trimmed beard, the woman round-faced and long-armed, built for carrying burdens. She wore a long brown gown, but a woolen mantle lay close by to be put on in the cool evening. Bronze clasps lay ready to fix it on. He wore *loose trousers like a warrior of the Viking fleets, but his leather shirt was cut into thongs at waist and sleeve, for show. This is how most folk live now, the Shef-mind thought. "Their names are Afi and Amma," said the voice.*

Again they invited the newcomer in, offered him food, plates of bread with fried chops of pork, ready-salted, the grease from the frying running into the bread—food for heavy laborers and strong men. Then they retired for the night, all three lying down together on a straw mattress with woolen blankets to pull over them. In the night Afi snored, sleeping in his shirt. The traveler turned to Amma, wearing only a loose gown, whispered in her ear, took her soon with the same speed and zest as before.

Again the newcomer went on his way, left Amma to swell, to bring forth children with silent stoicism, as strong and well-built as herself, but maybe more intelligent, ready to try a new thing sooner. Her children tamed oxen, timbered barns, hammered out ploughs, made fishing nets, adventured on the sea. From them, Shef knew, came the race of carls. Once upon a time I was a carl too. But that time has gone as well.

On the newcomer went, his road tending now to the great plains. He came to a house set back from the road, a garth round it of hammered posts. The house itself had several rooms, one to sleep in, one to eat in, one for the animals, all with windows or broad doorways. A man and a woman sat outside it on a well-crafted bench, called to the wayfarer, offered him water from their deep well. They were a handsome couple, with long faces, broad foreheads, soft skin unmarked by toil. When the man stood to greet the stranger he overtopped him by half a head. His shoulders were broad and his back straight, his fingers strong from twisting bowstrings. "These two are Fathir and Mothir," said the voice of the god.

They led their visitor in, onto a floor strewn with sweet-smelling rushes, sat him at a table, brought him water in a bowl to wash his hands in, set before him roast fowl, griddle-cakes in a basin, butter and blood sausage. After

*they had eaten, the woman spun on her wheel, the man sat
on a settle and talked with his visitor.*

*When night came the host and hostess seemed under
some compulsion as they guided their guest to the broad
feather bed with its down bolsters, placed him between
them, lay while Fathir fell asleep. Again the visitor turned
to his hostess, fondled her with fingers, served her like a
bull or a stallion, as he had the two before.*

*The visitor went, the woman swelled, from her belly came
the race of jarls, the earls, the fighting men. They swam
fjords, tamed horses, beat out metal, reddened swords, and
fed the ravens on the plains of slaughter. That is how men
wish to live now, thought the Shef-mind. Unless it is how
someone wishes them to live . . .*

*But this cannot be the end: Ai to Afi to Fathir, Edda to
Amma to Mothir. What of Son and Daughter, what of Great-
great-grandchild? And Thrall to Carl to Jarl. I am the jarl
now. But what comes after Jarl? What are his sons called,
and how far down the road will the wanderer go? The son
of Jarl is King, the son of King is . . .*

Shef found himself suddenly awake, perfectly conscious
of what he had just seen, perfectly aware that in some way
it related to himself. What he had seen, he realized, was a
breeding program, designed to make better people as men
bred better horses or hunting-dogs. But better in what way?
Cleverer? Better at finding new knowledge? That was what
the priests of the Way would say. Or quicker to change?
Readier to use the knowledge they knew already?

One thing Shef was sure of. If the breeding was done by
the tricky, amused face he had seen on the wanderer, the
face that was also that of his god-protector, then even the
better people would find there was a price to be paid. Yet
the wanderer meant him to succeed. Knew there was a solution, if he could find it.

In the dark hour before dawn Shef pulled on his dew-
soaked leather shoes, rose from the rustling straw pallet,
wrapped his blanket-cloak round him and stepped out into

the chill air of the late English summer. He walked through
the still-sleeping camp like a ghost, with no weapon except
the whetstone-scepter, cradled in the crook of his left arm.
His freedmen did not ditch and stockade their camps like
the ever-active Vikings, but at the edge sentries stood. Shef
walked up to the shoulder of one of them, one of Lulla's
halberdiers, leaning on his weapon. His eyes were open but
he paid no heed as Shef walked quietly past him and out
into the dark wood.

Birds began to chirp as the sky paled in the east. Shef
picked his way carefully through the tangles of hawthorn
and nettle, found himself on a narrow path. It reminded him
of the path he had followed with Godive the year before, as
they had fled from Ivar. Sure enough, it led to a clearing
and a shelter.

The day was up as he reached the clearing, and he could
see plainly. The shelter was a mere hut. As he watched it,
the ill-hung door opened and a woman came out. An old
woman? Her face was worn with care, and had the pale,
pinched look of the chronically underfed. But she was not
so old, Shef realized, standing silent and motionless under
the trees. She looked round, not seeing him, and then sank
down in the feeble sunlight by the side of her hut. Put her
face in her hands and began to weep silently.

"What's the matter, Mother?"

She started convulsively as she heard Shef's question,
looked up with terror in her eyes. As she realized there was
only one man, unarmed, she calmed.

"The matter? An old story, most of it. My man was taken
off to join the king's army . . ."

"Which king?" asked Shef.

She shrugged. "I do not know. It was months ago. He has
never come back. All summer we were hungry. We are not
slaves, but we have no land. With Edi not here to work for
the rich, we had nothing. When the harvest started they let
me glean grain from what the reapers missed—little enough.
But it would have been enough, only it was too late. My
child died, my daughter, two weeks ago.

"And now this is the new story. For when I took her to the church to be buried, there was no priest there. He had fled, driven out, they say, by the pagans. The 'Way-folk'? I do not know the right name. The men in the village were happy, they said now they would pay no more tithes, no more for Peter's pence. But what good was that to me? I was too poor to tithe, and the priest would give me a dole, sometimes, from what he had. And who was there to bury my child? How could she rest without the words said over her? Without the Christ-child himself to take her part in heaven?"

The woman began to weep again, rocking backwards and forwards. How would Thorvin answer this? Shef wondered. Maybe he would say that the Christians had not always been bad, till the Church went rotten. But at least the Church gave comfort, to some. The Way must do that as well, not think only of those who tread the path of the heroes to Valhalla with Othin, or to Thruthvangar with Thor. He fumbled at his belt for money, realized that he had none.

"You see now what you have done?" said a voice behind him.

Shef turned slowly, found himself confronting Alfred. The young king had dark rings under his eyes, his clothes were stained and muddy. He had neither sword nor cloak, but still wore mail, with a dagger at his belt.

"*I* have done? I think she is one of your subjects, this side of the Thames. The Way may have taken her priest away, but you took her man away."

"What we have done, then."

The two men stood looking down at the woman. This is what I have been sent to stop, thought Shef. But I cannot do it by following the Way alone. Or not the Way as Thorvin or Farman see it.

"I will make you an offer, king," he said. "You have a purse at your belt and I have none. Give it to this poor woman here, so that at least she may live to see if her man returns. And I will give you your jarldom back. Or rather we will share till we have defeated your enemies, the Cross-wearers, as I have already defeated mine."

"Share the jarldom?"

"Share all we have. Money. Men. Rule. Risk. Let our fates run together."

"We will share our luck, then?" said Alfred.

"Yes."

"There must be two conditions on that," said Alfred. "We cannot march under your Hammer alone, for I am a Christian. Nor will I march only under the Cross, for that has been defiled by the robbers of Frankland and Pope Nicholas. Let us remember this woman and her grief, and march under the sign of both. And if we conquer we will let our peoples find comfort and consolation wherever they can. In this world there can never be enough for everyone."

"What is the other condition?"

"That." Alfred pointed to the whetstone-scepter. "You must get rid of it. When you hold it, you lie. You send your friends to their deaths."

Shef looked at it, looked again at the cruel, bearded faces that ornamented each end: faces like that of the cold-voiced god in his dreams. He remembered the mound where he had got it, the slave-girls with their broken spines. Thought of Sigvarth sent to die by torture, of Sibba and Wilfi sent to the burning. Of Alfred himself, whom he had knowingly allowed to march to defeat. Of Godive, rescued only to be used as bait.

Turning, he hurled the scepter end over end into the deep undergrowth, there to lie once more among the mold.

"As you say," he said. "We will march under both signs now, win or lose." He held out his hand. Alfred drew his dagger, cut free his purse, threw it with a thump onto the wet ground by the woman's feet. Only then did he shake hands.

As they left the woman struggled with feeble fingers to pry at the lashings of the purse.

They heard the commotion before they had gone a hundred yards down the path: clash of weapons, shrieking, horses neighing. Both men began to run toward the Wayman camp, but the thorns and thickets held them. By the time they arrived, gasping, at the edge of the wood, it was over.

"What happened?" said Shef to the men who turned disbelievingly toward them.

Farman the priest appeared from behind a slashed tent. "Frankish light cavalry. Not many of them, maybe a hundred. They knew we were here, came all at once out of the wood. Where were you?"

But Shef was looking past him, at Thorvin pushing through the crowd of excited men, holding Godive firmly by one hand.

"We came just after dawn," said Thorvin. "Got here just before the Franks attacked."

Shef ignored him, looked only at Godive. She raised her chin, stared back at him. He patted her shoulder gently. "I am sorry if I have forgotten you. There are things—if . . . soon . . . I will try to make amends for what I did.

"But not now. Now I am still the jarl. First we must set guards on the camp, so we are not surprised again. Then we must march. But before that—Lulla, Farman, all priests and leaders to me as soon as the guards are set.

"And Osmod, one thing before that. Send twenty women to me now."

"Women, lord?"

"Women. There are plenty with us. Wives, friends, drabs, I don't care. As long as they can push a needle."

Two hours later, Thorvin, Farman and Geirulf—the only priests of the Way present among a half dozen English unit commanders—stared unhappily at the new device hastily stitched onto the army's main battle-banner. Instead of the white Hammer standing upright on a red field, there were now a Hammer and Cross, set diagonally, one across the other.

"It is dealing with the enemy," said Farman. "More than they would ever do for us."

"It is a condition made by the king for his support," said Shef.

Eyebrows raised as the priests looked at the shabby, solitary figure of the king.

"Not just my support," said Alfred. "The support of my kingdom. I may have lost one army. But there are still men who will fight against the invaders. It will be easier if they do not have to change religion at the same time."

"We need men, for sure," said Osmod the camp marshal and leader of the catapulteers. "What with this morning and the desertions we've had—seven, eight men to a team left, where we need a dozen. And Udd has more crossbows in store than men to use them. But we need 'em right now. And where are we to find them? In a hurry, like?"

Shef and Alfred stared uncertainly at each other, digesting the problem, groping for an solution.

An unexpected voice cut the silence from the back of the tent. Godive's.

"I can tell you the answer to that," she said. "But if I tell you, you must grant me two things. One, a seat on this council. I do not care to be disposed of in future like a lame horse or a sick hound. Two, I do not want to hear the jarl say again, 'Not now. Not now, because I am the jarl.' "

Eyes turned; first, in amazement, to her, then in doubt and alarm to Shef. Shef, hand fumbling automatically for reassurance to his whetstone, found himself looking into Godive's brilliant eyes as if for the first time. He remembered: the whetstone was no longer there, nor what it stood for. He looked down.

"I grant both conditions," he said hoarsely. "Now tell us your answer, councillor."

"The men you need are already in the camp," said Godive. "But they aren't men, they're women. Hundreds of them. You find more in every village. They may be only drabs to you, as the jarl said before. Needle-pushers. But they are as good as men for some things. Put six with every catapult-team. The men released can go to Udd, to carry a crossbow, or the strongest of them to Lulla, to use a halberd. But I would also advise this to Udd: pick as many of the youngest women as you can, those who are not afraid, and put them with your crossbows as well."

"We can't do that," said Cwicca incredulously.

"Why not?"

"Well—they aren't strong enough."

Shef laughed. "That's what the Vikings said about you, Cwicca, remember? How much strength does it take to pull a rope? Turn a lever? Wind a pulley? The machine gives the strength."

"They'll get frightened and run away," Cwicca protested.

Icily, Godive overrode him. "Look at me, Cwicca. You saw me climb into that dung-cart. Was I frightened then? And if I was, I still did it.

"Shef. Let me talk to the women. I will find the ones you can trust, and if need be I will lead them. Don't forget, everyone"—she looked round the circle challengingly—"it may be that women have more to lose than any of you. And so more to gain."

In the silence Thorvin said, still skeptically, "This is all very well. But how many men had King Alfred here when he marched against the Franks? Five thousand? Trained warriors. Even if we use every woman in the camp, how can a third of that number hope to win? People, men or women, who have never shot so much as a bird-bolt before? You cannot make a warrior in a day."

"You can teach someone to shoot a crossbow in a day," said Udd unexpectedly. "Just wind 'em and point 'em."

"Just the same," said Geirulf, Tyr's priest. "We learned this morning the Franks will not stand still to be shot down. So what are we to do?"

"Listen," said Shef, drawing a deep breath, "and I will tell you."

Chapter Eleven

Like a great steel reptile, the Frankish army moved out of its base at Hastings, a little after dawn. First, the light cavalry in their hundreds, armed only with steel caps, leather jackets and sabers: their duty, to search out the enemy, hold the flanks, exploit breakthrough. Then, file after file of archers, mounted like every man in the army, but expecting to dismount for battle, when they would close to within fifty yards of an enemy line and pour in the arrows from their breastbows: their duty, to fix the enemy, make them raise shields to cover faces, crouch down to cover unarmored legs.

In the center, the heavy cavalry, the weapon which had brought the Franks victory after victory on the plains of central Europe. Each man with mail-shirt and thigh-guards, back and bowels protected by the high-reaching saddle, each man with helmet and longsword, and above all, shield, lance and stirrups. The kite-shaped shield to cover the body, the lance with which to strike overhand or underhand, the stirrups to brace the feet for the stroke. Few men, and no Englishmen, could at once wield a lance in one hand, strap the other arm into an unmoving shield, and control a war-stallion with thigh-pressure and the fingertips of one hand alone. Those men who could, they believed, could ride down any infantry in the world, once they came out from their ships or their walls.

At the head of his main battle, nine hundred riders strong, King Charles the Bald turned in his saddle and looked back at the banners flying immediately behind him, at his guarded base beyond, at the ships clustered off the beach. His scouts had brought him good news. The last army south of the Humber, marching to meet him, careless and unprepared, but ready to give battle. That was what he wanted: one decisive shock, the leaders dead on the field, then surrender and the transfer of all the reins of government to his own hand. It should have come sooner, after the defeat of the gallant but foolish Alfred. Then the summer would not have been so far on.

At least the time was ripe. Maybe overripe. But today, or at worst, tomorrow, the decision would be made. Charles realized that his view was blurred by rain drifting in from the Channel. He turned, rode on, waved the English renegade up to ride by him with the translator.

"You live in this God-forsaken country," he said. "How long is this rain going to last?"

Alfgar glanced at the drooping banners, noted the slow wind from the southwest, thought to himself that it looked as if it was settled in for a week-long soak. Not what the king wants to hear, he realized.

"I think it will soon pass over," he said. The king grunted, urged on his horse. Slowly, as the army picked its way over the unharvested fields, the damp earth churned into mud—the advance-guards leaving a broad black swathe across the turf.

Five miles northwest, on a ridge a little south of Caldbeck Hill, Shef watched the Franks moving toward him. His banner flew from an ox-cart, the Hammer and Cross athwart each other. He knew the scouts would already have picked it up, told King Charles where he was. He had moved forward at dusk the day before, after the marauding Frankish light horsemen had pulled back to their base. His men—and women—had taken up their positions at night. Almost none of them were with him. This was a battle he could control no more. The real question, he knew, was whether his army could act according to plan—and keep on acting after they had lost touch with him and with each other.

One thing Shef was sure of: there were more people in his army than he knew about. All day the day before, he had overtaken little groups of men heading toward the battle-ground, churls with spears, woodsmen with their axes, even grimy charcoal-burners out of the Weald, called out by Alfred's summons of the *fierd*, the ancestral levy of Wessex and its dominions. All were told the same thing. Do not stand up to them. Do not form a line. Wait round the edges. Press in if you see your chance. It was a simple order, and they had taken it gladly, the more gladly from their king in person.

But the rain, thought Shef. Would it help or hinder? He would know soon enough.

The first shot came from the shelter of a half-burned hamlet. Fifty Frankish light horsemen, well forward and to the flank of the army's main advance, crossed the sights of "Dead Level." Oswi squeezed the trigger, felt the thump of release, saw the great dart flash half a mile. Driving clear into the solid target of horsemen. Instantly the team—seven men and four women—were rewinding, dropping the next bolt into its slot. Thirty slow heartbeats before it could shoot again.

The leader of the hobbelars saw his man on the ground, shaft driven below his ribs, and bit his lip with surprise. Siege-engines, in the open. Yet the answer was clear. Spread out, scatter the targets, ride round behind them. The shot must have come from the right, the open flank. He spurred his horse, shouting, sent his men pouring across the fields.

Thick hedgerows, designed to keep the cattle in and the wild pigs out, channeled his rush into a sunken lane. As the hobbelars swept by, faces looked out from the thorns. At ten-foot range, the crossbow bolts thumped into leather-jerkined backs. As soon as the boots left the stocks, the shooters turned and ran, not even waiting to see if they had hit. In instants they too were astride ponies, spurring hard for cover.

"Ansiau's in trouble," remarked the leader of another conroy of horsemen, watching the growing turmoil. "An ambush. We'll hook round behind it and catch them between him and us. Teach 'em a lesson; they won't try it again."

As he began to lead his men round in a wide sweep, there came a thud in the air and a sudden terrible shrieking behind him: a great dart from nowhere, striking a man in the thigh, driving through, pinning the screaming man to his dead horse. Not from the ambush. From somewhere else. The leader stood up in his stirrups, searching round the featureless landscape for something to show him where to charge. Trees, fields of standing wheat. Hedges everywhere. As he hesitated, a crossbow-bolt, shot from a steady rest by a man under a hedge a hundred and fifty yards off, caught him full in the face. The marksman, a poacher from Ditton-in-the-Fen, made no attempt to leap to his feet and run. In ten heartbeats he was twenty yards away, crawling like an eel in a half-filled ditch. The waxed and twisted gut of his crossbow, he had already

discovered, had took little harm from the wet. As the horsemen hesitated, spurred in the end toward the place where they
thought the shot might have come from, the sights of another
twist-shooter trained round.

Slowly, without horns or trumpets, like a cogwheel tight-
ening a rope, twenty separate skirmishes began to grow into
battle.

From his vantage point on the ridge, Shef saw the Frankish
main force still riding forward: but slowly, at no more than
a walk, with many checks. They did not like to advance
without their flanks secured. And on the flanks, for long
moments, there was scarcely anything to be seen. Then
horsemen would appear, spurring round a copse, or charging
a burned-out village in extended line. What they were
charging or spurring after was usually invisible. Then, as
Shef strained his one eye in the blurring rain, he caught a
flash of movement far out to one side: a pair of horses side
by side at full gallop, one of the twist-shooters bouncing behind, its team drumming their ponies with their heels in a
long trail behind. Oswi and "Dead Level" pulling out at one
end of a hamlet as the Franks poured in the other, the flanking movement that was meant to cut him off delayed and
confused by shots from other directions. The catapult disappeared behind a dip in the ground. In seconds it would be
unlimbered again, once more menacing a wide arc anywhere within its half-mile range.

Shef's strategy depended on three things. One was local
knowledge: only those who lived, farmed and hunted over
the landscape knew where there were passable tracks, safe
lines of retreat. Every group he had sent out had attached to
it a man or boy picked from those who had fled the area.
Others were scattered in hiding places everywhere over
twenty square miles, told not to fight but to guide and pass
messages. The second thing was the shooting-power of the
torsion-catapults with their great darts, and the new crossbows. Both were slow to load, but even the crossbows

would pierce mail at up to two hundred paces. And they were best shot by men lying down in cover.

The most important part of Shef's strategy was his realization that there are two ways to win a battle. Every battle he had ever seen—every battle fought in the Western world for centuries—had been won one way. By shock. By forming lines and clashing till one line broke. The line might be broken by axe and sword, as the Vikings preferred; by horse and lance, in the Frankish style; or by stone and dart, as Shef had introduced. Breaking the line meant winning the battle.

This might be a completely new way to win a battle. To have no line, to produce no shock, but to wear and shred the enemy away by missile attack. Only Shef's unprofessional and unwarlike troops would do it: it went against too many ingrained habits of lifetime warriors. Ground was not important. It was there to be yielded. Face-to-face courage was not important. It was a mark of failure. But there could be none of the usual battlefield boosts to morale—the horns, war-songs, leaders shouting, most of all the sense of comrades alongside you. In a battle like this one it would be easy to desert, or simply to hide, to come out when all was over. Shef hoped his teams would keep on covering each other: they had gone out in bands of about fifty—a catapult, twenty crossbows, a few halberdiers together. But it was in the nature of the battle that they would split up. Once that happened, would they come back again?

Remembering the dogged, snarling attacks that the Yorkshire peasants had put in against him in the snow outside York, he thought they might. The men and women out there could see the country over which they were fighting, see its unreaped crops, its burned barns and cut-down orchards. To the children of the poor, food and land were sacred. They had too many hungry winters to remember.

As he watched the battle develop, Shef felt an odd sense of—not of freedom, but freedom from care. He was only a cog now. Cogs had to turn when they were wound. But they did not have to think about the rest of the machine. That would wind, or it would break, and the cog could do nothing about it. It had only to perform its part.

He dropped a hand on Godive's shoulder, standing beside him. She looked sideways at his ravaged face, allowed his hand to lie there.

King Charles, still moving forward toward the ridge of Caldbeck Hill—where from time to time through the rain he could see the taunting banner of his enemies displayed—held up his hand for the twentieth time for his main battle to halt. The leader of his light horse cantered up to him, rain now soaking through his wool and leather.

"Well, Rogier?"

The hobbelar shook his head disgustedly. "It's like fifty dogfights out there all at once. No one stands up to us. We chase them out and chase them out. Then when we reform and fall back they come back after us, or they come in behind."

"What would happen if we just held together and rode forward? Up there." The king jerked his thumb at the banner on the skyline a mile away.

"They'd shoot the hell out of us all the way."

"But only as long as it takes us to ride a mile. All right, Rogier. Discourage these varlets and their bows as much as you can, but tell your men to ride forward in line with the main battle now. Once we have broken their center we can turn and deal with the flanks."

Turning, the king raised his lance and swept it forward. His riders cheered hoarsely, once, and began to push their horses into a trot.

"They're coming now," said Shef to Alfred, standing next to Godive. "But it's soft ground and they will save their speed for the last rush." Barely fifty people stood by the three leaders on the ridge, mostly runners and message-bearers, but he had kept one pull-thrower team by him, with its clumsy, immobile machine.

"Swan-stones," he ordered.

Glad to move after hours of inactivity, the team—men and women together—sprang to their places. They too had only one role to play today. Early in their practicing, Shef's English machinists had discovered that chipping grooves in the stones their engines lobbed produced a strange warbling note as they flew through the air, like the noise of a swan. For their own amusement they had competed to see who could carve out the loudest. Now Shef meant to send a signal to his scattered troops that all could recognize.

His team loaded, braced, loosed. Launched one eerily whistling stone to one flank, heaved the machine round, launched to another. The dart-thrower and crossbow teams still lurking in ambush in front of the Frankish advance heard the signal, hitched up, retreated and swung round to join their leaders for the first time that day. As they appeared one by one, Shef pushed aside the farm-carts which he had set on the skyline, set the machines in the gaps, posted crossbows inside the carts. For every man, woman and machine, a horse or a horse-team stood no more than five yards away, horse-holders ready.

Shef walked up and down the line, repeating the order. "Three shots from each catapult, no more. Start at extreme range. One shot from each crossbow, on the word."

As King Charles reached the foot of the ridge, his spirits rose in spite of the rain. His enemy had tried to harass and delay him, and now he was counting on the slope and the mud to take the force out of his charge. But the hobbelars had done their job in taking the casualties of skirmishing. And the English still did not appreciate the plan of the Frankish charge. Setting spurs to his horse, he drove up the hill at a canter rising to a gallop, overtaken in seconds by the counts of his bodyguard pulling ahead.

The catapults twanged, black lines streaking through the air, swirls in the massive body of metal plunging up the hill. Still they came on as the levers twirled behind the farm-carts. Again the musical notes, the streaks, the cries of pain from men and horses, the rear ranks hurdling over those who fell. Strange, Charles thought as the obstacle in front of him came into focus. A barricade, but no shields, no warriors. Did they think to stop him with wood alone?

"Shoot," said Shef as the front ranks of the charge reached the white sticks he had planted that morning. Then, instantly, in a Brand-like roar, drowning the simultaneous thump of the crossbows, "Now run! Hitch up and run!"

In moments the slope behind the ridge was a flood of ponies, crossbows well in the lead, catapults taking seconds to hitch up, one team-leader cursing a sticking toggle. Then they too were away. Last of the throng, Godive suddenly turned back, jerked the Hammer and Cross from its frame, swung astride her gelding, and pounded off, banner dragging behind her like a lady's train.

Eyes glaring, lances poised, the Frankish cavalry swept up to the ridge-line, furious to strike at their harassers. A few drove their horses straight at the gaps in the enemy line, whirled round, stallions rearing to strike with their steel hooves at the foot soldiers who must be lurking there.

No one. Carts. Hoofprints. One single siege-engine, the pull-thrower Shef had abandoned. More and more squeezed through the gaps between carts, some finally dismounting and hauling the obstacles away. The king gaped up at the stout wooden frame from which Godive had hauled the Hammer and Cross. As he did so, tauntingly, the same banner rose again, on another ridge-line above a tangle of wood and gully, a long half-mile away. Some of the hotheads in his ranks, fury undispersed by action, yelled and began to spur again toward it. Sharp orders brought them back.

"I have brought a knife to cut beef," the king muttered to his constable Godefroi. "But what is set before me is soup. Thin soup. We will go back to Hastings and think again."

His eye fell on Alfgar. "I thought you said this rain of yours would stop."

Alfgar said nothing, looked at the ground. Charles glanced again at the high frame from which the Hammer and Cross had been torn, still standing sturdily on its cart. He jerked a thumb at it. "Hang the English traitor," he ordered.

"I warned you about the machines," shrieked Alfgar as the hands seized him.

"What's he say?" asked one of the knights.

"I don't know. Some gabble in English."

On a knoll well to one side of the track of the Franks, Thorvin, Geirulf and Farman conferred.

"What do you think?" asked Thorvin.

Geirulf, priest of Tyr, chronicler of battles, shook his head. "It is something new. Completely new. I have never heard of such a thing before. I have to ask: who puts it in his mind? Who but the Father of Warriors? He is a son of Othin. And such men are dangerous."

"I do not think so," said Thorvin. "And I have talked to his mother."

"We know what you told us," said Farman. "What we do not know is what it means. Unless you have a better explanation, I must agree with Geirulf."

"This is not the time to give it," said Thorvin. "See, things are moving again. The Franks are retreating."

Shef watched the heavy lancers turn back from the ridge, with foreboding. He had hoped they would come on again, take more losses, weary their horses and exhaust themselves. If they pulled back now, there was too much chance that they would reach their base and come out another day of their choosing and renew the attack. Instinctively he knew that an irregular army cannot do one thing: defend territory. He had not tried to do so today, and the Frankish king had not tried to make him, sure that both sides desired the traditional, decisive clash. But there must be a way to make him attack. An undefended population all over southern England stood at the king's mercy.

He needed victory today. It meant taking greater risks for greater gains. Fortunately, retreating armies are vulnerable in a way that advancing ones are not. So far, hardly half of Shef's forces had been engaged. Time to commit the rest. Calling his errand-lads around him, Shef began to pass his orders.

Down on the sodden slopes rising from the sea to the downlands, the Frankish hobbelars were learning sense. No longer did they ride in bunched groups presenting easy targets. Instead they too lurked in cover, moving only when they had to and then in short gallops. By a path through a dripping copse, one group tensed as they heard running feet. As the barefoot lad rushed by, intent only on his message, one rider spurred out, slashed savagely with his saber.

"He had no weapon," said one of the Franks, looking down at the body draining blood in the rain-pocked puddles.

"His weapon was in his head," grunted the sergeant in charge. "Get ready to move again."

The boy's brother, running fifty paces behind, hid quiet as a vole behind a red-berried rowan tree, watched them go. Slipped off to find avengers.

The Frankish archers, so far, had done nothing but endure random shot, their bowstrings long since so wet as to be valueless. Their commanders, now, were using them to hold strategic spots as the army fell back. They, too, were starting to use woodcraft.

"Look." One pointed to a conroy of hobbelars falling back over a field, one of them suddenly clutching his side and tipping from his horse. The archers, behind a wrecked barn, saw a figure suddenly slip from a hedgerow, seize a pony, and ride off unseen by its victims. But straight toward their ambush. As it came round the edge of the barn at full gallop, two men drove their short swords into the pony's chest, seized the marksman as the pony collapsed.

"What devil's work is this?" asked one, snatching the crossbow. "See, a bow, arrows. What is this at the belt?"

"Never mind the belt, Guillaume," shouted one of his mates. "Look, it's a girl." The men stared at the slight, short-kilted figure.

"Women shooting men from cover," muttered Guillaume.

"All right. We've time to teach her a lesson. Give her some memories to take to Hell with her."

As the soldiers crowded round the writhing, splayed-out figure, a dozen churls of the Kentish fierd crawled closer, wood-axes and billhooks ready. They could not stand up to mailed horsemen. Mere prowlers and robbers they could deal with.

Leaking men and horses, the great steel reptile oozed sullenly back toward its base.

King Charles, sunk in thought, did not notice the check in front of him till he was almost on his own archers. Then he paused, looked down. A sergeant caught his stirrup, pointed. "Sire, they are in front of us. Standing, for once."

The village reeve Shef had found was positive that a day's rain and the passage of thousands of horses would turn the brook between the Brede and Bulverhythe into a quagmire. Shef had decided to take the chance and believe him. His runners had got through—most of them. The pull-thrower teams with their heavy guards of halberdiers had closed in from the far flanks where they had waited immobile. Assembled their weapons, lined up five yards apart along a hundred and fifty yards of front. On a fine day, in the open, against cavalry, suicide.

Osmod the marshal, peering through the rain, judged the Frankish vanguard within range. As he called the order, twenty beams lashed the air together, slings whirled, stones shot into the sky.

Charles's horse reared as the brains of a dismounted archer flicked its face. Another stallion, leg broken, screamed and pawed at the air. Almost before one volley had landed another was in the air. For a moment the Frankish army, surprised again and again, came close to panic.

Charles rode forward bellowing, ignoring the stones now aimed deliberately at him. Imperiously he drove the archers forward, launching feeble arrows. Behind them, following his example, his heavy lancers broke into a slow trot. Into the quagmire where a brook had been.

Charles himself was pulled clear of his bogged horse by two counts of his stable, stood in the end to watch. His men floundered through, some on horses still, some on foot, to reach the machines that flung an unending rain of stones. They were met by a line of men in strange helmets, swinging and stabbing with huge axes like woodmen's tools. Robbed of the élan which was their birthright, the Frankish knights stood and fought them weapon to weapon. Slowly, the big men in mail forced their smaller, strangely armed adversaries back. Back. Almost to the line of the machines, which they must stand to defend.

Horn-blasts from both sides. Floundering through the mud, Charles tensed, expecting the counterattack, the desperate last charge. Instead his enemies turned suddenly, all together, and ran. Ran unashamedly, like hares or leverets. Leaving their machines to the conqueror.

Gasping with exertion, Charles realized there was no way to carry the things off. Nor to burn them. "Cut them up," he ordered. An archer looked doubtfully at the heavy timbers. "Cut the ropes! Do something to them."

"They lost a few," said one of his counts. "And they ran like cowards. Left their weapons behind."

"We lost many," said the king. "And how many swords and mail-shirts have we left behind us today? Give me my horse. If we reach base with half the strength we started, we'll be lucky."

Yes, he thought. But we're through. Through all the traps. And half, behind a safe stockade, may be enough another day.

As if to encourage him, the rain began to ease.

Guthmund the Greedy, sweeping down the Channel under oars alone, ignored the rain and welcomed the poor visibility it brought. If he was going to go ashore he would much prefer it to come as a surprise. Also, in rain or fog, there was a chance of snapping up information. In the prow of the leading ship, he pointed off to starboard, called an order to in-

crease the stroke. In moments the longship was alongside the
six-oar fishing-boat, its crew looking up in fear. Guthmund
pulled the hammer-pendant from round his neck and showed
it, noted the expressions fading from fear to wariness.

"We are here to fight the Franks," he called, using the
half-English pidgin of the Wayman camp. The expressions
relaxed another degree as the men realized they could understand him, took in what he said.

"You're too late," a fisherman called back. "They fight
today."

"You'd better come aboard," replied Guthmund.

As he took in the sense of what the fishermen told him,
his pulse began to beat stronger. If there was one principle
of successful piracy, it was to land where the defenses were
down. He checked again and again: the Frankish army had
been seen marching out that morning. It had left camp-
guards and ship-guards. The loot of the countryside, Canterbury included, was in the lightly guarded camp. The
fishermen had no hope that the Franks would find anything
but victory. Still, Guthmund told himself, if his friend and
jarl was defeated, it could do no harm to rob the conqueror.
And a stroke in the rear might be a vital distraction. He
turned to the fishermen again with another string of questions: The fleet drawn up in a bay? The stockaded camp on
a hill? The nearest inlet to it? Steep sides but a path?

In the drenching rain the Wayman fleet, rowed now by
chained Ragnarsson survivors, pulled one by one into the
narrow mouth of the stream below Hastings and its camp.

"Do you mean to climb the walls with ladders?" asked
one of the fishermen doubtfully. "They are ten feet high."

"That's what those are for," said Guthmund, waving cheerfully at the six onagers being slung over the side by derricks.

"Too heavy for the path," said the fisherman, eyeing the
way the boats heeled.

"I have plenty of carriers," replied Guthmund, watching
keenly as his men, weapons poised, unshackled the dangerous Ragnarsson galley-slaves a few at a time and made
them fast again to the onagers' frames and carry-bars.

As the narrow inlet filled with men, Guthmund decided to make a short speech of encouragement.

"Loot," he said, "lots of it. Stolen from the Christian Church, so we'll never have to give any back. Maybe we have to share it with the jarl, if he wins today. Maybe not. Let's go."

"What about us?" said one of the chained men.

Guthmund looked at him attentively. Ogvind the Swede: a very hard man. Threats no good. And he needed these men to use their full strength up the steep hillside.

"This is how it is," he said. "If we win, I'll let you go. If we lose, I'll leave you chained to the machines. Maybe the Christians will be merciful to you. Fair?"

Ogvind nodded. Struck by a sudden thought, Guthmund turned to the black deacon, the machine-master.

"What about you? Will you fight these for us?"

Erkenbert's face set. "Against Christians? The emissaries of the Pope, the Holy Father, whom I myself and my master called to this abode of savages? Rather will I embrace the crown of holy martydom and go . . ."

A hand plucked at Guthmund's sleeve: one of the few slaves taken from York Minster who had survived both Ivar's furies and Erkenbert's discipline.

"We'll do it, master," he whispered. "Be a pleasure."

Guthmund waved the mixed party up the steep hillside, going first himself with the fishermen and minster-men to reconnoiter, the Ragnarssons struggling up next under their ton-and-a-half burdens. Slowly, still cloaked by the rain, six onagers and a thousand Vikings moved into position four hundred yards from the Frankish stockade. Guthmund shook his head disapprovingly as he realized that there were not even sentries posted on the seaward side—or if there had been, they had all drifted over to the other side to watch and listen to the far-off rumor of battle.

The first sighting shot from an onager bounced short, kicked up and flicked a ten-foot post stump-first out of the ground. The minster-men pulled out coigns, lifted the frames a trifle. The next volley of five twenty-pound boulders smashed down twenty feet of stockade in a moment. Guthmund saw no point in waiting for a second volley. His army headed straight for the gap at a run. The startled Franks, mostly archers, bowstrings useless, faced with a thousand veteran warriors ready to fight on foot at close quarters, broke and ran almost to a man.

Two hours after setting foot onshore, Guthmund looked out from the Frankish gate. All his training told him to parcel the loot, abandon the now-unnecessary machines, and get back to sea before vengeance fell on him. Yet what he saw looked uncommonly like a beaten army streaming back. If so, if so . . .

He turned, shouted orders. Skaldfinn the interpreter, priest of Heimdall, looked at him in surprise.

"You're taking a risk," he said.

"Can't help it. I remember what my grandpa told me. Always kick a man if he's down."

As his men saw the Hammer ensign break out over what they had thought was their secure camp, Charles the Bald felt the morale of his army break. Every man and horse was soaked, cold and weary. As they straggled out of the copses and hedgerows and formed once more into ranks, the hobbelars could see that at least half their number were still lying out in the sodden fields, dead or waiting for death from some peasant's knife. The archers had been mere passive targets all day. Even the core of his army, the heavy lancers, had left a third of their best on slope or in quagmire, with never a chance to show their skill. The stockade in front of him looked unharmed and heavily manned. No assault would go in willingly.

Cutting his losses, Charles stood in his saddle, raised his lance, pointed toward the ships drawn up on the beach or anchored in the road. Sullenly, his men changed their direction of march, angled down towards the beach on which they had landed weeks before.

As they reached it, one by one, the dragon-boats cruised

round from the inlet where their crews had re-embarked. Rowed into position, halted all together on the calm sea, swung bows on with the skill of veterans. From a vantage point by the stockade, an onager tried a ranging shot. The missile plumped into the gray water a cable's length over the cog *Dieu Aide*. Gently, the onagers trained round.

Looking down on the crowded beach, Shef realized that where the Frankish army had shrunk, his had swollen. The dart-throwers and crossbows were in place as he expected, hardly fewer than when they had started. His stone-throwers were coming up at a rush, recaptured from where the Franks had left them, unharmed or hastily re-rigged and now carried along still assembled by hundreds of willing hands. Only the halberdiers had lost more than a handful. And in their place had come thousands, literally thousands of angry churls out of the woodlands, clutching axes and spears and scythes. If the Franks were to break out it would have to be uphill. On weary horses. Under withering fire.

Into Shef's mind, unbidden, came the memory of his duel with Flann the Gaddgedil. If you wanted to consign a man, or an army, to Naströnd, to Dead Man's Shore, you cast the spear over their heads as a sign that all were given to Othin. Then no prisoners could be taken. A voice spoke inside him, a cold voice, the voice he recognized as the Othin of his dreams.

"Go on," it said. "Pay me my due. You do not wear my sign yet, but do they not say you belong to me?"

As if sleepwalking, Shef drifted over to Oswi's catapult— "Dead Level," wound and loaded, trained on the center of the Frankish army, milling in confusion below them. He looked down at the crosses on the shields: remembered the orm-garth. The wretched slave Merla. His own torments at the hands of Wulfgar. Godive's back. Sibba and Wilfi, burned to ashes. The crucifixions. His hands were steady as they pulled out the coigns, trained the weapon up to launch its missile over the Frankish heads.

Inside him the voice spoke again, the voice like a calving glacier. "Go on," it said. "Give the Christians to me."

Suddenly Godive was beside him, hand on his sleeve. She said nothing. As he looked at her, he remembered Father Andreas, who had given him life. His friend Alfred. Father Boniface. The poor woman in the forest clearing. He looked round from his daze, realized that the priests of the Way, all of them, had appeared from somewhere, were gazing at him with grave and intent faces.

He stepped back from the catapult with a deep sigh.

"Skaldfinn," he said. "You are an interpreter. Go down and tell the Frankish king to surrender or be killed. I will give them their lives and passage home. No more."

Again he heard a voice: but this time, the amused one of the wanderer in the mountains, which he had first heard over the gods' chessboard.

"Well done," it said. "You defeated Othin's temptation. Maybe you are my son. But who knows his own father?"

Chapter Twelve

"He was tempted," said Skaldfinn. "Whatever you may say, Thorvin, there is something of Othin in him."

"It would have been the greatest slaughter since men came to these islands," added Geirulf. "The Franks on the beach were worn out and helpless. And the English churls would have had no mercy."

The priests of the Way sat again in their holy circle, around the spear and the fire, within the rowan cords. Thorvin had picked great bunches of the freshest berries of autumn. Their bright scarlet answered the sunset.

"Such a thing would have brought us the worst of luck," said Farman. "For with such a sacrifice it is essential that no loot or profit be taken. But the English would not have regarded that. They would have robbed the dead. Then we would have had against us both the Christian God and the wrath of Allfather."

"Nevertheless he did not shoot the dart," said Thorvin. "He held his hand. That is why I say he is not a creature of Othin. I thought so once. Now I know better."

"You had better tell us what you learned from his mother," said Skaldfinn.

"It was like this," Thorvin began. "I found her easily enough, in the village of her husband the heimnar. She might not have talked to me, but she loves the girl—concubine's daughter though she is. In the end she told me the story.

"It was much as Sigvarth told it—though he said she enjoyed his attentions and she ... Well, after what she suffered it is not surprising that she spoke of him only with hatred. But she bore him out up to the time when he lay with her on the sand, put her in the boat, and then left her and went back to his men and their women on the beach.

"Then, she said, this happened. There was a scratching on the boat's gunwale. When she looked over, in the night, there was a small boat alongside, just a skiff, with a man in it. I pressed her to know what sort of man, but she could remember nothing. Middle-aged, middle-sized, she said, neither well-dressed nor shabby. He beckoned to her. She thought he was a fisherman who had come out to rescue her, so she got in. He pulled out well clear of the beach, and rowed her down the coast, saying never a word. She got out, she went home to her husband."

"Maybe he was a fisherman," put in Farman. "Just as the walrus was a walrus and the skoffin was a foolish boy afraid of keeping watch on his own."

"I asked her—did he not want a reward? He could have taken her home. Her kin would have paid him, if not her husband. She said he just left her. I pressed her on this, I asked her to remember every detail. She said one more thing.

"When the stranger got her to shore, she said, he pulled the boat up on the beach and looked at her. Then she felt suddenly weary and lay down among the seaweed. When she woke, he had gone."

Thorvin looked round. "Now, what happened when she lay in this sleep we do not know. I would guess that a woman would know by some sign if she had been taken in her sleep, but who is to say? Sigvarth had been with her not long before. If she had any suspicion, she would have nothing to gain by mentioning it. Or remembering it. But that sleep makes me wonder.

"Tell me now." Thorvin turned to Farman. "You who are the wisest of us, tell me how many gods there are in Asgarth."

Farman stirred uneasily. "You know, Thorvin, that is not a wise question. Othin, Thor, Frey, Balder, Heimdall, Njorth, Ithun, Tyr, Loki—those are the ones we speak of most. But there are so many others in the stories: Vithar, Sigyn, Ull . . ."

"Rig?" asked Thorvin carefully. "What do we know of Rig?"

"That is a name of Heimdall," said Skaldfinn.

"A name," mused Thorvin. "Two names, one person. So we hear. Now, I would not say this outside the circle, but it comes to me sometimes that the Christians are right. There is only one god." He looked round at the shocked faces. "But he—no, it—has different moods. Or parts. Maybe the parts compete against each other, as a man may play chess, right hand against left, for sport. Othin against Loki, Njörth against Skathi, Aesir against Vaenir. Yet the real contest is between all the parts, all the gods, and the giants and monsters who would bring us to Ragnarok.

"Now, Othin has his way of making men strong to help the gods when they shall stand against the giants on that day. That is why he betrays the warriors, chooses the mightiest of them to die. So they will be in his hall the day the giants come.

"But it is in my mind that maybe Rig too has his way. You know the holy story? How Rig went through the mountains, met Ai and Edda and begot on Edda, Thrall. Met Afi and Amma and begot on Amma, Karl. Met Fathir and

Mothir and begot on Mothir, Jarl. This jarl of ours has also been thrall and carl. And who is the son of Jarl?"

"Kon the Young," said Farman.

"Which is to say *Konr ungr* which is *konungr.*"

"Which is King," said Farman.

"Who can deny our jarl that title now? He is acting out the story of Rig in his own life. Of Rig and his dealings with humanity."

"Why is the god Rig doing this?" asked Vestmund, priest of Njörth. "And what is Rig's power? For I confess, I know nothing of him but the story you tell."

"He is the god of climbers," replied Thorvin. "And his power is to make men better. Not through war, like Othin, but through skills. There is another old story you know, about Skjef the father of Skjold—which is to say, Sheaf the father of Shield. Now the kings of the Danes call themselves the sons of Skjold, the war-kings. Yet even they remember that before Skjold the war-king there was a peace-king, who taught men how to sow and reap, instead of living like animals by the chase. What I think has happened now is that a new Sheaf has come, however we pronounce the name, to free us from sowing and reaping and living only from one harvest to the next."

"And this is 'the one who comes from the North,' " said Farman doubtfully. "Not of the blood or tongue. One who has allied himself with Christians. It is not what we expected."

"What the gods do is never what we expected," replied Thorvin.

Shef watched the gloomy procession of disarmed Frankish warriors filing after their king aboard the ships that would take them home. With them Alfred had insisted on sending not only the papal legate and the Franks' own Churchmen, but also the archbishop of York, and his own Bishop Daniel of Winchester, Erkenbert the deacon and all the English clerics who had failed to oppose the invaders. Daniel had screamed threats of eternal damnation for the excommunicate at him, but Alfred had remained unmoved. "If you cast me out of your flock," he had remarked, "I shall begin my own. One with better shepherds. And dogs with sharper teeth."

"They will hate you forever for that," Shef had said to him.

"That is another thing we must share," Alfred had replied. And so they had done their deal.

Both men single, without heirs. They would be co-kings, Alfred south of the Thames, Shef north of it, at least as far as the Humber, beyond which there still lurked the Snakeeye and his ambitions. Each named the other as his heir. Each agreed that within his dominion, belief in the gods should be free, for Christians, for Way-folk, and for any other that should appear. But no priest of any religion should be allowed to take payment, in goods or in land, except for a service agreed upon beforehand. And Church-land should revert to the crown. It would make them the richest kings in Europe, before long.

"We must use the money well," Shef had added.

"In charity?"

"In other ways too. It is often said that no new thing can come before its time, and I believe it. But I believe also that there can be a time for a new thing, and then men can stifle it. Or churches can stifle it. Look at our machines and our crossbows. Who could say they could not have been made a hundred years ago, or five hundred, in the time of the Rome-folk? Yet no one made them. I want us to get back all the old knowledge, even the numbercrafts of the *arithmetici*. And use it to make new knowledge. New things." His hand had clenched as if on the haft of a hammer.

Now, still watching the files of captives embarking, Alfred turned to his co-king and said, "I am surprised you still refuse to wear the hammer of our banner. After all, I still wear the cross."

"The Hammer is for the Way, united. And Thorvin says he has a new sign for me. I will have to see if I approve of it, for the choice is a difficult one. He is here."

Thorvin approached them, flanked by all the priests of the Way, behind them, Guthmund and a cluster of senior skippers.

"We have your sign," said Thorvin. He held out a pendant on a silver chain. Shef looked at it curiously: a shaft, with five rungs sticking out from it on alternate sides.

"What is it?"

"It is a *kraki*," replied Thorvin. "A pole-ladder. It is the sign of Rig."

"I have never heard the name of that god. What can you tell me about him that should make me wear his sign?"

"He is the god of climbers. Of wanderers. He is mighty not through himself but through his children. He is the father of Thrall, of Carl, of Jarl. And of others."

Shef looked round at the many watching faces: Alfred. Thorvin. Ingulf. Hund. There were some not there. Brand, of whose recovery he still had no news. His mother Thryth. He did not know if she would ever wish to see him again.

Most of all, Godive. After the battle a group of his catapulteers had brought him the body of his half brother—his mother's son, Godive's husband. Both he and she had looked for a long time at the purple face, the twisted neck, trying to find in it some memory of childhood, some clue to the hatred in the brain. Shef had thought of lines from one of Thorvin's old poems, said by a hero over the brother he had killed:

*"I have been your bane, brother. Bad luck lay on us.
Ill is the Norns' doom, I will never forget."*

But he had not said the words. He meant to forget. He hoped one day Godive would forget too. Forget that he had first saved her, then deserted her, then used her. Now that the constant stress of planning and action was over, he felt inside himself as though he loved her as much as he ever had before he rescued her from Ivar's camp. But what kind of love was it that had to wait for the right moment to be admitted?

So Godive had thought. She had taken her husband and half brother's body for burial, left Shef unsure when or whether she might return. This time he would have to decide for himself.

He looked past his friends at the prisoners still filing by—the sullen, hating faces—thought of the humiliated

Charles, the enraged Pope Nicholas, the Snakeeye in the North with a brother now to avenge. He looked again at the silver sign in his hand.

"A pole-ladder," he said. "Difficult to balance on."

"You have to do it one rung at a time," replied Thorvin.

"Hard to climb, difficult to balance, to reach the top. But at the top there are two rungs to grasp on to. One opposite the other. It could almost be a cross."

Thorvin frowned. "Rig and his sign were known in the ages before there ever was a cross. It is not a sign of death. No. It is one of reaching higher, of living better."

Shef smiled, the first time he had done that for many days. "I like your sign, Thorvin," he said. "I will wear it." He slipped the Wayman's pendant round his neck, turned and looked at the misted sea.

Some knot, some pain within him was released, fled.

For the first time in his entire life he felt at peace.

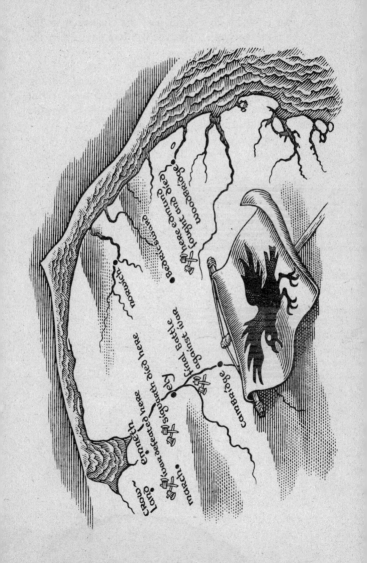